Poetry by Peter Fortunato

A Bell or a Hook
Letters to Tiohero
Late Morning: New and Selected Poems
Entering the Mountain

Carnevale

PETER FORTUNATO

Fomite
Burlington, VT

ISBN- 978-1-947917-08-8
Library of Congress Number- 2019933282

Fomite
58 Peru Street
Burlington, VT 05439
www.fomitepress.com

This book is for my family, alive and in the spirit,
and for all who have called the Hudson River Valley home

The wrath of the lion is the wisdom of God.
The nakedness of woman is the work of God.

(William Blake)

PART 1

CHAPTER 1

S NAKE EYES WERE HARD, but you could win big with a pair of aces, except on your first throw, which didn't make sense to me. The name of the game is craps, but *craps* means you lose. My father tried teaching me to play, and I liked to throw side-arm, snapping my wrist and from my fist letting the dice fly. It was like *morra*, he said, that hand game older than the Romans: you had to trust in Lady Luck and see in your mind the point you were shooting, say it out loud. *Quatro! Cinque! Sei!* He said all kinds of things to make the dice do what he wanted. Sometimes they obeyed.

The men played craps on the pool table at the Villa, bar towels stuffed in the holes and small bills scattered on the felt. They cheered after making their points and jiggled the rocks in their empty glasses. They bought refills with moola stuffed into my father's pockets, afternoons before he or Gracie Laporta would open the bar. One of the guys, Georgie the Mick, a bricklayer, brawny and blond, took a long time to shoot. "Baby needs a new pair of shoes," he'd shout, even though he didn't have a kid, and Gracie, well, I doubted he'd ever bought anything for her. My father, a real comedian, towel swinging from his belt like a scalp, high on his own booze, would whoop the loudest when he was losing. "Gotta work hard for my *o' lady,*" he'd wisecrack. "Didju know she's *I-rashina?*" Blowing into his fist, pumping the air before his throw. And this one, a wisecrack he used to distract the Mick: "Don' getta hitched, Georgie, my friend. Stay playboy!"

I was watching from a booth at the back of the cocktail lounge, my shadow box I called that spot, waiting my turn, not to drink or to chance a buck on the bones, but to try my luck at love. I wasn't a kid anymore when Gracie Laporta started working for us, "Georgie's girl," or so the Mick liked to say.

GAMBLING HAD A LOT to do with luck. Making your point was the goal, the trick, the art, and how you held the dice or flicked your wrist was your play. Your bet was how you beat the other guys. Your prayer, your faith, your fate, your *luck,* these were invisible things, and *the odds* were a central mystery in any game of chance: how did you play the odds, and when they were against you, how did you beat them? I thought of *the gods* from Greek and Norse mythology, and not of *il Signore,* Our Lord, because he was for everybody, wasn't he?

Meanwhile, I could see why some people thought that gambling—dice or cards, playing the horses, betting on high school football games, or on the name of a pretty woman sitting alone at the bar, all of the stuff my father and his pals did for fun and profit—might have something to do with the Devil. He was the one who played favorites, my grandmother told me, and it was best not to think you could beat him. When she said that, Nonna made the horns with her fingers, pointing them down, and spat.

My father could be a good shooter. Part of his play was to hold the dice high and talk to them in Neapolitan. Sometimes he made kissing noises over his fist and called out things like "Come onna my house, baby!" My mother thought there shouldn't be gambling at the Place, even in the off hours, but she could get excited about a game of chance, and sometimes she would roll for him when he asked. Sometimes they won that way.

Once he asked me to bring him some good luck, and I got out one of my snakes in a big empty mayonnaise jar. Jacky Bosch and Red Grant laughed and were impressed, and my father slapped me on the back, but George McInnis got really nervous. "Get your kid and his thing outta here!" he said.

My father calmly raised the snake into the light and examined it through the glass. He didn't say a word. As he gently turned the jar inspecting it, the little red and white milk snake coiled on itself like a bit of ribbon and flicked out its perfectly forked pink tongue. "Thank you, my son," he said quietly to me. And to the Mick, in a funny way: "You ain' got a chance now, Georgie! That little-a snake she tol' me."

My father did sometimes win big, but more often he lost. *"Donna Fortuna,"* he said, nodding his head, resigned to the Lady's whims. He kept gambling, he said, because someday he'd "get in good" with her. He tried a lot of ways to do that. His career as a comedian was one.

A friend of his once told me that I was "a lucky son-of-a-bitch." He was sitting on a barstool, staring at the bottles doubled in the mirror before him, drunk. What does a drunk know, I asked myself, but then it hit me, he was right. I thought of my mother who always said she was lucky to have me. After one of my parents' big fights, when my father claimed that since we were so deeply in debt, our best bet was to torch the place for insurance money, after

5

he pounded an angry fist on the kitchen table and slammed out of the back door, I was scared he meant it. I asked my tearful mother, but she said no, he was just an unhappy man. She stroked my hair like she used to when I was little, and the look on her face made me want to cry too.

SOME PEOPLE SAY THAT love is the answer to every question, but I'm not so sure how many know about the power of love. Buddhists say that what everybody basically wants is to be happy and to avoid pain; even your enemies and all the evil people in the world are trying to get their own particular brand of happy. Maybe it's their idea of love, maybe money and the freedom it could buy, or maybe they just want to deaden the pain of living with drugs or booze. I think the greatest mistake is to believe you can be happy by getting power over other people—whenever I catch a whiff of that I grow suspicious. I've been this way since I was a kid; it was one of my problems with the Catholic Church, and it's also why I have a hard time at the Hudson River College, where I teach art. "Playing politics" is the polite term for what I'm talking about. Hell, maybe Leo Declare started the place because he was on a power trip—I never thought of that until now.

For better or worse, he was my first example of a real-life painter, and he was someone who, like my father, often was unhappy. True, an artist can never be too easily contented with his work, but it's also true that it's during the pursuit of your ideal—that is, when actually making art—that you are likely to be happiest. I don't know if Leo ever said that to me exactly, but I learned it from being around him. I know what's best in his painting, but I contend that his greatest success was the creation of the Hudson River College.

Although he and his buddy Bob Badget were never regulars at the Villa, because they were for a while partners at the Half Moon Café and Saloon, up in Poughkeepsie, they were among a circle of my father's and mother's business acquaintances. While Leo would later claim that he didn't remember meeting me at any time before I showed up at the café looking for a job, and more importantly, asking for private art lessons, he was wrong. I saw him see me at the Villa when I was about eleven years old. I didn't yet know he was a fairly famous artist, but I did notice how he was dressed: paint splattered, white, baggy pants, white tennis shoes streaked with drips of color, no socks, white tee shirt taut over his bulging belly—very unusual for the Villa Giustovera. His eyes were on me while I was cutting grass one day outside the recreation room on the south lawn. I was in my bathing suit and sneakers, sweat pouring out of every pore on an August afternoon, walking behind the Gravely mower, big as an ox. He watched me wheel it around and come back down a long row as precisely as I could make the cut. I was performing and he was watching and I liked the attention.

Leo wasn't one to dice and drink with my dad and his pals; Bob might have, I don't know. It's easy for me to attribute any character flaw I can think of to Bob Badget—and then, because I've worked so long on this, I have to let it go. Live and let live: that's what Bob and I have tacitly agreed, a necessity for us since Leo's death. It's not that we're friends today or that we ever really were friends, but Bob Badget is unavoidable when it comes to talking about Leo Declare.

I KNEW A LOT about reptiles and amphibians. Behind the Villa, among stone walls that looked so ancient they might have been built by English settlers or by the Dutch before them, on huge rocks piled by tough farmers long ago after the last of the natives were pushed from the Hudson Valley, snakes of many kinds might be coiled under the summer sun or lying flat out in the heat. In that state I discovered they could be either quick or slow, relaxed or ready to strike. Sometimes they ran through my hands smooth as warm rubber, limp as macaroni. You had to be calm when you grabbed them and ready for anything. I was startled more than once by a snake suddenly springing at my face. Although I was never seriously bitten, one time a small king snake struck my index finger and stuck, its teeth hooked bloodlessly until I peeled it off. I can still remember the sensation and the way the little red and white snake seemed dead when I dropped it, and then how it came back to life.

Some serpents have fangs, and through these hollow fangs, the vipers inject venom with their bites. They don't suck blood. I collected more facts than specimens, and although I never found a copperhead or a rattler on the land, I reckoned they could be around, and so I was prepared. Garter snakes and milk snakes I found aplenty, black snakes and water snakes too, amazingly quick on dry land, and beautiful, emerald green snakes. Box turtles old as the Villa Giustovera I captured, and painted turtles slick and bright, and baby snapping turtles like tiny dinosaurs to swim around in a glass bowl until I set them free; the dangerous grownups left over from the saurian age, I left alone to rule the ponds. Among the amphibians were bullfrogs and leopard frogs, tree frogs, cricket frogs, and all of their tadpoles. In those days the Villa's ponds and bogs were filled with tadpoles that I gathered into my aquariums, releasing them after they grew legs. I also collected toads, newts, and red efts that I thought might actually live in fire like the salamanders of myth, and once, under a flat stone in a swamp I found a yellow-spotted salamander big as a newborn puppy.

IT WAS THE BETTING about Gracie the barmaid that got my mother so mad.

The men had been drinking all afternoon, playing cards. My father was unshaven, in his kitchen clothes, rowdy as the rest. My mother hated him when he was like that, looking like a dishwasher, she said. When he was in that condition, she never knew what to expect. He could be vile or he might cower before her like an over-grown child, ashamed of himself and apologetic. "Go and change yourself," she'd say. Then he would return looking like a first class *barista,* having shed his greasy apron and found his self-respect, having donned an outfit from his days on the cruise ships of the Italian Line.

Gracie came in at about four thirty to open. Her black hair was teased a bit and sprayed into place, arranged specially in a new style, so that a carefully groomed tress hung along each pow-dered cheek and framed her heart shaped face. A hoop of gold glittered in each ear lobe, her lips were red, her luminous eyes rayed with black mascara. To say she was "dolled up" doesn't do her justice, for the Italian American ways of young women looking for marriage in the 1960s, the ways of a certain class of dark haired, hard working, practical and seductive beauty bred in Astoria or Bensonhurst or Greenwich Village, *una bella donna* well versed in the conventions of romance, the ways of a young woman such as Gracie Laporta can seem to ignorant people cheap, if you say the girl is "dolled up."

Gracie was beautiful.

She wore a black waitress uniform piped in white that clung to her curves in the neon half-light behind the bar. The hemline had been shortened to show off her long legs in their black stockings. I was certain she was wearing a garter belt, and indeed, when she bent over and the satiny material of her skirt grew taut around her hips, I could see its snaky lines under her skirt. Brand new black-and-white heeled pumps completed the outfit. That day, I was practically frightened of her beauty that lit up the Place like a bolt from beyond, like the legendary ball of lightning that flashed through the Villa Giustovera once upon a time.

I had always had a way of warming up to the waitresses and barmaids, chambermaids and salad-girls who worked for us, and although she was a fairly recent arrival, Gracie and I were becoming pals. When I was small, "the girls," as my mother always referred to them, could see how often I'd be left alone in the busy evening hours, and it was common for them to keep an eye on me. But I wasn't a little kid in Gracie's time, and I knew a *bella donna* when I saw one.

I'd been daydreaming at my post in the cocktail lounge, doodling aimlessly on the pages of my sketchbook, just hanging around in the shadow box while the men played their game, but now, since I couldn't *not* look at her, I started to draw in earnest. My pencil point, as if it had a mind of its own, followed her every silken movement.

Gracie had a head on her shoulders, everybody said so, and she could be all business, which was why my mother liked her so much. That day Gracie must have known that George was there, must have seen his car out front when she arrived. They were going together, and since it was obvious to me as it was to my mother that Gracie had a brain, I couldn't believe that she'd fallen for George McInnis, no matter how much he looked like Paul Newman, as my father liked to say. Without seeming to notice him or anybody else in particular, in her sexy heels she'd crossed through the restaurant's main foyer and tapped over to the barroom behind the table where they were playing rummy. I watched her change into a pair of flats, loved seeing the bend of each leg and the way her skirt rode up to her stockings' garter snaps. Then she wrapped a neat white apron tight about her hips. I felt like a thief, filling my eyes from where I sat in the shadows. Now she flipped on the lights, dimmed them a little, and plugged a quarter into the jukebox. "Moon River" came on, the instrumental version.

Suddenly one of the men's voices climbed above the rest and with fake politeness said he wondered what color bra Gracie was wearing. Rude laughter broke out, George said something, and they went on about this as if they really thought she would show them. She ignored them all, set out a tray of glasses, checked the refrigerator for lemons, put some yellow slices into a crystal bowl, counted ashtrays. Humming along with the music, she polished the bar.

"Georgie says black. Hee-hee-he's gonna bet a *f-f-fever* on it. Can we see?" A loud voice, tittering stupidly. Danny Resnick? Or that other guy from Highland, the fat one who wore cowboy shirts with pearl buttons. But the loudest laughter was unmistakably Georgie's. He sounded like a donkey braying, and from then on that's what he was to me: Georgie the Mule.

Meanwhile, I burrowed into my drawing with a fever all my own. Although I was aware of something like a storm gathering nearby, I felt as if I could hold Gracie, not too tight, not too loose, with the power of my pencil. I sketched furiously, hoping she wouldn't notice me in this act of adoration. Now I realize that she must have known what she was doing that day: she wanted Georgie to be jealous of all the other eyes on her.

"*Oh!* Are you guys-a gonna play this game o' *that* game? Leave-a poor girl alone so she ken work. Okay?" My father.

And then, suddenly, my mother's voice: "*Zizi, ma che Cristo fai?*" A storm cloud visiting blame like hail stones and fire on my dad's head. "You don't see the girl is ready to open? Jesus H. Christ! Game's over, fellas! You want some customer walk in here and tell the cops, shut us down?"

My mother's footsteps on the hardwood floor of the barroom, my mother growling as she passed behind the men. Then: "Everything all right, Gracie?" No reply but a nod of her head as Gracie bent to the sink to wash glasses.

"Guido, what the hell are you doin' here? It's five o'clock!"

I'd expected that, and I looked up at her, sighing audibly, as I'd taken to doing so often in those days. I closed the sketchpad without saying a word to anybody. The Place was silent, the music gone, the men having quickly collected their things and made apologies as my father shooed them out a side door. He himself without another word had slunk away into the kitchen.

I slid from the booth and snuck another longing look at Gracie. She knew that I'd been drawing her, and I had seen that she was interested. In truth, we were only a few years apart in age, though at the time this was a huge barrier. She was free to work behind the bar, and after five I was banned from being anywhere near it. She smiled at me. To my mother she said, "He's making my picture, Anna. I should come in early some time so he can finish it. Right, Guido? Your son's an artist, Anna."

"Eh? What's that?" My mother was riffling through some papers near the cash register, squinting fiercely because she'd forgotten her reading lenses, or else because of the stack of receipts and bills, or because of my father in his greasy apron bent on chasing Lady Luck with his pals, or else because—she paused in the midst of her work with her right thumb raised to her lips. It was an automatic gesture, acquired years ago when a sewing machine at the Bleachery in Wappingers had pierced it, leaving its nail forever deformed. Looking up from her accounts she realized Gracie had said something about me. She saw that I was still nearby, and I expected another reprimand, a parting shot before she left for the kitchen.

In those busy desperate days, I didn't believe that my parents took much notice of me. I had relatively few chores and quite a few privileges around the Place, as well as the envy of friends who thought that because we owned a resort my family must be rich. My most important responsibility was to assist my ailing grandmother, to whom I was devoted. I was an honors student in high school, I was a devout Catholic who confessed himself weekly and never missed mass, but I was also growing secretive and evasive. What I could hardly admit to myself was that I wished I were still the center of my mother's attention, and I suffered on account of this particular contradiction. I wished we could go back to the way it had been when my father was working in New York City, back when my grandparents were both healthy, and when on special nights my mother and I would have dinner out and take long aimless drives on country roads.

I had recently experienced a growth spurt that added three inches to my height, and with a new found interest in barbells, I developed the upper body of a football player during my sophomore year. I hated school teams, but pumped iron at home and before a full length mirror admired myself. I began to call my reflection *Cellini,* a nickname inspired by the autobiography of the tough-guy

Renaissance artist, Benvenuto Cellini. On a visit to Florence, I had seen his bronze masterpiece, *Perseus*, at the Piazza della Signoria. By virtue of my weight lifting, I thought to sculpt my body to resemble the Greek hero. I was never so obsessed with body building as to realize that ideal, but I reveled in the hours I spent lifting weights before my mirror. When I could be sure of my privacy, I worked out in the nude. I fused in my imagination the form of *Perseus* with my idea of the artist who'd created him. On my feet I saw the winged sandals of Hermes. In my right hand, a sword, jutting forward at my hip. Of course, the focus of the statue is the demi-god's exhibition of Medusa's head, upraised in his left hand. Even in death, this had the power to turn the unwary to stone. The fact that Medusa's hair was a nest of snakes further increased my fascination with the statue and its maker.

I learned that Benvenuto Cellini was often referred to as *incorrigible.* I had thought that the word meant something like "super-courageous," but when I looked it up I found its meaning was "irredeemable." This sent a shiver through me, for I had a terrible fear of Hell. Throughout his life, Cellini had been at odds with all forms of authority, including the Church, although he'd apparently had no problem compromising when it was to his advantage. As an artist and a man he was rebellious, courageous and daring in many ways, purposeful as a falcon falling on its prey—at least according to his autobiography. And Cellini seemed never to have doubted himself.

At about this time, I won third prize at a county wide art competition for a fanciful self-portrait I did with colored pencils and oil pastels. I had managed to shadow my face by smudging graphite over the features so that, as one of the judges said, the piece was "compelling yet also concealing." The prize validated my talent, but exhibiting this self-portrait had a peculiar effect on me. Everyone had always said I was an excellent draftsman, that my pictures were "so lifelike," yet this drawing embarrassed me: I felt that I had shown part of myself that heretofore I'd kept secret, and the more I looked at what I'd done, seeing the picture as if through the eyes of a stranger, the more it disturbed me.

Sometimes I hardly knew which Guido I was: Cellini, the fearless one who stalked snakes in the forest and was a wizard with his pencil, or the lonely boy, pining at night in his bedroom, angry at his family, especially his mother, for reasons not particularly clear. Surely, I was also an ordinary teenager subject to his hormones, watching from the border of the cocktail lounge while grown men bucked the odds for money and Graziella Laporta looked on like a princess at a tournament of lancers. In my mirror I might meet the guy whose eyes glinted in the Villa's black ponds at sundown. Staring back at this face I might move my lips to say, "Who are you?" and when he replied, "I'm you," as often as not, I shied away from this fact.

I would not grow up to inherit my parents' restaurant business—they as much as told me how unhappy it would make me—but what if I failed as an artist? Grown up independence I imagined as a condition beyond doubt, where the will of such a one as Benvenuto Cellini could accomplish marvelous things, and I yearned for this. The Villa Giustovera had been a childhood adventure land of forests and fields and happy summers when the hotel was filled with uncles and aunts and cousins and family friends, but now that my grandfather was so sick, my grandmother also ill, and my parents financially strapped, it saddened me. I wanted to help them, but at the same time I wanted to break away.

After the game, after the men were gone, after everyone had been scalded by my mother's flashing temper, I loitered rebelliously in the lounge. My mother was done at the cash register, and now with a wad of papers in her hand she headed through the dining room for the kitchen to begin cooking for the night ahead. She was the complete restaurateur, adjusting tablecloths and inspecting place settings as she passed, glancing at a piece of paper in her hand while probably doing a mental calculation, looking up to pull open a dining room curtain for two more inches of light.

Your son's an artist, Gracie had said.

"I know," my mother replied, softening the furrow between her brows and suddenly stopping mid-stride to rest her hazel eyes on me. It felt as if she were seeing me for the first time in a very long while—perhaps from a new distance where she saw me more clearly. "Guido," she said gently, "make her a beautiful picture."

CHAPTER 2

A T SCHOOL OR AMONG my friends or in public places my father might insist on speaking to me in Italian, or worse, in his broken English during a time when I was acutely conscious of such trivial things as the length of a sweater. Worst of all, he might begin one of the comic routines we used to perform by addressing me as "Spaghetti," as in *Ehi, Spaghetti, how's come you gotta da meatballs inna you pocket?* I hated to be seen with him. Sometimes he wore his work clothes when we shopped together in the supermarket, looking to me ridiculous in his tight *barista's* waistcoat as he squeezed tomatoes, fondled eggplants, and flirted with cute cashiers. At night at the Villa, plump and oily in the white jacket and black cummerbund from his salad days in the dining rooms of Italian luxury liners, he could be impressive, almost smooth, until he broke into one of his zany bits, suddenly seeming to become an overgrown child. I could laugh readily with him when we watched Lou Costello, his idol, on television, but I didn't want my father acting like a chubby "bad boy" around anybody I knew. I wasn't the only Italian kid at school, and I could take a ribbing, yet one particular event stands out: when I was a high school sophomore a hood called me "a greasy Guido," and trying to provoke a fight, mocked my father as "a *real* Guido." Trembling with rage at his insult and filled with disgust at how nearly he had hit the mark, I blushed deeply and, ashamed of myself to this day, walked away.

Although my father was ordinarily prone to silliness when he was drinking rather than to anger, he would never let epithets go unchallenged. I remember very well one afternoon at the Villa with his buddies when I was around ten years old, when my curiosity about the bar and its habitués was just beginning. I didn't know the cause of his anger, but I saw him all of the sudden put on a demented looking grin, as if lowering the visor of a battle helmet. Turning to his supposed friends he improvised a scathing routine about "micks" and "krauts," lampooning them to their faces. I was astonished at how deeply he cut, and even a little afraid. I shrank away into my corner of the cocktail lounge to watch him go completely "Louie." That day he was both frightening and terribly funny. "I know what *you* is, but ken you fellas please-a tell me what is a *guinea?* I never learn-a this word, *guinea.*"

My mother, who'd heard the uneasy laughter and come to the side door of the lounge saw my discomfort and came over to put her hands on my shoulders. "Never mind," she whispered. "He knows what he's doing." That had not occurred to me.

In those days, even when we were at home as a family, I'd begun to use English rather than Italian as much as possible. I knew there was a certain power in the Italian we used among ourselves—"our other tongue," as my mother called it, *la lingua nostra*—and it continued to live in my imagination. My tongue was forked, I thought—no that wasn't right, it meant you were a liar. Then again, maybe I was. I shuddered to think that maybe I had been deceived by the Old

Serpent himself, Satan. Was I actually one of the damned? *My other tongue.* I used it to describe beautiful women to my cousin Cristiano, whose own Italian was far inferior to mine. Sometimes in my fantasies I conducted whole conversations with *le belle donne.* Of course I was in love with Sophia Loren and Gina Lollobrigida, international movie stars of the day, and I also imagined that my linguistic skills would help me to win Natalie Wood or Ann-Margret if we ever met, say, at a movie premier in Manhattan.

I couldn't deny the pride I felt when someone who was blond and light of skin and with a last name like Olson or Van Buren admired anything that was Italian. Then I would happily tell about my visit to Florence and how I'd seen Cellini's *Perseus.* In Rome I'd been to the Pantheon and Saint Peter's Basilica; in Milano, I'd been to the great opera house, *La Scala,* where my cousin Amadeo sang. Then it was enviable to have dark hair and skin that tanned easily like a movie star's, and if some ignoramus taunted me about my name or my nose or my father, I could laugh it off, but I also began to carry a pocket knife, inspired by the sword of Cellini.

According to my grandmother, a well-behaved *signorino* was supposed to suppress his anger and disdain rough and tumble confrontations. I was taught to be polite and respectful to my elders, and also I was expected to be generous with my friends: during elementary school, my birthday parties were often rather lavish affairs held in the Villa's main dining room; as a teenager, in the summers I hosted swim parties, and in winter, my friends and I sledded on the Villa's slopes. I was also supposed to be a model student who would when asked recite his lessons in both English and Italian for my parents and grandparents. I went to public schools but attended religious instructions, made my First Holy Communion, confessed myself on Saturday afternoons, was Confirmed, and like every teen-age boy I knew, thought constantly about sex. After puberty, from about the age of twelve onward, I had wet dreams almost nightly—I knew what they were and what caused them, but I dared not mastur-bate for fear of damning my soul.

I was a perfectionist, and I remember standing before the full-length looking glass to judge every aspect of my appearance. I was hypercritical of myself, and I also became rather thin skinned around others. My face could be colored by the smallest aggravation. My grandmother's mention of my clothes or hair style, my mother's glance at some pimple on my forehead, an offhand observation by my father about a friend of mine, even a compliment about a girl whose party I was attending, could cause me to flush with embarrassment. My anger and general unhappiness began to feel uncontrollable and one day exploded: I had plunged my hands into a tub of hot dish water that my father had just filled, and burning myself, I cast an angry eye his way. "Christ Almighty!" I shouted.

He slapped me so hard that I bit my tongue to bleeding. Stifling my sobs, humiliated in front of the salad girl at work nearby, I fled to my bedroom. I expected him to chase me and I locked the door against him. But nobody followed. *Wake up, stupid,* I told myself. *They don't really care.* I resolved to run away.

I didn't. I went to Confession instead, and when the priest asked me about my home life, I told him, "Everybody there is unhappy." The Business was struggling, my grandfather was so ill that he rarely spoke, my grandmother was ailing, my parents seemed to hate each other and I thought they both hated me. "Hate is an awful word," the priest said kindly, "and their problems aren't your fault. Try being nice to them." For my penance, he gave me a few

Hail Marys and Our Fathers and told me to be helpful rather than so critical. God would be watching, he said.

Stubborn, smug and resentful I was during this period, as well as preoccupied with what I'd been told were "impure thoughts." I kept a running tab on my imperfections, and every other Saturday, trembling with fear that my sins might be unforgivable, I purged myself in the confessional. I was an anxious adolescent, a lonely, only kid who spent as much time trying to please the adults around him as he did avoiding them.

It's obvious to me now that these contradictions within me, particularly my ambivalent relationship with my father, helped color the background against which Leo Declare would one day appear in my life. I sought him out, of course, because I wanted to be an artist, and I needed a model. Years of teaching have taught me that regardless of what I try to impart to my students, my very presence—and to some extent, the example of my own art—has the ability to instruct and inspire in ways I can't totally anticipate. Parents know about the importance of the examples they set—well, I'm not sure my father really understood this—and while I am not a parent, I have had a formative role in the lives of many young adults. Leo certainly instructed and inspired me. I had thought that being an artist meant being a nonconformist, a radical thinker, an anti-authoritarian, an outlaw even, and I spotted all of these traits in the man, as well as others I hadn't bargained for. And yes, he was a damn good painter when he wanted to be. A visionary too, in terms of what he saw the Hudson River College could be and actually was for a brief period in the 1970s.

"REPTILES ARRIVED ON THE scene 250 million years ago, and amphibians have a 50-million-year head start on them." I memorized these words, and other fascinating facts about these creatures "who are vertebrates, just like us" from a book that to this day remains in my possession. From my field guide, I learned to recognize various species of turtles, frogs and snakes, newts and salamanders, toads, swifts, skinks—the harmless as well as the venomous. With my *Big Book of Reptiles and Amphibians* I studied the beautiful, the loathsome, the tiny and large, the deadly. At the Villa, I stalked them through acres and acres of woodlands and meadows, hunted them in creeks, swamps and ponds.

My mother had also once been a child here, during the ghostly past when the fallen-down barns had housed cattle and sheep and flocks of chickens on her parents' farm. I marveled like an archeologist poking among the skeletal beams of the caved-in dairy. Its nearby pond was muddy green and filled with reeds and cattails where livestock once-upon-a-time drank and wallowed. I squatted motionlessly for a timeless time and stared through the surface scum, through the dark water that held my own eyes, stalking swift leopard frogs.

Snakes were always my particular favorites among the reptile family. That they "undulate languidly" or "coil in the warm sun" or "streak through the grass like running water," as my big book told me, was thrilling. That their tongues "flash like forked lightning" was poetry. What I read and imagined and saw with my own eyes and drew with my own hands, I took into my heart. I began to think of myself as an expert on snakes, and I considered becoming a herpetologist, a "doctor of snakes," as I explained to everybody. I connected my words to the pictures of the copperheads and rattlers,

I connected myself to them, dreaming over my books. In the field, I watched for poisonous species and was always careful when I scaled the stone walls, while always hoping to encounter one. I knew what to do in case of a venomous bite: in my pocket I carried a blue plastic kit whose lid was embossed with Mercury's caduceus.

Out behind the Villa Giustovera, I found two huge breeding grounds of garter snakes: flat rocks in the sun, crevasses, loose shale where they burrowed and multiplied, rugged stone shelves where they shed their skins and I collected them. Some of the skins were remarkably long and intact, translucent and smooth, dry to the touch—and one year I found so many that I thought of making a costume for the Villa's annual Halloween party. I'd scare people silly, emerging suddenly like some wild man from behind the curtains that separated the cocktail lounge from the barroom. I've always liked to make a strong first impression—my father taught me that a good entrance *jumps* your act.

Whatever he meant about showmanship, I knew how to get the jump on the snakes I hunted: on a warm summer day, one quick move and then gently, gently especially with the little ones, plucking them to my breast like flowers. Even the largest could be made calm with quiet hands, although some were too wild to attempt a catch. Mature garter snakes when frightened will shake their tails like rattlers, open their mouths wide and weave their heads. Non-venomous though they are, the threat of being bitten is not something to ignore. I collected plenty of them. Some starved in captivity despite the frogs and crickets I supplied for my cardboard box terrariums, some escaped, and most I released, believing there would always be more out back on the rocks.

You could lose bad at craps. You could be lucky with sevens and then crap out with them on your next throw. Box cars were special, but it was hard to shoot a pair of sixes when you wanted, and it seemed that snake eyes damned your luck more often than not.

Once I overheard Uncle Jacky from Brooklyn tell the Mule, "That one's got her eye on you." He was talking about Gracie, and he put down his cigar and cleared his throat. "Be careful, Georgie-porgie."

I thought about Gracie—ever since my mother had encouraged me to do her portrait, I was thinking more and more about her, and when I did, a thrill ran tingling all the way down there, where it seemed that nowadays I was always tingling. Why, why, *why*, was she with George McInnis, that insensitive, ignorant, unworthy Mule— there was something awful about Georgie, disguised as it might be by his all-American good looks. It made me want to puke, the way he talked to Gracie, calling her *Baby Doll* and *Puss* and *Smarty Pants*. *Georgie's girl*—ha. I never tired of looking at her. I was a secret agent man, spying on Gracie as she bent over to wash glasses, following her with my eyes from my corner seat, and I imagined my mission, which I had dutifully accepted, was to help her escape the Mule. While the difference in our ages kept me grounded, I sometimes flattered myself thinking how in a few years time this wouldn't be such a big deal, and that maybe she could be mine.

I was a wild animal hunter and snake handler, a snake *charmer*, on his way to becoming an expert, and maybe I would go to Africa or India to hunt cobras in the jungle and make drawings for a book I would write. In my own backyard I set a challenging task for myself at the garter snake den. I had observed a particularly large individual on several occasions, and I was convinced that this was the King of the Snakes, whom I would capture. Of course, I would then release him—well, after I'd shown a few people exactly what I could do.

It was early May, and the first really warm weather of the year brought them out of the ground every afternoon, out onto a shelf of hot slate where they slumbered and dreamed the dreams of snakes, older than Adam' s and Eve's. Sometimes, I would stride like a giant among them, plucking up any of the smaller ones that I chose to play through my hands. After a few early sightings, spotting the King became more rare, but then one day it happened: I found him stretched out in his striped suit, greenish-black and gold, maybe two feet long, thick and drowsy in the dust. He wasn't alone. Laced neatly about him was another snake, a smaller one, looped in figure-eights, like the snakes of the caduceus. Twined together tail to tail they made one thing, a magical, two headed beast.

Boldly, I reached down and swiftly took the King behind the neck. Then I grabbed the other one in my left hand. I lifted the pair and shook to untangle them until I saw where they were stuck together with what looked like white glue. There was no resistance, no squirming, no tail-whipping, so absorbed were they in each other. I separated them, and though they did not come unstuck easily, finally both tails fell limply toward the ground. The stunned reptiles dangled, one from each of my fists, dripping the white juice that reeked of snake sex. When it dawned on me that they'd been fucking, the fact that I'd broken them apart bit me with sadness. I put them down before they woke from their trance of snake love, and wiping my sticky palms together, I prayed that they could make again what I had put asunder.

I didn't learn until later—when I consulted one of my books—that the larger one was almost certainly a female, the Queen of the Hill, and perhaps the mother of them all. I wonder if I would have dared snatch her had she been fully awake, and not preoccupied with other matters. At first I regretted what I'd done, and yet, after a while, I began to grow rather pleased with myself.

CHAPTER 3

BEFORE I APPRENTICED MYSELF to Leo, there were other painters I studied through reproductions of their works. Although I grew up not far from New York City, I never set foot in any of its museums and galleries during my childhood, but I had lived for a time in Italy, the homeland of the Renaissance, where masterpieces abound. My lineage includes Cellini above all, whose autobiography I read and reread, and then Botticelli, whose works I first attempted to copy with colored pencils when I was a teenager. Leonardo Da Vinci's significance for a boy who fancied himself an artist and a naturalist goes without saying; however, I don't think I consciously put together my reverence for Leonardo with Leo Declare until a long time after I joined his crew at the Half Moon.

By the time I reached HRC, however, I'd mutinied against the captain: I was by then fully under the influence of the Aquarian Age, and for all its emphasis on peace, love and understanding, it also is a spirit of rebelliousness. "Question Authority" is still a motto among today's independent minded students; during my undergraduate years at HRC, I refused to take classes with Leo—a paradox perhaps, since I had once thought he epitomized our revolutionary times.

I am blessed in that I knew Leo best when he was at his best—the bossy, irritable, inspiring captain of the Half Moon—but in remembering him, I have to include my own self portrait. Call this vanity if you like, but most of us will, happily or not, retain certain pictures from our youth that summon powerful emotions and personal associations with the events of the day. In 1967 and 1968, Leo Declare and I were master and disciple, painter and model, and fellow revolutionaries. Many years later in 2005, I tried to find my way as a painter, and left my job teaching part-time at HRC. What I did mostly, however, was to write. Leo had died the previous year, and his death was, if not completely a surprise on account of his drinking problem, a grief to me. My sympathetic dean, Liotta Smythe, refused my letter of resignation, and instead, offered me the possibility of returning from an unpaid leave to my former position without being regarded as a new hire. As any adjunct faculty member can attest, this was a sweet option. After a year during which I'd written a little, painted less, but had somehow managed to arrange a midlife retrospective at a gallery in Chelsea, I returned to the Hudson River College.

When the Dean proposed I write a scholarly monograph about Leo, I felt coerced, but moreover, I demurred: how could I do justice to Leo without writing about our relationship and revisiting the seedy alleys down which it led us in search of a brave new world?

"But haven't you already started your story?" Liotta asked in her silky Southern voice.

PRIMAVERA, SPRINGTIME. IN ITALY, it's the season of the first true warmth, a time of fecundity, as Botticelli's masterpiece depicts. In Kinderkill it was on a spring evening at the Villa that we celebrated the 69th birthday of my grandmother, Maria Giustovera. This was a couple of years in advance of my departure for the Moon, when I treasured the rare occasions that our family might be together at the dinner table, which is, of course, a second altar for Italians. It was a Monday night, the Place always being closed on Mondays, and the guest list quite limited: besides my grandparents, my parents and me, here were my Uncle Tony (my mother's brother and only sibling), his wife Josie, my cousin Cristiano (four years my senior, cocky and aloof), and his sister Tina, five years younger than I (the family darling, whom my mother once referred to as a "surprise baby," and which for all her life she has remained.) Also with us that night were Carlo Manaperta, my grandfather's oldest friend, who lived at the Villa in the summers, as well as Mr. and Mrs. Lupo from up the road, and my grandmother's special guest, her dearest gentleman friend, the suave signor Ernesto Caballo.

I have never completely untangled their mutual attraction, but like Nonna, I was fascinated by the elegant signore, and dream about him until this day. (Whether or not they ever were more than Platonic friends remains a mystery; when I inquire, the Tarot deck offers the Two of Cups as a symbol of their faithfulness to each other, something my own eyes confirmed.) Usually, he visited us only in August for two weeks of holiday, and whenever he appeared, his presence brought back to the Villa an aura of the Old Days, about which I heard so many stories. His very scent, a manly cologne I supposed he compounded at his *farmacia* in Queens, was to me an invitation to adventure—or at least to my having a beard someday that I might sculpt before laving my skin with an equally irresistible aroma. He was more youthful than either of my grandparents or Mr. Manaperta, and possessed vigor as well as stylishness that were admired by all. "*Raffinato,*" people said of him, "well bred," as if they were speaking of a race horse. He was also the model of a thinking man who had made his way across the Atlantic to success in America, a success very different than that of my grandfather, a butcher and farmer, a Sicilian innkeeper, for Mr. Caballo was a chemical engineer who'd once had his own company in Verona. All my life he has served as an engine of my imagination, and his interest in me was a great boon to my youth.

At about this time, still in my early teens, I became obsessed by the idea of manufacturing gunpowder with my Gilbert chemistry set. I wanted to cause a serious explosion rather than some fizzling sparks. I had potassium nitrate, charcoal and sulfur, and yet some element of *savoir-faire* eluded me, and so I failed repeatedly. Alas, Caballo was silent on this subject, and instead preferred to talk with me about the masters of Renaissance art and how they had prepared their own paints. He loved the work of Sandro Botticelli, and it was Mr. Caballo who gave me the marvelous, illustrated edition of Vasari's *Lives of the Painters* still on my bookshelf. As well, it is to Caballo that I owe my life-long interest in Florentine hermeticism and alchemy; in fact, I used to believe that his vigor and riches might be attributable to his possession of the *Lapis Philosophorum*.

Although undoubtedly "very comfortable," as my mother once told me, he was not ostentatious in his wealth. During his summer visits, he dressed with simple panache for dinner: a thin woven waistcoat neatly buttoned under his jacket for cool nights, or dazzling white shirtsleeves when the weather was warm, with always a necktie worn when at table. When he took his evening walk along the country roads after dark, he would often drape a jacket over his back like a cape and carry a black cane. Even in the heat of summer his trousers were of tailored wool, a fact that surprised me: "Worsted," he explained, "is basic to elegance because its fibers are so fine and hard."

When signor Caballo was about, Nonna wore pearls and dresses of taffeta to table. Even after her left leg had to be amputated as a consequence of diabetes, donna Maria, in Caballo's presence, shone like a much younger woman. She concealed the artificial leg under ever more lovely skirts—created herself from imported fabrics—so that no one could have guessed its difference from her good leg. Her 69th birthday party was a celebration of her indomitable life, and what better gift was there for my grandmother than a visit from her great friend?

CAKE HER DAUGHTER BAKED has been eaten and coffee sipped, having been served in the exquisite blue and white china that came with Nonna from Milano, and so now my grandmother commences with after dinner chatter. *Chiacchierone* she is not, yet she embroiders her tales compellingly. Her bearing is naturally aristocratic, sometimes imperious, but she also possesses a sanguine humor and ever ready wit. She is accepting of life's vicissitudes, and she laughs on many occasions that I fail to see as funny. Although she was not raised for it, her years of country life in the Hudson Valley have come to suit her. Big-boned, tall and energetic, her movements are nevertheless graceful and deliberate. ("Dancing lessons, *quando era attuzetta.*") Despite the loss of a leg and the prosthesis she wears, she seems to have grown still larger since my grandfather's illnesses began to diminish him. It is I who have noted that Nonna resembles in profile George Washington of the US quarter dollar. When I pointed it out to her, she was flattered and giggled that she had truly become an American. Proud of my discovery, she kissed the bridge of my own longish nose. "We both have a nose like *Giorgio*," she said, though that did not relieve my self-consciousness about its size.

Tonight the Place has the feeling of earlier times, "before the War," she explains to our guests, "when everything seemed possible." Most stories begin *doppo il Ventisei*, after 1926, which is when my grandfather, Antonio Giustovera, with his brothers Renaldo and Palermo purchased the farm in Kinderkill. That these times also followed a Great War and the hardships of immigration is rarely mentioned. Back then my mother and Uncle Tony are still very young, and of course, my father has not yet sailed from Naples for New York City. While the Twenties are still roaring, my grandfather, *Nonno*, eventually moves his wife and two children upstate from the Little Italy of Manhattan to live in the Hudson Valley.

It's my grandmother, infinitely charming, who first invites their friends to the Farm to take the country air. Soon, the friends of friends are also coming in the summertime. Together they make democratic hay with Mr. Grady, the resident farmer, and pitch it into the barn. They let their sweat run freely, men and women both in shirtsleeves and straw hats. *Salute!* They raise their glasses brimming with my grandpa's wine, toasting each other's health, praising the fresh food on the table. After dinner, couples take their *passigiata* on a starlit lane at a place they themselves have christened as the Villa Giustovera. For them, my grandmother becomes *donna* Maria. My grandfather, self-effacing and gentle, a man of few words, even before his stroke, acquiesces at last to *don* Antonio. He gives the farmhouse wings to accommodate all of the guests, most of whom will eventually elect to pay rather than to work for their room and board.

But all of this is well known, the reminder of the happy past. Tonight donna Maria yearns for the *coloratura* that her friend Ernesto can supply. Accordingly, the signore accommodates himself to the role of honored guest and begins a fascinating discourse on the mysteries of the atom, which, he says, modern science has only just begun to comprehend. Everyone but Mr. Manaperta is awed by his erudition. Carlo Manaperta listens without comment, smokes and stares at the ceiling, drains another glass from the carafe of wine stationed before him.

I HAVE HEARD THAT signor Caballo had a wife and daughter who perished in Italy as the result of a fire that began in his pharmacy, and that blaming himself, he charged into the First World War seeking oblivion. I have heard people say that nowadays he's "involved" with someone in New York, and that he also "has a woman" in Verona, and I myself have noted that, whatever his age, he still looks fit for battle as a *cavaliere* and handsome as a movie star. His silvery hair is long and combed straight back with brilliantine. He wears a mustache and a short beard, *una barbetta,* whose contours I have watched him shape with the light strokes of his straight razor, a splendid tool with an ivory handle. I have just begun to shave, and my father has given me for Christmas a hefty, metal, safety razor with a faceted handle; however, it's the blade of Caballo I covet.

Many are the gifts he has brought to our home. I remember my grandmother clapping her hands like a child when he unloaded from his green Buick packages of imported cheese and *biscotti.* To my mother he regularly brings fashion magazines from Italy, and recently a bolt of lavender silk. Besides art books, to me he has given a tiny ship complete with sails carved from buffalo horn, and a nugget of yellow stone I had presumed to be fool's gold, but which he informed me was sulfur, "taken straight from the womb of the Earth."

Caballo is speaking now of the opera *Tosca,* of the fatal beauty at its heart, of Tosca's fire and magnetic personality, of passion that seeks to surpass all limitations, of Tosca's "ultimate triumph." Having destroyed the tyrant Scarpia, she leaps from the walls of the Castle Sant'angelo, to be reunited in death with her lover, Cavaradossi. Thus, signor Caballo pronounces, her beauty and their love become "deathless."

NOW MY MOTHER SPEAKS. "At the Villa our business has always been pleasure," she says gaily, introducing a bottle of cognac to the table. Although this night belongs to Nonna, still it has been born through my mother's efforts. At the restaurant we must, my mother always insists, pay attention to details, and she is the exemplar of this practice, of which her mother is so evidently proud that her eyes moisten. "White candlesticks in silver holders," my mother Anna insists—and yet the daughter of Maria and Antonio Giustovera is hardly an aristocrat. "One to a table, unless more than a party of four." Practical she is, although for tonight's occasion, we dine by the light of several branching candelabra that I myself have arranged on the long tabletop. "Guido knows how. Guido is smart," she says, beaming at me. Candle light is important, I agree, nodding my head, a little tipsy from my first sips of the cognac. To be allowed alcohol at the dinner table is not without precedent; however, tonight is special in so many ways—it seems that I am being invited into the grownups' conversation.

Although I certainly agree that pleasure is a fine livelihood, I see also how rarely my parents actually enjoy themselves at the Villa.

My mother knows what it means to be in the hospitality business, and she claims she understands what the public wants, which is why I have so often heard her exhorting my father to put on some "personality" for our customers. He can be very charming, warm and funny, although he depends on whiskey and soda to meet many of her demands. I have come to believe they were happier together in the days before I was born. No one has told me this, but I believe it.

Nonna takes an interest in my parents' affairs, but mostly she keeps her eye on me. I'm intent on pleasing her and because I try to be perfect, I hate making mistakes. I am not conceited, although I've been accused of this by certain kids in school due to my natural aloofness. Watchful of others, I am also secretive, and certainly Nonna's manner with me has helped instill the notion that I have inherited some special power from her.

Bending this way and that through time, our family history is recalled around the table. It has the lulling effect of a fairy tale for me and incites dreamy visions of a past I wish I had lived. Nonna recounts my father's first visit to the Villa Giustovera with happy approval, for she above all others loves his genuine talent for *commedia*. Now he has married my mother and then I am born, and when I'm five, before I start school, my mother and father and I make a lengthy visit to Italy. Sitting across the table from me, now, my father gestures with both hands by his cheek, inquiring whether I'm sleepy. It is an affectionate gesture, and his eyes shine with the candle light, but I'm not a little boy. I sit up immediately and drink from my tiny glass of cognac.

I keep my eyes fixed on Nonna and Caballo. I have no intention of following my younger cousin Tina from the dining room—at eleven years of age, moody Tina is not allowed the same freedoms as

Cristiano and I, although she is indulged in many other ways. The baby of the family, the surprise, the darling, my mother has told me more than once that her father is spoiling her and that Uncle Tony is also too lax with Cristiano who, she says, "needs a firm hand to guide him." Usually, Chris has his own plans, especially now that he has a car, but tonight he wants to stay at the dinner table and hear the old stories, and this makes me very happy.

As far as I'm concerned, the evening won't be complete without the tale of the Lightning, and it's this my grandmother now commences. "We were sitting here, in this room," she says, "finishing our meal just like this. The thunder was so loud as it approached. Geppina—do you remember her with her wild eyes and raven hair?—Geppina had just cleared the table when suddenly the house shook terribly; falling glass shattered and silver knives rattled in the drawers. The girl dropped her tray, which was loaded with dishes, right here, on the floor next to your chair, Tony. Then, as if shot, she fell to her knees." Nonna points to the ground: when I look I see the black haired girl, who takes on for me the dark and deathless beauty of Tosca, stunned on her knees amid shards of white China. Is she hurt? My grandmother continues the tale: "Maybe there were several cracks of thunder and then like a cannon ball it came at last into the room!" She throws her arms wide. Her eyes track the ball of lightning through the air overhead.

Taking his cue, Mr. Caballo rumbles the tabletop with his two fists. Our plates and glasses tremble. "*Era la forza del destino!*" he intones with mock gravity. He casts a look at Nonna, who is also smiling to recall that extraordinary night.

This took place before I was born, and over the years of my childhood, I have heard various accounts of the blasting thunder and the fireball that seared the air as it flew through the long dining room, although it is always to Nonna's version of the story that everyone defers. "*Così strano, così straordinario,*" she says, stroking the flesh of her left ear where an ornament of white gold quivers. I think it's like a tiny chandelier, I think that in Milano, all the women wear such jewels—which must be why my grandfather's eyes have lights in them, looking at his highborn lady. His hands, big butcher's hands that he washes carefully like a surgeon's, rest on the table before him as he listens.

"The electric went out, and the candle flames flew off into the darkness. The windows were open, you see. It had been so hot. *Non si poteva respirare.* We wanted rain, we wanted a cool wind. We had prayed for the rain and then it came. I say it was not a bad thing, that tempest and its miraculous bolt from beyond." Nonna glances at my father, but he's gazing at his empty wineglass, tapping it with his fingers, his thoughts apparently elsewhere.

"Then it was suddenly cold, colder than you would like sitting here tonight, believe me. The chill ran up the women's dresses and bit their thighs." She pinches her own face like a naughty schoolgirl. She often says things like that, and my grandfather lowers his eyes while everyone else laughs, my father too, and even Manaperta, amid his cloud of cigarette smoke.

"So cold that I grabbed myself—Nino was far from me, you see, at the opposite end of the table—and I sat frozen like this." She laces her arms across her bosom and grows completely still. A breathing statue she's become with dazzling gray eyes. Old Tommy Lupo is transfixed, and his moon faced wife Lena seems quite dumbfounded by Nonna's sudden intense silence.

Then: "Sitting at my right was *la signora* Dolcepane. May she rest in peace. On my left that night was her skinny little boy, Paulo, the one who became a police chief in the Bronx. That night he cried *Mamma!* and when his mother reached for him, he flew beneath the table to nestle in her skirts like a baby bird.

"Next we heard a great sigh, *un sospiro grande,* as if something long imprisoned had been let loose—isn't that right, Nino?" My grandfather nods. Nonna leans forward on both hands to address us. "If you've ever sat with the dying"—she leans back and crosses herself—"you know how much one sigh can mean. At such a moment, the condition of your own soul might be called into question. . .

"The lightning had not come through one of the open windows," she says abruptly, looking around at everyone. "You remember? The windows were open, but it crashed through the wall. Like a shooting star it burst into our midst, with its blue and white fire like a bridal gown trailing. Yet it did not hurry: it made its stately way about the central pillars of this room illuminating everything. I sat completely still, expecting I knew not what from the hand of God.

"Incredibly, without so much as touching a candle wick, it finally flew out through the same opening by which it had come. There! Exactly there!" She points to the wall, and with x-ray vision, I see the ancient hole behind the plaster. "That extraordinary moment passed, and sitting stunned in the darkness, we could hear the rain falling outside, the storm rumbling distantly, like a battle far off. We stirred awake, and Ernesto, you leapt to your feet, ran to the window, and signaled all clear."

She takes a quick whiff of the air. "I can still smell the electricity, and perhaps there is something else. Fear, perhaps." Her voice whispers away into eerie silence.

I have been to this place before, where Nonna's eyes glitter with lightning and the condition of my soul seems bright and dark at once. And sometimes, when the big dining room is packed with a hundred guests, gazing into the ether above their heads I myself have seen the lightning in its orbit, or else alone in bed, staring at the ceiling of my room I can see it like a comet making its way back to us. *Perhaps it was an angel,* I have thought, but also I have told my friends it was like the ghastly thing hurled at Ichabod Crane by the Headless Horseman of Sleepy Hollow. When someone objects, "How can you know so much about this? You weren't even born!" I recollect my grandmother, all of time at her command, and I too become a breathing statue.

There is usually some particle of mirth in Nonna, even on the most solemn of occasions, but tonight as she concludes the tale, there is a coolness, practically a chill. I'm puzzled by her last words. My grandmother afraid of something? I sniff the air, but I detect only the scent of burning candles.

At last, her audience rustles in their chairs. I hear Manaperta strike a match, cackling to himself as he often does. Then my father offers his pack of Old Golds to the other grownups. My mother excuses herself and leaves for the kitchen through a swinging door that waves goodbye.

CHAPTER 4

KITCHEN DOORS THAT SWING this way and that, opening and closing eyes on a scene—or like the shutter of a camera taking an image, like the stutter of film rolling through the ratchets of an old movie projector. How often my memories take form through such apertures! How many entrances and exits through such doors did I witness at the Villa and later on when I worked as a kitchen boy at the Half Moon! Why, I have only to blink my eyes and through my mind the reel of my choice can play.

"DONNA MARIA," CABALLO BEGAN, straightening himself in his chair, lifting his snifter of cognac. "I toast your long life and happiness!"

With Nonna, etiquette meant a great deal, and when Mr. Caballo raised his glass to my grandmother, we all did, pronouncing with him, "*Salute!*" Then Caballo nodded to my grandfather, and then like a true *cavaliere*, to each of us in turn. Mrs. Lupo and Aunt Josie giggled; Uncle Tony and the other men tipped their glasses with respect. I wore a serious expression to show that I was also a man, which by his appraising glance, I saw that Caballo confirmed.

"What a wonderful story, Maria. I can think of little to add to your poetic picture. Except for my humble sound effects." Again, with his two fists, he rumbled the table to amuse us. "Well do I remember the explosion of thunder, the shattering glass. And that fallen angel, Geppina—of course I remember her."

"That one was always a problem," Nonna said stiffly. Her tone was not lost on me, and I was intrigued: until tonight, I had never heard of Geppina, who lived with the family and worked at the Villa just before the Second World War.

"*Era saporita.*" Manaperta spoke up suddenly. "A sweet girl. A good cook." He kissed his fingertips in that Italian way.

I sensed the conversation veering toward the sort of topic reserved for adults, and I dreaded being told to leave.

"*Davvero,*" Caballo said, but without looking at Manaperta. "Exceptional pastry. How well I remember the sight of her white hands working swiftly on the flour board. A very talented and attractive girl."

I glanced at my cousin, but Chris just shrugged his shoulders. My grandfather raised his chin a little, smiling mischievously, as if to say, let us hear more about Geppina of the white hands.

"She wasn't born in this country, you know, but she spoke English quite well. She'd had some education. Oh, we talked, we talked. . ." Caballo's voice trailed off. Was he perhaps *involved* with this strange girl?

"Her independence and a certain haughtiness in her carriage incurred your displeasure, I know, Maria. Certainly, she must have deserved the scoldings you gave her. Anna was her friend, and I remember how the two of them seemed inseparable one summer. But Geppina had ideas all her own. . ."

Mr. Caballo looked up suddenly, as if he had just remembered my mother. She was still in the kitchen, and so his dark eyes narrowed, resting on mine for an instant. Then he said to my father in Italian, "Nunzio, your son, does he know about men and women?"

I was uncertain what he meant, although I had memorized certain biological facts and gazed long at diagrams pertaining to reproduction. And even though my father and I had never had a talk about such things, I knew about love—I was fifteen years old, after all.

My father answered Caballo in Italian, "He has eyes and ears."

Then the signore turned to my grandmother, whose unease he must have sensed. "Despite her, ah, problems, you kept her on, Maria, out of pity I'm sure, although this Geppina *was* a baker of the first order. One of her *panettone* was fragrant as an orange grove, and do you remember what she did with anchovies! I drank a flagon of white wine so that they could swim through me! What was she, perhaps nineteen? Unmarried, and—" he too kissed his fingertips—"it must be said, that any man was bound to notice her. Am I right, Tony?"

My uncle shifted uncomfortably in his chair. I recognized instantly that this comment had the potential for upsetting my temperamental aunt, well known for her emotional outbursts. It was said that Aunt Josie, bespectacled and always anxious, was quite a beauty in her youth, and while that seemed impossible to me then, later when I saw a photograph of her and Uncle Tony taken after the Second World War, I was impressed by her looks and terribly puzzled by the changes time had wrought.

Signor Caballo's comments had missed the mark, and Uncle Tony cleared his throat. He rested his arm behind Aunt Josie's chair. "I was working in the city then, at Cousin Johnny's butcher shop. I was here hardly at all, but I do remember this Geppina. She and Anna were girlfriends, but Mamma never liked her."

"*Scusi,*" Caballo said, a tight smile fleeting across his lips. "My recollection must be clouded. Or else I'm thinking ahead. I hear that storm approaching, and, well, I feared the lightning would strike before I could do justice to the girl." He smiled ambiguously.

"Most men only talked with her," Manaperta mumbled from the other end of the table next to my grandfather. I swung my eyes to Cristiano, who, smirking, raised his eyebrows in return. Manaperta leaned back on the hind legs of his chair, humming to himself. My grandfather, sitting beside him, was almost deaf, and anyway, he never objected to his oldest friend, Carlo Manaperta.

Mr. Caballo recomposed himself. Then: "The beautiful girl struggles with a heavy tray of plates and glass and silver. She falls when the fire from heaven strikes. On the floor, Geppina cowers, and trembling, she clutches my trouser leg. As I would calm a frightened animal, I stroke her black hair, looking down into her eyes—what large, wild eyes! She shivers and her head jerks from side to side as if to say, *No, oh no!* Then her lips shape the words: *My God, forgive me!*"

Caballo paused and I expected the dramatic drumming of his fists once more, but instead, in a serious tone of voice he continued. "I'll tell you this, the fear of the Almighty was in that girl."

As if to shape the hurtling ball of light, he gestured with his two hands overhead. Then he looked toward the floor at the tormented figure. I looked also. Geppina was there, more vivid than before, destitute and beautiful, with the terrible lightning overhead.

"In fact, later on we *did* speak at length. Of course, she could rely on my discretion. Even until tonight."

He raised his face and threw a pointed look directly at Manaperta, who snorted with incredulity. The cognac bottle had migrated to Caballo's elbow and he refilled his glass. It was usually plain to me when grownups, especially my father or Manaperta had had too much to drink, but with Caballo I couldn't tell. I had supposed he would never commit a breach of etiquette, but I sensed that now he might be very close to something like that. There was a rustling around the table, and yet I saw that everyone wanted him to continue, even Nonna. Whether it was because of Manaperta's various challenges, or because of Caballo's wish to offer up something truly special for the occasion, or because his tongue was exceptionally well lubricated, or, dared I suppose it, for the benefit of my cousin Chris and me, "our two young gentlemen," as he called us, he pressed on.

Reaching for his glass, he said, "After the tempest passed, we counted our blessings. No fire, no human injury that a brandy or perhaps a cup of chamomile couldn't soothe. No electric lights in the house, either, and so by candle light we hastily patched the hole that the incredible thunderbolt had made. Carlo, I will never forget the speed with which you handled hammer and nails." He tipped his glass to Manaperta who was humming in that private way of his, eyes on the ceiling of the dining room.

"As we were each preparing to retire for the night, Geppina took me aside, and still trembling, asked if I would come to her room in one hour. I didn't think of refusing the troubled child, and at the appointed time, taper in hand, I rapped softly, *tock, tock* upon her door. She opened and ushered me within. There was what looked like an altar arranged on her dresser top. Two votive lights burned before a large wooden cross, whose anguished Christ was painted to show all of his bloody wounds. The crucifix wasn't standing, but rested on its back, and it seemed to glisten, with the poor girl's tears perhaps. I could imagine how she might have clutched it to her bosom, but who would have supposed such piety in her before that night?"

Geppina humbly thanked Caballo for his visit. She seemed somewhat ill at ease to have him in her room, but knowing that he was a gentleman—Caballo gave a quick glance at Cristiano and me—knowing she could trust the signore, she began to unburden herself of a sad, involved story.

She was raised in a convent orphanage in Italy, which accounted for her education and culinary skill. She came to America at thirteen when a childless couple acquired her; although she was supposed to have been like the daughter they had lost, she was instead treated more like a slave. They brought her to New York and confined her in their apartment. She was not allowed to attend school, and only through an iron-latticed window was she able to socialize a little with those in proximity of the building. One day she fled. Her only refuge, she supposed, was with a nearby order of nuns.

Caballo raised the pitch of his voice to mimic the poor girl: "More than sanctuary, I hoped that the sisters would give me purpose and guidance. I wanted to love and serve Our Lord, but as much as I prayed, I never could find God's favor. Mother Superior said I prayed selfishly and that I was vain. Purity, she said, was not to be found in my mirror." The signore took a drink, and resuming his baritone, continued: "Her efforts to banish self-love proved futile. Her imperfections seemed to her indelible, and she was convinced of her unworthiness. She couldn't possibly take the vows of a novice, and after a little while she left the convent. Her recourse was to beg her way back to her adoptive parents."

At this point in her story, Geppina had begun to sob and Mr. Caballo had put his arms around the girl. He reminded *quella poverina* that he was not a priest who could offer her absolution for a sin she might feel the need to confess, and while he expressed his sympathy for her sad history, he tried to assure her that better days had dawned now that the family Giustovera had taken her in. Gently he asked why she wanted this visit with him in her room.

She hesitated, tears rimming her lovely eyes. She needed the aid of a gentleman, she said. Caballo told us that if he had gone to her room with anything in his heart other than pity and honor. . . His brow was lined, and he lowered his gaze for a moment in private reverie.

I struggled to contain my excitement, fidgeting my legs, bouncing them like a cantering horse I sat astride. I too was anxious to help Geppina, and I felt that nothing must be concealed from me.

Mr. Caballo stroked his pointed beard. "She had been deeply affected by that visitation of heavenly fire, as were we all. For me, Geppina's need, whatever it might entail, must become a commission. Now. . .*Now*—" he pulled on his whiskers distractedly—"I might well question the veracity of some things she said."

Geppina's people agreed to take her back. In order to supplement the family income, she was allowed to have a job in a laundry. One day, at a lunch counter on Mulberry Street she met a man. He seemed kind, and so she spoke to him of her life. They agreed to meet again, and then again, and then he suddenly proposed marriage. Geppina did not love her suitor; still, the girl recognized an opportunity. Surprisingly, her people were interested in the idea of her marriage. They could offer no dowry to her groom—quite the contrary. They struck a bargain with her suitor and traded her off like chattel.

After a civil ceremony—"Why not," she had told Caballo, "when God seemed nowhere to be found?"—on the courthouse steps her husband jested that the paper he held in his hand was proof of possession. She laughed. She said that this was the only time she ever laughed during her marriage. When the brute left for his job each night at the shipping docks, Geppina went to hers as a taxi-dancer in a seedy dancehall operated by her husband's friend. She'd been told she must obey and that if she ran away she would be hunted down and killed. She refused to prostitute herself, even though the money would have been better than what she made as a dancer. Brancano, the club owner, even forced her to hand over her tips. Once again she tried calling on God for assistance, but hearing nothing in return, she devised a plan on her own. She began to keep tiny amounts of money from her husband and her employer each week. She was a thief, she thought, but if God would not help her then she must help herself.

I was startled by the logic of Geppina's reasoning. I myself had often discussed with God my disappointment at his absence when I called on him, and Geppina's stance actually struck me as rather heroic. Here was the logic of an outlaw, its gist being that when those in charge of the law have abandoned you, you yourself are responsible to set things right. My own private code of conduct was beginning to shape itself around Caballo's tale, not only with regard to what I gleaned about gentlemanly honor, but also through Geppina's example.

"Can you imagine such an ill-starred life?" Caballo asked us. Everyone, including Nonna, sighed. "*Ebbe.* Of course the girl took with her whatever she could when she escaped that swine. And by your good graces—" Caballo looked at each of my grandparents in turn— "*and* perhaps the unsuspected grace of God, she made her way upstate and found sanctuary here at the Villa. Whatever her disagreeable traits, she earned her keep, did she not? When the Lightning struck, her soul was stirred profoundly. She told me she must make amends for a particular misdeed. It was for this that she requested my aid. I agreed to deliver a package for her. I was to give it into the hands of her father, and only to him, personally. I was not to reveal her whereabouts."

"Ah, *Caballo mio!*" Nonna interjected. "You should have suspected something was wrong with the girl. Because of your wish to be of assistance, you didn't question her, but I tell you, that one's mouth was filled with honey, and those dark eyes bewitched you. She was a liar. She was a sly girl who contradicted and disobeyed me. 'Geppina, why did you wash the linoleum with *javela* when I asked you to use plain soap?' 'Oh, signora, the floor smelled of fish.' Or else the most preposterous stories: 'A man came to the window when I was in my bath upstairs.' I told her: 'Well then, he must have been standing on a long ladder!' 'Ah, *si!* That explains it.' "

A ripple of laughter dispelled the tension at the table. It was clear that my grandmother had never been taken in by the girl. Thirty years later she was being indulgent of her friend's folly, but she was also offering him the opportunity to reconsider his lapse of judgment.

"You must remember the unusual circumstances," he replied. "Lightning is a phenomenon that science has yet to fully comprehend. For example, why did the ball leave through the same hole by which it had entered? God's will? Perhaps. Perhaps we should regard all such extraordinary events, as evidence of His inscrutable will. Did you know there are various miracles ascribed to the power of lightning? Cases when the blind or deaf, the paralyzed, the *impotent* have been cured. *Allora. . .*"

Aunt Josie stood suddenly, anxious to leave at this juncture. "It's getting late, Tony," she said, smoothing down her dress with both hands. She nodded politely to my grandmother and grandfather, made a strange face at Caballo, and wobbling a little, stepped back from her place, calling Tina's name loudly into the unlit rooms of the Villa's ground floor. I knew that my cousin would never be found unless she wanted to be, and I hoped that no additional commotion, as was typical of Aunt Josie, would end the evening.

My uncle, who had been enjoying himself like the rest of us, looked over at his son. "Chris, you wanna go home with your mother and sister?" I knew that my fate was tied to Cristiano's. *If he stays, I stay too.* My cousin shook his head *No*, and Uncle Tony smiled at the both of us. "You go home, Josie, take Tina. We'll come later."

Rebuffed, my aunt drew a long breath and said, "She probably fell asleep in the television room. I'll go see." She cleared the dessert plates, motioned Mrs. Lupo to stay seated, and left through the dining room's doors to join my mother in the kitchen.

"Shall I continue?" Caballo asked. My grandfather nodded. "She might well have contemplated the veil as an answer to her troubles, for the convent was what she'd known as a child. And I can well believe she thought marriage could be a means of escaping her awful people." He glanced at my grandmother, and then said, "Maybe she *was* one of those who trades on her charms, but to me she did not seem evil. Certainly she had a powerful instinct for self-preservation, but this instinct is something humans possess as do the animals."

Caballo looked into the faces of Nonno and Manaperta, the two men who had known him the longest. "Isn't it possible that the Lightning was drawn to the girl? Surely you know that some persons can call the thunder and make rain, and that some, through no intention of their own, are struck by lightning and even survive being struck more than once! Such phenomena might be attributed to the supernatural, or else dismissed as strange coincidence, but to the wise, nature's wonders invite scientific scrutiny.

"At the court of the Medici's in Florence, Marsilio Ficino explored the ways that cosmic energies correspond with terrestrial life. He was considered a magician, but he was undoubtedly a scientist and sage who held sway with many great persons; Sandro

Botticelli, for example. Some have a gift—isn't it true, Maria?—by which they are able to explore mysteries sealed to the rest us. And how blessed they are who find a tutor for their talents."

I have never forgotten what happened to me in the next instant: when Caballo concluded this speech, it seemed to me that his voice continued inside my head. *You, Guido Diamante, can become such a man.*

"When I left the Villa two days later," the signore resumed, "I carried with me Geppina's small packet, which had been addressed in her fine hand. Next day, I took a taxicab to that place, a rather shabby tenement near Canal Street. I knocked on the apartment door, persisting until the tumbler turned in its lock, and the door cracked open on a chain.

"A single eye peered out at me. A gruff voice demanded, 'What is it?'

"'I'm seeking Mr. Andrea Bosca,' I said.

"'Why, what do you want of him, eh?'

"'I have a package. . .'

"'What package? Let me see it!'

"'*Signor Bosca?*'

"'Yes, yes,' he said.

"'I bring Mr. Bosca something from his daughter.'

"'My *daughter?* Ah. Give it here.'

"The chain lock fell open, and he stepped out into the grimy hallway with one large paw reaching for the packet in my hands. He was about my age, with heavy shoulders and arms. I glanced past him into the apartment. I suppose I thought the girl's mother might be somewhere within, but no one else was visible. The place was squalid, which didn't surprise me, for the fellow himself was unshaven and stinking for a bath. I held my ground, moving the package behind my back.

"'One moment. A personal delivery like this requires that I have proof of your identity.'

"'Proof you want?' He had a porcine smile and his three-day whiskers bristled. 'Wait a moment, *signor Postino.*' He closed the door, then reappeared with an envelope addressed to Mr. Andrea Bosca. I recognized Geppina's hand at once, and also, immediately doubted this was her father."

Caballo paused and took some cognac. "What could I do?" he asked us.

The question had to wait, as my mother and aunt returned chattering into the dining room and reseated themselves. Unaware of the dramatic moment they had interrupted, my mother leaned over toward me as if she might mention that tomorrow was a school day and how early it would begin.

"*Figlia di puttana!*" My father suddenly blurted out, passing his judgment on Geppina, throwing his right hand up with that crazy gesture he used to dismiss any of life's unsavory features. He looked strangely handsome at that moment, his dark brows drawn together boldly, daring anybody else at the table to disagree with him.

"Zizi!" my mother said. "Please!"

He looked at her with disdain. The table buzzed with a peculiar excitement, for the rest of us were also deliberating about the proper course of action that Caballo ought to have taken under those circumstances.

"Punch Bosca in the nose!" Chris said.

"Fight him?" Caballo fixed his eyes on my cousin. "Nooo— *tsk, tsk.* I couldn't argue with a man that I wished were somebody else, even though I wished that other person had not existed in the first place. No, Cristiano. Whatever we might now think of Geppina, this man Bosca, wasn't he entitled to the package she had sent him?"

"It stinks like dead fish. Maybe the girl put some of those anchovies into the package," my father said, causing us all to laugh. He poured another cognac for Caballo, and quieting down, he said, "You handed it over, of course."

"*Certo.* I'd given my word. I was performing a service to help Geppina." Caballo looked directly at me.

"Bah!" Manaperta said. "Women always makin-a trouble fuh you!"

My grandmother reached over and took her friend's hand. "*Caballo mio,* you were compassionate, you were honorable, but that one, she had the devil in her. I'm certain that she stole from us. I lost a ruby brooch and a sapphire ring while she worked here. And signora Buonparoli lost a necklace of pearls. I could never prove that the girl was a thief, but I always suspected her. Especially after she vanished so suddenly." Nonna cut her eyes toward my mother, whose face at that moment was turned toward the unlit corridor beyond the dining room, leading out of the Villa's main entrance. "All that talk about God! How she deceived you, Ernesto! No wonder we've chosen to forget her until tonight."

"Maria, please forgive me for disturbing you," Caballo said. "Still I beg your indulgence a moment more. For a long time I've held my words about this matter. And these young gentlemen—" he motioned with a swing of his hand toward Chris and me—"they might learn some important things from my story."

"*E giusto, e vero,*" my grandfather said, stirring unexpectedly. *Fair and true.* "Good fuh kids ta heah." His slurred words conveyed a surprising strength.

"I was to give the package directly to Bosca, and now I handed it over. *Ah, me!* A small packet, but large enough to hold some pieces of jewelry, yes. He examined the neat writing, the tight knot of string, and then raised his eyes to me, smiling like a pig.

" 'My *daughter*—do they like her where she lives now?'

"I said curtly, 'She's among good people. Her talents, her piety are well respected.' "

" 'Piety?' he said. Then he laughed aloud in a revolting manner. 'Oh yes, I can believe she's on her knees often.'

"I had all I could do to restrain myself. The man was an ugly beast, and the thought of that beautiful girl having any connection with him was revolting. 'Perhaps, if you are fortunate,' I started to say, but I was disgusted, and without another word, I turned on my heel and departed.

"How it saddens me, Maria, to think that I might have played a role in some affair that injured you or don Antonio. I regret it deeply." He bowed his head.

The rest of us looked to my grandfather but he remained silent—it was his way of settling almost any distress, and it worked once more. Then my grandmother placed her hand over that of her friend. Her face displayed nothing of jealousy or rebuke. With her white hair rolled near the nape of her neck, the bun resting on a splendid lace collar, she looked regal indeed.

All the same, her friend remained agitated. "Let me try to explain," Caballo persisted. "I've always trusted in my own heart, and if my head might doubt, believing it knows better. . . Strange but when I think of her pathetic life I am still disturbed." He tapped his breast with the fingertips of his free hand. "If Geppina *was* nothing more than a liar and thief, your graciousness shines all the more brightly."

Caballo tipped his snifter of cognac to Nonna and drained the last of its fire. He inhaled deeply the vapors of the empty glass and summoned his familiar bearing. Drawing himself upright, glancing toward my grandfather, he took both of my grandmother's hands.

I stared at the topaz ring she was wearing, but I saw the absent sapphire of the story. I saw the lost ruby brooch, and I burned for that fallen angel, Geppina.

"That was years ago," Nonna said, forestalling further discussion. "Let us instead remember our joy at being together tonight."

CHAPTER 5

ARLO MANAPERTA HAD BEEN first of all the friends of my grand-father, a *paisano* he'd met on the journey to New York City from Nonno's village near Palermo. Their friendship was the beginning of America, they liked to say, a pair of old men now, smiling and clapping each other on the back. Mostly it was Mr. Manaperta who said such things, while Grandpa and I listened, Nonno silently urging him on with a thrust of the chin or a finger he lifted like an exclamation point.

Manaperta had helped him right from the start, had even helped him find a wife, encouraging his friend to do more than stare at those three pretty Milanese on the boat; the very same ladies who were now waiting with them on Ellis Island, waiting for America on the long concrete floors. "Look who's here," he said to my grandpa: Maria Belangeli and her sisters, how beautiful they looked even under these circumstances, their light hair piled atop their heads, their fine clothes bundled against the cold.

"You could see she like him, but your granpa so quiet, always a gentleman," Manaperta said. Nonno squared his shoulders and cleared his throat. The three of us were playing a game of rummy.

In America, people such as my grandparents, whose own parents had perished "on the other side," were as free from Old World customs as they wanted to be. Back there, back then, a Sicilian butcher would not even have been considered Italian, much less a prospective husband for an educated woman of Milano. But here, *negli Stati Uniti*, Antonio had prospects, Manaperta explained to me. Eyes on his cards, he called "Gin." After he laid down his hand, he continued to relate my grandparents' story.

Maria had traveled here with her two sisters and a spinster aunt, having survived the First World War as well as the Spanish Influenza, which had taken her mama and papa in the same week. Nonna's younger brother, Guido, the one for whom I was named, also had succumbed. Meanwhile, Antonio—his family called him Nino—already had a position with his brothers at a butcher shop in Brooklyn: this he told Maria and her sisters and aunt the day he came courting in a jacket and bow tie.

Their neighborhood on the lower east side of Manhattan was rather different from Palermo, he explained. Had they been to Palermo? "Ah," he said. "It's beautiful. As Milano must be," he added, never having been to the North. "Only more beautiful because of the sea and Monte Pellegrino. My village, Tomasso Natale is nearby."

An improbable pair, still my grandparents found in each other things of which they had been deprived on the other side. My grandmother's glamour enfolded Nonno; his strength and stability lifted the grief she carried for all that was lost in the War and in the terrible epidemic that followed. Here was a man of the soil on whom she could depend; she'd never known such a one in Milano.

Carlo Manaperta with his carpentry skills and sailor's English proved himself a valuable friend. He helped remodel the store on Mott

Street where the Giustovera brothers had set themselves up with the help of their cousin, Domenico, and he steered them clear of the local protection racket. Antonio's eldest brother Renaldo never quite trusted Carlo, but Manaperta proved loyal and continued in his role as a family retainer even after Nino and Maria moved upstate to Kinderkill.

I gave Mr. Manaperta the affection and respect due an uncle. Many people, however, tolerated his ways only for the sake of my grandparents. He drank much and had a wicked tongue. Caballo didn't bear him true enmity, but even when they played cards, they hardly seemed friends. Manaperta often cackled or mumbled, or spoke with a mocking grin, and once, after he'd made some incomprehensible remark, I heard an exasperated Caballo ask if he were "capable of speaking a human language." Manaperta pulled a monkey face and emitted several grunts; then, before Caballo could truly take offense, the rascal slapped his own cheek and made the Sign of the Cross. "*Pardona me, padrino,*" he said. Nonna laughed, but she quickly ushered me away from them, chatting about something quite unrelated.

Behind the cards they played on quiet afternoons, they killed time and filled time, choosing carefully what to say and what to ignore, while I, watching at their sides, tried to learn their game of scopa—*whist, whist,* like a broom sweeping points. I loved the Italian deck with its ornate figures of kings and queens and mounted *cavalieri,* whose stories would compose themselves before my eyes, and although I would occasionally be included to complete a foursome, I much preferred to let my imagination gallop away.

YOU MIGHT THINK THAT since I was brought up around card players and craps shooters and consider myself gifted with what as a boy I called "secret information," that I would have an appetite for gambling, but such is not the case. Whether with lottery numbers or blackjack or the stock market, whether shooting dice or blind-betting on horse races, my visions and intuitions do not serve me this way, and this has probably been for the best. Long ago, my grandmother predicted that my good fortune was assured if I would always keep good company. This she saw in my cards, literally, spreading open the Tarot, her *Tarrochini*, the "dear little ones" who'd come with her from Milano, and which are now in my possession. Sometimes she would arrange a few of the Major Trumps in a specific pattern and ask me to contemplate them while she whispered in Milanese dialect; sometimes she slipped the cards face down one after another from the pack onto a table top and asked me to tell her when to stop. Then, without turning up that ultimate card, she proceeded to tell me a story whose life-lesson I might well consider to be obvious— and yet the sound of her voice was always transporting. I considered myself a practicing Catholic into my college years, but I have never thought the Tarot impious, and why would I? Did it not have the blessing of my grandmother, donna Maria Giustovera? She herself did not attend mass except on special occasions; however, she assured me that *il Signore* understood her reasons, and of course the rest of us never questioned this. Her Tarrochini and palm reading, the auguries she read in the flights of birds, her knowledge of wild mushrooms and herbal cordials and her various idiosyncrasies deeply colored the *carnevale* of my youth.

My mother, however, did not condone Nonna's "superstitions," and it was indicative of a great change in all our lives that when the Villa was expanded in the mid-1960s and began to welcome customers previously unknown to the family, many of my grandmother's antics were suppressed. She was no means a witch, at least, she would have never called herself a *strega*, but the best my mother could say about her mother's repertoire was that "the old Italians go for this stuff, and so Nonna likes to give it to them." The fortune telling and the rest were meant as entertainments, she explained, "You know, *commedia*."

A card game in the cocktail lounge before the bar was open or late at night after it closed, these my mother could tolerate, especially if my father were winning rather than blowing a hundred bucks. But unlike my dad or my grandmother or me, my mother didn't believe in courting Lady Luck or in seeking supernatural assistance beyond the occasional votive candle she lit in a rack at Saint Mary's.

I turn to Nonna's Tarrochini as often as I like; and indeed, when I was first at work on these chronicles, they often inspired my memory. However, after long familiarity with the deck I have discovered that it is rarely necessary to open a complete spread, for the appropriate card in response to a question will usually appear in my mind's eye. With the gift, intuition is always available as a resource, and fortune telling tools, while they might at times serve as props, especially when employed for the benefit of others, in private feel superfluous. For example, at some level I already know what I need to say in this story—my story is already written "in the aether," so to speak—but the process of unfolding it card by card or word by word is something else.

I SKETCHED CARLO MANAPERTA's face once while he was engrossed in a game of gin. Everybody praised my drawing, and it was then that Mr. Manaperta called me Leonardo Da Vinci. All agreed that I'd captured the rascal's creased, oily mug, his black pupils magnified behind the brown frames of his lenses, the perpetual cigarette in the corner of his mouth. Into its plume of smoke shaped like an inverted bottle overhead I'd drawn a sailing ship—my grandmother especially liked that—and I had done his hair as if it were the sock-cap of a sailor. (Caballo once joked that Manaperta dyed it with something from his shop, and indeed, his hair was an odd color, almost orange, its long strands pasted back as if they'd been shellacked.)

There was much more to Mr. Manaperta than his odd appearance and rascal antics, however. Alone with him in his shed, he spoke to me with care and kindness, or if he were pointing out some aspect of his woodcraft, there was a certain dignity that one might not have expected. I could easily understand why my grandparents were so fond of him. Also, I sensed that his argument with Caballo had something to do with my grandmother and that it went a long way back.

I AM STANDING BESIDE the old man near his bench straining to see the precise work of his hands, anxious for the finished product, a present he's making for me, a boy of ten. He works with a coping saw, with chisels unwrapped from a shred of tartan blanket, and he carves with a curved knife. Sometimes he whistles or hums; sometimes he asks me to fetch him things—a glass of water, a fresh pack of cigarettes— or he sends me to the house to ask if dinner will be ready soon. "Don't stand on my feet," he says, puffing smoke from his nostrils. I back away, letting my eyes wander among the objects crowding his shed: boxes of tools, articles of furniture awaiting repair, and that great trunk of his strapped shut, padlocked in its iron buckle. I practice with my x-ray vision to pierce its bulwark, believing that the chest must hold a cutlass, a pistol, perhaps a treasure map. . .

"Try this," he says, handing over to me the wooden sword.

My heart jumps when I grasp it. I'm surprised it is so long and heavy; the tip sinks to the floor before I can jerk it high again. "Harhar!" I swing it clumsily, banging the leg of the workbench.

"Too long. *Dáme*. Give it back, Guido."

"Big is good to swing at the enemy," I protest, yet I pass back to his hands the hickory root he's been carving.

He takes up his saw to trim off a length from the butt. Then he drills into the hilt and sets a cross-piece that he's whittled as a guard. Watching, waiting to begin my own adventures, remaining at his side patient as I can be, I ask, "Was signor Caballo once a horseman? Did he ever ride in the cavalry?"

"Caballo? Maybe his people had horses in *Espagna*, long ago. I'm sure he ken give you some cock-in-a-bull story."

Wanting more, I prod: "How did he come here, anyway?"

He doesn't answer, but pauses and turns from the workbench. My spirits sink when he puts down his tools, but once he has a fresh cigarette, he pulls a chair forward for each of us and motions me to sit. He shakes his head, regarding me affectionately, and then, staring into the rafters of his tarpaper coated shack, he begins:

"*C'era una volta,*" which means one time there *was* . . . "One time there was a soldier on his horse, and behind him a war. So he comes to a beautiful *paese* and on a hilltop finds *un castello magnifico*. The road his white horse goes is lined with flowers and fruiting trees. *Posto di felicita,* he thinks, and he sings for the first time in many days. Open the gate, the people say. Here is a gentleman, we must treat him well. Children run to see the *cavaliere*. And his beautiful horse, a tall white horse, every lady horse is watching: he make them shake their tails when he calls: *Nrhrhrhrh, nrhnrhnrh.*"

"And what's his name?"

"His name, eh? Don Alfredo, an he. . ."

"The horse, Mr. Manaperta, what's the horse's name?"

"*Il cavallo?* Ah, *si,* always you think of the horse. So. . . This horse. This was when? A long time ago. We call him. . . *Trent'uno.*"

"'Thirty One? That's his name?"

Manaperta takes a long draw of smoke. He exhales slowly.

"Okay," I say. "Trent'uno and don Alfredo. What happens next?"

"I tell you what I know. *Alfredo il cavaliere* meet Prince Domenico and his *Principessa,* donna Rosa, so beautiful. Prince is a good man and he got good woman. Don Alfredo gives to them much respect, and to don Alfredo in return everyone is good. In this place people like to laugh. Very different from his *paese.* Something very sad when he thinks of his home, and this la Principessa sees. Oh, yes, Guido, he's a brave soldier, *capitano,* killed many men. Many friends also dead—that's war, and don't forget."

Suddenly Manaperta splays the fingers of his right hand, pushing the palm out, facing me: a straight blue scar runs through the fleshy part of the hand down the outside of his wrist and under his shirt cuff. I have seen this before, but always it startles me. Then he glances toward the small ebony and silver crucifix hanging high on the shop's wall.

"Maybe you ken understan: Alfredo so happy now, but also his pain. Princess takes care of him, good woman. Prince, he likes Alfredo too. '*S'accomodi, amico mio.* Be comfortable, my friend. *Cortesia,* no? Then one day, Prince he say, '*donna mia,* I go to my brother's country. *Cavaliere, vi prego,* take care of my lady.'

"He go and Alfredo stay. *La bella donna* sings. She plays the guitar, yes, yes, in those days, play like this." Mr. Manaperta strums an invisible instrument with his spidery fingers and moves his mouth to make me laugh. "Laugh alla time in those days. At night she tell many stories. Don Alfredo also has much to say, and so they pass-a the time."

It has become a love story. I know that many stories of brave men become histories of love, that many knights are inspired to glory by lovely ladies, and that such tales are also sometimes terribly sad. Even my father, who is happiest when Abbot and Costello are on TV, sometimes has tears in his eyes during the opera on Saturday afternoons.

"One night, Lady Rosa, she say to him, 'Give me your hand.' She will read the future. Alfredo smile. This one, always she's-a play games. He does not believe she is *strega*, no. She is like a girl with her games. 'Oh,' she says, bad things have finished well . . . but, signore, you must still fight for happiness.'

"'Will I be successful?'

"'Perhaps. Perhaps it will not be so easy.'

"So then he knows, Guido. The Prince does not return, no word from him. And she, his friend for many days, always together with him, she has love for don Alfredo, he has felt it. Can you imagine? *A-mor-e.*"

"What will he do?" I ask. Mr. Manaperta shakes his head. Excited, I say, "When the Prince returns, how can she stay with him? Don Alfredo has to take her away, because—a-ha!—the Prince is bad!"

"No, no, *ragazzino.*" He begins to cough and cough and spits an amber colored gob into the sawdust near his workbench. It shines for an instant. He inspects it, then he kicks it under. He clears his throat. "Prince is *good* man, *strong* man and he cannot be defeated."

"But she loves don Alfredo."

"Sure. But love makes a problem, I tell you. Prince is Alfredo's friend—*ma*, he's not gonna give his wife! And anyhow, friend cannot take wife. If he is friend *should not* even think about his wife . . . And donna Rosa is too good, not gonna let that happen. That's all."

That's all? That is not enough as twilight deepens and the shadows reach our feet through the open door of the shed on this warm spring night. I can smell my mother's cooking, and I know that we will soon be called for dinner.

I think there must be a great duel. I think that swords must flash. When the Prince finally returns, I think donna Rosa resists him and admits she never loved him, that she is meant to be don Alfredo's lady, everybody can see this. I think that Alfredo will first refuse Domenico's challenge to a duel, but then he will defend the lady when he sees the Prince's temper. He is an evil sorcerer who has bedeviled Rosa, and he must not be spared. I think that even when the Prince is pierced nine times by the good cavaliere's sword, and lying in his boiling blood that blackens, hissing on the castle floor, he will yet curse the lovers. But they have pledged their true hearts, whatever the future might bring. And when the castle vanishes, and all the villagers vanish into the air with their fake smiles, now that the sorcerer is dead, Alfredo and Rosa will stand together in a field of flowers. The beautiful horse Trent'uno will paw the ground, ready to carry them off. They will have many more adventures. That's what I think. I tell Mr. Manaperta.

He laughs. "Good story, but not this story."

"Then what?" I ask.

"You cannot always have what you want," he says.

He says that at last don Domenico has completed the business in his brother's country and that he returns more prosperous than ever as a result of his travels. He is happy to be home as are the Princess and his people happy to have him back. A great celebration is planned in his honor, but the Princess sees that something in Domenico has changed. In truth, she does have *the gift*—the second sight. Mr. Manaperta tells me that in some women this power is due to their pure hearts, but that the gift chooses for itself the one it belongs to. Some who have it are fools. Others are evil.

"And what of don Alfredo? I tell you," Manaperta says. "The cavaliere is not unhappy with Domenico's sudden return, for he thinks, 'My temptation will be removed.' Yes, he thinks one thing, but feels another." At the feast, Alfredo's jealousy grows uncontrollably, for Rosa belongs completely to Domenico that evening: without so much as wishing goodnight to their guests, the couple slips away from the party to enjoy their reunion.

Manaperta squints at me through his lenses. He fishes out a fresh cigarette from his crinkled pack of Old Golds and inserts it between his lips, tossing the packet away onto his crowded bench top. In the soft darkness, the match light flares, and his lined face holds a hundred knowing smiles. Then he disappears in a cloud. He coughs, thumps his chest with a fist, spits and coughs and curses in *Siciliano*. He sucks long on the cigarette and points to his medicine on a shelf. I bring it with the sticky porcelain cup, but he pulls directly from the bottle, gargles, and swallows. Then he stares through the failing light at his wristwatch.

"Soon they will call us to eat. Okay. You be surprised what happens." He takes another draught from the bottle and smacks his lips. He says that it's true, Domenico has changed, there is something stern about him; it is as if, having been burned by fire, he can now command fire. He is more like a king than a prince, he has hardened. "*È duro,*" Mr. Manaperta says. Noticing my confusion, he assures me I will understand what this means when I'm older.

A few days after his return, Domenico gathers the lords and their ladies and leads them, torch in hand to a special room in a tower of the castle. Some of them have been here before with the Prince and Princess, some are anxious for the séance, others dread it, but they comply because their Prince has commanded.

Alfredo is curious. He remembers the game—he thought it was a game—when donna Rosa held his hand and studied the map of his soul. It is plain that don Domenico does not have games in mind, there is a serious air tonight. The Princess too seems quite changed; with a black veil over her head, the long tails drawn over her shoulders like wings, she looks as if she might be a witch after all, mysterious and unearthly.

In the tower room, a single candelabrum is lit. The guests settle at a round table and are instructed to join hands. Rosa sits with Domenico at one side and Alfredo at the other. Before her is a large crystal ball into which she gazes. She tells the circle of guests that already the spirits of her dead ancestors, *i Morti*, have arrived to help her. Everyone is encouraged by Domenico to ask questions. One wants a son: "Not yet," Rosa tells him. Another wishes to know if her mother will survive an illness: "Already she walks to the open window," Rosa says. But it does not seem as if she herself is speaking.

Now the Prince bids Alfredo: "Ask a question, for my lady sees the future. Ask!"

Mr. Manaperta stares at me. "I tell you, Guido, Prince is powerful. Alfredo must obey. He look onna face: very black! Look onna woman he loves—like a statue she is. Like the one we put on the point of a ship, to take us through the storm. I tell you, this is a big deal, and you cannot break the circle! Everybody shakin'. Then Alfredo, he says, '*Bella donna, vi prego*: Will I have what I most desire?'"

Donna Rosa does not look up. She is transfixed, staring into the future, eyes locked on the glass globe. There is a long period of silence before she speaks, though it is not her own voice that issues from her lips. It is like the cold wind moving through the bare branches of a tree. Maybe the winter moon has a voice like this, Mr. Manaperta says. It is like the ghostly voice blowing down from the topmast of a shipwreck. Sitting in the dark with the old pirate, my surroundings feel suddenly unfamiliar, while he sings the eerie words emanating from Donna Rosa's mouth: "*L'uomo è andatto cacciare una bestia.*"

What does it mean? The man has gone to hunt a beast: what does it mean to Alfredo? And there is more: "*Spada in aria, sta'attento, sta'attento.*" Be careful, be careful! A sword is raised.

No one moves at the table, this I know without being told. Mr. Manaperta sits quietly letting the tension build. The lords and ladies all watch the Prince to see his reaction. Domenico is silent, but he looks at Alfredo, who has closed his eyes in concentration.

At last the cavaliere speaks. Mr. Manaperta repeats his words: "*Sì. . .Sì. . .*" And his mouth softens, his face brightens gradually. "Tomorrow morning I hunt. With the boar, I must take care—his tusks are sharp as swords. The message is clear, is it not?" He looks around the table. He forces a laugh.

"Domenico, he laugh too," Mr. Manaperta says. "All break hands from the circle. Donna Rosa smiling, she stand. Everything okay now."

I sense he isn't through, but we are interrupted. "*A tavola! A tavola!*" It's my mother summoning us to dinner from the back porch, just outside the kitchen. The shed is only a short distance from the house, and I hope she won't come here looking for us. I sense that Mr. Manaperta has some more to say.

He raises his wrist to check his watch, shakes his head and

stands. "That's all," he says firmly. He scans his workbench, peering down through his lenses, holding them on his nose with a long yellowed finger. When he finds his cigarettes, he stuffs the pack crackling into the breast pocket of his shirt. With his other hand he motions me out the door. I glance back at the wooden sword waiting to be finished.

CHAPTER 6

THE VILLA WAS "OUR house," and I knew how strange a place it was compared to the ordinary houses where other people lived. For one thing, privacy was rare amid the busy, peopled rooms, and the idea of "family" sometimes felt as vague as it did inclusive, because our house was also the Hotel, the Resort, the Restaurant. Although there were three different bars over the years in three different rooms and a cocktail lounge that was continually remodeled, the Villa Giustovera was never called the Bar, except by my father and his pals. To my mother, it was usually referred to simply as the Place or the Business—but it was also, indisputably, her home since childhood.

When my grandparents and great uncles were alive it was still occasionally called by them the Farm, for they had owned it together in the old days: as a boy I yearned for those times and for a horse to ride and cattle to herd like a cowboy. We lived on a dirt road until the 1960s, the houses were few, and cars rarely passed by. Indeed, most of the traffic on Widener Road was destined for the Villa Giustovera. The Lupo's, the Buonaparte's, and the Canale's were among my grandparents' local friends, all with their homes down the road beyond the Villa's long driveway and gate. There were still several working dairy farms back then, and from the nearby barns of Old Man Clausen and Mr. Stromm you could hear the calls of their cows at milking time and smell the aroma of the barns when the wind was right. I loved this odor, although the city kids who came in the summer said "shit" and called me a hick. Where Widener Road turned for the hamlet of Kinderkill and ran toward Route Nine in Wappingers Falls, there were a handful of newer houses, modest ranches or two story houses with dormers for the kids' bedrooms. Three miles from the Villa was the Hudson River heading south some seventy miles to New York City.

At the base of the hill on which the Place stood were two stone monuments, four and six feet tall respectively. Built by Felix Lundi, my grandfather's *paesano,* one of the markers was of polished rosy granite, cut to read VILLA GIUSTOVERA, BENVENUTO, A.D. 1931. The other, taller, more imposing, a later addition also executed by Lundi, was chiefly of red brick, but its marble face was inscribed VILLA GIUSTOVERA, POSTO DI VILLEGGIATURA, APPERTO TUTTO L'ANNO. A.D. 1950 ("Place for a country holiday, open year round"). Lundi had made his fortune carving gravestones in Mineola on Long Island, and the fact that one of the markers showed my birth year filled me both with pride and an eerie apprehension, as if I saw my own gravestone.

For a boy, the Villa's grounds and surrounding landscape, some of it mowed and gardened near the house, much of it over-grown with brush amid which the ruins of the old barns and crumbling out-buildings kneeled, were endlessly intriguing. Under the laundry shed I once found a pair of laceless work boots whose mute tongues, cracked and misshapen, whose blind eyelets of rusted metal I sketched and presented at school to win a prize.

I also collected other artifacts such as the saber teeth of a hay rake, even though they were too heavy to play with as swords. (I have kept one until this day, polished and mounted as a sculpture, an homage to Brancusi.) Then there were the truly spooky things that obsessed me, like the horned goat skulls cached in the niche of a stone wall, which my mother told me she remembered from her own childhood. And in the ruined dairy barn, I found a lidded, blue, ceramic crock lined with stinking orange paste. I told Tina that with this magical substance, I could revive the dead. She was five years old then, my angel, and I regretted frightening her when I dipped a stick into the pot, and stirring the muck, uttered an incantation.

Despite my religiosity, or perhaps because of it, I thought I might encounter a vampire at the Villa, and off-season with a crucifix in hand I poked about the hotel annex, "the Other House," as we called it, set back in the woods at some distance. I sniffed through those unheated rooms, whose mildew smelled oddly sweet to me, like the flowers at grave sites. In the vacant annex, which during the summertime housed so much life, I sensed another world, another layer to the here and now, and it wasn't the Heaven or Hell spoken about in church. I believed in ghosts, in the Holy Ghost I certainly believed, and in God the Father and in *Gesu Cristo*, and in the Blessed Mother, but also in the Devil, who must be rejected. In my solitude I also came to believe in some unnamable, invisible stratum of life that has enthralled me ever since. (Whether its importance to me is a type of wish-fulfillment, as a psychologist later suggested, or conversely, a projection of my fears, to me that world is very real, and its presence has consequences for the other world seen by the light of day.)

Even when my mother said to cease with my stories because I was scaring my little cousin and would give myself nightmares, I didn't stop. Back when I'd overheard my fifth grade teacher, Mrs. Badget, tell my mother that I seemed to be "something of a dreamer," I thought it was compliment. What might a dreamer be capable of? I had always had very vivid dreams and what's more, I believed that if I concentrated with enough intensity my dreams could become real, like the sword that I wanted and which Mr. Manaperta then made for me. And yet I was also afraid that what I dreaded might materialize. I was especially terrified of vampires, and worse, of turning into one of the damned myself.

Divided by fear and desire, I often mooned about the Villa, wandering among the hotel's empty upper floors in the winter time or poking among its barren fields with a stick in hand, hoping to unearth some sort of treasure. An only child, alone much of the time, I had ample occasion to explore. I liked to think I was bold, but I could also be overwhelmed by the thought of having gone too far and then having to face terrible consequences for my transgressions. After I reached puberty, because my fantasies had so much to do with sex, and were further abetted by vampire movies wherein beautiful undead women wandered all night in negligees, I felt that I needed continually to cleanse myself with confession; weekly, meekly I would repent my impurity and all the "milk" I had spilled while I slept.

Many mirrors populated the Hotel. Every guestroom had one and most notable of all was the full-length looking glass outside of my bedroom and that of my parents on the second floor. There I met my double regularly, relieved to see by my reflection that I hadn't unexpectedly joined the ranks of the undead. Mornings, my double promised to be the good boy whom everybody praised; at night he dared me to emulate Benvenuto Cellini.

Before this same gilded frame that was carved to look like a great wreath, tied with a bow at the top, my father inspected himself each evening before work. I studied the way he adjusted his tie or smoothed down his hair. Didn't he always say that his own father, a poor but proud tailor, had always cut a fine figure? *Bella figura.* Posing in my Sunday best before the glass, I too wanted a beautiful face to show the world, and I too hoped to make for myself a fine fate, which was something different than simply relying on luck.

I HAD SPENT NINE months in Italy with my parents, celebrated my sixth birthday in Naples, was feted with *molti regali* and later with fireworks outside my father's house while the neighborhood kids looked on in awe. The two-week long ocean crossing had christened me a traveler from afar. I'd been dashed with saltwater on the decks of the ocean liner *Roma* and below, in its theater, I had watched the film *Ulysses* three times, transfixed by the mythic images that came to life in the dark. When our ship sailed through the Pillars of Hercules at Gibraltar, I felt as if I myself were coming to meet the ancient gods.

In Italy I visited catacombs where skulls and bones were moldering, and at the summit of Mount Vesuvius I sniffed sulfur and peered down the stony cone into what I thought must be the underworld where Ulysses had consulted the dead. I discovered Pompeii's ruined glory, vowing to return someday to see the artworks of a certain house to which my father alone was admitted. At Saint Peter's Basilica, I drew a long breath of Catholic sanctity and descended to the tombs of popes whose stone effigies admonished me *Don't forget, don't forget* (or was this my papa's voice?) It was my papa who hoisted me with strong hands onto the kitchen table at his papa's house for that birthday celebration: me, the one and only Guido Diamante. With my family around me, America was celebrated that had been so good to Nunzio Diamante, to his young wife Anna and their lively son, but of Italy we also sang, welcomed home by uncles and aunts and a dozen cousins.

With this pack of memories I returned to America. On a big pad of paper I used to draw maps of whole *paesi* underground, and I pictured oceans there, islands, even imagining a sun and moon and stars for my subterranean world. I was also fascinated by any token of chivalry, and in my boyhood drawings I gave life to an entire medieval pageant. I acquired an army of plastic warriors, my favorites being a pair of jousting black and silver knights mounted on wind-up chargers. When I was nine I taught myself to play chess and did quite well and dueled in the cocktail lounge with smooth old Mr. Frosch, who sometimes allowed me to defeat him. I was, however, a poor loser. I would grow surly, despite the fact that Mr. Frosch cheerfully informed me that anyone could be beaten. I wanted to be infallible, I replied. "Like the Pope," I announced proudly. I regretted this immediately, and later that night I attempted to pray a Perfect Act of Contrition, insurance against damnation, in case I were to die in my sleep.

I suspected that despite my family's pride in me, I might actually be a bad person. Didn't I persist in my sorry ways, no matter how often I took the sacraments? Didn't I regularly keep the company of buccaneers, and with my wooden saber slice my foes in two, pierce their black hearts, stab at their eyeballs like grapes on my plate after dinner? And did I not lust after half-naked pirate women, purring to them in a hodge-podge of Italian inspired by Manaperta? I dreamed about towns such as Hispaniola and Port Royale, where I might meet a sassy wench for purposes that were not as yet completely clear.

I have always been entranced by that type of woman who can sit at a bar by herself smoking and drinking and simply being beautiful. There were a few of those who came to the Villa—maybe they were only waiting to be picked up by smooth talking men, but to me they looked like the pictures of freedom. Even before the days of Graziella Laporta, I was obsessed with their *belle gambe,* the beautiful legs of these women, bobbing their feet in open-toed shoes, and I yearned for a glimpse of their lingerie. *Lingerie*: the word seized my tongue. Repeating it in my best French accent, I felt a watery confusion of pleasure and regret. I would inevitably take that awful, impure mixture into the confessional every Saturday, but what was my sin? That I wanted to draw pictures of naked women? That I wanted to kiss their feet and paint their toenails pink? I was ashamed of my ignorance, and in the booth grew reticent; afterwards I wondered if the priest had misunderstood me, if perhaps I'd been absolved of sins other than those I had actually committed, and so I felt compelled to confess them again and again. Of what was I guilty? Of living, it seemed. Such was a pirate's lot.

SOMEONE FAR MORE PIOUS and knowledgeable than I, one day asked me why the stone in Jesus' sandal pained Our Savior so excruciatingly as He dragged his cross to Golgotha.

"Was it because he focused so much attention on it?" I replied.

My interlocutor was a nun, a Sister of Charity, Sister Vincent by name, and from her I was receiving instruction to prepare for the sacrament of Confirmation. I was about to become a "Soldier of Christ," inducted into Our Lord's legion by the Bishop of the Archdiocese, referred to as His Eminence, who would soon visit the local parish from his seat in New York.

Sister Vincent was clothed head to toe in black, and wore a black bonnet on her head, its black strings laced tightly under her very white chin. She and her sister nuns sometimes also wore short black cloaks— too small to be as cool as Zorro's furling cape, but still, I liked the way they could fly behind the sisters as they walked. Chris had called the nuns "bats," but I couldn't think of them like that: I was respectful of these "brides of Christ." My cousin also told me that some of the nuns were actually much younger than they appeared, and that some had to be "sworn in" because of troubles in their lives. He had winked know- ingly, and I, naturally, thought about Geppina. Could she be among these very nuns? Cristiano also said that since they were married to Jesus their ages didn't matter anymore, because Jesus is eternal.

I had no idea how old Sister Vincent might be, or why she had a man's name, but she smiled a lot when she spoke to me, and she was the only nun with whom I had ever had an actual con- versation apart from the questions and answers pertaining to my study of the Baltimore Catechism. At those times, I felt as if she were talking to me personally rather than to any boy whom she was trying to keep more interested in his upcoming Confirmation than in girls. Her eyes were pale blue and her face and hands very white, as if they had been floured, white as my grandmother's skin. It occurred to me that being a bride of Christ might somehow keep nuns perpetually young, and that except for her powdery looking skin, Sister Vincent might have the body of a teenager under her habit. It was a disturbing thought.

I liked talking with Sister Vincent, and I tried several different answers to her question about the stone in Jesus' sandal.

"Was it sharp as a nail digging into the sole of his foot?"

She shook her head no once again, her pale pink lips pursed, and continued to gaze at me expectantly. Then she gave me a clue: "Put yourself in Our Lord's place, His body broken under the weight of the cross that He's dragging to Calvary. He has all the sins of the world bearing down on him and He's preparing to offer His own life in exchange for our redemption. He's the son of God, but He's also suffering terribly just as you or I would." She blessed herself slowly when she said this.

"Was it because the pain of life can be worse than we ever imagine, and it's not so bad if we pretend that little stuff is more important than it really is?"

That got her attention, and she lowered her eyes while she considered it.

I looked down at my own feet in case something awful and miraculous might be happening to them at that very moment. During recent months my body had been changing rather dramatically, sprouting hairs and bulging muscles and smelling strangely so that my imagination often ran wild with the possibilities of what beast I might be turning into. Especially I dreaded the sudden boners that could appear at any time and in any place, and which Father Ryan told me to ignore so that they would wither on their own.

I was about to say something about choosing to ignore the stone so that it wouldn't be so painful, when Sister Vincent piped up. "No, no," she said, as if she were talking to herself rather than to me. She shook her bonneted head.

I liked the smooth folds in the satiny wimple, and just then, while her face was downcast, I had a terrible urge to slide my finger back and forth, deep inside one of the bonnet's tight creases. When sister Vincent suddenly looked up, I felt terribly ashamed of myself.

"It's the little things in life that can hurt so much," she said "But all of it, all your suffering can be offered up to Jesus." She crossed herself and raised her face heavenward, her pale eyes glittering with moisture.

We had been standing together in the hallway of Saint Mary's School, alone for a few moments before my class got underway. I thought our conversation wasn't yet over, and indeed I wanted to spend more time alone with her, but before I could could say another word, the bell sounded, and Sister ushered me into the room to take my seat. I had wanted to ask why the Romans let Jesus keep his sandals on; I had deduced this was so that the pebble could add to His torture in its tiny way.

THERE IS A PARTICULARLY painful episode from my early adolescence that I have never related in detail to another soul, but the recollection of Sister Vincent's allegory has put me in mind of it. My double, Cellini, would have laughed in my face rather than believe that this childhood indiscretion could be the cause of such long lasting torment—but then he could only see from his side of the mirror with its cold light that neither asks for nor offers any mercy. To put it simply, I thought I might have committed the sin of adultery, a mortal sin, and so I sweated with the fear of eternal damnation.

I have always loved my cousin Tina, and I have loved her in many ways beginning when she was the toddler whose pudgy hand nestled in mine, the little girl who listened wide-eyed to her older cousin Guido's fantastical stories—my cousin like a sister whom I love to this day, difficult though she is, and whom I resist like an addict in recovery. (It pains me now to write this because Tina might someday read it, and yet, I confess, it also thrills me strangely.)

I am the original cause of the distance that Tina and I now keep from each other, and it is largely due to an incident that occurred when I had just turned twelve and she was seven. It was Christmas time, near the Feast of the Epiphany that Italians celebrate as the day of gift giving, and Tina's parents, my parents, our grandparents and several of our aunts and uncles from the City were gathered at the Villa. We children were left mostly on our own, and since the ground was frozen and bare, the Villa's playroom, although unheated, became our haven. I'd already been Confirmed, and therefore as a Soldier of Christ I ought to have foreseen the danger. Tina has never spoken a word about what happened when we two played in there alone, and so, as troubled as my cousin's life has been, I cannot suppose that this regrettable incident is a source of her problems. I have explained it to myself many times, and yet, writing about it at last, I am still aware of this scar over my heart. Many times after the Incident occurred I thought that I'd attended to the pain as Sister Vincent advised, offering it up to Jesus, and yet the stone in my shoe always returned to cause me further agony.

Even after Tina was old enough not to require constant supervision, I persisted in regarding her as my special responsibility. A darling child, everyone indulged her, a smiling, dimpled girl with thick, curly, black hair. When she was small, I especially loved her plump thighs with their smooth skin, and in all innocence, I would lovingly pinch and even bite them pretending to be an ogre who wanted to eat her. Then I would tickle her until tears of laughter sprang from her eyes.

When the Man in the Moon was still quite young—that's how the story began, the one that was her favorite, and which I embroidered that day while we rode together on our imaginary pony. Tina sat astride my legs, facing forward, her thighs squeezing the flanks of her mount while I bounced my knees rhythmically. We had sealed ourselves away in the unheated recreation room. She had on her snow suit: a short, wooly plaid skirt of a piece with thick blue pants that buttoned tightly at the ankles over heavy socks and chukka boots. I told her it was perfect for riding—I think I should have noticed then the unusual excitement I felt when she mounted me.

The story featured two brothers, one from the Moon and the other from Mars, who had come to Earth to learn what it was to be human. My fairytales were often rather moralistic, and in this one, Gregory of the Moon had to learn to love his wayward brother, Carlo. They both had mighty powers, though Carlo Mars, because of a mistaken wish that Mother Earth had granted, was invisible to everyone except his brother. Gregory was good, but, Carlo, ah, me.

Gregory was adopted by a kindly, childless couple and lived with Mr. and Mrs. Grady on their farm. Carlo the Invisible always hovered around Gregory, and he was very curious about Earthlings, which to him were something like minnows or tadpoles to scoop up in a jar. Carlo once made tracks like a lion in farmer Grady's yard. Another time he took Mrs. Grady's flour sack and spilled it out into a big spiral on the kitchen floor. He played spooky music on the piano with invisible hands, scaring the Gradys, who believed they had a ghost in the house.

"He was like a cat sitting next to a fishbowl," I said.

"He wanted friends," Tina added.

"Yes."

The Royal Family were to pass through the village for everyone to see. Besides the King and Queen there would also be the Princess

Frey, who was said to be very pretty. With the church bells ringing loudly, proudly at noon, the villagers cheered as their beautiful coach rolled past. Carlo flew to the carriage, and like a gust of wind he pulled aside the coach's curtain to see the lovely Princess Frey.

However, at that moment, it was Gregory the Princess saw: she looked right through his invisible brother Carlo, and Gregory stared back into her blue eyes. Her shining hair was spun from gold, her cheeks were pink and white. In her ermine collar, in her blue cape brocaded with a thousand pearls she was like a living doll. Gregory raised his hand hello. Princess Frey waved back. He was in love with her, but so was Carlo. So was I, I suppose, in love with my creation, which I offered up to Tina.

Here's what happened the day that the dish ran away with the spoon: we were galloping beside the royal carriage to get ourselves a look at the Princess—up and down, up and down on our pony— when all of a sudden I pushed Tina off my lap, half-lifting her onto her feet, pushing her at arm's length out before me, stopping the story abruptly.

I said nothing about my reasons for this, I was incapable of saying anything. Expecting an explanation, with elbows akimbo and her eyes fixed on me, Tina resembled a miniature version of our imperious grandmother. I spoke not a word, but moaned and then doubled over, clutching my abdomen as if in intense pain. I think Tina saw that I was putting on an act—cousin Guido could be very funny—but she was puzzled and didn't laugh. Her inquisitive eyes crinkled while she continued to watch and to wait for me to say something. In fact, I *was* in some pain, for I'd been hurt when she bounced back hard against my erection. But that wasn't my only problem. My crotch was suddenly soaking wet.

Convulsively, in an effort to save us both from plummeting directly into Hell, I'd thrown Tina onto her feet. Then I'd lowered both hands to cover myself, and bending at the waist, had begun to groan. At this point, Tina could no longer contain her laughter and it spilled over me, multiplying my shame. Clutching my belly, I actually did begin to feel nauseous. In my heart I asked, *Oh, God, what have I done?* Of course, I had had the opportunity to prevent the incident in the first place—and that, I reasoned, was what made it a sin. I wondered if I had gone psycho, and having become a deranged pervert, was now doomed to commit other despicable acts. Eventually, I would probably be locked away in Mattawan Penitentiary for the Criminally Insane—it was just down the river near Beacon and loomed monstrously in my mind.

I knew I had made a big, big mistake, and that I would never, never ride Tina on my lap again. I told God right then that I was sorry, and many times thereafter I would tell God how sorry a soul I was. What was most awful, most shameful and incomprehensible was that I had persisted despite the arrival of my boner. For days afterwards, while I worked up a strategy to confess without actually having to go into the shameful details, I argued in my defense that I had felt no sexual passion, that the Incident had been purely a biological phenomena. Furthermore, I had not had the intention to affront God, and therefore could not technically have committed a mortal sin. Yet I was stupefied by the swiftness with which I'd lost control of *il sesso* while Tina bounced and bumped on my lap.

Meanwhile, my cousin's eruption of laughter attested to her innocence. She seemed not to have noticed the wet place near my crotch, which I was prepared to call ambiguously "a leak." She shook with giggles while her cousin Guido played a joke, holding himself like someone who'd been run through the belly with a sword. "Yes, that's it," I cried at last, kicking my legs on the cold, dusty floor-boards. "Carlo stabbed Gregory because he was jealous," I gasped. Then I died.

A moment later, when I'd recomposed myself somewhat, Tina was ready for some other childish *divertimento*. We left the freezing rec-reation room, me with my hands lowered as nonchalantly as possible in front of my groin and planning how I would escape to my bedroom to change my clothes. We would never return to the tale of Gregory and Carlo and the Princess Frey. Our magic pony was abandoned too.

From a corner of the playroom, the silent upright piano grinned with black and ivory teeth.

I hadn't harmed her. I was certain. I was the one who suffered and prayed many Acts of Contrition, avoiding the near temptation of every sin as best I could, and during my confessions accounting all my impure thoughts and then inventing many impure acts that I substituted to counter balance the actual details of the Incident. Gladly, I recited the penitential prayers I was assigned, sometimes saying them twice over in order to insure my clemency. In fact, as I learned many years later, I was suffering from a painful compulsion that the Church recognizes among those who strive to be perfect: Scrupulosity. And so I repeatedly confessed myself, not only in Wappingers Falls, but also when I had the chance in Poughkeepsie and in Arlington and in the little basement church near my cous-in's Susanna's apartment house in Manhattan, a place where I was certain sins more terrible than mine were regularly admitted and forgiven: Hell's Kitchen. Nevertheless, I was always afraid to say exactly what I'd done.

CHAPTER 7

WHAT DIDN'T I DO—THAT is, what about my sins of omission?
Did my inability to confess all the facts of my transgression
compound my crime? Perhaps it was pride rather than shame that
prevented me, and so, perhaps I sinned even more deeply by denying
my soul the opportunity to be properly shrived. I might continue to
torment myself in this manner were I still under the spell of Roman
Catholicism, and then this chronicle might very well be thought
of as a confession. It is not, nor am I an exhibitionist interested in
making art of my pain. My work has less to do with guilt than it does
with justice—all of my ghosts demand justice and truth, maybe Leo's
most of all, for his is the one provoking my return to these pages.

Tina is still alive, of course, but where she might be found
I can't say at this moment, since she goes where she will—and yet,
with a shift of my eyes into the aether overhead and to my left, I have
her instantly in sight. As for Leo, poor dead Leo, I see him to my
right and down near that hand. Memory, imagination, fact and fancy
are distinguishable to the healthy mind, but the act of recognition is
also an act of creation—of *re-creation,* some might say, or as Nonna
would put it, "consideration." It's why a story changes every time it's

told, even when the teller is sworn not to lie. Although I aim to present a fair and accurate portrait of myself and of those who have had a great impact on my life, I am well aware how indefinite the words are. Maybe I started out as a visual artist because of the comforting illusion that what I could set down with pencil or brush transcended the need for references to other facts. The problem is that a painting, whether abstract or naturalistic, is still subject to interpretation—as is a photograph, so often mistakenly assumed to present objective truth. I'm lecturing now, but it has to be said: we find meaning in an experience according to our own lights; both seeing and not-seeing are inherent to us and comprise what we ordinarily refer to as reality.

Oh, Leo, I do wish we could smoke a joint and talk about stuff like this once more!

THERE USED TO BE three apricot trees out on the north lawn of the Villa, between the bocce court and the pool, ideal for climbing, since the first forks were all low. An entire orchard had stood there before my time and before the Villa Giustovera itself—the trees dated back to my grandparents' farm and maybe earlier. Because they were old and neglected, the fruit of the remaining three was scarce and vermin-infested, and throughout my childhood, as they died, one by one the trees were felled. Nevertheless, I ventured along the limbs for what apricots I could find, and like the lord of the manor, considered them my private stock. Even the sap of these trees was sweet to me, and I can still taste the sticky wood-specked drops I plucked from the long splits in their bark.

It was up in one of these trees that I might take refuge from the influx of summer guests to spy on them. Sometimes there were children who came with their parents for a holiday, but usually they were younger than I, since there wasn't a lot for teenagers to do. On the other hand, there were kids I'd known for years, but since children change so rapidly, our cyclic reunions weren't guaranteed to be happy. Some years we were a crew of hearties glad to ship together once more, and from the treetops we all took turns on watch. Some friendships ended because a weeklong visit was never to be repeated, and in this way I also learned one flavor of grief.

Card playing—gin rummy, poker, scopa sometimes—was a prime diversion of many adults on vacation, and in groups of four or eight or more they would gather at a large picnic table in the shade near the pool, pausing only for meals, and after dinner, after dark, moving indoors to the recreation room until bedtime. For a few of our guests, whole weekends, weeks even, would pass in this way. One clan in particular, the Maggio's, always squared off against each other with fathers and daughters and mothers and sons competing, and I wondered what scores were settled or debts incurred like this. To a child lolling along the limbs of a tree, the seriousness of these games seemed incredible, and though the stakes rarely ran high, concentration always did, with hardly an extra word exchanged during a hand of play. Woe to the kid who pestered, or shouted, or snapped a branch during one of these contests.

FRANCO OSTIANO MUST HAVE been about fifteen, a year or so older than I. He was at least a head taller, however, and brawny, pale—so very white, I remember, as if he never had been in the sun. A city kid, he arrived in white shirt and dress trousers, but soon switched to ridiculous plaid Bermuda shorts with socks and black shoes. Oily beads of perspiration ran from his combed hair, and, in sum, he looked gooney and foreign. Our fathers introduced us. They thought we should be friends and that I could help him with his English. Shaking his hand, I agreed, although I had no real interest in that, and anyway, Franco wouldn't need many new words to earn my enmity.

A bully he turned out to be. He wanted always to defeat the younger kids at bocce, and he tried to take over any other game as well, whether or not he understood the rules. Often he sent his kid sister crying to their parents, who were supremely tolerant of Franco's bad behavior. I refused to lend him my archery equipment, out of selfishness it's true, but also out of fear: he told us that in Rome with arrows made from the metal stays of an umbrella, he had hunted alley cats. Uninhibited by my lack of cooperation, Franco fashioned a bow from sumac wood and household string and then purchased some arrows in the village. Joey Scarpetta and Mickey Santucci became his lieutenants; turncoats, as far as I was concerned. Worse, my father loaned Franco my thirty-pound bow while I was visiting my city cousins for a week that summer. When I returned, an awestruck Joey described how "the King of Bocce" had launched an arrow up into a flock of birds and skewered one through the neck.

One day Franco saw me with my wooden saber in the yard behind the kitchen where hotel guests almost never came. I was slashing at invisible enemies, and when I became aware of him, I sought to refine my thrusts and cuts, showing off my skills.

"So, you like fencing!" he called in Italian. "I'm the champion of my friends. I have a real sword at home. Let me see that thing of yours."

Hesitantly, I showed it to him, keeping it from his hands when he reached for the hilt. It was stout and pointed, its edge beveled, and Mr. Manaperta had told me that I could hurt somebody if I wasn't careful with it. But I envied Franco for having a real sword; in fact, I also thought that making arrows from umbrellas was fantastic.

"Want to duel with me?" he asked good-naturedly. "I'll use a stick. I'll teach you how it's really done." He searched through a pile of brush at the edge of the yard, found something suitable and broke it to length with a snap over his thick white thigh.

We squared up. I was confident that I could easily swing my heavy saber through his stick, and I waited for him to come at me. Franco only rotated the point of his weapon before my face. At last I lunged. I missed and he struck, poking me sharply in the shoulder. So it went for several rounds. As I began to lose my composure, he mocked me, calling me a little boy whose toy sword was useless. Rapping me on the head, in English he said, "You die! I kill you!"

Infuriated now and heedless, I ran at him with my sword raised, swinging it hard like a baseball bat. He deftly stepped aside and laughed at me some more. At last I stopped trying. Humiliated, I turned away to catch my breath and wipe my watery eyes. "You win," I said, hoping he would leave me alone.

"Wait," he said. "I teach you, like school."

He sounded earnest. I knew I had a lot to learn about fencing, but I couldn't. I tried to find something of what Mr. Manaperta meant by the word *duro*, something like the hard outline of honor, in order to survive my defeat and save face, but I couldn't. Nor could I open the Earth with a word of power and disappear before my adversary's eyes.

Beaten, I shook my head dumbly and walked away, hiding my face. Afterwards, I resolved to have Mr. Manaperta instruct me in battle with a real weapon, with the blade I knew he must have hidden in his seaman's chest. I muttered to myself and cursed vilely like he did in Sicilian, but I couldn't bring myself to challenge Franco for a rematch, nor would I become his friend.

WHEN IT WAS HOT, things started early in the morning at the pool: children were in their swimsuits right after breakfast; parents toted out lawn chairs and towels, coolers and transistor radios appeared. Blankets were spread on the tables in the shade and the card players began to kill time. On one particular morning, however, this routine was dramatically interrupted by a strange discovery: perched on the stump of an apricot tree was a large, moon-faced owl.

Like a sculpture fixed to its base, the immobile bird took no notice of us, even though everyone at the Villa eventually came by to see it. Well, not everyone: my grandfather, fading fast, was confined to bed that summer, but Nonna came, wheeled most of the way in her chair by Mr. Manaperta. Rising on his arm, she walked slowly over to greet the unexpected guest. She agreed with the rest of us that the bird's presence was most unusual. She had never known an owl to remain so near to people in broad daylight. My grandmother believed in omens, but she resisted interpretations that sunny morning, and simply joked that since the barns were gone, the owl wouldn't be charged any rent if it were content to stay outdoors.

All day we dipped in and out of the pool, returning again and again to watch the motionless bird. Behind pale inner eyelids, it seemed asleep. The curved beak and sharp yellow talons were fearsome and its strange presence fascinated us kids. At first we kept a respectful distance, but soon we edged closer in our dripping swimsuits, crouching in the shade before the great *gufo*. "I hope you are well, *signore*," my cousin Tina said, as with a curtsey she placed a gold berry at the owl's feet. Parents occasionally turned from their cards to see that the bird remained on the low stump, occasionally called a word of caution to their children, but they finally accepted the odd visitor, saying only that since it was blind by day or else sick, it was best to leave it in peace.

Of course Franco tried to disturb it. "Can it fly?" he asked, addressing the air. He began by tossing pebbles toward the owl and then directly at it. They pocked off the brown barred feathers of the breast, and the owl blinked its eerie eyes but remained stationary. A couple of the men grumbled that he should leave it alone, the boy couldn't predict how it might react. But Franco kept on, finally poking its chest so hard with a stick that the owl had to beat its wings in order to keep its roost. At last the bird grabbed the stick with its beak, and Franco jeered, twisting it away triumphantly. I felt powerless, and sorely wished that the creature would teach some manners to this ignoramus. Nursing the wounds to my pride, sick on sour dreams of revenge, I was condemned to watch. Joey and Mickey and all of us did, as Franco grew more bold and finally tried to put his stick into one of the creature's eyes.

The outer lids above the yellow membranes closed tightly and then the eyes opened completely and then suddenly the great bird leapt off the stump. Beating its wings flightlessly, it hopped about the lawn as Franco pursued it. This threw the smaller children and their mothers into a panic of shrieks and protests. Finally the card players could tolerate no more and their voices rose as one in complaint, a complaint that was ultimately directed to Franco's father who stood up, shouting terribly at his son. He grabbed Franco by an ear and cuffed him several times on the back of the head, banishing him from the pool, shaming him in front of everybody.

When peace was restored at last, the owl found another roost. In the high fork of a maple tree, he could be seen but not reached. There he remained unmolested throughout the lunch hour and into the afternoon.

All day he was in my thoughts. I wondered if he had originally chosen the apricot stump because of some special magnetic attraction. Surely, his appearance was a sign of something, and when everyone else went indoors for dinner, I hung behind, contemplating the day-struck creature. I wished he would take up permanent residence with us at the Villa.

I WAS LATE FOR dinner and ate alone unnoticed in the kitchen at the long table. I always enjoyed such moments, becoming more or less invisible while the Place bustled around me. My mother and her waitresses were seeing to the guests' meals, and I knew my father must be on duty in the cocktail lounge, because Gracie was tending bar. My grandmother had already joined my grandfather upstairs. Mr. Manaperta washed dishes at the big steel sink, probably a little drunk, singing to himself as he worked. His clothes, earthen colored and faded, hung from his thin shoulders, and I noticed his bony brown elbows, capped with whitish calluses. He looked harmless, an elderly man happy to be of use, swaying at the foam filled tubs, carefully wiping the plates and bowls with a sponge.

Outside the dusk had thickened, and I knew that if the barn owl wasn't sick or injured he'd soon be off, off on the hunt. I had a brief, keen sense of the bird with outstretched wings, of its sure, swift plunge with open talons. Didn't magicians transform themselves into such creatures of the night? Was I not a student of alchemy and shape-shifting? I passed my empty plate to Mr. Manaperta, who stared at me, his eyes large and unperturbed behind brown rimmed spectacles. "*Vai, vai, vai,*" he said. It sounded like *fly, fly, fly*—and I did, out the kitchen's screen door into the darkness, sweeping around the building's corner, finding the maple tree empty, and then running to the swimming pool.

"He go. È partito. " Franco said quietly, standing in the dew soaked grass near the stump where the owl had first appeared.

The place felt unbelievably vacant. "Did you see him go?" I asked. I was still panting after my sprint.

"No," Franco replied. "Nobody sees."

I had watched as Franco was shamed, slapped down by his father, and tongue-lashed in two languages by a crowd of angry grownups. I had watched the blood rush into his neck and face—*bruta figura*, an ugly picture, sobbing under his father's heavy hands—and I had been glad then, but now I shared with him a sense of loss.

"Maybe he'll be back in the morning," I offered.

"One time. No more," Franco answered in a whisper. He kicked the short stump with his black shoe.

I could just make out the rings of the old wood, and I wondered how many years those trees had actually stood, and how long it would be until every other trace of my grandparents' farm vanished. The night was black and vast. Out of it, the owl had silently come and into it returned. Behind us, lights were shining in the recreation room, and I could see the shapes of people moving behind the windowpanes. Kids would be playing Ping-Pong, and the adults with their decks of cards would begin again to kill time. Franco and I stood together for a few moments more, and then, with nothing more to say, we headed back separately.

Next morning, a Sunday, dawned bright and hot once more. Before mass, I hastened directly to the pool. I still had some small hope, had at least my curiosity to satisfy, but the owl had not returned. It practically hurt to remember him. Franco and his family were gone when I came home from church, and I never saw *him* again either.

CHAPTER 8

MY PARENTS HAD BEEN to the lavish wedding of a cousin on Long Island, and my mother had come back to Kinderkill crying for the faux-Camelot and movie picture Roman elegance so stylish in the early 1960s. Taking a second mortgage on the Place, she proceeded to remodel most of the ground floor of the Villa. She refurbished the front porch, facing it with artificial pastel-colored stone, and just inside, she had her builders add a wall of thick glass into which was set a magnificent transparent door. Other interior walls fell and new ones went up, reshaping the foyer and lobby of the restaurant, which was now decorated with red and gold pat-terned velvet paper. A cloakroom was built adjacent to the cocktail lounge, which was itself refurbished with turquoise blue uphol-stered booths. From the lounge you could look through venetian louvered windows onto the front patio with its maple trees like col-umns reaching to the sky.

Inside, the Place gleamed under batteries of lights. In the main foyer, a chandelier was hung that weighed "hardly a feather," as my mother put it proudly, "because it's plastic!" New lighting arrays appeared everywhere and were wired to a single control box that housed a complicated switch board as well as two huge dimmer wheels. Specially constructed planters were added in the dining room and were filled with actual soil to hold green polyethylene vines that made their way on rubber tendrils along the walls, and they too were given florescent tubes humming with light.

My mother's crowning achievement was the installation of her orchestra on a stage at the front of the remodeled dining room. Old linoleum had been scraped from the floor, and the boards sanded down until they were blond. Waxed and polished weekly, they shone under the feet of the couples who soon discovered the Villa Giustovera's new *ballroom.* They would dine and dance on Friday and Saturday nights, as well as on Sunday afternoons, if they were invited to one of those gala affairs over which the Larry Bell Boys, my mother's chosen orchestra, now presided. I had never seen her so happy.

Lorenzo Bellocielo, as he was also known, had a day job working at a dry cleaning joint in Wappingers, but he'd always fronted a band, and according to everybody, he was going to go places with the Bell Boys. Tenor sax was his axe, but he could also croon at the piano or sway dreamily on his feet at the mic, cradling the horn like a baby in his arms while he sang. And if Larry still sometimes had to take heat from a jerk who made the inevitable joke about his *cello,* well, he laughed it off good-naturedly. That's what a regular guy did. Larry Bell was no greasy guinea ready to bristle up for a fight, but was instead smooth and friendly with everybody, including me. I told him that when the Boys were swinging, he could bet that I was with it, hanging out at the back end of the ballroom, when the kitchen was dark, when my mother and father were both at the bar, and my grandmother asleep.

I dug his sound, and I told him so. "You make the walls come tumblin' down."

"Cool," was what he said.

For once it seemed that timing, which has so much to do with luck, was on our side: IBM was going *boom* along the Hudson, and with its expansion came an echoing explosion in the region's population. "Let these people dine and dance at the Villa Giustovera," my mother said, turning her right hand into the air, its index finger raised like an exclamation point, "where people have always come for a good time."

MY GRANDFATHER DIED THE year before the music arrived. A series of strokes had been for some time erasing him from our midst, and as his mind dimmed, his physical functions also deteriorated to the point where sitting upright was the major exertion of his day. By then he was confined to his bedroom where he might be propped up in a heavy chair well padded with pillows, his lap draped with a familiar crimson blanket, his hands motionless on the broad wooden armrests.

In his last months he seemed to think I was getting younger rather than older, and he treated me, a tall fifteen year old, like a baby. I loved this gentle man with his cloud of snowy hair and scratchy unshaven face, but whom, in fact, I had only known to be fully himself when I was very young. Back then, every night at bedtime, I was expected to visit him with a kiss. The exact moment, the exact place where I would be asked to plant it varied nightly. It was a game we played, with me waiting for the finger that tapped his right cheek, or his left, or his chin.

That makeshift throne gave to Nonno in his final days some of the regal aura that his wife naturally radiated. This old farmer from Sicily, this homesteader and winemaker, meat cutter and sausage grinder, this grandfather and father and husband and brother good as cold water on a hot afternoon, rested easily near the end, never complaining. It seemed to me that having accomplished his life, he deserved to doze all day, to dream away his remaining time in royal contentment. Beyond his bedroom, bereft of his presence, his *paese* grew daily more unrecognizable, but what did it matter? He could still recognize me (even if it was an earlier version of myself), and he needn't speak anything but my name.

Dino it became—shortened from *Guidino*, itself a diminutive of Guido. Through a few stained teeth and a loving smile he would mumble in Sicilian, "*Dino, vene ca.*" His index finger would show me where to plant my kiss among the rows of stubble.

One day I awoke to a general commotion outside my bedroom door: many feet raced on the stairs, there was an alarmed voice calling distantly down the second floor hallway, and then my father abruptly entered my room. He sat beside me on my bed, crying softly as he broke the news. His tears so surprised me that to this day the reality of Nonno's passing, the emblem of his end, is my father's face wet and puckered. It's still odd to think what Nonno might have meant to him: my father had always been an outsider at the Villa, and it was with my grandmother, delighted by his comedy, with whom he had a natural rapport.

"Never forget *il Nonno*," he intoned gravely. "Never forget!" And I too broke into tears.

At the funeral parlor, my mother asked me if I would kiss Grandpa for the last time, where he lay in his coffin. "You're not afraid?" she asked when I hesitated. In fact, I was embarrassed; I thought I was too old for that, that such a display was *Italian* in the very worst sense. Yet I was obedient. I was also curious about the facts of death, and I did it, touching my lips to cold skin that was not skin, loving the grandfather who was not this waxen statue in a satin lined box.

My mother and grandmother took Nonno's death well. For my mother, whose hands had been full with her father's decline and who still had Nonna's diabetes to contend with, there was some obvious relief. Unfortunately, it was during this same period that my grandmother's "sugar" began to progress rapidly, and never to be forgotten by any of us was how she had lost her first leg due to the disease. Arturo, a long time waiter, had volunteered to massage her legs and feet nightly for the benefit of her circulation. By accident he had rubbed raw the skin inside her big toe, leaving an open blister that would not heal. "Just like that," my mother would later say, "just like that, gangrene set in, the foot went bad, and then they had to take her leg." This happened about a year before my grandfather grew so gravely ill, and though it was for him a great sorrow to see his wife lose a leg, the loss could not debilitate donna Maria Giustovera. She adapted quickly to the prosthesis, and although she often relied on her walker or wheelchair, she could stand and move well with only her cane for support.

Under the thick beige stocking that it wore, with its permanent black shoe laced on tightly, the false leg fascinated me. When Nonna was sitting, it looked very real beneath her ample skirts; when she walked it moved a little stiffly, but the illusion was still convincing. Close up the prosthesis was a mechanical curiosity, a modern wonder, science truly in the service of humanity. The flesh-tone plastic under the elastic stocking was modeled as a shapely, ageless female leg, hinged with stainless steel at the knee, its mechanism concealed by the brown stocking. More than once I tried to draw a picture of the "fake leg," as everybody including Nonna called it, but it seemed impossible to capture what was artificial without sacrificing what looked so real.

Meanwhile, Nonna took to dressing very carefully once again, as she'd done in the old days of my childhood, especially for the evening meal when she would often appear in the family dining room wearing makeup and jewelry. Never haughty, donna Maria was, however, always a presence to be reckoned with; never exactly beautiful, she was the picture of a handsome woman even in her seventies when she sported false teeth as well as a fake leg. At times she looked stunning, especially when wrapped in her crocheted black shawl, which had come with her from Milano. Its silken fringe twined about her wrist and accented the oblong topaz in the ring on her right hand, the strong, blue-veined hand with which she gripped the pearly crook of her cane. She did at times thump that stick imperially when she entered a room.

Encouraged by my mother and father to take a sense of pride in my caretaking duties, I was now donna Maria's constant companion. If I chaffed at times under this yoke, nevertheless, the loss of my grandfather had impressed on me the impermanence of life, and I did truly treasure these years with Nonna. Like a hospital orderly, I served her insulin and hypodermic needle each morning and evening after my mother had disinfected the works with boiling water in a special stainless steel apparatus. Before bed, I relieved her of the prosthesis and took it to its corner to sleep standing like a horse. With clinical detachment, with an anatomist's eye, with an artist's curiosity I studied it closely. I have no doubt that my lifelong fetish for women's legs and lingerie was shaped by this early fascination.

Nonna reciprocated my attentions with lavish signs of affection, behavior I could never have mentioned to my friends, for it bespoke something far different than the independence we all craved. She was always affectionately resting a hand on my shoulder or kissing my forehead, smoothing my hair away from my face as we conversed. Her ideas about boys, about girls, about young gentlemen and *donne raffinati* originated in the *alt'italia* that she recalled from the turn of the century. Her family was of a class whose ambit included La Scala, the great Opera house where our cousin Amadeo still sang. From her I learned my table etiquette—"Never touch the fork against the teeth"—the foundations of French, which she taught me from a moldering French-Italian grammar, as well as how to collect the edible fungi that we gathered under backyard trees—"Speak to them as children." If I ever raised my voice to holler for my busy mother, Nonna leveled her gray eyes on me, and without a word I understood my fault. When I moped or whined about some dissatisfaction or other, she might laughingly ask if I had become a puppy dog. It was also she who confided to me that my father, believing too much in Lady Luck and not enough in his own talent, nevertheless had things to teach me about the value of hard work.

For Nonna's sake I studied and excelled in school. American though I might be, with interests all my own, a teenager, a hothead, yet out of love I played my role as her companion, her young gentleman whom she tutored in her country's old ways, and to whom, in turn, I would recount my experiences at school. She could be sharp with me or with anyone else, with my mother especially, and yet we all thanked God for Nonna's unfailing sense of humor. "My bad leg," she once said, shaking her head as if she were referring to an underling who had disappointed her, "I had to let it go."

When the music came to the Villa Giustovera, when the people came to dance, once or twice Nonna joined them on the ballroom floor abetted by her walker. Awkwardly at first, leaning on the metal bars, she shuffled her feet, and then at last raised her arms to sway in time with the beat. At the wedding of my cousin Margherita, relying only on my arm for support, she took to the dance floor, and for a few measures of "Finiculli, Finiculla" banished the facts of mortality. All her life, my grandmother seemed to defy gravity.

At the farm—no place that she as an educated young woman from *alt'italia* had ever planned to spend her life—she had decided the ground was to be trodden, husbanded and harvested. At the farm and then at the resort, troubles were to be trampled under foot. And if or when things came tumbling down, well, after all it was into the ground we were all eventually going, and it was up to God to judge us and do what He would with our immortal souls. She refused to be burdened by life, and in this way was of a different type than her daughter—which was another reason why the music became so important to my mother.

WITH THE INFLUX OF new people into the Mid-Hudson Valley, local farmers sold off their herds and pastures, and contractors made fortunes, erecting houses that appeared overnight like mushrooms after the rain. Widener Road was finally paved, a shopping plaza opened where it met the Albany Post Road, and Route 9 became a highway, ever after to be broadened and straightened and clogged with cars, ever on their way to the newest shopping plazas and malls. Much of southern Dutchess County was prime real estate, although the Village of Wappingers was largely ignored as Route 9 became a major artery and drew the New York City people ever further north. Kinderkill was whittled away but kept the tiny post office that marks it as a hamlet; today, it appears to passersby as rather quaint, a pocket of Americana, with its handful of colonial style buildings, each one boasting antiques for sale.

Although summer was still high season because of the resort business, the Villa in the 1960s was open year round, its restaurant and bar populated by a new breed of customer. One night, watching these people with their beehives and bowties pour into the ballroom for another of their loud office parties, Nonna, beside me at the kitchen door, asked in all seriousness, "Who are these strangers?" There were many of the white-as-Ike types that IBM imported to serve its growth in the Valley: crew-cut bachelors who subscribed to *Playboy Magazine,* cute bachelorettes for whom dating games were the preamble to their split-level dreams of suburbia, as well as frugal young families with one night a week to escape the middle-class tedium they had successfully achieved. My mother and father worked hard in an attempt to persuade them that their nights at the Villa were well worth their money.

I felt as out place as Nonna did, but for my own reasons. I was no longer the boy-hero of my imagination, and although I was the young gentleman in Nonna's life, that didn't mean I was allowed in the bar or lounge or ballroom after five o'clock. Naturally, Cellini fumed, always threatening to explode. I learned to masturbate at this time, and while I was conflicted in my Catholic heart, it helped to vent my frustrations. Most of all, I relished my solitary, ritual escapes to a place in the woods where I had stowed a box of nudie magazines I'd found in one of the hotel's bedrooms. And I never missed an opportunity to study the real-life women of the cocktail lounge and bar and draw them. My creativity has always been joined with what I referred to back then as *il sesso*. It's probably true that all artists are voyeurs, but more importantly, there's something truly erotic in the way that observation and creation can be simultaneous acts.

A taboo is always fascinating, and the bar in the evening seemed to me like that place in Paradise where the forbidden tree stood. It wasn't the alcohol that tempted me, for I had easy access to booze in the Villa's storerooms, and what's more, I often drank wine at the family table. On the other hand, I think that if I hadn't had Nonna's companionship and my sense of responsibility for her, I might have become a drunkard out of boredom, for my solitary fantasies were becoming less and less satisfying as my prospects for realizing them were not so apparent. Was it cowardice that prevented me from seeking to satisfy my sexual desires? Or was it conscience? Perhaps my angel has always understood me better than my devil and I am not fit for a life of careless love and debauchery.

I watched and waited at futurity's gate, tantalizing myself until I could no longer bear it, and with my grandmother looked away from the world outside the kitchen door, choosing instead to turn time back, preferring her memories of the distant past to the possibilities that lay ahead for the Villa. If I had finished my homework and Nonna and I weren't required to make salads and antipasti, if a hired dishwasher were on duty, she and I would retire quietly to the family quarters to play cards or watch TV and talk until bedtime. "Bonanza" was her favorite TV show, *"L'Abbondanza"* she called it, this myth of abundance, this vision of America.

CHAPTER 9

I HAVE MENTIONED BOB Badget a couple of times, and eventually I would have my own relationship to him, but it was first of all through my cousin Cristiano, his acolyte, that I learned about the man.

Chris had been held back in school twice, and at the end of his junior year, he decided to quit and leave home. Although his parents argued that he would never get anywhere without an education and warned him that he might be drafted for Viet Nam, they gave in. This was a source of irritation to my mother: she thought that Cristiano had been spoiled by Uncle Tony and Aunt Josie, who were also in the process of doing the same to his young sister, Tina. My mother had had a bad time with Chris during the summer when he worked as a waiter and pool boy at the Villa because of his inattention to the details of his job. He was also inattentive to his little sister who couldn't yet swim (and who was almost always placed in my care anyway), but the worst thing about Cristiano, so my mother said, was that he didn't show respect for his elders, most of all his one surviving grandparent. This was the beginning of a schism if not quite a feud between our two branches of the family. I myself rarely ignored or disobeyed my parents, both of whom had "big hands" that they were quite ready to use on me, but God knows I thought a lot about leaving home, even if in reality I could never have followed my cousin's example.

Cristiano was several years older than I, but when we were young we spent a lot of time together, especially out in the woods: as *ragazzi,* the country of our childhood had been unbounded and the source of many adventures. The family property—including the Villa and the surrounding fields and forest that belonged with it, Uncle Tony's house down the road and his land that adjoined the Villa's, our great uncle Renaldo's woods and his hunting cabin, and the various cousins' parcels that made up the rest—insulated us so well as boys in the 1950s that a trip into the village of Wappingers Falls felt like an expedition.

Chris taught me to shoot, and although I never took to hunting as he did, he convinced my father to buy me a .22 when I was eleven. (The symbolism wasn't lost on me, for I was confirmed as a Soldier of Christ at this time, when puberty was upon me.) Awed at Cristiano's skills, I watched him bag rabbits and squirrels, gutting and skinning them as his father and grandfather before him had done, swiftly and cleanly, unperturbed by the blood that ran on his hands, ignoring the steaming entrails that shone like ingots and jewels. But things changed between the generations, and Chris had no ambition to become a farmer or butcher, or a Soldier of Christ, for that matter. His only interests seemed to be cars and girls, and perhaps it was as my mother said, that he was in danger of turning out shiftless. At the time, I thought it was a funny word to use because of his car and all, but the look in her face told me this possibility would be a sad outcome for my cousin.

At the Villa, we Diamante's stayed put and people came to us because hospitality was our business, and what's more, the restaurant depended on our retaining what was genuinely Italian. It was this insistence on tradition and a failure to adapt to demands for speedy service and customer volume that would eventually help kill the Villa as well as my parents' marriage. By contrast, my uncle Tony was American in ways that neither of them were, and his wife, Josie, was smart enough to stand to the side of his determination. He was always on the go, changing jobs to cut meat at one new supermarket or another, taking another new job with a raise, even in a shopping plaza as far away as Peekskill if the money were good. After the War, his patrimony had included fifty acres of land and liberation from his parents' hotel business. Uncle Tony was perhaps the only man ever to resist Nonna's power, and she never once remarked on the distance that he kept from us, always referring proudly to him and his family. "See how good they live?" Nonna would say. She was as content with her son's independence as she was with her daughter's unwavering devotion.

All of this had something to do with why my uncle let Cristiano quit school and leave home. Uncle Tony let him go and find a job, let him rent a room with his own kitchen, let him have the old Chevy whose engine Chris and his friends rebuilt. All this despite Aunt Josie's hysterical protests that her son might starve to death like a bum, *un disgraziato*. Of course, my aunt kept cooking for him even after he moved into Wappingers, but if she hoped to lure him back home with platters of eggplant *parmagiana*, she was mistaken.

My cousin had wheels, and in his overhauled jalopy, he was, as we used to say, *hauling* along the county's newly paved roadways. It wasn't simply an act of defiance or a haphazard rebellion. In fact, he did what he had told his parents he'd planned to do and right away got a job. He worked outside Poughkeepsie in Arlington at a store that had once been called Conklin's, a clothing and shoe store that had reopened under new management, and was now called Badget's Bazaar. It was run by Robert E. Badget, a former high school teacher who regardless of Cristiano's academic failures, liked him, and was happy to have him "on board." Chris said that together with Bob he was "going places," and, as he wisecracked, "I don't even have to join the Navy."

According to Chris, Bob—"everybody calls him Bob"—had realized that "the future is retail," and he was giving Chris the opportunity to get in on the ground floor. Chris was always quoting him, and because he'd been a teacher and because his wife Connie still taught elementary school in Wappingers, Uncle Tony and Aunt Josie must have thought that teaming up with the Badget's was a good bet for their son. Uncle Tony had hopes for him, but he also realized how thick-headed my cousin was, and so he was basically left to sink or swim.

Chris had always been interested in girls, and I knew that he'd had "extensive experience," with a girl named Shirley from Arlington. She was his first steady, and he had swept her away in the Chevy, far away from my curiosity. Although I rarely got to ride with Chris, he and his hot engine conferred on me a certain notoriety, and once, when one of the village hoods told me my cousin was "all aces," I felt myself flush with pride. Shirley was history by the time Chris left home, and Aunt Josie was relieved to learn that "what's-her-name-from-Arlington" wasn't pregnant: "Thanks be to *la Madonna!*"

I remembered well the summer when Chris worked for us, because it was the year our cousin Carol, almost unrecognizable to me once she'd "filled out," spent a week at the Villa with her red-headed friend, Laurie. They were both from Brooklyn and teased their hair with rat-tail combs, and smoked cigarettes in the dark by the swimming pool, and danced the "Locomotion" near the jukebox in the recreation room. Chris later told me that all week Laurie had been teasing his cock, and that the night before she left he'd gotten what he wanted. Had he actually laid her? I was so much in awe of this possibility that I never asked him directly.

I too was interested in "the ladies," I told him, and bragged that I'd met plenty of *belle donne* at the Villa—but Cristiano only smiled and said I didn't know what I was talking about, that I probably didn't even know what a French kiss was.

"Can you go to Hell for that?" I asked naively.

He laughed and grabbed me behind the neck. "Naw, kid. You go to Heaven."

AT ABOUT THIS TIME, I began to fancy myself as "Guy Diamond, that guy from the Villa," and trying to look suave before my mirror, I recited my line as if I were James Bond introducing himself. I thought about the pretty girls at school and considered which ones I might want to "entertain" at my swimming pool. I had kissed a few girls and although I could only imagine what it meant to French kiss and pet, I planned to get a girl alone, exactly who I hadn't yet decided, upstairs in one of the Villa's bedrooms. I was learning to put on a pretty good act as a teenager.

Everybody knew I was a budding artist, an honor student, a performer, and so on, but also I had another talent that I kept private. This was my *secret information.* Although it was yet to become useful with the opposite sex and sometimes felt like nothing more than good guess work, my power could also prove amazing. Once my father had won big at dice when he followed my advice on every pass and bet. However, my secret information could also yield unexpected or unwanted results. For example, on more than one occasion when I was asked for a sketch-portrait by a customer at the Villa and I added certain background details—shadowy forms, other human figures, animals, images that I believed belonged with the main figure—my pictures were received with puzzled silence and even rejected.

I'd been especially hurt way back in sixth grade when I gave the class heartthrob, Sarah Crawford, one of my artworks. With a razor knife I'd cut her photo carefully from the black and white class composite, mounted it on green paper, and then crayoned a pale moon rising behind her. I portrayed her as a beautiful blossom amid a dreamy landscape and titled the piece "Moon Flower." I inscribed it "To Sarah, from the artist Guy." While she thanked me for the piece, she never again mentioned it. After she moved away, in seventh grade, I heard she'd been diagnosed with leukemia and had died, which saddened me terribly and confirmed my sense that she was never quite of this world.

Generally, I hated being asked to explain my pictures or the "meaning" of the clay figurines I arranged in dioramas—weren't Adam and Eve and the Serpent obvious?—but I would sometimes spout off about my art as if I were interpreting someone else's work. I might embark on stories that I thought highly entertaining, but which could elicit looks of confusion. If I were in a bad mood, I might seek a subtle revenge on my audience and begin to talk about their secret fears—snakes were always a good bet—or warn them they should be careful to avoid being struck by lightning.

Where do you get these ideas? That was a question that could stop me, whether spoken by family or friend, by chick or chump or foe. The truth was, I couldn't say. When I was making art, I simply *saw* things. Afterwards, I just said whatever came into my mind. Eventually, though, I learned to keep quiet about my insights, since nobody except Nonna wanted to hear about them.

Throughout my youth I drew pictures of people and pictures of animals, and I knew that animals could speak. In many fairy tales they spoke human words, but as a country boy I knew how they could communicate with their eyes and bodies and animal voices. I knew that they have lives something like our own, with love and children and hunger and fear and death. We ourselves are animals, and so the Indians often adopted for themselves the names of the forest animals and birds. I liked to think of myself as "Hawk," and I used to pretend that I was a Wappinger Indian when I was alone in the woods and fields. Wearing a loincloth that I'd made from a piece of chamois, slinking forward on my belly in the grass, I stalked deer and rabbits, and as I've already said, stocked many terrariums with turtles, salamanders and snakes. Sometimes I ran completely nude through the woods and swam in an old duckweed covered pond that had once been a watering hole for Nonno's cattle.

Those were the days before sex, or rather before my want of it would preoccupy me so completely, days when boners and wet dreams were surprising and uncomfortable, but when I was still afraid to masturbate because I'd been warned it would lead me to Hell. I was an only child and secretive about my private life, and I fell prey to many misconceptions. I was afraid to bother my older cousin Chris with questions about sex and sanctity, and anyway, he was rarely straight with me. He liked to poke at my insecurities, attempting to loosen me up, I realize now, although most of the time I didn't get it.

I learned how to handle my gun, but I killed nothing except a single woodchuck who had devastated the vegetable garden, and this gave me no joy. I had seen what the land could yield to the hunters in their red jackets who came from the City in late autumn every year. I relished the game birds and rabbits and venison my mother served with cornmeal polenta, cooked *a la cacciatore* for them. Whatever vague fears I had about the appetites of the flesh—was I potentially a glutton, as well as sexual deviant?—and however much I loved the wild animals in the woods, I knew that to partake of a harvest feast was sacramental, the very source of the Thanksgiving holiday.

I was passionate about many different sorts of things, some of them quite contradictory, and this curiosity was a quality of my innocence. My boyhood heroes included the great artists of the Renaissance, I was always interested in the religious themes of their work, and yet I was also fascinated by swords and whips and wild stallions, by pirate ships and Saint Elmo's Fire that flashed among the topsails, by fairytales about Arabian princesses who needed to be rescued from evil magicians. In the stacks of the public library I hunted old books that smelled as if they must hold the secrets to real magic: treatises on the work of ancient alchemists who had supposedly formulated the elixir of immortality and claimed they could transform lead into gold. I thought that I might someday accomplish such feats with the Philosopher's Stone, and I wanted it badly, this fabulous elixir of immortality, this miracle-making substance. When I mentioned my aspiration to signor Caballo, I took his silence to be part of his professional code and held him in still greater awe.

With girls my own age I was always popular, but no more adventurous or confident than other adolescent boys. By the time I was sixteen, I'd had my share of kisses in the dark, and yet I was obsessed not with school girls but *le belle donne*. I had begun to notice how Sandro Botticelli, "the divine Sandro," as Vasari refers to him, somehow conveyed the beauty of women as *more* than their outward appearance. While I tried to copy him, I couldn't figure out how this other sort of beauty was to be portrayed. Odd as it seemed, I supposed this special quality had something to do both with spirituality and *il sesso*—but with whom could I discuss my hypothesis? It would be a little while until I had Mr. MacDonald as my high school English teacher, and though I couldn't exactly talk to him about this topic, his lectures would inspire me to think analytically about such matters.

At about this time, I made with colored pencils a portrait of my grandmother in her wheelchair, wide-eyed, smiling, girl-sized. This was during her last good year, before her second leg had to be amputated, before her health began to fail completely. Long ago that drawing was lost, but I still have it in mind quite clearly, and can see it in the space directly above my eyes. The stump of her first amputation protrudes beneath her skirt. Swaddled in a linen napkin that I have embroidered with the words, *Villa Giustovera*, her thigh is meant to resemble an infant: she herself used to call it "the tiny one," *piccinin*, a joke she often made with me, probably to diffuse revulsion, which in fact I never felt. I thought that the stitched scar resembled the way the skin at the end of a salami was tied, and in turn I joked about this with her. In that portrait, Nonna is pictured almost as a cartoon figure, and issuing from her mouth within a balloon are the words to a nursery rhyme she used to sing. It's about a tiny child who danced upon a penny: *Piccinin che l'era, balava voluntera, balava sul' quadrine, anche l'era piccinin*. Above her head is a leg surrounded by musical notes to show that it is dancing. This is the limb that was removed, the phantom that was no longer the flesh of my beloved grandmother. Below the flounce of her skirt is also her good leg, laced into a fanciful heeled shoe. It is, however, with the other leg that I have taken the greatest pains, perhaps making it too shapely for a grandmotherly leg, but, as I thought with pride, looking very much alive.

Nonna was silent a long time with my drawing in her hands, holding it near and then at arm's length, inspecting it as she rotated it slowly. I could see she was pleased, and she told me so, but she didn't praise me lavishly as if I were still a child. Regarding me carefully, she said at last in Milanese, "You look like my brother, your great uncle, Guido. The same eyes, the same nose. Like a hawk."

"Is any sentence of a story exactly the same when you reread it? Does a painting always communicate the same experience?"

Mr. MacDonald posed such questions while striding thoughtfully about our classroom. We had been studying the mythological references in Botticelli's painting *La Primavera*. I had thought it beautiful precisely because it was unchanging, and daily I fell more deeply in love with the figures depicted in this famous tableaux, also known as *The Allegory of Spring*. But now I had something entirely new to contemplate.

Mr. MacDonald—neat, dark, alert—projected for us a slide of the painting. He informed us that the actual image was even larger than what the movie screen at the front of our classroom could show. In the Uffizi Gallery of Florence, the figures of Venus and several other goddesses, plus Mercury with his caduceus, and mysterious Zephyrus seizing a nymph, were nearly life-size. He said that the "transporting effect" of the painting in person was not reproducible;

nevertheless, he explained, "the slide projection conveys some of its grace and power." I thought I could feel "the living thing connected to your own experience," that MacDonald said he wanted for us, his students. I thought that every word MacDonald spoke was worth taking down in my notebook, and surely he was an important model for my own eventual career as a teacher.

"This work occupies a psychic space, continuous with both the painting and the viewer. However, this special place can't exactly be located," he said. "I can only suggest with my words where you ought to seek."

His nervous fingers traced across his chest and then leapt to his mouth, as if he had somehow said too much and were now embarrassed. It was a habit of his, this touching of the chest and then the lips, as if he were wiping his mouth clean before dropping his hands quietly to his sides, leaving behind a strange smile. He lowered his head as if in a bow and continued: "This kind of beauty is a paradox. This is more than a beautiful sentiment, unless by that you mean to suggest the Platonic Realm. In which case. . ."

I didn't really know what he meant to suggest, but in the dazzled darkness of that high school classroom I felt something truly inspiring. MacDonald probably wished he were teaching college kids and I don't know why he wasn't. Our class was his eleventh grade honors English class, and although he was a patient logician, or because he was, I think many of the students were bored. Not me. From him I learned to think about literature, art and religion as variations on one theme: the life of the soul. He said thinking need not be opposed to feeling but that they could complement each other and complete your passion. *Your passion*—that's what he said. I shivered.

I did well in MacDonald's class, absorbing everything from him that I could. I loved it that he'd once studied to become a Jesuit priest, but failing to prove that God exists, or so the story went, he'd had to leave the Church. I was as much in awe of this as I was by anything else he taught us. I can still see him in his charcoal tweeds pacing while he lectured, his handsome, lined, brown face, his eyes darting about, daring his students to meet them.

"Some works, such as this one, attain a classic stature due to another paradox," he said, gazing at the masterpiece that he'd materialized before us. "They seem immortal *because* of time's passage."

I was very conscientious in keeping the journal assigned to us by Mr. MacDonald, and in mine I included some of my drawings, just as Leonardo had done in his notebooks. I was inspired also by Washington Irving's collection of stories, *The Sketchbook,* a classic of Hudson Valley lore, and in one of my entries I theorized that although such specters as the Headless Horseman might be said to haunt specific locales, "they could also exist in a psychic space that can't exactly be located." I hoped that this idea would please Mr. MacDonald. Then I wrote that I'd had "some personal experience of such things."

When he read my journal, MacDonald spiked the margins with exclamation points and question marks. He did give me an A for my work, but in one place he wrote, "Come off it," and in another, where I had dared to muse about reincarnation, "Many have fallen into the same sort of wishful thinking." I don't recall ever having had a private conversation with him, and two years after I graduated, he left our school, the rumors being that he'd gone off to teach at Loyola University, or else had suffered a breakdown and been institutionalized, or that both things had happened after he departed. He was one those figures whose *style*—half what he projected, half what I interpolated—helped me more than I could appreciate at the time. Back then, I was simply dazzled. Now I am also grateful.

I remember that it was in MacDonald's class where I first faced a paradox about self knowledge that still puzzles me: while I could accept that the world was constantly changing, it didn't make sense that *I myself* could change. I believed that the "I" whom I had known as "myself" for my entire life—who seemed at his core more or less permanent—would grow up in one continuous stream of days and nights and that eventually I would conclude, *Yes, I am really that guy.* I wondered if this unchanging yet gradually emerging inner self must be my soul, essentially changeless and therefore timeless. But what about my body, growing somehow outside of this *me* while also housing it? It was *my* body, but also, it wasn't completely in my control. Therefore, I reasoned, it was somehow not my own—or not yet, anyhow, since obviously I wasn't completely free to do with it as I wanted. That freedom would come with adulthood, I believed.

My body-in-process awaited me in the full length mirror of the hall outside of my bedroom. As I have previously said, this looking glass was quite magical—I well remember witnessing my father do a little dance before it as he transformed into his comic alter ego, Mr. Confetti. His belly rolled like that of a jolly child, and he moved his arms ever so slightly as if they were tied to the strings of helium filled balloons; his smile was silly and irresistible like that of a big baby boy. And he talked in that peculiar way of Mr. Confetti, addressing himself in the mirror and then replying. This was at about the time we first formed our act together, back when I was only ten years old and still so very impressed with him.

The mirror had always stood in a dark little foyer at the head of the stairway leading up from the main entrance of the Villa, and sometimes as a teenager when I was alone, I risked standing before it completely naked. I examined myself with a mixture of scientific curiosity and autoerotic excitement. My double's brown eyes stared back. I had heard a little about homosexuals and I felt certain I wasn't one of them, but I admired my own body often and thought about the bodies of other boys I had seen naked, comparing myself to them. Of course, there was also the ideal form of Cellini's *Perseus*.

Despite my successes in school and all the options offered me by a nation on its way to the stars, and despite my so-called secret information, I couldn't clearly envision a destination for myself. Artist? Wasn't that a little queer, a somewhat foolish aim for a boy from Kinderkill? I knew no one personally who was actually an artist—well, there was Joe Corelli, a friend of the family, a barber in Wappingers who also painted landscapes in his spare time—and so what business did I have wanting to follow Cellini and Botticelli and Leonardo? Shouldn't I abandon my hope and try to catch a rocket to the moon like every other guy in America? One thing I knew for sure was that I didn't want to end up running the Villa Giustovera. "Business is bad," I heard my parents say repeatedly. *Business is bad*: a motto I internalized.

What was it Mr. MacDonald had said when we read *The Brothers Karamazov*? Something about that chapter called "The Grand Inquisitor," something about the poor soul who binds himself to doubt without ever having known faith.

CHAPTER 10

DESPITE OUR RECENT ESTRANGEMENT and the disapproval that my mother felt for him, I made a big effort during my junior year to get close once again to Cristiano. My parents gave me permission to take the bus from school into Wappingers on some afternoons in order to visit him. Chris was supposed to drive me home on those days, but out of fear of pestering him, I often volunteered to walk the mile and a half. I took it as a sign that I was on the path of independence when he merely said, "Suit yourself," and let me go. Those long walks after dark were not entirely pleasant, and I could have used some brotherly affection from Chris, but I didn't know how to ask for it.

We grew reacquainted slowly at his rented studio apartment in the attic of a rickety colonial. It wasn't a pad, he explained, but a base from which to plot his next move. Under a rather low sloped ceiling, Chris and I sat on his sofa bed. Across from us was a tiny sink and next to it a hot plate on a stained Formica countertop; below that, the smallest refrigerator I had ever seen. A small sashed window looked down three stories into a tidy alley. The bathroom Chris used was down a steep stairwell through a narrow hall in the main part of the building. This feature suggested that his digs were in a tower.

His Digs Himself, I thought, conferring a kind of nobility upon my cousin, although I never called him that to his face. We were blood and this was never in doubt, but there remained a certain distance, partly because of our ages, that I couldn't bridge. Nevertheless, I studied Chris and copied him in small ways, wore white crew-neck tees under my permanent-press school shirts, combed my hair wet, bought a pair of sharp black shoes, the kind we called torpedoes.

"Bob's place isn't anything like Conklin's old store," Chris told me. "You remember it, right? In Poughkeepsie, near Arlington? Shoes and clothes are only part of it now. Bob wants to keep expanding. The latest in everything. Lemme tell you, Bob has an eye for the hip. Out back he's got a room full of this ritzy-looking junk he just picks up off the sidewalks in Manhattan. Brass lighting fixtures, antique candlesticks—he even finds valuable stuff in garbage cans.

"Course, we've got plenty of shoes, that's the backbone of the inventory, but what he really wants is his own department store—that's what Connie, his wife says. Connie's the one who picks out the wild threads, knows everything about the New York styles. 'She's got the knack,' Bob says. 'She knows what people want.' He means females, mostly. Puerto Rican girls. Colored too. 'Connie sells seashells and glad rags,' according to Bob. *Fashions.* He's gonna have a sign made for her, and that's all it says: *Fashions.*

"The place isn't exactly jammed, but we do good business. They come in looking for shoes, then we hope they get interested in the other stuff. 'We're selling an idea,' Bob says. He knows what he's talking about. *Variety.* And musicians come in too—Larry Bell and the Boys. Boots with Cuban heels. But you ought see what the *girls* are wearing in Poughkeepsie. You should see Connie when she's decked out."

Connie. *Mrs. Badget.* Mr. Badget was Bob. They were Bob and Connie. What had my father called her? Standing in the corridor outside my fifth grade classroom, talking with her at an open house. I was so shy of her beauty that I couldn't look directly into her eyes. I stared through the open tips of her shoes at her painted toenails until she coaxed me to look up, up across her magnificent chest and into those warm brown eyes. Her hair was honey-blond, an unreal color, and she was wearing it up. She praised me to my parents that night. And then, not so long ago at the Villa, I had seen her doing the Frug in a fringed black skirt. She was Puerto Rican, a Latin, dark like us: she'd never looked like Mrs. Bob Badget. *Concetta,* that was what my father called her, flirting in the hallway at my school.

Women, independence, money—and after work, Chris hung out at the Half Moon, which was run by Bob's best friend, Leo Declare. Leo, the artist. I'd heard the place was a pick up spot for horny Vassar girls, which Chris confirmed for me. My cousin was the picture of success, I thought, and he took all of it in stride. He'd always been quiet and calm like a true Giustovera, and now he was genuinely cool. As for me, I *yearned.* I had *passion.* My fantasies about Gracie Laporta had become so intense that lately I could feel my face glow whenever we spoke. I would actually lower my eyes when she arrived at work with her black hair teased up like a crown, and when she asked, "How's my artist buddy today?" I could barely reply.

I knew that after hours, Larry Bell sometimes played at joints like the Half Moon, very late at night when the band was through at the Villa. *Making jazz:* it was an expression I'd heard Larry use. He would snap his fingers starting up the band, and in a whisper at the mic tell the crowd what they were up to: "Makin' some jazz." Then he'd put the horn to his lips and blow something crazy. At my spy hole, I might catch them wailing away, so loudly they rattled the plastic chandelier in the Villa's lobby. My father hated that—but then, it wasn't *his* orchestra. My mother said there were customers who liked it, who came here for that, and Larry liked that, and she wanted Larry happy so that he'd keep playing, so that she could keep dancing. "Huh! Let's see if customers buys some booze," my father said. And shouting over the soaring music: "Don' hurt people's ears, *eh, Lorenzo?*" Truth be told, I think both of them had crushes on Lorenzo Bellocielo, me too.

Whenever I could, I got Chris talking about the scene at the Half Moon or about Bob's store. When I stayed for dinner at his digs, it was like camping, cooking on the electric hotplate, a can each of spaghetti with sauce. In the woods, we had eaten stuff like this, but never at home, it would have been a perversity, a sacrilege. Chinese food out of cans, too—Chris actually ate that stuff. Pepsi and cold cuts, huge heroes packed with salami and provolone were staples.

Tell me more, I prayed.

I was careful not to annoy him, and I gave him plenty of leeway whenever he opened up a little. I yearned to touch the new world Cristiano had discovered. I could smell its earth and green trees, as a sailor on the original Half Moon might have done, plying the Hudson through fog at dawn, enchanted with the emerald beauty of the valley.

Tell me more about the women, I prayed. *Give me their perfume and voices, the colors of their eyes, the curves of their breasts and bottoms and thighs. Outline the bones in their chins, the lobes of their ears like fruit on the trees of Eden. Give me the long smooth hair that Vassar girls pile on their heads, their clean hair pinned up to the sky and just waiting to tumble down. Is it true, Cristiano? Give me their blue jeans tight in the crotch, their cashmere sweaters and bare white torsos peeping out underneath. Give me the sound of their bras unsnapping, their wet French tongues—tell me it's true, give it to me straight, Cristiano.*

Ah, how I prayed and tortured myself.

For as long as I could remember, for my whole boy's life, if I dared allow myself to look, to really *look twice*, I was able to see twice as much and more of any female on whom I fixed my eyes. Secret information of a special type—I knew it was dangerous to the health of my soul, but I had never not been interested in the opposite sex. On the Bay of Naples at the age of six—*six*—when I watched two young women enter a beach cabana to change out of their swimsuits, laughing that the door wouldn't latch, drawn near by the clap-slap of the blue door cracking open, oh, what I saw. *Cristiano, you should've been there!*

In an awful tone, Father Ryan had hissed that I must prevent myself from even thinking about girls in this impure way. Because I would touch myself, wouldn't I, when I had such thoughts, and such acts were displeasing to God who saw everything. I wasn't a *toucher*, was I? he asked accusatorily. I hadn't been much of one until then, but I began to think of myself like that and to keep track of every so-called impure thought and action until their total weight on my conscience could be discharged in the Saturday confessional.

Meanwhile, up in Poughkeepsie, Chris was surrounded by angels in short skirts. Well, surrounded by angels and old men. At Badget's he'd been put in charge of a special line of orthopedic shoes. "These weird shaped comfortable shoes for old guys," is what he said. "At special prices, straight out of a foot doctor catalogue." He could earn commissions on these expensive sales, and Chris was successful at the job. Bob had told him, "It's the shape of Italy in your soul, man."

I sensed there was something awful about such work, and Chris confirmed it could truly be rotten. "The first time I ever pulled off an old guy's shoe, the toes were all stickin' out of a stinkin' holey sock," he said. "The toes had black scabs on them."

And he had had to hold the guy's leathery foot and do all sorts of things with it, measuring and outlining it for a pattern in order to customize the insoles. He'd held his breath as long as he could so as not to inhale too much of the rot. The way Chris showed me, pretending to hold the foot in one hand and hiding his nose with the other, all the time acting polite and professional, cracked up both of us.

Chris said he thought it would be hell if he had to do that every day, and he thanked God nothing so bad had happened since. But it bothered him that he had to get down on his knees in front of people. He went on about this kneeling, showing me how he was learning to stand, squatting half-erect so that he wasn't bowing to them. This hurt his back, and he'd begun to wonder if kneeling were simply part of the job. "If that's the case, I'm not in it for the long haul."

"The girls," I sputtered out at last. "What about the girls?"

"*Whattabout the pretty girls,* eh, Guido? *Whaaa?*" He patted me on the back of the neck, grabbed me playfully. "You little snake! You were always interested in the pretty girls. *Le belle donne,* as you like to call them, my little guinea-wop cousin! Okay. The girls! Ta-da!"

He got up suddenly as if he were going to the door, as if to let them in, but instead, he swiveled on his heel and reached for another slice of pizza from the pie we were sharing.

"Connie is *prima*—no doubt about it." Eating and talking, he averted his eyes. "*Mrs. Badget.* You remember her from school, right? Didn't she give you a hard-on?"

I prickled with embarrassment. I could practically feel my forehead breaking out. He was right about Mrs. Badget, *Concetta,* but nobody talked to me like this. Oh sure, my cousins Nicky and Giacco, Brooklyn Mario's sons, used that kind of language to rib each other, and Cristiano had been part of that, smoking cigarettes and all, stealing bottles of beer from the walk-in cooler, sniggering about rods and hand-jobs and *fica.* But they'd thought I was too young that summer and ignored me.

"Yeah, Connie gives me a boner, too." He said it so matter-of-factly that he might have been talking about the hard biceps under his shirtsleeves. He was a young bull, and I thought his thick lips, like grandpa's, gave him something of that look. His light brown hair too, combed back wet, with its tight natural waves gave to his head an animal grandeur.

"Don't get me wrong, kid. Connie, she's a lady, you know? And she's Bob's wife, and anyway she's not even at the store very much. Sometimes after school, *maybe* I might see her. Connie does the books. And there's a new girl who's works there too. *Leenda,* Connie calls her. She's so cute. Leenda graduated from Saint Anne's last year. Bob likes her a lot. She's got something, *bazooms,* anyway. He makes a big deal when she does anything smart. Like it was her idea that we sell the school uniforms, you know, the plaid skirts and blouses, the knee-socks and shoes the Saint Anne girls have to wear. And just like Linda predicted, once they come into the store for their uniforms, they buy all these other things. Bob says Linda will take over someday. He teases her all the time.

"Then there's the Vassar girls. " He paused for effect and stared at me. "How do you tell a Vassar chick?"

I could barely imagine myself in the presence of such a mythical creature and missed that he was joking.

"By the crack in her china," he said. He swilled some Coke. "You see them Saturday nights at the Half Moon, posing in their baggy sweaters and dungarees. Now they're wearing ribbons around their heads, like Indians or something, a new style the hippies imported from California, Connie says. And Bob, what does he do? I tell you this guy is an operator. He goes around to their tables at the Moon and he invites them personally to come to his store. And don't they spend the *denaro!* Vassar chicks all got money or else they couldn't go there, see?

"Linda waits on them, not me. With the old guys, it's really pretty easy. As soon as they feel how comfortable their feet can be, they don't care about much else. But the young ladies want *style*. They wanna look good, so you convince them: by spending their money, they look good. That's the way it should be done, anyhow. Bob thinks Linda could sell a little harder. Connie says let the fashions sell themselves. But Bob tells Linda, 'Be a model.' You should see the outfit he dressed her in last Friday—you know what cleavage is?"

Chris raised his bottle to his lips, tilted it back and stared at me.

"Linda has cleavage?" I asked nervously. I reached for another piece of pizza.

He looked at me, smiling as if I must be a complete idiot, but after his drink he went on. "Yeah, kid, like I said. Christ, did Connie get pissed off! Good thing Linda was already finished for the day, because as soon as she split, Connie started in, spitting Spanish in Bob's face. 'What? What?' he says back at her. 'The girl looked great, so I snapped some pictures.'

"They take it into the office. 'You're in charge,' Bob yells to me. I can hear them arguing, but then it gets quiet, like maybe they're making up." Chris winked at me. "In a little while a customer comes in, somebody I've never seen before. Real snooty look on her puss."

"College chick?" I asked.

"Nah. Older. Moneyed. You've seen the type: gets her hair done with a little flip, puts on make-up first thing in the morning. Nice to look at. We don't see many of them in the store, but hey, like Bob says, if she's buyin', we're sellin'. Nobody leaves Badget's empty-handed.

"First she just walks around looking, picking up stuff from the racks of cosmetics, not really interested. I figure maybe she'll leave. Then she's over in ladies' shoes. 'Is Bob around?' she says. I go, 'Uh, no. But I can help you.' Without looking at me, she asks, 'Do you have these in a six?'

"Of course, I've gotta wait on her. When Bob and Connie argue, you don't interrupt them. And when they make up, you don't interrupt them." Another wink to make sure his little cousin had gotten it. "'Have a seat, please.' I get a pair of size six heeled pumps for her. I can feel her eyes on me. I've sold plenty of shoes before, what's the difference if it's a woman?

"What's the difference?" Chris repeated, looking at me intently. I stared back waiting for the answer.

"Man, oh man, lemme tell you," he said quietly. "I squat down in front of her, see. Now she's staring at me, but I won't look her in the eyes. There's something blank about her pretty painted face, and that's fine, I think, this business is easier if you don't get too personal. But here's where it gets tough. She wants me to do *everything* for her. Points her toes so I can take off her pricey flats. *Jesus*, help me out a little, I think. And then I can smell her perfume, and—I know this sounds weird, Guido, but these are facts of life I'm layin' on you—the smell of her hot feet in the nylons. I start to sweat. In one hand I've got my horn and with the other I take her right foot and slide that warm tootsie into a pump. I can tell the shoe is too small, and I look up at her to see what she thinks, but her pretty face is just blank. Okay, on goes the other one. All this time she's got her legs crossed tight under her skirt, but then she uncrosses them really slow. I'm kneeling now, and I hear her stockings rub together when she slides her legs, and, oh, man, it's too much! I jump up like Jack-in-his-box. She gets up slow, and I know the shoes must be pinching her, but back and forth on the carpet she goes. The shoes are nothing flashy, skinny heels, but they put a wiggle in her ass. She knows I'm watching—I know, because she makes a little show. By now I'm startin' to think she actually is a pretty nice piece, but what am I supposed to do?"

"I dunno," I said earnestly.

"I tell you, Guido, it was trouble, or an invitation to trouble. And she never looks at me. She stands in front of a floor mirror, looking at her feet. What is she thinking? That they don't hurt? Finally she asks for a half-size larger, and we do the whole routine again. Then she wants to try the smaller pair. Then the larger size, and she does her walk all over again. *Swish, swish.* At first I was hoping that Bob or Connie would come back. They don't. And there I am for who knows how long, kneeling in front of her, and getting a good look up her skirt, I might add: panty-hose and pink panties underneath. I'm pushin' the shoes on and off. She's making these little noises to herself like *Hmm. . .Uh-uh. . .No, no . . yes. . .*

"Jesus!" Chris said, nodding his head vigorously and reaching his arm around me. "*She likes this,* likes me on my knees, sliding her feet in and out of the pumps, whether or not they fit at all. She actually laughs out loud and thanks me: 'I don't know what I would do without you.' Damn straight! She probably has servants at home, I think. Maybe she lets them sniff her. But, yeah . . . this beats waiting on old guys. I mean, here I am, with her feet in my hands, listenin' to her stockings sing. I don't even have to tell her how good she looks, like Linda would, to make the sale. She looks too damn good in her pink skirt, in those heels, swishing her tail."

His voice trailed off and I followed his eyes across the floor: there she was in his digs, strolling back and forth with that sexy wiggle, right there.

"New takes getting used to, and then it's old—that's the trick with style, Connie says. Maybe it's the same with people. Anyhow, whattid she come in here looking for, asking for Bob—lemme tell you, he knows a lotta chicks—and I start to think, maybe what she really wants is to get laid."

Oh, God, I thought, steadying myself, *here they come, the details . . .*

He took a swig from his bottle. "All those days on the floor in front of old men, doing my job, the thing that helps me, see, is that I'm a *professional.* I can get the job done. And I'll tell you, there was something else. I really started to feel like I was helping their miserable feet. You remember the story about Jesus washing people's feet? Maybe you know what I mean, helping Grandma with her fake leg and her insulin and all that. It takes something, Guido. You should feel good about yourself. I couldn't do that. . . Christ, I should come over to see her, you know, before it's too late. . . Anyhow, I was thinking that helping those old geezers made up for some stuff. Then this ritzy piece of ass breezes in. Goombye!

"Now of all the bad times is when Connie comes back. She catches on right away, and very polite, business-like and all, she says,

'Everytheeng all right, Ma'am?' 'Yes,' the lady says. 'I'll take this pair, thank you.' She says it to Connie. 'You wanna wear them?' I ask. 'They look good on you.' I mean it, but she gives me this stare, like I insulted her or something, like I shouldn't have spoken before I was spoken to. 'Just wrap them, please,' she says, and pulls them off herself. Tosses them on the floor next to the box."

"Shit! What happened next?"

He looked me in the eye and nodded. "I do what the lady says. I wrap them nice and neat. I take her money at the register. I'm a professional, I keep telling myself, but I'm gettin' mad—mad at myself. I feel like a jerk, really heated up at how the whole thing went. What was I thinking? The sale rings in my ears, loud enough to hurt, and I know Connie's watching me, like I've never sold shoes before.

"Finally I'm through, the customer leaves. When the door closes behind her, I take a long breath. Connie puts her hand on my shoulder, and staring after her ladyship, she goes, 'Don' fall off your high horse, honey!' She laughs and squeezes my shoulder like she knows exactly what happened. Then all of a sudden she kisses me on the cheek and it goes on fire."

He took another drink from his bottle, emptying it, holding it up to his lips for a long time.

"Yeah, Connie," he said finally. "She's A-One. The best."

CHAPTER 11

Easter would come early that year, which meant *Carnevale* would fall near Valentine's Day, and since this was Nonna's favorite holiday, my mother, who, for a change had a lot to celebrate, decided to do just that. She and Nonna planned a masquerade party. I was ecstatic when told I could attend.

My mother had already set the stage and planted her orchestra there. With their brass horns swinging *dong, dong, dong* the Bell Boys were pulling crowds into the Villa every weekend. Big parties and gala affairs had become common, and the Christmas season that year was especially successful. For the first time in her life, my mother was making real money. After the New Year balloons fell from the ceiling and the confetti was swept off the floor, once the artificial trees with their plastic ornaments, their tinsel and beads were raveled and stored, after *l'Epiphana,* with its magical kings and boxes of oranges, planning for *Carnevale* commenced in earnest.

It was agreed that we would use the Italian spelling and pronunciation in all references to the masquerade, for Nonna and my mother had something elaborate in mind that would evoke the festival for which Venice is so famous. Seamstresses both, they set to designing their costumes immediately, but these were a secret they kept from my father and me, even as they nagged us to choose characters for ourselves. Regarding the menu, my mother decided to do something unprecedented: she would prepare only a few specialty dishes like *caponatina* in honor of her Sicilian roots, and *risotto Milanese*, for Nonna's sake, but the chef who now worked for us, Mr. Schnock, would be in charge of the rest. Nonna argued that the party should have the homegrown flavor of the old days, meaning that my mother, with Schnock's help, should cook the entire buffet ahead of time; that way Mr. Schnock, an irreverent Austrian whose company Nonna greatly enjoyed, could join her table for the festivities. My mother flatly refused: she had her own plans for the night, which included her freedom from the kitchen.

I'd never seen her so much in control—of the Business certainly, but also, remarkably, of her life. Within a span of two years, she'd contended with the death of her father and with her mother's amputation, she'd gotten her husband buckled down, soothed relations with her brother and his family, and had had the Villa made over to suit herself. *Ann*, as she was now called by many people, Ann Diamante was in charge.

My father and I were requested to revive the comedy act we did together back when I was a kid. As Mr. Confetti and Mr. Spaghetti, we were going to perform at an after dinner stage show. Larry Bell and his Boys were to back us with music and special effects inspired by Spike Jones. Amazingly, during our rehearsals we fell easily into the timing and goofy improvisation of our best days, back when my father and I dreamed of hitting the big time together, after we'd won a talent show at the Knights of Columbus hall in Wappingers. For the Carnevale I wrote a silly skit that I called "Best Foot Forward," trying to script our lines and our timing. When I sought to introduce it at one of our rehearsals, Mr. Confetti was way ahead of me.

"*Ma*, Spaghetti," my father called, addressing me as he entered the ballroom, "you know, I no know, my bess foot—if it's-a right foot—" he shook it rubbery in the air at waist height—"or th'otha." He looked down with great wonder, pulled up each cuff a few inches, and then took some funny steps, acting as if his ankles were hobbled together. "Inna that case, how you know fuh shoe the best foot to make a-head?"

"*Ma*," I began, taking on my role as the straight man, scratching my head at my partner's obtuse logic. My mother was watching, and playing on the pun—the word *ma* means *but* in Italian—I turned toward her, pulling her into the act. "*Ma*-Ma, this guy heeza talk like he gots someplace to go. Hey, Confetti, whassamattayou? You know, I know you know that when you gets someplace, you *gatz* to stand on you own two feet!"

My father, pushing his cap down bashfully over his eyes, became a little boy shocked at my street slang. He grabbed his crotch—*gatzo* means penis in Neapolitan—and waddled off a few more ridiculous steps. "You so smart, my fren, a real wise guy. How come you so funny? I toll you I wanna buy a new pair a shoes fuh baby, but you act like you grown up. Now I miss the big craps game because you no ansa simple *questione*. Em I wrong o right? Whatsa best left behind? Right foot, march!" And with this doubletalk he strode toward me, kicking my ass playfully with the side of his foot as he passed.

I stood there, jostled silly, rubbing my head like a clown. I'd let myself go, for a change, and I had to admit it was fun.

We began to rehearse regularly in the afternoons when I got home from school. One day, when we'd finished and my father was on his way to the bar, he asked casually, "So whatta you drinkin', my dear son?" I knew he would make himself a whisky and soda like he did every night.

"Same as you, Dad," I said.

He looked at me, paused, made the face *I guess so*, and poured a drink for each of us. Sipping his, he went about his work, checking his ice bucket, polishing and then shelving a rack of heavy-bottomed tumblers. At the family table, I'd often had wine and a sip of anisette, and on special occasions *grappa*, or a finger of the witch, *Strega*, or a drop of cognac in a small snifter whose lip was rimmed with gold, but after our rehearsals it had always been ginger ale or Coke. I'd always supposed that one day we'd have a real drink together, and now the time had come. My father watched as I sauntered over and plugged a dime into the juke box, choosing "Volare," the original recording, by Domenico Modugno. A seal had been broken and out flowed sweet liquor indeed. Even though I was only drinking soda with a wisp of whisky, I was flying.

On another afternoon, at our rehearsal, my mother showed us the printed program for the Carnevale, beginning with the cocktail hour and scheduled through to "Ballroom Dancing, for which Our Guests are Requested to Remain *in Maschera*." Affixed to the back of the professionally produced card, inside a lacey paper heart was the black and white picture of two svelte ladies in evening gowns. With sinuous slender arms, long white arms clad in long black gloves, they beckoned. A second look revealed that the image was that of a single woman before a full-length mirror.

"*Fantastico,*" I said to my mother and father. *Fantastico,* I would say throughout the coming days, whenever the Carnevale was mentioned.

AGES AGO, GRAZIELLA LAPORTA had said she wanted me to do her portrait. I still had the sketch of her I'd first done, and although I'd barely traced her gestures that day, dashing a few lines across the page, this drawing was unlike any other of mine, and it inspired extravagant fantasies. I wrote in my journal that Gracie had "smiled on me like a priestess of love." I never shared that rudimentary sketch with her or with anyone else, nor have I have ever forgotten the feelings it aroused. In my solitary contemplation, I asked myself if an artist were like a magician who could bring phantoms to life on an empty page. Without realizing it, I had in fact verified for myself something essential about a true work of art: its existence and one's relationship to it create a vibration between the objective and subjective realms. The "greatest" works are the most effective at amplifying this vibration which brings them as meaningful objects into one's life. At the time, I thought I'd done nothing more than doodle while under the spell of Gracie's beauty, and yet here in my hands was something whose power was undeniable. Leonardo Da Vinci doodled, and some of his revered sketches were even referred to as "cartoons," but dare I compare what I had done to the maestro? I chastised myself for the sin of pride, yet I couldn't disown my sketch. I had unknowingly created a symbol.

In any case, I hadn't expected Gracie to remember the afternoon when my mother broke up the betting about her lingerie and chased away my father and his cronies, but one afternoon in anticipation of the Carnevale, she appeared in the foyer wearing her costume for my mother's approval. Hearing her voice below, I listened from outside my bedroom while she discussed the portrait of herself that she wanted her buddy, *the ahtist* to do. I hadn't the nerve to come downstairs, but I heard my mother happily approve of Gracie's idea—these days she was happy about almost everything—and when my father arrived on the scene he also applauded the costume, and the notion that Graziella would pose for me.

I was scared shitless.

After Gracie had gone, I was informed that I should set aside a couple of hours on the coming Wednesday afternoon when she would sit for the portrait. That meant I had two days to prepare for my undoing, two days until I would be revealed as nothing but a doodler. I considered an alternative career as a snake handler in some traveling sideshow that could take me far away from Kinderkill. When I recalled it was a large woman in a skimpy exotic outfit that I had once seen perform such an act, I was further mortified. My freakishness felt unbearable, and the spirit of Benvenuto Cellini was nowhere nearby to encourage me. If I ran away for a life on the road, I had no doubt that my parents would send the police after me, and then what? Confinement in a mental hospital. Mattewan probably.

I decided instead to go down like a man.

Gracie arrived at the Villa on the appointed day. My mother, wreathed with smiles, made a great fuss over her entrance—I now realize how fond they were of each other, and that my mother had high hopes for Gracie, who, as I have said, had a head on her beautiful shoulders. I came forward shyly into the foyer to meet her when I was called. I guessed that Gracie in her full skirts and petticoats must be a character from *Gone with the Wind*; however, batting her eyes at me, she said she was Little Bo Peep. In a cute voice that killed me right there at the foot of the main stairway, she pined for her lost sheep: "Where, oh, where have they gone?" She looked at me, as if I might be one of them.

Her dress had seen better days with a theater company—it had come from a trunk at Badget's Bazaar—but the satiny blue fabric was still rich, and the skirt belled upon its crinoline, sweeping side to side when she moved. For the complete effect, she put on a blond curly wig, and on top of that, an oversized bonnet. This silver and white cap was touched with the same red ribbon that gathered her gown's puffy sleeves. Over the dress she wore a bodice of blue velvet, snug at her waist and laced fetchingly below her ample bosom. *Cleavage.* My father who'd joined us in the foyer predicted that if Little Bo Peep were to serve drinks during the Carnevale, we'd do a fortune in bar business, but Gracie replied to him demurely, "Anna told me I could have the night off, Zizi."

Then she looped her wrist around mine, twining my fingers, and then the reality hit me. With a voice barely recognizable as my own, I said, "Let's go. We only have until five." I actually did feel like *that guy from the Villa* while I led the way upstairs to Room Eight, which I used as a studio because the light was so good.

Behind me the *tap, tap* of Gracie's footsteps taunted me. I thought about the black and white heeled pumps she often wore, and I imagined her luscious legs under the long skirts; with my mind's eye I saw how she would need to clutch the folds of her gown to raise the hem, which would reveal her feet in those fabulous shoes. I fought against this image, refusing to look back over my shoulder at her, and this resistance was my first success of the afternoon.

In the room, I situated Gracie on a chair that I'd previously arranged near the window. The bed was beside us to my left and I used it to hold most of my drawing tools, but I kept the pad on my lap, along with a bunch of colored pencils in my left fist. I sat as far away from her as I could, found the reins to my runaway heart, and settled down to work. Gracie told me she'd been preparing by practicing various poses, and she struck several which were reminiscent of movie actresses in *Photoplay*.

She had kept the blond wig on her head, but not the oversized cap, and inexplicably this helped put me at ease. Like the gown and bonnet, the wig too had lived in a theater once and was well made. I asked her to change her gesture a couple of times, and to place one of her hands on the back of the chair so that she was only partially facing me. Then I did something that a few minutes earlier would have seemed unthinkable: I touched her chin gently and turned her face a little in the light so that she was gazing out the window.

Smiling sidewise at me, quieting herself, she was already moving into that peculiar distance that models inhabit while posing—then, abruptly, she snatched off the blond wig and tossed it aside. With two quick strokes of her free hand, she raked her own shorter, black hair into place, glanced directly at me as if to ask for my approval, and looked away once more. Her right hand was extended toward me, resting on the back of the chair with the index finger pointing at my heart. Her nails were newly painted with the same red that accented the gown and bonnet.

A thaw day outside, water dripping slowly from the roof eaves over the window. I had wanted natural lighting, and although it wasn't a bright day, the light from the melting snowfields was lovely. There was a copse of firs at the edge of the Villa's south lawn, and Gracie let her eyes rest there. Beyond these evergreens was Mount Beacon, a blue-gray cone on the distant horizon. I had drawn this landscape many times, and the presence of Gracie in the foreground now inspired me beyond all my previous efforts. I decided that her portrait would be my masterpiece—yes, my own *Mona Lisa*.

I studied her as a way to steady myself whenever a pulse of *il sesso* shook me, and I worked hard that afternoon to truly become Gracie's buddy, the artist. When I nonchalantly asked her to cross her legs and lean back a little so that I could finally get a glimpse of her ankles and feet, my subsequent disappointment became another cause for sobriety. With stumpy heels and low vents, the shoes that she wore made her feet look long and narrow, almost ungainly. Looking back at her pretty face, I devoted myself to capturing the line of her chin, and felt again the skin I had touched and the firm ridge of her jaw. I imagined her warm lips—but I held back my longing and in the most curious way I felt powerful because I was able to do so.

I've already said that Gracie was no dumb flirt and that her working class charms, the Queens accent I adored but which she labored to hold in check, the elaborate manicures and the nails that she seemed always to be filing, as well her scent, Water-of-Lilies, these were incomparably sweet to me. Although I must have seemed like a kid to her, a young admirer still in high school with whom she drank sodas and chatted at the bar before she opened it for business, today she was here alone with me because I was *an artist*.

I continued to wonder how could she possibly be interested in George McInnis, who brayed like a mule when he laughed, and whom I'd rarely heard speak to her, except to say things like "Crush," and "Gimme," and "Feather," the words of their secret language. I refused to believe that they were going to be engaged, and how I wished that she would drop him, preferably from a tall building.

My father did not regard Georgie, many years younger than himself, as a close friend, and yet, like Gracie, he too saw something in the Mick that I could not. Georgie was a regular at cards and craps, and also during the recent renovations of the Villa, his cement work on the two patios had sealed their bond. While he was nothing like Manaperta in relation to my grandfather, still I had to concede that George McInnis with his tanned good looks and wavy blond hair, with his skills and "personal friends in the trucking business" was always welcome at the Villa. A high school dropout like my cousin Chris, he had one time given me a compliment because I excelled in school and was clearly headed for college—but I had brushed it off.

If like the mythological Tantalus I only starved myself before the thing I could not have, there would be no portrait of Graziella Laporta. But when I dared to think about her in my embrace, the blood would pound in my chest until I had to stare off at Mount Beacon to cool down. And so, as Gracie herself grew more abstracted, settling into her pose, I too became more withdrawn and committed to my work.

At first I struggled with the figure emerging on the page before me. I was involuntarily resorting to clichés that my pencil could perform from memory, reproducing an image from a book Cristiano had unexpectedly given me: *Glamour Girls and How to Draw Them.* Intended for fashion designers and commercial artists, it was a step by step guide, like others I'd used for landscapes and horses. The author illustrated how the foundations of the figures were geometrical solids, how these forms developed into heads and torsos, thighs and ankles, and were finally brought to life with the addition of "telling details," the arch of an eyebrow, or "cleavage insinuated with a single stroke." As for the stylish clothes that glamour girls wore, they were analyzed into a set of common parts, the bib and bodice of a dress, for example, or the vent of a skirt. The author, Gary Sebastian—"Mr. Sebastian, as he's known in Hollywood"—wrote that "the basics are altered easily, according to the demands of fashion." While I had no

interest in becoming a fashion designer, I practiced my lessons devot-
edly, and yet I also wondered how I might observe my subjects and
draw them without resorting to lenses prescribed by others. It was
the sort of question Mr. MacDonald might ask his class.

Almost two tense hours passed during which Gracie and I
hardly spoke. She managed to sit very still at first, but it was tiring
work, and we took breaks as often she liked, keeping relatively quiet
so as not to break our concentration. Gracie pushed open the window
so that a little fresh air blew in, and she smoked cigarettes. I asked for
one—it was not my first—and from the proffered pack of Salems,
I shook out a cig for each of us. I felt serious and sensitive, and I
couldn't risk coughing, so I took short puffs and blew out bursts of
the mentholated smoke, fumigating the place with artistic intensity.

We went back to work for one more session. I hadn't let her
have even a peek at the drawing. I had managed to ignore my disappointment with what I'd done at first to her figure by focusing
instead on the drapery of the gown. Whatever my reservations, I
went on. I'd learned about impressionism and expressionism recently,
and had decided to call myself a Naturist. As for portraiture, well, it
had always been a talent of mine, and I was quite happy with the face
itself: I'd gotten the half profile; the nose was good, and the right eye
expressive, which hadn't been easy, since it was obvious to me that
Gracie had something on her mind.

Then it happened, suddenly as was usually its way, and I began
to see more than Gracie's form on the page. The head of a tawny lion
appeared above her, circled in a silver cloud that became its billowing
mane. The beast was roaring, but although it was open-mouthed
with teeth bared looking straight out at the viewer, it was glorious
rather than frightening. I outlined the figure in yellow pencil which

I rubbed with my fingers until a golden nimbus shone. In the end, I was happier with the lion than I was with the lady, but the two figures fit together well.

Visibly relieved to find it was 4:45 when she glanced at her wristwatch, Gracie took a deep breath, sighed, and looked expectantly at me.

"Yeah," I said. "It's done. It's a mess, but it's all I can do."

"Can I see it now?"

I passed it over and came around to look over her shoulder. Our faces were almost touching and I inhaled her fragrance of lilies mixed with the scents of cigarette smoke and her outfit's musty past in a theater wardrobe. I tried to see out of Gracie's eyes. Did the drawing have anything at all to do with her?

"You made me look like a girl on a movie poster!" she said. "Lemme tell you, bud, you got some talent!"

"Yeah, well I'm sorry I didn't do it better, you're more beautiful than that." I felt my face redden, and I backed away from her. "It's not completely realistic," I added.

"I couldda had a picture taken with a camera if I wanted that, Guido. This is *art*, it doesn't have to look exact. But what's with the lion? I mean I like the lion, but what is this, MGM?"

"No. . .no," I began, hesitantly. "You could think of this as an allegory, like the Old Masters did. Courage, you could say." Then I blurted out the rest: "Listen, Gracie, you got a lot going for you and if you stay with George McGinnis, you're gonna need it, because he'll always hurt you. He's dumb as a mule even if he is as strong as one."

"Who says he hurts me?"

"I could see it in your face."

"Howda you know he hurts me?" she repeated, disbelieving.

Then she got ahold of herself. A torrent of tears was waiting, but sniffing once sharply, she held it back. A host of old pains gathered at the corners of her eyes, remaining there until she could forge a smile.

That's how she does it, I thought. *That's how she stays with him.* But I had no idea why.

For the first time that afternoon she looked directly at me. In the dark irises of her eyes was something bright, something that George had put there, and I saw how much she needed that. Her eyes ate that light, just as my own eyes did, feasting on whatever it was that I loved. Which was why I made pictures.

Was Georgie enough for her? Did they really have the sort of love that the singers all sing about, or was it something within Gracie herself that made a life with him seem possible? Courage, I'd have said a moment ago. Face to face with her now, I really did feel like a kid, and yet I couldn't deny that Gracie was genuinely grateful for the funny valentine I had produced.

"You're a sweet guy, Guido, and I hear what you're sayin', and even a little more than the words. This picture is great. I'm gonna roll it up right now and maybe later I'll get it framed. Thank you so much. I owe you for this. But if you will excuse me, right now I gotta get changed and ready for work."

She was still somewhat flustered and fumbled to secure the scroll of paper with an elastic hair-tie. Then she slipped it into her bag like an arrow into a quiver. Retrieving a pack of Wrigley's, she offered me a stick, took one herself and pushed it into her mouth. She began to hum while she chewed the gum and gathered her things together. "We will talk latuh. Meanwhile, I'm a very happy customah, Mr. Artist buddy."

"Don't show it to him," I said quietly. "Please. He wouldn't get it."

"Well, okay, but you think about this. You did this for me, and I'm proud of it. I might wanna show it off. Georgie can be mule-headed, like you say, but he's also very nice to me. Believe it or not, he can appreciate pretty things."

PART 2

CHAPTER 12

GUESTS AT THE CARNEVALE were to be offered a free dinner
buffet, dancing to a live orchestra, a stage show, and a glass of
complimentary champagne. "Free?" my shocked father had asked.
"We gonna give them dinner and champagne fuh *free?*"

"Yes, Zizi," my mother had replied, stroking his arm. "And
we'll make it back at the bar. You'll see."

My mother invited many, including her brother and Aunt
Josie and even Cristiano, old enough to drink. If they were to attend,
I had no idea what Tina would do, but she was almost thirteen and
I supposed she could probably be trusted at home alone. Certainly
I wasn't going to babysit her! In any case, none of them did attend,
which was fine with me, since my life was functioning very well
without my little cousin's presence.

Just before the party, Nonna had her hair done professionally
so that it shone with silver and blue lights. I was somewhat surprised to learn that she'd invited signor Caballo, and I was glad of
it, for we hadn't seen him since the sober day of Nonno's funeral.
Although he and Mr. Manaperta were once so important to me, I
had begun to regard them, as I did my own grandfather, like relics

of my childhood. Manaperta had moved back to Brooklyn a while ago: he'd been ill, so ill in fact that he'd been unable to come upstate when Nonno died.

One afternoon, my father and I were having our final fittings for Mr. Confetti's and Mr. Spaghetti's costumes. The blouses—*Shirts, Ma, please, men wear shirts*—were of glossy fabric printed with the traditional diamonds of Harlequin, black and red and white. Each of us also had an oversize black bow tie, floppy, but somehow dandy looking, and instead of knickers we were in black baggy trousers that my father loved because of how the loose fabric moved.

"*I pantelone miei sono grandi perche io sono grande!*" he roared, hands in his pockets, the pants billowing, while my mother pinned their hems.

" *Zizi, basta!* You know you can't do that in front of people," she chided. Yet she was laughing.

He stepped down from the stool in front of her so that I could take his place.

"My pants are big because I'm big!" he roared once more in Italian. My mother and I covered our ears. Then she had me up on the stool to measure my trousers.

"Daddy wants us to wear lipstick, but I think that's stupid," I said to her when my father left the room.

"That's so your mouth will look big—though I think yours is big enough already."

My father's idea repelled me, and I persisted. "How ridiculous do we have to be? I mean Jesus H. Christ!"

"What did you say?"

"Lipstick, geeze—I don't like it."

"The mouth, Guido. The mouth. Lipstick might be an improvement."

She wasn't angry. I could read her thoughts: *Che confidenza—* what impudence! But today she loved her imp enough to forgive him most anything.

"After this, Mom, I need some help with my other costume," I said.

"Your other one?" she asked, pins between her lips, eyes on my cuff length, fingers tugging the fabric into place.

"I'm gonna be a pirate. Chris got me this cool leather vest. It's like something from Shakespeare. Bob Badget found all these costumes at a theater that went out of business. He told Chris I could have the vest. These baggy pants I'll stuff inside my cowboy boots, and there's that wooden sword, you know, the thing Manaperta made for me. How about one of your scarves for my head? And I need a big clip-on earring and maybe like a necklace or amulet to hang around my neck."

"It sounds like you have a lot of plans."

"Well, yeah. So?"

"After dinner, you get into your costume for the show, and then, you know, the rest of the night is for grownups, honey."

"I can't stay up? Caballo will be here with Grandma, they'll stay up, everybody will."

"If you want to sit at Grandma's table, okay, but I don't want to see you wandering around. *Capisci?* "

"Oh yeah, sure, I get it. I can make everybody laugh, but I don't get to have any fun."

My mother stood up and regarded me sternly. "Everyone will have a good time," she said. "You too, unless you ruin it. Now get out of these so I can sew them."

"What about my pirate outfit?"

"Okay," she said patiently. "Okay, but you know what I said. And remember, Nonna relies on you. When she's ready for bed, that's your cue, too."

IT HAD BEGUN TO rain that morning, sometimes mixing with sleet, but by Saturday afternoon, the weather had let up a bit. Anyway, it couldn't deter the final preparations. Kitchen staff arrived at noon, though the chef, Mr. Schnock, had been at the Villa all day on Friday working with my mother to lay up platters of veal *saltimbocca*, pounding the medallions of meat, seasoning them. By three o'clock on Saturday the Place was humming nonstop. I'd helped my mother hang pink and black streamers from the ballroom ceiling and we'd mounted a pair of large black, lacy hearts on the glass panels at the main entrance. I thought the large hearts resembled the panty clad bottoms of women bending over, and slyly I pointed this out to my father. He concurred and made much of this similarity, stroking his "beauties."

Because they would be starting to play during the cocktail hour, the band came in early to set up, and like a crew of serious workmen carried the tools of their trade to the ballroom stage: music stands and cased horns and a heap of boxed drums. For tonight, Larry had added a second trumpet and trombone—two Black guys I'd never seen before—and so the band numbered nine. Their sound would be really big. On the stage they put up brand new solid music stands in two tones of blue, stenciled with black enameled letters: *The Bells*. That's who they were. *Cool.*

Once they'd set up, Larry, smooth and genial even when he worked seriously, had them rehearse a Latin dance number. The music purred soft and brassy, backed by swishing maracas, and Jojo

Aubrey—one of the Black guys, who'd skinned my hand when Larry introduced us—punched the beat on a cowbell. *Wow.*

It was the kind of music you hoped would never stop, and it was during this number that signor Caballo suddenly appeared at the Villa's porch door. I was in the main foyer riding the rhythm when I saw him at the cloakroom brushing water from his sleeves. He undid his dripping overcoat, gently shook it out, and when he saw me watching, with a flourish he whirled the coat about so that for a splendid moment it seemed to become his dance partner.

"I have returned to the Villa Giustovera, where life is always good, and it seems that things change only for the better. My ears tell me there's an orchestra in the house, but do my eyes deceive me? Can this tall young man be Guido Diamante?"

"*Benvenuto, signor Caballo,*" I said, smiling broadly as I went out to greet him. He was now completely white of hair and beard, but he had remained slim, and not in the cadaverous way that some slender people become with age; actually, despite his hair, I thought he looked young as ever.

"How you have grown, my friend," he said affectionately. "And how much you resemble your uncle Guido." Caballo draped his coat on a cloakroom hanger, and then he stepped forward to take my hand.

I shook his damp palm firmly, looking him square in the eyes. My great uncle Guido had died in Milano after the War—so Caballo must have known him! And known my grandmother, of course, at a time before she'd ever met Nonno!

Then my mother was there, welcoming the signore with a kiss on each cheek, and I was sent off to summon Nonna. In the office where she'd been awaiting her friend, she clapped her hands and immediately rose from her chair. On her cane she came rather quickly out to the foyer. I saw her gray eyes sparkle at the sight of Caballo, and heard a sob when he embraced her. I too felt an emotion long suppressed flutter in my throat.

When Caballo hoisted his suitcase my mother motioned for me to take it, and I did gladly, proud to show off my muscles, suddenly eager to be near my old friend as much possible. "Room Twenty One," my mother said.

"Twenty One? Ah, that room has memories. Lead the way, signor Guido."

Once we were in the bedroom, I said excitedly to him, "You know this is a masquerade party? You brought a costume, right?" Of course I wondered how he would dress.

Caballo stood at the window with his back toward me. "The vineyard has not been pruned," he observed. And then turning: "Now that don Antonio, bless his soul, is gone, and your grandmother. . . But say, Guido, do you still draw and write a story for the pictures?"

"In my sketchbooks, yes, like always."

"Like always," he repeated, fixing his eyes on mine. "You know that Leonardo wrote a strange hand, and his notebooks are legible to others only when read in a looking glass. But have you viewed his drawings and paintings by this means? Well then, you will discover some fascinating aspects. The master claimed that with a mirror he could better discern any flaws in his work. Perhaps other aspects are revealed, as well? You still have the edition of Vasari I gave you?"

"*Sicuro.* I tried to make copies of some works by Botticelli. They're terrible, but my art teacher told me to try."

"Good," he said. "Show me later. Now what is our schedule for tonight?"

He glanced as his wristwatch. I had promised to work in the kitchen on the salad crew and I realized I was late. To Caballo I said, "There's a program, it's printed with times and everything. I'll get one for you."

"Thank you," he said, stroking his beard pensively. I noticed the signet of the emerald ring he was wearing, a winged lion.

"I almost forgot to tell you! My father and I are doing a skit together."

"Ah, you will play the clown tonight," he said, looking me over yet again. "Very well. But I see something else: a pirate, correct?"

RAIN AND SLEET CONTINUED to fall outside, darkness had fallen too, but indoors the Villa simmered with excitement. The ballroom's floor was buffed and shimmered like a skating rink. The green and amber wall lights were dimmed in the lounge, and "Eleanor Rigby" was playing on the jukebox while the Bells sat together drinking. In the kitchen, the ovens steamed, and at a long table I helped finish assembling antipasto plates. My mother checked on us, and when she was certain we were managing without her, went off to dress. This was a signal we'd all been waiting for, and we hurried to finish our work so that we too could don our costumes. Schnock, in his perpetual chef's uniform, stayed behind to man the canapés.

Up in my bedroom, I began my metamorphosis. I could hear the first guests arriving downstairs, some of the costumes prompting *oohs* and *ahs* from Judy at the coatroom window, whose own skimpy, dance-hall outfit had already caught my eye. Anybody at the Carnevale who might need a mask could have a black satin domino, and also there was a box of Valentine cards available in the cloakroom: another girl, Lulu, was instructed to make special deliveries if requested. On my dresser, I had a piece of burnt cork to sketch a mustache and beard, which I did holding a little mirror before me, turning it side to side to search for any flaws in my disguise. I was decidedly pleased and believed I must look at least eighteen years old, maybe older. I reveled in the power by which I had transformed myself, and I thought of Benvenuto Cellini in prison using his own blood and a splinter of wood to secretly keep his diary. Nothing was impossible for us! A yellow silk scarf was already tied on my head; it matched the shirt my father had loaned me, whose sleeves were large and loose under the leather jerkin. The embossed medallion my mother had loaned me swung from a chain around my neck, and one of her big gold hoops was clipped to my numb left ear; over my head I slipped the eye patch I had purchased at a drugstore.

Out came, "*Har, har!*" Out came the sword of Manaperta as I lunged at my double in the hallway mirror. "I was only testing ye," I assured him. I slid my weapon home through a loop of leather I had cleverly hung on my belt. Back in my bedroom I grabbed my small telescope and then left, slamming the door behind. The big medallion swung and bumped on my breast, and when I steadied it, stroking the roseate pattern with my thumb, I could feel my heart beating beneath. Then I stomped in my boots to the stairway landing and trained my spyglass on the scene below.

CHAPTER 13

FOR MY PORTRAYAL OF a pirate on the night of the Carnevale—when I was on the lip of manhood, when I was a rascal for the final event of my childhood—for my *big man, har har matey, what's that yer tellin' me?*—for my impersonation, I received a grade of A plus from Nonna and Caballo. They toasted me with wine at their table in a corner of the ballroom: "A perfect pirate," Caballo pronounced, and to this odd locution he added a conspiratorial wink.

Nonna was swathed head to foot in black, her costume devised from a lace tablecloth, jet-dyed, cut and layered into a mantel that totally obscured her identity. Her voice indicated she was female, but Nonna would not answer whenever asked exactly who or what she was. Her body was an illusion within an illusion, and no one who did not know her could have guessed that beneath her costume, one leg was fake, her teeth were false, and that she needed regular shots of insulin like fuel injection. To top if off, when finally she did lower her veil, we could see how her cheeks had been powdered white and how a bright red was applied to make her mouth look like it had been painted by Toulouse Lautrec. A mauve beauty mark rode just above the jawline on the left side of her face, and it moved up and down when she laughed. I thought it resembled a tiny horseman in the snow; her nose was an Apennine ridge he must cross on his way to her lips.

Throughout the evening she took people's hands and told them the stories she found in their palms. Her little deck of Tarot cards was nestled in her lap, and sometimes she would choose a card at random, turn it over on the table before her, and whatever the card, proclaim, "*Buona fortuna!* I see good things ahead." A pair of gold hoops gleamed against the borders of the veil. It had been quite a while since anyone had seen her so animated, and her high spirits brought a special flavor to the festivities.

Caballo's transformation was jarring and delightful in its own way, as a true masquerade ought to be: even if we know the person behind it, we're happy to collude with the artful imposture. He was outfitted in the long brown cassock of a medieval friar, and from a stout white rope about his waist there hung a simple wooden cross. His silver hair and *barbetta* were well oiled, and it seemed he had applied makeup to his dark eyes so that they looked sunken and fervent like those of a religious hermit. On the ring finger of his right hand he wore the emerald ring with the winged lion, and it twinkled as he gestured expressively. His impersonation was a thorough piece of theater, and rather than the ageless gentleman I had greeted earlier, he now seemed an old ascetic with gaunt face and thin shoulders. He purported to be nothing more than a humble mendicant. His rich baritone was suppressed and instead he spoke in muffled tones, almost a whisper. I thought he rambled as if he might be daft, and I was utterly disoriented by his act. He was a brother of the open road, he said, who didn't look backwards at life, but forward to the reward that awaited him. We laughed at his jokes about fallen angels and heavenly helpers, but I thought that this friar's idea of Heaven must be very different from that of Father Ryan. Here was a priest who could befriend a pirate. Suddenly, I wished Manaperta had also been with us.

Now he would speak of Saint Valentine and of the original pagan holiday appropriated in his name. "To begin with," Fra Ernesto began, "we will need another bottle."

Nonna called over the aged waiter Arturo, whom she'd long since forgiven for the unfortunate role he had played in the loss of her leg. Although he had wanted to quit the Villa back then, Nonna insisted that my mother keep him on. These days Arturo only worked for us on party nights. I had noticed he could scarcely look anyone directly in the eyes, but obedient as ever, when Nonna sent him to the wine cellar he returned promptly with the special vintage my grandmother had requested. I was delighted when my glass was filled, quite prepared to consume my share of Nonno's '58. We drank a toast to my grandfather's memory, and when I recalled my father's injunction never to forget, never to forget *il Nonno*, I glanced at Caballo. While Nonno was alive, my grandmother and Caballo had never concealed their mutual affection, and tonight, well, might there be the occasion for something else?

With a fresh bottle at his elbow and a full glass in hand, Fra Ernesto started in on the tale of Saint Valentine. "He was originally a Christian of the third century A.D., at the time when Emperor Claudius II persecuted the sect relentlessly. Valentinus was notorious because of his ministrations to the faithful. These were the days when they practiced below ground, in catacombs and secret chapels, like so many mice undermining the foundations of the Empire. When he was captured, Valentine was singled out to be made an example— but you must remember that the highest aspiration of these early Christians was martyrdom, the ultimate imitation of Christ."

Who could doubt signor Caballo's authoritative tone? Nonna plucked back her elaborate veil and let it hang like a mantilla while she listened. Entertained, as we had so often been by Caballo, we sipped our wine throughout the cocktail hour while many costumed guests—courtesans and sheiks and giant bananas—filed into the bar or sat together at lamp lit tables or stepped out on the ballroom's bright floor. The Bells played something cheek-to-cheek and Caballo paused to eye the dancing couples. "The pleasures of the flesh are fleeting but sweet," he mused with one hand on his beard. "Is it any surprise that the first great lover in the history of cinema was called Valentino?

"But to continue: who remembers how *Saint* Valentine suffered the blows of a torturer's cudgel? No doubt he was asked to recant his faith, for the Emperor might be merciful then, but accepting such a proposition was out of the question. Praising God, praying for the salvation of his persecutors, a saint surrenders his life. Even afterwards his face might continue to smile, and the halo about his battered head light up the torture chamber. Perhaps the perfume of roses permeates the place, and the frightened executioner hastens away. Perhaps the man will soon seek forgiveness for what he's done, and embrace the Christian faith and later will himself go gladly into the mouth of a lion."

I thought Valentine's story was like so many hagiographies: a shred of cassock, a splinter of bone, a glimmer of legend preserved for children. More fantastical to me just then were the sights and sounds of the Carnevale whirling about me, made brighter by all the wine I consumed.

But why is a saint remembered on the day of lovers?

"A good question," Caballo said, seeming to read my thoughts.

"His feast succeeds the Roman celebration of Februata Juno. On her holiday, boys would write down the names of girls they cherished and offer these billets at Juno's shrine inscribed with prayers that their love be requited.

"You can see how the Church would frown on such a practice among the unmarried, and so the Feast of Saint Valentine was substituted. The names of various saints were to be written on cards and exchanged by pious youths. For whatever the reason, that custom didn't last. The Cupid who launches his arrows at lovers has far more to do with pagan Rome than with the Church. Botticelli knew this of course, and his masterpiece, *La Primavera* alludes to it.

For added emphasis Caballo rapped the tabletop with his knuckles. Nonna giggled appreciatively, like a young girl ever enthralled by her darling friend.

"The origins of Carnival are similarly pre-Christian," he said, casting an appreciative eye to the fantasia revving up all about us. "Impossible to eradicate, the Church tolerates it as an end to New Year revelry and a preamble to Lenten austerity."

Now a certain figure entered the room: Gracie Laporta, passing through the archway from the bar, rustling past the bandstand and the dancers as she fetched up her skirt, a blond Bo Peep wearing a black domino. And, as I might have expected, at the opposite side of the crowded room, George McInnis was waiting; just beyond the door in the main lobby he embraced her. He was some kind of overgrown sailor boy in white; his costume was a size too small and his muscles bulged beneath it. He wasn't wearing a mask, but his face twisted with disgusting pleasure when he pressed his mouth on Gracie's. I turned away.

"Guido, right after dinner, upstairs and change for your act."

My mother had alighted at our table. I'd hardly seen her

tonight, but now, startled from my reverie, when I looked, I barely recognized her. Her brunette hair had been darkened and expertly coiffed into a bouffant style. In mascara and blue eye shadow, this was the woman known by her friends as *Ann*. There was even a dash of silvery glitter above her eyelids, and her lipstick was pink—pink, for *Chrissakes!* In her left hand she held her mask on a stick, something acquired I know not where, but Venetian in style, a domino of white leather studded here and there with gems, its brows feathered: a piece of real craftsmanship. Her dress, handmade by her, had a low neckline, probably cut to resemble an outfit of her favorite movie star, Ida Lupino. Her shoulders were bare. My mother in a cream colored gown on a February night in Kinderkill looked positively tropical, and, I was afraid even to think it, *sexy.*

I could not maintain eye contact with this person, feeling embarrassed, almost repulsed. I answered her with an indistinct "Uh, huh," and let my eyes sweep out over the room, spotting here and there people whom I thought I could recognize. I had lost track of Gracie, my father was nowhere to be seen, and practically the only person I could identify with any certainty was Larry Bell—but just then he put down his familiar soprano sax to pick up a clarinet.

"Are you all right, Guido?" my mother asked. And then in Italian to Nonna she said not to let me have anymore to drink; she regretted that I'd had any wine at all in the ballroom, even among family members, for what if the ABC Board should hear about this?

"Fine. I'm fine," I said. "After dinner Diddy and I do our act. Got it," I said, still refusing to meet her eyes.

At last she eased up, smiling at me, *you-know-what-I'm-talking-about-my-son,* and raised the mask to her face. Now she seemed a complete stranger. The coral pink mouth had one more thing for me: "After the show, you think about bed. I'm sure Nonna and Mr. Caballo won't be up late."

"Sure. . .*Mom,*" I said angrily. And standing, feeling the floor come suddenly to my feet, rolling like the deck of a ship: "Excuse me. I have to go to the *head.*"

THIS PART I REMEMBER quite clearly from that overfilled, endless night: in the first floor men's room leaning over the toilet with one arm against the back wall, I took steady aim and through me drained Nonno's '58—that is, my water that was his wine. After I zipped my trousers, I rested with my forehead against the cool tiles, eyes half-closed like a somnambulist. There are portions of this night that I will never forget, other parts that I have only in fragmentary form, others altogether absent from my memory leaving only blank spaces, and then also there are those moments I have conjectured and with the help of Nonna's Tarochinni have reconstituted over the years.

I do know this, that when I regained my sense of balance and turned to the bathroom sink and its mirror, the one I met there greeted me unequivocally with this: *Yer drunk, matey.* "Drunk I yam, an' drunk I'll be!" was my reply. But while I admired myself, washing my fingers under the faucet, my stomach suddenly churned violently, and just in time I turned to the toilet, crouched with hands on knees, and puked.

I thought at first I had vomited blood, so red were my stomach's contents with hardly a solid morsel to be seen. It looked as if I had emptied my three glasses of wine into the toilet—or was it four?—gushing a long stream whose acid burned my throat, whose

fumes seared my nostrils. The torrent echoed in the porcelain com-
mode and from afar a small voice within me remarked that this must
be the greatest upchucking ever to have occurred in this place—*Nay,*
in the whole history of the world. . . Then I slumped against the near
wall. I think I lost consciousness for a time, yet I did not fall. My
angel was in that angle.

When I opened my eyes, what a peculiar state of consciousness ensued! What a strange energy had entered my limbs! Light
headed as I was and greatly relieved of the turmoil in my stomach,
I found that the shining beige and brown tiles of the walls and floor
were quivering in the most fascinating way. If I stared, I would grow
queasy; if I closed my eyes, however, the after-images summoned
me toward a dream. Somehow I navigated these states, flushing
the toilet, and then at the sink cleaning up myself. I avoided the
eyes in the mirror as I wiped my mouth, careful to salvage what I
could of my perfect pirate's mustache and beard. Just then, I heard
the flat of a hand thumping impatiently outside on the bathroom's
door frame. When I glanced once more at my face, I saw that the
shadows about my lips and chin had been transformed into a more
rakish stubble than I had originally drawn. I liked this guy, inspecting his teeth in the mirror!

Outside the men's room, crowded in a narrow hallway, a
line had formed. A very white and pink faced gentleman in a green
military uniform—General Eisenhower?—gave me a mock salute,
and behind him, wrapped in aluminum foil I spotted a visitor from
another planet, the male of the species, which the sign of Mars upon
his breast proclaimed. I pressed my way through various masqueraders, male and female, all waiting for the restrooms at the end of that
small corridor. I squeezed between the Lone Ranger and two tall, furry

creatures—a pair of woodchucks? beavers?—and then was squashed up against the bosom of a fruit crowned woman—Carmen Miranda, naturally—who exhaled a loopy giggle, and with a large hairy hand adjusted her falsies. At the outlet of the corridor, an authentic female in a scarlet sequined leotard and fishnet stockings slouched smoking against the wall. I supposed by the whip in her hand that she was a lion tamer, and I nearly threw myself at her feet, which were caged in the tallest pair of silver heeled sandals I had ever seen.

The Villa's main foyer was filled to capacity when I entered the swell out there. Then, all together, we began to surge toward the dining room where the buffet dinner was now being served. No one questioned my place among them, and for the first time in my life I enjoyed a peculiar form of freedom at the Villa Giustovera: anonymity. Tall for my age, with my swagger well lubricated, with a patch over my left eye and a yellow kerchief knotted on my head, my apotheosis felt complete. I rested my left hand on the hilt of my saber, and feeling slightly quaky reminded myself to *keep walking, matey, yer sea-legs strong below ya.* Even the dreaded ABC Board with its undercover agents would never suspect me, for I was very sly, was I not?

I have long since lost the wooden saber Manaperta made for me, yet in my possession these many years later is a greater treasure that unites us: the silver and ebony crucifix that hung on the wall of his workshop, the one whose gaunt Christ plants his feet on a skull-and-crossbones. *Jesus of the Pirates,* as I have always referred to it, thinking of the outlaw murdered by the Romans for subverting the laws of Judea, he who in the supreme act of rebellion, rose from the dead. *Har, har!* This talisman must already have been reaching out to me with its protective power that night.

Throughout my youth I was never a trouble-maker or wise

guy—much less a genuine delinquent like my cousin Cristiano, who might have been thought of by some people as a hood and prospective criminal. I did, however, believe that I was pretty funny, and I could crack wise with the best of high school clowns—I had the sharpest of wits, if I do say so myself—but also I exulted in the power of my self restraint and in the private pleasures of my artistic life. Lord Byron's poetry spoke to me as did Aubrey Beardsley's graphic world, and yet I was never completely at home in their company either. Although I was somewhat obsessed with vampires, and into my teen years irrationally afraid of them, as are many horny kids, I never truly aspired to be one of damned. *Perfect pirate*, Caballo had called me, and with that benediction, that night I cut myself loose from any other designation, including my wish to be known as a "regular guy."

My dream has come true, I told myself as I floated, one eye patched closed, the other shining, as I drifted, a head among many heads, drifting among the horned and hatted and flowered, among the mysterious and beautiful heads and the ridiculous ones filled with flotsam like that of the raggedy doll bobbing beside me on the waves. A tide of strange spawn, up we surged toward the feast my mother had spread upon the waters.

CHAPTER 14

MASQUERADERS SWARMED ABOUT ME. I had recovered from my surprise at being truly intoxicated for the first time, and now I managed to take some bearings. Women of all sizes and shapes had me surrounded. Was this only because most of the men had charged ahead to pile their plates at the buffet tables while the ladies hung back? Whatever the explanation, it was a blessed state of affairs: more of my good luck.

Like any gentleman who sails under the black flag, I wanted "the comfort of a woman my equal in appetite." I had read in one pulpy romance how a buccaneer might fondle "a pair of sumptuous love apples and stroke to erection the coral-tinted nipples" of his favorite Hispaniola wench. I was definitely on the hunt that night for what Cristiano called *first hand experience*. As well, I had seized upon a particular word, evocative of all my yearning, something that Chris, whom I had never seen with a book, might nevertheless comprehend. *Seraglio*. I imagined myself raiding an Asiatic sultan's harem and rescuing a prized beauty. Having learned the origin of the word was Italian and that it meant literally "a cage for wild beasts," I grew more excited and growled it out like an incantation: *Seraglio*. Surely there will be a harem girl tonight, I told myself. Her midriff naked, a jewel for her navel, her long legs in sheer, silken, pantaloons. *Fantastico.*

"Eva Lynn," she said, holding out an open hand. "We've met before. My aunt Julie? I'm here with her tonight." The young lady whose warm hand I found myself holding gave a sidewise nod to a tall woman swathed in white whom I recognized as one of my mother's friends. Julie Rosenbaum, her attractive aunt, lived in Hyde Park and ran the interior decorating company that had helped to remodel the Villa.

Eva Lynn's forwardness took me by surprise, and I sputtered in reply, "I'm Jack. Hi. Which is true."

It must have taken her but an instant to recognize my state and probably to deduce my age: she was obviously somewhat older than I, at least eighteen, which in 1967 would mean that she could drink legally. "How did you ever get served?" she asked, evidently amused.

"At the table. Julie Rosenbaum? Her niece?"

We continued to float among the other heads. My feet knew how to move, my single beaming eye to see. There was a lowered, pink, half-veil attached to the pillbox fez Eva Lynn was wearing, her costume clearly inspired by the popular TV show, *I Dream of Jeannie.* She was a strawberry blond, of very fair complexion with a rather pointed chin. Her mouth looked overly large, but it was a sweet face—and suddenly she came into focus. I remembered her from the previous summer at the pool with her aunt Julie, a henna-haired *bella donna* in a black bikini. *Eva Lynn.* Now I looked into her green eyes, the first truly green eyes I'd ever known. Now she was smiling broadly and now I thought, *What beautiful teeth!* And then I glanced at her breasts.

"You all right? You look a little shaky. Come 'ere, kid: let's sit you down in the cocktail lounge, and then I'll go and get you a bite to eat."

Still holding my hand, she led me, half pushed me against the tide of revelers into the lounge, which was completely empty now that dinner was being served. Once we were settled in a booth, I made an effort to clear my head and calm the tremors that had beset my limbs. I took several strenuous breaths, looking ridiculous I'm sure, my chest puffed up like one of the cock-birds in Uncle Tony's pigeon coop. Eva Lynn and I burst out laughing simultaneously. It must have something to do with being drunk, I thought: you don't need to take things so seriously!

Reach over and stroke her face. Tell 'er in Italian that she's beautiful. Brush her bangs back from her eyes.

You'll regret you didn't, matey!

"I did some heavy drinking on an empty stomach," I boasted.

"Uh-oh. Bad idea, *Jack*," she said. "I remember once. . .Ever been to the Half Moon up in Pougkeepise?"

"Sure." I lied. I would never have been allowed in the place. And I would never have tried to use a phony ID, since I had heard many times from my parents about the *bruta figura* of getting caught. It was at this moment that the difference in our ages hit home, yet I continued brazenly: "Yeah, the ole, the good ole, Moon. S'what everybody calls it, ya know. My cousin Chris, he's got friends there."

"Right—so you're Chris's little cousin. . . *Jack*."

"That's me. Black Jack—*yar*. My grandfather was Giovanni Nero, but my father changed it after the fire. I mean, you know, Nero's fiddle. He hated that. My father, I mean. After the old man died he changed his name. My father has a great sense of justice."

She stared at me. I was absurd and she was enjoying it.

"I *am* Chris's cousin—on the other side," I said, feeling terribly woozy.

I COULDN'T REMEMBER HOW it had come to pass, but I was lying on my back in my own bed. There was a harem girl seated beside me, reading under the amber cone of my night lamp in the corner of the otherwise darkened bedroom. Spattering my window with sleet, I could hear the ice storm continuing. From downstairs, I could hear the din of the Carnevale.

"How long have I been asleep?"

"Years," she said idly, turning a page of the movie magazine on her lap. "Last Fall at a mixer in New Haven, somebody had to put me to bed before dinner. I missed the rest of the party. How ya feeling?"

"What are you doing here? My God, what time is it? The show! If my father. . ."

"Your father's got a great sense of justice, just like you said. He put you to bed. He was a bit surprised to see you passed out in the booth with me. I don't mind telling you I was relieved when he got you onto your feet. You don't remember that? First time you were ever blotto, huh? Your dad laughed it off. Unbelievable! My father would have had a shit fit. But your dad was cute, the way he stood you up against himself, and how he moved your legs talking to you in this funny voice, step by step up the stairs. Don't worry: you didn't make a scene or anything. Everybody else was in the ballroom or the bar."

"Did he do the show alone?"

"The show? I guess so. I've been up here with you. He asked me to sit with you for a while. I wasn't having such a good time anyway. Too many hands, if you know what I mean. "

"How long ago was that?"

"Maybe like an hour?" She came near and peered into my face. "You'll live, Mr. Black. You seem fine, and so I'm going back downstairs before my aunt starts looking for me. She won't stay long—she can't—she's got cancer. Shit, I shouldn't have said that."

"I'm sorry," I said. I sat up on the edge of my bed, rotating my head in small circles, rubbing my neck. Sheepishly, I looked up at her. *She's what—a student at Vassar? A Vassar girl is babysitting me?*

I held onto the thought that my father had laughed about my condition, and that, amazingly, he himself had put me to bed. He'd probably gotten a real kick out of Eva Lynn, too. I was praying that he would keep this fiasco from my mother and make up something about why I hadn't played Mr. Spaghetti. I was his straight man, but he really didn't need me, and that script I'd written for the two of us stank.

I hung my head and ran my hands through my hair: the kerchief was gone, the eye patch was gone. My sword and spyglass also were nowhere nearby, but my mother's medallion still dangled about my neck. I'd been blown far off course on my maiden voyage, shipwrecked, but I'd survived.

Take a risk. She likes you.

I let my eyes move over Eva Lynn's sumptuous breasts. I glanced up at her lips.

"Listen," I said, "listen to what the band is playing. It's 'Moonlight in Vermont.' I love this song. Let's go down together."

I lunged unsteadily—not toward Eva Lynn, but up onto my feet, smiling somewhat stupidly as a sign of my victory over gravity. I regained my balance under the hand with which she steadied me. She slid her fingers off my shoulder when I took my first step.

She smiled indulgently. "You'll be fine, Jack. I really do have to go before my aunt starts getting worried or something worse. I've got to drive us to Hyde Park. Maybe I'll see you again sometime, maybe at the Moon, huh?"

Evaline Samuels. Eva Lynn, she preferred to be called. I would in fact meet her again, much, much later, but that is another story.

MY FATHER, THE LOOPY life of the party in Harlequin togs and pointy hat is—amidst his whoops and wisecracks—behind the bar calling out loudly for Gracie Laporta to come to his aid. Then he sees me at the entry way to the bar, and shouts over the heads of the crowd, "Okay, kid?" He never calls me kid unless he's very busy. He motions me to come closer, among the customers—this is, of course, terribly irregular, but then, this is Carnevale. "Seen-a Gracie around? Seen-a Georgie? That guy, he get so mad. . . Do me a favor, Spaghetti. You go find her, yeah? Tell her I need some help in here." He laughs and pats me affectionately on the cheek. "Ah, *Guido mio.*" His hands are busy with bottles and glasses and bunches of bills. I stand there dumbfounded, aware that I am not to be punished for having slept through our floorshow, but rather feeling as if I've somehow been promoted.

More seriously, he says, *"Fa presto.* See if-a Georgie's car is in the parking lot. See if they's havin' a cigarette. Tell her I need some help in here, okay?"

I'm greatly relieved to be let off the hook, and now the best I can do by my father is to immediately carry out the mission I've been assigned. I have wits enough to notice that the night's rain has become sleet, and I remember Caballo's overcoat in the cloakroom. Judy is not at her post, and so I fumble among the wraps hanging on the long rack, sniffing out Caballo's coat with its telltale scent of cologne. Putting on the overcoat, I feel its woolen warmth.

Outside, the patio is slick with a thin layer of ice and so I must be cautious. The effects of the alcohol continue to tingle through me, but after my unusual interlude with Eva Lynn, my nap as I am choosing to call it, I feel somewhat reinvigorated. Now I think longingly about Gracie Laporta, and my old anger at George McInnis begins to pump through my bloodstream. I feel ready to fight him if George is so much as raising his voice against Gracie. I swear to Jesus of the Pirates that I will kill him if he has a hand on her.

Sliding from car to car in the parking lot I search for George's black GTO.

At last I find it and grab the tailpiece, cold as a shark fin, to steady myself. The engine is idling, and the sound gives me cover as I catch my breath and slip to the driver side window. It's fogged, but looking in through the clouded glass, I can see plenty. Gracie is bare to her waist, the bodice of her silvery costume folded down like the petals of a great flower. I can't see her breasts completely, because she's pressed tightly against George.

I watch from behind George's white sailor-suited back, relieved that the Mick can't see me, but now I'm shivering with the sleet falling on my bare head and cold water dripping inside the back of my collar. Although I yearn for a look at Gracie's bare breasts, I'm revolted by the sight of the Mule's fingers squeezing her nude shoulders, and my lust suddenly contracts, far away from the scene. Unsure whether or not I am about to become a hero, I study the situation for a long moment.

Now Georgie has his hands at her neck.

But she's smiling.

Now he's pressing his mouth against hers.

Carnevale

It's his pathetic way, slobbering.

Now his tongue is in her mouth.

She's French kissing back.

Now his mouth is on the breast he's squeezing.

Her pearly flesh! His lips on the nipple!

Now Georgie lowers his face, a breast in each hand. Hungrily, he slides his tongue around the aureoles, first one then the other.

Gracie throws her head back, pleasure on her face, but then, surprisingly, I see that her thoughts are flitting elsewhere: she squints at the wristwatch on an arm she raises overhead.

And now she has spotted me.

Well—she sees *somebody*, and it prompts her to avert her bosom quickly. Then her gaze returns, for she has indeed recognized who is standing outside the car in the freezing rain.

Here is the look that was foretold when Gracie was my silent model, the look I can never forget. It is a look of compassion but not of comprehension, and a look of expectation also. It is an expression startled but unashamed, and her self-possession affects me greatly. This is the first time a woman has looked at me as if I were a man, looking not for a valentine of paper and crayon, but instead perceiving in my heart the nearest thing to love of which I am at this time capable. Whether or not she could have intended any of this, the effect on me will be indelible.

THEN THE UNIVERSE SHIFTED. In the next moment, all of time and space took up a new abode. Gracie was mouthing some words to me. I silently repeated them: *Not. . . on . . . the. . . window?* I stepped back, afraid suddenly, but then I reconsidered and thought I had gotten what she meant:

172

Knock on the window. I made a gesture with my knuckles, as if to rap the glass, and she seemed to be nodding to me, *yes,* her eyes widening like she was smiling, but then a sudden displeasure flashed across her face.

"No, Georgie! That's enough. I gotta go in and help Zizi, I promised," she said loudly.

I was startled into action, and stepping back from the car, I simultaneously extended my arm its whole length to bang on the driver side window. *"Graziella!"* I shouted, in a voice that I thought was like my father's. *"Graziella, oh!* My father needs you at the bar. You okay, or what?"

"Jesus H. Christ!" Georgie exploded. "Who the fuck is out there?"

I could see that he was pulling up his pants, and I had a split second when I could have run, but I didn't. "Gracie," I said, emboldened, "everything okay?"

Gracie began to say my name, but George snarled, "You shuddup!" Then, rolling down the window, he turned his anger directly on me: "Kid! Get your ass outtahere now or it's grass. Capeesh?"

"Georgie, take it easy, honey. Don't go talkin' to him that way. Zizi musta sent him—you tell your father I'll be right in, Guido. You go back inside now, honey. I'm okay."

"I said shuddup or you're gonna regret it!" Georgie shouted. Her dress was back in place, she was fussing with her compact when he grabbed her roughly at the base of the neck with one hand.

"Fuck you, you mule headed shit," she spat through chattering teeth.

"Leave her be!" I said, putting my hand through the rolled down window onto Georgie's back.

And he did—turning on me instead, throwing open the door, stepping out of the car to confront me. "That's it! First you and then her!" He raised a fist.

Now, the voice spoke in my head. *Stand your ground and let him have it, matey.*

I stared with terrible purpose into Georgie's eyes, stared with snake eyes, and with the fingers of my left hand I made the sign of the horns and pointed them at him. "I curse you. And my curse will be a great sorrow to you, George McInnis, for no one will love you, and all women will scorn you until you have humbled yourself at Graziella's feet."

And then he knocked me down.

IF I HAVE FORGOTTEN certain portions of this night that I would remember, then also there are other portions I would as soon erase but cannot. One part is this, the part that has me falling on my face, thudding to the ground, shocked not so much by the force with which George McInnis hurled me aside, but also by my body's instinctive contraction when I met the earth, my fetal recoil, my helplessness. I see now, however, that this pathetic posture might have prevented George from doing me further damage.

Gracie opened her door and came around the car to me, but I was on my feet by then. Looking me over she said, "You slipped and fell, Guido, that's all. You're okay, you're okay," she said nervously. "Now get back inside. You tell your father I wasn't feeling well and Georgie had to take me home. Tell him I'm sorry—I'm sorry I can't help him . . . "

She cast a look back over her shoulder as she got into the GTO. Georgie was at the wheel, a cigarette in his mouth, grumbling.

I had already been humbled earlier that night when I'd blacked out and a Vassar College girl had been assigned to babysit me, and now this: it might have broken my pride completely, but I didn't let it. Of course I knew that Gracie was not going to be my woman—I had no illusion of wresting her away from Georgie—but also I knew with what force I had cursed the Mule. I exulted in that, and I knew that it was not the power of my hatred that I had focused on him, but rather the terrible force of Justice, and this thought was my consolation after Graziella got back into the car and they roared away.

The Carnevale had taken yet another decisive turn, and I wondered if Gracie would be safe, and I believed she would be: I'd seen that lion, after all, the sign of her courage and strength. Then I remembered why my father had sent me out into the storm. If I told him what had just happened, I didn't know what he would think, and so I made a decision then and there to concoct my own version of events. It had stopped raining, and although I was cold and soaked through to my skin, I felt surprisingly intact. My blood was up and I could feel it pulsing hot in my ears. I took a few deep breaths. I could feel my curse at work, like a falconer who knows the bird that he released has sunk its talons in its prey.

Crackling the icy pebbles of the parking lot, sliding and skating, I made my way to the patio steps. Through an open window in the lounge I saw the face of a clock. It was only ten minutes past ten. I would have to decide what to tell my father, but I couldn't let him or anybody else see me like this, and so I would need to wash up. By now he would have figured out something behind the bar, probably with one of the other waitresses to help out, or maybe Judy, the hatcheck girl. I bundled Caballo's coat around me as I picked my way over the slick patio cement. Since it was actually fairly early, I thought that my grandmother and Caballo might still be up and about, and I decided to find them. I was betting that my father had made excuses to my mother for my absence at the stage show and that she would be mollified to think of me asleep in my bed. Plus she had other things on her mind: after all, it was her party.

CHAPTER 15

I PAUSED WITH MY hand on the front railing and looked up to see the face of the Villa. Despite the many renovations within, her outward appearance remained rather undistinguished. Yet tonight, because the ice storm had drenched and glazed the facade, and because the moon had emerged after the rain, by that light, she seemed transformed. A pole-lantern near the main door cast the entryway into shadow, and I thought it a spooky looking mouth. With their shades lowered, two lit windows in the second story gave the impression of a woman's heavy lidded eyes—bedroom eyes, indeed. On the roof above were three crenellations that suggested a crown. Then a ragged cloud stole the fat moon from the sky, the white clapboards lost their sheen, and the face was reduced to a skull.

Maybe my curse on George will backfire! Maybe I'm a tool of the Devil rather than an agent of la Giustizia. . .

I was more of a boy that night than I would have liked to admit, but I was purely myself, Guido Diamante, that guy from the Villa, a perfect pirate, a secret agent. I patted myself smooth, wiping the rain from my cloak and found a smile like the one my father would wear on cold mornings-after, hung over, but gamely at work cleaning up the bar with a bucket and a mop, whistling a Neapolitan folk song. I tugged Caballo's coat close and told myself I was a sea-changed sailor, told myself that I had moxie, and I thanked Jesus of the Pirates. I was being looked after, and if I had sinned, or if my curse were to boomerang, I wanted to be sure Jesus and I remained on good terms.

But I couldn't go in through the front door of the Villa, my clothes sopping and torn.

I slinked around back, hoping that the kitchen would be unlocked, that Mr. Schnock would have hung up his apron for the night, and I would find the kitchen empty. I got lucky on all counts. I could hear the party swinging at full tilt in the ballroom, and when I peered through the porthole of the swinging door, I saw my mother glide by, in the arms of a guy who looked like the Mouse King from *The Nutcracker*. I thought about my father and felt bad, but I'd decided that there was no way I was going to report back to him tonight.

I stepped into the bathroom adjoining the kitchen and peeled off the coat and my clothes underneath. I scrubbed my smeared face a long time with soap and warm water, but I couldn't remove every trace of the soot-sketched beard. I toweled my body, inspected my bruised left hip which was taking color and beginning to throb; I washed my scraped wrist, extracting grit like buckshot from a stinging wound. When I got dressed I saw that the pants my mother had so carefully tailored were ripped at the knee, and I felt sorry. I had also lost the earring she loaned me, but not the amulet, which had worked its way under my shirt, and I clutched it now, stroking its splendid boss before I buttoned the shirt over it and secured the jerkin. I hung Caballo's coat to dry near the radiator.

In the kitchen I noticed that the cellar door was wide open. Most unusual. The cellar, like the bar, was generally off limits to me, and therefore, infinitely fascinating. As a child, I was certain there must be passageways through that great abyss which gave access to the first floor rooms of the Villa. The cellar was like a catacomb, and I had also imagined that it communicated with a hidden cavern where a hoard of treasure was stashed and a dragon might reside. Two large cavities in the dirt floor abetted my suspicions, although I'd been told by my mother that they were only the sealed entrances to the root cellar and ice-hold that were once necessary at the Farm. Down in the cellar with my father I was sometimes allowed to check on the furnace whose hot rancid smell was indeed like the breath of a dragon, and whose fire sparkled like diamonds behind an isinglass door. With him I also visited the fuel oil tank and thumped its red metal flanks so the sound could tell us how much the beast had drunk and how much more it required.

Down a short corridor with a low ceiling was a substantial room carved into the earth where a coal furnace had lived a long time ago. Later, Nonno had made his wine and grappa in this cell and racked many dust laden bottles, some of which we were still consuming. Each was numbered in his hand with the year of the vintage. Other articles of his craft had been removed, including his distillery, which I could remember with its vats and coils and firebox. There remained a sturdy wooden table in the center of the cell surrounded by chairs with a bare light bulb on a wire above. As a child, I wondered what special purposes this room might yet serve, and my imagination supplied many possible scenarios. Whenever it was stirred, the hanging bulb cast an array of creepy shadows through the racks of bottles, and once when I'd dared to bring Tina down here for a "séance," we both grew so uneasy that we fled.

Throughout my childhood I was haunted by the thought that there were secret goings-on around me at the Villa—and there were, of course, by definition, since as a child I could only brush unknowingly past the adult worlds from which I was excluded. But now I could hear voices and laughter climbing the narrow stairwell to me from below the kitchen. When I looked in, immediately I could smell the cellar's familiar odor compounded of damp earth and fuel oil, and something else too: I smelled the potato crib in its dark corner where spooky white eyes crawled out of the potato heads.

"Hello," I called.

"Eh?" My grandmother's voice answered me, breaking off her conversation. "*Buona sera. Buona sera, Guidino!* Come!" Her voice sounded odd with its echo attached like a tail.

When I descended, I could see them in the wine cellar, looking up toward me, gathered at the table with some bottles and glasses under the glowing bulb. Nonna's headdress was tossed back and hung behind like a mane of long black hair. Mr. Caballo, at Nonna's right hand, was still dressed in his coffee colored cassock. How very much at home he looked down here, I thought, remembering the story of Saint Valentine in the Roman catacombs. Schnock wore his chef's uniform, and he waved to me with both hands, motioning me forward with short rapid gestures, as if he were rolling dough in the air.

I ducked under the timbers of the lintel to enter the chamber. "Don't hit your head, sonny boy," the cook tittered, as I found my way to a chair.

My grandmother regarded me with some concern and asked if I'd like a glass of water. I realized how terribly thirsty I was and nodded eagerly. *Everything had better seem fine,* I thought, *or else the party's over.*

Mr. Caballo poured me a glass from a bottle of Nonna's seltzer. It was usually nearby, since it helped her to shape the small controlled belches that eased her nervous stomach. Her constant belching, as well as her habit of cleaning wax from her ears with a hairpin, her jokes about the amputated leg, her appetite for peanut butter and whipped cream, were among a growing list of her eccentricities. Also, a deck of greasy playing cards were sooner or later in her lap or on any table at which she sat, solitaire being necessary to her, it seemed, as her insulin kit. More recently, perhaps in anticipation of the Carnevale, she had unpacked her ancient Tarot from storage, and I had seen her sitting as if entranced, shuffling the cards endlessly without spreading them, and talking to herself so strangely that I was afraid to interrupt.

Caballo looked over at me. "You didn't make the floor show with your father. You changed your mind?"

I was feeling slightly dizzy. I replied, "My father does okay without me." I gulped carbonated water and burped loudly and everybody stared. I felt somewhat sleepy, somewhat nauseous.

"*Si, si,*" Caballo said. "Your papa is a soloist. And you, I think, are not so interested in being a comedian."

"He has many talents," Nonna chimed in. She reached over to take my hand. She had removed most of the gaudy makeup and now her visage was more like that familiar one on the quarter dollar: stately, composed, as masculine as it was feminine.

"Dreamer boy, yah. I know ze type," Schnoch said, eyeing me. "Vhy you don't learn to cook? Someday this place will be yours, sonny."

"Oh," Caballo said, "our Guido will feed people."

"You met that pretty girl." Nonna spoke blandly now as she peeled cards onto the table before her. "An Arabian dancer? Did you give her a valentine?"

"Strawberry blond, very fair," Caballo said. His face was animated, and he gestured with the hand that wore the flashing emerald. "Very pretty. A Jewish girl, I think. Not too old for you?"

"Yah, yah, very pretty, chewish," the cook said smiling. "Always you Italians see how pretty!" It was meant as a joke, but nobody laughed. Putting his foot in further he added, "I have no prejudice. I see things how they are. Listen, sonny boy: don't think you are too good to work in a kitchen."

He turned toward Nonna for some sort of approval, but her eyes remained fixed on the Tarochinni.

Mr. Schnock was visibly rebuffed. "So sorry. I meant no offense, *signora*. My apologies. Only this world is a sad place for dreamers."

"Dreams are a mirror for the soul," Caballo said, pushing his glass out and back before him, tilting it, raising it, rotating it hypnotically. Half an inch of grappa caught the light of the bare bulb and sent sparks flashing amid the racks of bottles.

I shuddered with a wish that I was unable to voice. *I wanted you to be my father.* It was not to him I said this, but to a knight on a plunging steed, the picture card on the table before my grandmother and me. *Caballo mio,* Nonna liked to call him.

I have a blank space here about what happened next—perhaps I nodded off? But then, my grandmother was stroking my hair. *"Madonna!"* she said, holding her hand to my forehead. "He's so hot! Ernesto, feel."

"Ebbe," Caballo said. "A small fever. Too much exertion, I think." He withdrew a bottle from beneath his cassock and shook two pills into the open palm of his hand. He gave them to me and with his chin motioned toward my glass of water.

Reassured, Nonna said to the shame-faced cook, "No offense taken, Gustave. We make a party tonight. I'm pleased you join us."

Her eyes twinkled and she added, "Antonio, my husband, *sa bened-ico*, would be happy for us. *He is happy.*"

Then, suddenly, I could hear my grandfather's voice. In life he had always extolled forbearance. *Ce voule pazienza.* A person has to have that, I was reminded. Patience, in order to counterbalance *la pazzia*, the madness of this world.

And then Nonna began a story I had never before been told.

Antonio Giustovera and Carlo Manaperta, while not exactly new arrivals to New York, had rarely been outside of the City, but then Nino purchased his first car. Several trips to the truck farm of a *paesano* on Long Island and to another near Peekskill got him thinking about country life. He talked up a plan with his brothers: he wanted cattle and sheep, he wanted to butcher and market them. He told his wife Maria he was looking for a farm and she encouraged him to find one.

Carlo would be happy to read the map he said, and he winked at Maria as if to assure her they wouldn't get lost "huppastate." It surprised no one who knew him that Nino preferred Carlo Manaperta's company to that of his straight-laced brothers. Nino was industrious like Renaldo and Palermo, but he was more ambitious, curious about America, and unlike them, a risk-taker. His friend Carlo was clever and never lacked for ready cash—that one was always up to something, some *servizio* at the docks, or over in Brooklyn for people whose names were best left unspoken. But Carlo regarded Nino and Maria as his dearest friends, and he was always available when they asked for his help. One time, Maria had slammed the palm of her hand against a wall, annoyed with a gossipy neighbor who had insinuated that Manaperta was her husband's *consigliere,* as if their partnership were somehow shady. She'd told that nosy woman that Antonio knew how to choose his friends and with a withering glare had silenced the crone. America was a big place, but just as in Italy, to go forward a man needed friends he could count on, people with big ideas. She was thinking of Renaldo and Palermo Giustovera, both of them older than her husband and cautious beyond their years. She was remembering how finely her own family had lived in Milano before the Great War, and she still had an appetite for fine things.

Now it was 1925. Automobiles being what they were, new drivers being what they were, some malfunction or other stopped Nino and Carlo just north of Irvington. A cold, sunny Saturday, early in the month of March, and it was almost noon when they decided to set out on foot for help.

"Where?" Nino asked, rubbing his palms together for warmth.

Carlo gestured up the empty road before them. "There must be a garage nearby," he said. They rolled closed the tin-lizzie's windshield, and although there were no locks for the doors, with a shrug Carlo told Nino, "The car will be safe until we return."

As they walked, they spoke in the old tongue, Siciliano. It was nearly spring and the river had begun to shed its coat of ice; when it boomed suddenly, Carlo cringed and covered his ears like a sailor under cannon fire. It was an old reflex. Nino understood and touched his friend's shoulder kindly.

They grew silent after walking a while, savoring the scent of evergreens and the sight of the Highlands cut out against the sky. But a half hour later they had still not encountered so much as a farmer toiling in a shed, and Nino began to grow concerned. "No gas station. I think we go back. Maybe she start."

"*Aspett'aspetti,*" Carlo said. "See that fine house of stone on the hill? Perhaps they can help us. Or they will have a telephone."

They knocked and a doorman appeared. Tall and ungainly, with the face of a pugilist, he was nevertheless dressed rather elegantly. By his accent they recognized him as a Sicilian *paesano.* The doorman tugged his jacket sleeves and touched his necktie repeatedly, seeming somewhat uncomfortable, but he was friendly to Nino and Carlo who were now speaking Siciliano with him, explaining their situation. Rocco, that was the ugly man's name: Manaperta would never forget it and would always recall this meeting, shaking his head and smiling slyly. Rocco said that he was in the employment of a certain gentleman. This important gentleman took a genuine interest in others who had come to America from the Old Country.

"Wait here, in the hallway. I see if don Trippa is free. Don't worry about the car. We take care of that."

Grateful, bowing courteously, they sat in the chairs they were offered. When Rocco had gone, Carlo turned to Nino and loosened a soft whistle. With one hand he gestured toward the palatial room just beyond the foyer where they sat. It was an atrium, glass walled, high domed, trimmed in dark wood. Among its leafy plants and splendid furnishings, several huge enameled vases held fresh bouquets of flowers.

"I'll own such a home myself," Nino said, jesting. But in America, he thought, why not?

"*Amico mio,*" Carlo whispered. "This is not a farmer's house. I can only imagine how some *paesano* of ours, with a trained ape to answer his door, has acquired such a fortune." He mimed the gesture of pouring and drinking.

"*Contrabbandieri,*" Nino said softly.

Antonio Giustovera was a lover of wine and a vintner all his life, and the Eighteenth Amendment to the U.S. Constitution was one of few things he could not accept about his new homeland. He believed that the fruit of the vine was essential to life, and moreover, after consecration during mass, did it not become the very blood of Our Lord? *Sangue de Gesu* was in fact a common expression of his, and he used it not as an imprecation, but rather as an expression of awe. Prohibition made no sense to him, and as he had done back in Sicily, in New York he continued to press grapes for wine and to distill *grappa* from the pomace. Nino provided for his own table, which was legal, and in a neighborly way, he traded bottles of his excellent spirits for favors throughout the city. In the eyes of the law, therefore, Nino Giustovera was himself a bootlegger, although his customers never called him that, nor did the beat cops, who got theirs and then some. Certainly he knew about racketeers and *that thing* which had come along with *some people* to America. But he was no criminal. And hadn't Gesu himself, for his first miracle, at the wedding in Canna made wine for his family and friends?

"Yah. Dat's a good story, very good story. Your granpa got some crazy idea from those guys and he made out okay. Vhy not?" Schnock was addressing me while he poured into his glass two more fingers of grappa.

"Did you know I was born in 1925? A very *gut jahr*." The cook stretched wide his arms, and tilting back his head, he yawned. "It's a big world, sonny, and if a man has blood in him—" he jabbed at his left wrist with his rigid index finger—"you want things from that world. She keeps turning, and you keep chasing. When you stop, they make a picture to remember. No more death mask today, only by Kodak a snapshot. But even if they put your name in gold on your headstone, you become nothing but a memory. That means a ghost, sonny boy."

When he was done blabbing at me, he looked over toward Nonna and Caballo as if for confirmation. Nonna had paused, and resting within a reverie, she stared blankly at the intemperate cook, forbearing his interruption, as it seemed I also was required to do. Caballo yawned behind the back of his left hand. I had no idea what he thought of Schnock, but the cook had obviously been invited here, and although I was annoyed by him, I knew I should behave like a gentleman.

Why Schnock needled me so persistently I could never quite understand. Is it possible that he really did wish to teach me his kitchen craft? Is it possible that in spite of myself, I learned something about cooking from him, but more importantly, paradoxically, that because of his irascible behavior I myself became more temperate, so that during the wild times that were to come when I worked in the kitchen of the Half Moon Café and Saloon, I kept my composure? Meanwhile, on the night of the Villa's one and only Carnevale, I had discovered my power to curse, and I felt something begin to twitch spontaneously in my left eyebrow as I regarded the cook. Instantly my chest throbbed and my mouth felt dry. I drank again from my glass of sparkling water.

"Let the dead sleep, sonny boy," said Schnock in reference exactly to what I did not comprehend. "If you hear unhappy things, maybe you won't rest so easy."

I gripped the edges of my chair.

Schnock nudged my foot with his. "Maybe ve're all criminals, huh? Vun bottle, and we become friends, but two bottles—how many bottles to make a fight? You like vor stories, sonny boy? How come you don't answer me, huh? You think I vas a Nazi, because I'm *Cherrman?*"

Of the cook's rare atmosphere I too must interrupt Nonna's story to speak. Of his apple strudel and the Black Forest cake that my mother called "sinful" because it turned us into gluttons, I must remember, my mouth watering, in spite of myself. Was he truly an old Nazi—I had actually called him that behind his back because of the way he bossed us helpers in the kitchen. Of the rancid odor broiled-in-with-roast-meat that penetrated his white uniforms which by evening's end were inevitably stained many colors, perhaps smeared with his famous honey-mustard sauce that he spiked with vodka and pronounced "dangerous," of these things I must also tell. Of his tasty and nasty doings, of the cook who was a little like Manaperta, but never so kind to me as the old shipwright. Of the veal *saltimbocca* that really did surpass my mother's and which he then taught her to make. Of the way he flashed a knife in the air to show how swiftly and painlessly he could slit the throats of calves and lambs—as my grandfather must also have done, bringing death to them so that we could eat, praising how tender was their flesh.

Uncouth, Mr. Schnock certainly was, but possessed of rare gifts that my grandmother obviously enjoyed, as did my mother, who raved about his culinary skills and wanted to keep him happy at the Place so that he would stay on and she could be free of the kitchen and dance in the ballroom. Then she could be Ann, wearing her strapless cocktail dress and peep-toe heels that caused me to look away, she was so pretty in them. Her liberator Schnock was trained in *haute cuisine*—as she reminded everyone—but when he was potted, nobody could stand to work closely with him. The salad-girls and I followed his orders explicitly or else we were subject to his lashing tongue. On party nights he usually had a bevy of assistants, and except for me, they were all girls, and, it's true, this was one reason I regularly volunteered for his crew. Once he was pickled he would pull me aside to share his observations about *jew-asses* and *chicky-breasts*. For a time, I smirked along, but then he pressed too close and his fumes began to sicken me. Ah yes, of the odoriferous chef I tell, of his rank body odor and his lobsters boiled alive and dressed in garlic that he would stuff us with, of his schnitzel and bratwurst in huge trays that allowed my mother to rest at the dinner table and later to relax at the bar with her customers, celebrating the art of her chef.

"Ho! Ho! Look at this, sonny boy!" he thundered to me one time: he had discovered under his counter a long forgotten cardboard box. Within it, choked in green and black mold were the remains of a white sausage casserole. "Now who could haf left this here?" he asked, as if I should have known, or cared. "You think the Board of Health wouldn't be interested?"

To me, the chef became a repository of all the unseemly essences of the kitchen and the ratty old butchery next door, even as with guilty pleasure, I fattened on his gourmet cookery and ogled the saucy helpers who accompanied him.

But consider him in a clean, starched uniform whose double breast of buttons gleams. Consider his thin blond hair, almost white, so neatly parted on the left side of his head, and through the part, his pink scalp that shines like a seashell. He was then a man younger than I am today: Mr. Schnock at the height of his powers. He begins each shift each night, having bathed at home and dressed for his work and kissed his wife and two sonny boys goodbye; he devotes himself to his art and I must respect that. He has weaknesses, he has his past of which so little was ever known, he has his starring role to play at the Villa. The wreath of odors he accumulates each night are an education to my adolescent nose, and his boorishness helps to teach me what I would not want to be.

But these quirks of character were not what most disturbed me about Mr. Schnock. Above all, the chef stank to me of collusion with my mother: because of his presence at the Villa, she moved further away from my father and me.

CHAPTER 16

NINO HAD A GOOD idea, a grand idea, and he had shoulders broad enough to carry the responsibility he was asking for. He reassured his brothers that they wouldn't need to work any more than they wanted at the farm in Kinderkill—*Where? Huppa state, near Pougkeep-a-sie. Where is that?*—Palermo and Renaldo would dig up, instead of the soil, a mortgage from the bank. They knew about that kind of thing, they had done that for the butcher shop on Canal Street. *Collateral. A lien, or was it a loan? Investors?* No, this they would keep among themselves. They made a deal: the house was Nino's to rebuild, the land was all of theirs to share. And someday each of them would have a villa of his own upstate—ha!

A hundred acres plus two barns, a house whose stone foundation they learned was "since before there was America." The brothers said that and more about her, and right away Nino was planning on moving his family to Kinderkill. And always it was *she* he talked about as sailors do about their ships. *Quella la,* Maria teased him, saying she was jealous of *that one,* and indeed she did become bothered by the money and time *that one* required of her husband.

Nino enjoyed physical labor. A well-built man in his early thirties, a full partner in the family business: the cleaver's rhythm made music to which his mind worked. But in the New York City shop his imagination was always with her, upstate, anticipating the Friday night drives with Carlo when they smoked in companionable silence or else sang—*Non la sospiri la nostra cassetta*—just enough to catch a glimpse of Tosca, enough to evoke the vision of a parlor room where someday on a new Victrola, they would be able to hear the opera whenever they wished.

That first springtime on Widener Road was mostly hammers and saws and sweat, beds in a bare room where they rose without washing to work long days, and then the late drives back to the City, tired but satisfied on Sunday nights. Things went well from the first. The bank had given the Giustovera's their mortgage, had given them a benediction, Nino explained to Maria: "People always gotta eat," that small bald man with the firm hand had said. Remodeling the kitchen, framing the butchery, with the strokes of his saw, Nino remembered those words. *People gotta eat.* And how many times, like a prayer, when he brought his knife to the downy throat of a calf or lamb, "People gotta eat," Nino would whisper.

When it grew warm they took off their shirts and knocked open a wall for a window and smelled the fresh fields. His friend Carlo surprised him continually, for he wasn't only a carpenter, but also a plumber, an electrician, a mason, and he seemed tireless. Nino decided then that the dining room they had stuccoed would be painted green. Maria would love that.

One day, when they were in the cellar to work on the foundation, they discovered a narrow passageway that ran parallel with an outside wall. There was wiring to do down there under the floor below the kitchen, and Nino did the crawling himself, while Carlo fed the wire in its beaded tube. "Here, *signorina*, I've brought you a necklace of pearls," Nino jested. On all fours he squeezed behind a stacked stone baffle. Then, sounding serious, he called to Carlo: "This is very strange. Up ahead, there seems to be a small room. Pass me some light."

Carlo crawled in behind him and handed over an electric cord and trouble light. When Nino extended his arm, the connection broke. "*Merda!* Go get the kerosene lamp, quick." A moment later he shined the lantern down into the tunnel before him. His friend peered over his shoulder.

"*Sangue de Gesu!*" Nino exclaimed, crossing himself. "It must be a tomb—there's a skeleton here on the ledge! Look, Carlo, see how well preserved. Holy God! On one hand, a ring. . . And what is this? A ruby! Come see the ruby on her breast!"

Manaperta squeezed past his stunned friend, taking the lamp with him. He inspected the remains, swinging the lantern back and forth over the skeleton in its rotted clothes and living jewels.

"She is dead many years, " Manaperta said. "*Madonna mia!* I bet we found some Dutch girl grave!"

After the initial shock, Nino said, "If we tell the police, then what? What would it mean to that one? Or to us? I think we should leave her alone, here where she's slept so long. Not a word of this, Carlo. Bless you, child, in the Name of the Father, the Son, and the Holy Ghost. Rest in peace. Keep peace with us and bring us *buona fortuna*. Carlo and I will remember you!"

"Amen," Manaperta said. "Well done, Nino. But, my friend, there is something important to consider . . ."

He was of course referring to the jewels, and Nino knew it. "Carlo," he began.

"*Aspett' un momento.* The dead have no vanity."

"But to steal from a grave!"

"Of course not, Nino, not to steal."

The man who had laid these stones and built the first house to stand on them was a Dutchman, and so they concluded that what they had found might well be his wife's tomb, or perhaps that of his daughter. "She look so small, so young," my grandfather would later explain to my grandmother. *La Principessa Olandesa,* Carlo called her, the Dutch Princess, who from then on, they would presume to be the daughter of a wealthy man. And now the place with all its contents belonged to Nino, yes? Carlo reminded him that his brothers had already agreed on this point. And was it not as if some unseen force had guided them here, where the electric stopped and crawling by lantern light they'd traveled back to long ago? Yes, they had been summoned, Carlo said, and it was good that Nino had immediately offered a prayer over the long forgotten bones. Was it not *giustizia,* then, to receive a reward?

"We are working men. Our dreams are simple ones," Nino said. Then from the ruins of the small ribcage where it had nested a long time, he lifted the brooch up into the lantern's beam. It was a faceted ruby set in a filigree of gold. On the back of his sweaty wrist, he wiped away the dust of time. Then he reached for the sapphire ring. He felt a pang of remorse, yet it slipped easily from the tiny knucklebone and shone readily when he held it in his palm under the light, spreading blue and white spangles.

Crawling backwards out from the tunnel, Nino and Carlo retreated upstairs to the kitchen and made strong coffee. They drank it while the spring breeze cooled them through an open window. Nino would always remember the voice he heard calling from the fields: it sounded like the happy voice of a young girl at play. He put the jewels away inside a flower vase. Then the men climbed downstairs with brick and mortar to reseal the crypt.

NONNA LAID THE QUEEN of Swords under her king. She had been turning the cards as she spoke about those early days when the Villa Giustovera was little more than my grandfather's dream.

To me she said, "In those days he wanted only to farm. Of course, your grandfather, God bless him, was reliable as oak—" she rapped the table with her knuckles—"but he could have been something more. And he knew this, did he not, Ernesto?"

We both looked over at Caballo, who was stroking his beard. His face was masked in shadows, practically unrecognizable. He said nothing, and after a few moments, to break the uncomfortable silence, I piped up about something I had recently read about horses who know when their masters are returning home.

Caballo remained silent, and Nonna, apparently losing interest in us, cast her eyes over the cards once more.

The tiny room felt close and I could feel myself perspiring. At least I was no longer aware of Schnock's fetid aura—and as for the chef himself, he was asleep, hunched over on one end of the little table, his face buried in his folded arms. He resembled something made of porcelain, perhaps a soiled piece of Dresden pottery that had survived the bombing of that city in World War II. He had not been a soldier. If he had been, would he have been so glib about Nazis? But a collaborator? Perhaps. Many were implicated in the Nazi atrocities, whatever their ages at the time. *Maybe he was one of those who came to his senses and fled?* It was my mother's voice I heard saying these words in my head.

The cards had become windows lining the stories of a palace, and within could be seen the comings and goings of various guests. *War is waste,* I thought. *War makes people stupid. At least my father was smart enough to switch sides with the rest of the Italians.*

"The Ten of Swords," Nonna said. She saw a man carrying a burden, a great weight whose worth he didn't comprehend. "Happier is the man who has love than the soldier of fortune." I knew that remark applied to both my father and me. She turned up the next card, one of the Major Arcanum, the Empress, which I have always associated with my grandmother.

Court cards and aces count most in an ordinary deck, but among the Tarot, there are twenty two trumps, the Major Arcanum, who rule the rest. These are numbered and have such names as the Magician, the High Priestess, the Empress, the Devil.

"It's a matter of completing what you've started," Nonna said to me. "For example, Caballo and Schnock have played their parts for tonight, and each has earned his rest."

Mr. Caballo's head was nodding forward on his chest, and the sleeping chef was snoring peacefully. I had to smile.

My grandmother's eyes were on me. Behind her stood the ghost of my grandfather. Dark haired as I had never seen him in life, he looked positively muscular, his black *mustacchi* waxed, the tips pointed slightly forward like the horns of a bull.

He placed his right hand on his wife's shoulder.

Domandi, Dino. Ask.

It was an automobile accident when she was fourteen that delimited my mother's childhood, and with it, her capacity for wonder.

After the Accident, as far she was concerned, and as she would often say, "Things can always go bad." It was an attitude rather than an entire philosophy, not exactly pessimism, and not the posture of a weary cynic, but an expression of her cautiousness. The Accident had included them all: father, mother, brother and her. Even with the steering wheel in the hands of her redoubtable papa, something had gone terribly wrong, confuting the course of ordinary life: their car inexplicably flew from a country road, rolled on its back, rolled over again, left them wrecked in a gully.

Pressed as a flower might be for safekeeping between the leaves of a heavy book, pressed tightly against her papa's body, bent strangely at the waist until she blacked out, she had eventually awoken in the hospital. Her father was in a coma for two more days, but her mother and brother were unscathed. Whatever *The Declaration of Independence* said, whatever the Bible assured about God's goodness and His watchfulness over every sparrow, my mother was henceforth uncertain about her natural right to be happy. In an effort to assuage her doubts and fears, she became over-scrupulous about many things in her life. "Your plans could be pinched," she told me once. "You have to watch out. The world is full of thieves," she said, even as she welcomed the world to the Villa and practiced hospitality like a religion.

Although she married, the marriage was not what she had hoped for. She never ceased to be glad for my existence, and yet she blamed my father for his disinterest in my upbringing and for their lack of other children. However, this dissatisfaction didn't stop her up with bitterness. Her perseverance and self-reliance I have inherited, as I did also her anxiety, not exactly a clinical disorder, but what I experience as obsessive self-scrutiny and a damaging perfectionism.

My mother once told me that God might be a good shepherd, but he didn't let his flock rest. "Maybe he's moving them to greener pastures," I proposed. "It's a nice thought," she said, tapping her cigarette's ash into the kitchen sink.

A lot of joy left my mother's life after the Accident, but also after that, every misfortune became by comparison more tolerable, like the pain she experienced for the rest of her life whenever her knees or ankles popped out of joint. "At least I didn't die or have to live in wheelchair." Although there was never a real possibility that she would remain in a chair, she never forgot that things could instantly go from good to bad. Many years later my uncle Tony would joke about the Accident, forgetting everything except *quella capriola*, that somersault his father had managed to turn in a brand new Ford. For my uncle, it was the Second World War that would leave its indelible mark: he had gone off "to do the job" that had to be done. He had survived, and returned to Kinderkill wearing a crooked smile ever after. Uncle Tony America.

No one would ever lay blame or criticize or speculate aloud how the Ford could have escaped my grandfather's control. For his part, after days unconscious he recalled only that he was driving a familiar road near Tarrytown, a road along which for years he'd hauled meat to Manhattan, crates of eggs, cases of wine, grappa and gin with never a mishap. But afterwards he was changed. To hear my mother tell it, her father's hair had grown white by the time he regained consciousness. The creases etched between his brown eyes, eyes so much like my own, the words that seemed from then on less and less frequent, his fine hair often left uncombed, bristling upward—according to my mother these were also signs to her that she was no longer a child. Now her father came to call upon his daughter for more and more help around the farm, and with her mother and brother she decided that the resort business must at last succeed hayfields and animal husbandry.

When I was still a teenager, I thought that I was very clever to note how my mother marked the beginning of her adulthood with the Accident, and yet always spoke of it as a young girl might have. I had heard the tale often enough to absorb its lesson about life's uncertainties, but with a casual, cocky cruelty, I protested to her that at fourteen she couldn't have been as naive as she made herself out to be. Whenever I witnessed her regression and her repetition of the story in almost identical language, her lack of reflection about the cause of the Accident as well as its consequences bewildered me. *So the crash put an end to your childhood*—I wanted to say—*so why didn't you get out from under your parents then?* At my age, I certainly wanted that, and I could believe that at some point she must have wanted it, and that furthermore Geppina, her girlfriend, had represented the real possibility of starting over, whatever adversity needed to be faced. Why hadn't the two of them run away together—but no, she had never been able to leave the Villa.

In later years I would grow impatient hearing her story, which might be repeated during any bout of despair, during any trial with husband, creditor, or doctor, her story replete with its stock images—*only a girl, new Ford, near Tarrytown, egg route, white hair like chicken down*—I wanted to interrupt her in order to spare us both. *Were you ever only a girl?* I wanted to exclaim, half out of anger, and half out of pity for the freedom she'd never enjoyed. *Tending your mother's hens, helping in the cow barn, feeding the sheep? Helping with all the cooking and washing dishes, changing twenty beds at the resort in the summer? And then, after school making money in town at the Bleachery, sewing on a machine that stabbed your thumb, working overtime for the boys overseas during the War? Were you ever only a girl, Mom? At sixteen you could run the whole place, and your mother would have been happy to let you do it, except that she was happier to run it through you. You worked for them, I wanted to say. You loved them, yes, of course you loved them, they were your parents and you did what was asked without asking why, but when were you only a girl?*

That is what I never said, yet from about the time I was twelve, I felt compelled to assess her constantly, as if I were doing geometry, calculating the shape of her life. I loved her deeply and wanted her all to myself, but I couldn't have her that way because, well, because no child has enough perspective to comprehend his parent, and all parents withhold parts of themselves from their children. My mother told me always to "say what you mean," and when I couldn't find the words in English, to search *la lingua nostra,* and in Italian find what I was feeling, but what I learned on my own was that she or anybody else might say one thing and instead reveal another.

Of course, my grandfather was changed by the Accident, my mother too, the whole family was. And if as a boy I dismissed the impact of the car wreck even after I heard Nonna's reminiscences on the night of Carnevale, it would not be until years later when I myself consulted the cards that I would deduce the cause. Someone had tampered with the car's brakes. Certain persons wanted Nonno's business, or wanted him out of theirs, and although he survived their attempt to kill him, he never sold another bottle of bootleg booze after the Accident.

The Devil doesn't shock me when from this pack of stories he steps out.

I know that souls are damned by their own ignorance, and that that they can free themselves with knowledge. I know that lust means luster and that fire burns the careless. I am in the middle of my life when I look him in the eye and the Devil replies that it's clear how capable I am. *Professore,* he addresses me, respectfully. He would not dispute with such a one as I, not with the grandson of *Don Antonio and Donna Maria Giustovera!* Not with him who can take up a serpent as if it were a flower to his breast, one whose words can curse or bless, seduce, instruct, console—the one who paints the very sky and earth to suit his purposes. *But you're lonely,* he whispers sympathetically. *And you're afraid you will remain alone.*

CHAPTER 17

I REMEMBER PUSHING NONNA up the cellar stairs, literally pressing my shoulder under her rump, while Mr. Caballo and Mr. Schnock each held a hand, tugging her up the narrow steps. My face was smothered in the folds of Nonna's black dress, and I heaved blindly up against her bulk when the men told me to push.

When we paused to take a breath, where I turned my face aside for air unfiltered by the costume's cloth, I saw a sign that read "Entrance Only"—it was one item of many stashed behind the exposed framing of the unfinished wall in the cellar way. Here were odds and ends that probably dated back to the first renovations my grandfather and Manaperta made: coffee cans overfilled with nails and screws and tarnished hardware, coils of rusty wire, clumps of coat hangers tied together with soiled lacey ribbons, a yellow wooden car that I recognized from my own childhood, a stack of rat-gnawed issues of *Il Progresso*, and the paper stencil forms that Nonno and my father once used to build a plywood Santa Claus, his sleigh and reindeer.

I still have the distinct sensation of fabric catching across my face, and where I leaned into the hinge behind the knee of the false leg, of bumping the metal with my forehead. I have also the sounds of our laughter, all of us succumbing to a type of comedy in which Nonna took so much pleasure, precisely because it was so unladylike.

"Pusha, pulla, pusha, pulla!" she huffed as we worked.

Bent over, laughing and gasping, we moved her carefully one step at a time up into the kitchen. There we found the lights were still on, just as Schnock had left them, and when Nonna was securely on her own feet, the four of us stood together for another moment, recovering from our exertions. The clock above the refrigerator told us it was after midnight. Her walker was retrieved for her by Mr. Schnock, who then mumbled goodnight and busied himself with closing down the kitchen.

Signor Caballo and I exchanged goodnights, and seeing that I was at a loss as to what my responsibilities might now be, Nonna said, "Ernesto can help me. Go to bed now, Guido." Then he took her by the elbow, as I would have ordinarily done, and guided her away. She looked over her shoulder at me once more, smiling gently, and I caught the glint of her gold earrings against the cloud of her white hair. Her veil was hanging about her shoulders like a shawl, and I saw how a Spanish comb had supported her headdress. From behind, it resembled a disheveled crown.

With my right hand I signaled *buona notte* to them as they made for the ballroom where the revelries continued. I was exhausted and had no desire to follow. The lights went black about me, and then the back door snapped shut when Schnock went out. I rested for a moment in the doorway to the family dining room. I could hear the muffled sounds of partiers in the hall outside the lounge, but the small dining room, one of the oldest parts of the house, was stone quiet. In the darkness, I could make out the forms of the table and high backed chairs that were so hard to push or pull in order to get my grandmother comfortable at dinner time. It must have taken quite an effort to have gotten Nonna down into the cellar tonight, but if my grandmother wanted something done, well, it was done.

To my left was a French door, curtained over its many small panes of glass, sealed tightly on the office that also served as our family room. I thought I might rest in there and then decide what was next, but I dozed off as soon as I sat in the easy chair. Sometime later, I was wakened by the sound of the door shivering in its sashes as it opened and shut. A whispered conversation followed.

"Do you still want me?" A man's voice.

"You know that I do." A woman's.

The rustle of clothing, the perceptible press of bodies. Her sighs and a slight, guttural sound from his throat. The thud in my own breast. The memory of Graziella and George.

She: "Got to get back, now, honey. Kiss me again."

Rustle, press, silence, sigh.

He: "Thursday afternoon. At the store. I wanna give you something."

The store? Was it Bob Badget? But the woman could not be Concetta with her Puerto Rican accent. *Who would choose the office for a secret kiss? Joan, the redhead waitress Schnock calls Chicky?*

It didn't sound like her, not even at a whisper. I was trembling a little, aware that I might be detected if I stirred. Outside in the parking lot, an engine coughed, a car pulled out quickly, its wheels spinning through the icy pebbles, and under cover of the noise I took a long breath through my nose: a scent as of pine needles or apples, or was it more like cinnamon? Who was wearing that tonight?

My mother?

The door opened and closed in the next instant and the two of them were gone. I sat up slowly, pushing against a tremendous force that seemed intent on holding me back. I felt that if I relented, I would be pressed down all the way to the center of the earth. A part of me wanted that: it would have been a great relief to sink into oblivion.

My mother?

Whatever else the Carnevale had licensed, I would never have believed this, and yet, and yet, I prepared myself for the worst of possibilities. *Things can always go bad.*

Suddenly I was angry not with her, but with my father. *This must somehow be his fault,* I thought, and then, to my surprise, my sympathies vacillated. In my mind's eye, I saw him put his hands up before a crowd of jeering onlookers. With his outstretched fingers shaping antlers on his head, he pranced pathetically, *come fosse un cornutto.* A cuckold. He wouldn't be able to endure it, however many laughs they might give him for his horns.

Had I also been betrayed by the woman called *Ann*—the glamorous one, excited and breathless, a woman in the dark asking to be kissed? Ann, who "adored" Ida Lupino and "devoured" *Photoplay* in the cocktail lounge while she smoked and drank vermouth? *Eeda:* she always pronounced the name in Italian, and always as if they were friends. Did I know that Ida had overcome polio? Did I know Ida had directed two episodes of "The Twilight Zone?" Now she was directing movies as well as starring in them! My mother idolized her. *Lupino:* the little wolf, British born, half-Italian—what a woman!

Was it really Bob Badget in the dark kissing my mother? Was he the masked Mouse King? Bob with his eyes always on the future—wasn't that where my mother also wanted to go?

I STARTLED AWAKE IN the armchair at first light. An adrenaline tingle put me on alert, and I could feel very strongly the beating of my pulse. With x-ray vision, I studied my hands and wrists, watching the blood tide through the vessels. Was I simply hung over for the first time in my life? Perhaps, but having witnessed my father's mornings after, I assumed hangovers came with a pledge to "nevuh let this happen again!" This was not my reaction.

I was in a state of considerable disarray, disbelieving portions of the previous night, disremembering others, and this morning still disjointed from ordinary reality. My head hurt, various scrapes and bruises stung, and between my ears I felt as if the Carnevale were continuing on its carousel of excess. Yet I was also exhilarated, and definitely more curious than regretful.

I felt strangely *complete*.

Although George McInnis had physically overpowered me and driven off with Gracie, I had made my best effort, and I dismissed my injuries with a cavalier attitude. I felt strong, for the moment at least, and ecstatically alive. I felt no boundary between myself and my surroundings, and then, spontaneously my consciousness floated above my body like a globe of light. It was as if I myself had become the ball lightning from long ago, returning to the Villa to pass effortlessly, and this time soundlessly, through its walls.

Benvenuto Cellini wrote that he participated in a midnight ritual among the ruins of the Coliseum, a dark magic that had summoned flying balls of light and awesome spirits so threatening that he had to flee—perhaps the only instance in his *Autobiography* when Cellini admits he was afraid. But I was not frightened of what came to me; I felt weightless, lucid, free.

No one else was up and about except for my father. He wasn't fully awake, but resting on the handle of his mop that streamed gray suds over the linoleum of the lounge floor. Standing in the froth, he contemplated the flotsam and jetsam, the cigarette butts and colored swizzle sticks, streamers and confetti and programs that littered the black and white tiles. He was still wearing his rumpled Harlequin blouse, and perhaps he had never been to bed at all. I saw too that he was weeping while he tried to do his work, and I knew at once the cause: he believed he'd lost his wife. She had been changing in recent days, remodeling herself, as it were, and he knew that, even if the causes were as yet incomprehensible to him.

His eyes were closed, his back hunched. Then I saw his entire collection of sorrows: he looked to me like a tree whose sagging crown was bent under the heavy fruit of grief. On his right shoulder sat his long departed mother's spirit. I had never before felt how much he loved her, nor with what insupportable guilt her memory bore down on him. I knew only that his mother had died a short time after he had gone to sea and left Naples behind. I knew my paternal grandmother Lucia Diamante only from the photograph of an iron-faced matron on my father's bedroom bureau. How vastly different than Nonna she had always seemed! And yet, her loss might have also been a reason why Nonna doted on my father, whose antics she above all others applauded. In the streets of Naples he had learned his comedy and earned his way performing in bars and cafés; on luxury liners he had waited tables and cracked jokes and first taken to the stage as Mr. Confetti, and then at the Villa—but his mother Lucia had never known what her son could do. On the other hand, his father, Nunzio *maggiore,* as he was called, had thought his son very clever to have married into such a family as the Giustovera's, with their villa on a hill in America in a town called Kinderkill. This morning, however, my father, Zizi Diamante, looked anything but *furbo*.

You have to be brave to keep on working against the odds. Even then, success might not arrive in the way you pictured it. When George McGinnis dropped me, I had refused to be defeated, and I thought that I'd found within myself the hard thing Manaperta once referred to, something like a diamond. Meanwhile, my father was slumping while he visited the regrets of his life and wondered where his wife was now, the glamorous hostess, *la bella dal ballo*. Suddenly, true to his training as a seaman, he straightened up and looked about himself; he rubbed his face to clear his thoughts and then with surprising vigor leaned hard into his mop to resume swabbing the filthy floor. (I watched, I waited, I wondered if he had any idea I was so near.) He patted his breast pocket as if he were searching for a pack of cigarettes or checking on an object in safe keeping. Then I saw a home-movie begin to play—and whether this was his memory or mine, I cannot say.

In the film I am three years old. A red blanket is tied about my shoulders and I'm wearing a woven straw sombrero while I dance and shake a maraca. How happy I look! My father, younger, thinner, his hair black and slicked back, jumps into the scene with me, smiling. He claps his hands and stamps the heels of his shoes. He clenches a smoking cigarette in his teeth, and chin up, hands locked behind his back, he dances into the center of the frame. He is wonderful, but I have stopped moving and stand back with a look that can only be described as bewilderment. Noticing this, my father urges me on, to continue dancing with him. Instead, I begin to cry.

HE DIDN'T GIVE HIS wife as bad a time as she in later years complained to me, and although my father couldn't praise her with all his heart as the capable business woman she was, he continued to love her. For Nunzio Diamante, Anna was supposed to have remained the dowry-daughter of the Giustovera's, the attendant, dependent, young lady he wooed and finally won by singing in German a bit from *Tristan und Isolde*. The only German he knew, he told me with a wink, but he was convinced it had done the trick.

In the early days, when I was still a little kid, he could work around the clock, cleaning the bar at dawn, shopping at noon, opening up for business at five. In the evenings, wearing a short white jacket as he'd done on the Italian Line, his waist cinched tight as a toreador's, he'd "mix things up:" a Zombie, a Stinger, a joke about that Canadian Club of the Kennedy's—whatever it was that his customers wanted, he would provide. He let everybody know he owned the place, though in fact my father was always afraid that both it and he belonged to my mother. When their debts began to accumulate and he thought he'd lost her, he also lost track of the fact that they could find their way out of trouble only if she led.

He never was the star that he'd set out to become, even if he did once clown around with Bud Abbott and Lou Costello when he ran into them at Grand Central Station, even if he did do a couple of spots for the TV show "Candid Camera," and one time Ed Sullivan had him audition his act as Mr. Confetti. In 1967 when the Villa was remodeled, new matchbooks were printed that on the back cover advertised *Zizi's Bar and Lounge—the happiest place in town.*

Many times I've asked myself if happiness is an act you have to believe in so that it becomes a reality—with a little more patience, a little more perseverance, could my father have been genuinely happy at the Villa?

It didn't last long, my secret visit to his world. The only other thing I remember from that adventure is that at its end I passed through the lounge to alight in a maple tree near the main entrance of the Place. In the clear sky a few stars were still shining as the faintest wash of dawn appeared. The terrestrial world was glazed due to last night's storm, and in this light, under the melting ice, it looked of a piece with heaven. I was waiting for the sun to rise when suddenly I found myself back in the office, burrowing into the cushions of the easy chair where I'd slept. I pulled a blanket to my chin.

The blanket, how? I opened my eyes. Down the hall, I could hear someone moving about in the kitchen.

I got up and went there. My mother's hair was the first thing I noticed: it was still perfectly coiffed, and from behind she was still Ida Lupino's sister, Ann, preparing coffee at the stove.

"Morning," I said tentatively.

With her back to me she said, "What happened last night?"

She was waiting for the little coffee pot to hiss and spout its fountain of black medicine; she was also waiting for my answer. I didn't know what kind of trouble I might be in, but I wouldn't argue, I was guilty, whatever it was.

"I decided not to do Mr. Spaghetti. Daddy and I decided." It wasn't exactly a lie, yet I began to shiver uncontrollably once I'd spoken.

"Your father said you had too much wine and fell asleep after dinner." Her eyes were on me now, searching my face as she might have done when I was very young, looking for a spot of dirt, an imperfection, some sign of impending illness.

That's all? I was preparing myself for a real explosion, waiting for the sort of fury she could serve my father on one of his mornings after. Nothing but coffee seemed to be brewing; now it began to gurgle in the vacuum pot.

"Yeah, well. . . he helped me up to my bedroom." I would say nothing of that harem dancer, that Vassar girl who had sat beside my bed reading movie magazines. There were several portions of the previous night about which I was uncertain, but Eva Lynn Samuels, in her Dream-of-Jeannie costume was not one of them. I flushed to remember my embarrassment, but only said, "Everything was cool. Daddy and I were, uh, *copasetic*." I was getting into it now, being someone who could tell part of the truth while the rest was still under consideration.

Copasetic was a word I'd copped from Larry Bell, and it made her raise her penciled eyebrows. "Are you all right? You don't look well," she replied. She didn't, as I was expecting, come over to rest a hand on my forehead, since the coffee pot began to hiss just then, the upper part filling rapidly with espresso. She waited another moment, and when it ceased to sputter, pulled it from the burner.

"Shit!" She'd touched the pot's handle. "Hot," she corrected herself. My mother was always correcting herself—a family trait that she inherited from Nonna, one that has been passed down to me.

"I'm freezing," I said, crossing my arms and chaffing them for warmth. "I didn't even eat dinner," I confessed.

Without looking at me she said, "And what, you slept in your clothes?"

So she didn't find me in the office? But the blanket? My father!

Now she was pouring coffee into a pair of tiny china cups; they were rimmed with green and sat in saucers in circles of green, the color of the sea. My parents used them every morning—at least this was the same as on any ordinary day.

"The heat'll be up in a minute. Come over here by the stove and get warm."

Her voice sounded tired and frayed, like the robe she tugged about herself while she worked. When she leaned forward I saw beneath the bathrobe her shimmering nightgown and within that the globe of one breast. I pressed the heels of both hands into my eye sockets, feeling this desire of mine always to see more as a curse.

"I'll make some breakfast in a minute," she said, putting the sugar bowl on the table. Then I heard the rattle of pills in a bottle: Empirin Compound, prescribed by Dr. Abraham for her "big headaches."

"I don't feel very good, Ma. I've got a bad headache too," I said. "How about a couple of your special aspirins?"

"In a minute. Come here and get warm. I'll make something for you to eat."

I hesitated, divided by my need for her, and, what else could I call it, my fear. Was this the woman who had kissed and whispered of love with Bob Badget? I hadn't slept in my bed, my father probably hadn't slept in his, and rather brutally I wondered where she had spent the night.

I stepped behind the counter. The iron stoves were always warm, like four black engines idling, waiting to be stoked and worked at full blast. Their pilot lights burned perpetually, and my mother constantly checked them to see that they functioned properly and that we weren't gassed to death in our sleep, nor the Place destroyed by an explosion and fire. Once the Villa was remodeled, she became more obsessive about checking the stoves: I had found her in a kind of trance one afternoon, passing her hands over the gas knobs, tightening them repeatedly and peeking under the stovetops to see that the pilots were still burning. Sometimes checking the stoves was delegated to me, and what a terrible responsibility it was! But on this morning, holding my palms outstretched near the burners' blue flames, I was happy to be warmed by them.

Standing behind me, she touched my neck. I could feel her breath, not quite a kiss, and then I heard another cup clatter in its saucer and smelled more coffee being poured.

"Here," she said, using *la lingua nostra*, as she passed a draught of sugary medicine to me. "*Prendi, figlo mio.*"

Standing at the kitchen counter, both of us sipped greedily. *Sweet demitasse, little cup, half-cup, very hot.* My hand was shaking, the cup and saucer rattled. *Sweet, very sweet, and bitter black,* I chanted to myself. Then a tune ran through my mind, words that everybody still remembered from the old days: *A la Villa Giustovera, si mang'e beve bene.*

"Sit," my mother said, in that tone of voice that meant the invitation was not to be refused. "You had quite a night, huh?"

I nodded. She must have seen that I was holding something back, but surprisingly she wasn't pressing me for details.

I sat with my coffee and waited for breakfast while my mother went over to the refrigerator. Then she turned back to the draught of coffee she'd prepared for my father, covered the cup with its saucer, turned again and pulled from the Frigidaire a carton of eggs, a bottle of milk, some butter, a jar of tomato sauce. It was like a dance in a movie musical, her sashay through the early light that cast her shadow, cone shaped beside her like a partner on the wall. I thought about the old black and white movies we both liked so much, about stars like Loretta Young and Heddy Lamar and of course, Ida Lupino. I drained the last of my espresso and hungrily spooned the grains of sugar and coffee from the bottom of the cup into my mouth. My thoughts turned toward Gracie then, and I felt slightly ridiculous by the light of day. *What curse? What endurance? The Mule knocked me down and drove away with his girlfriend. Then I limped off to find my grandma.*

Behind my headache Nonna's game of Tarot returned. She had warned me that whenever the Devil turned up, he had to be acknowledged. "Where will you find the strength?" she had asked. Caballo, never more sincere or enigmatic, added, "You should tame the lion gently, like the unicorn, with love."

My mother put before me a plate of eggs sunny side up in tomato sauce. *Occhi di bue* served with hot Italian bread and orange juice—"bull's eyes"—one of my favorite breakfasts. I looked up with thanks and she kissed my forehead. I ate, but I was also someplace else that couldn't exactly be located. I dipped my bread into the yolks and sauce, swirling the gold and red colors together like a sunrise.

I ate with pleasure, shivering in the cold kitchen, not yet aware that a serious bout of influenza was gaining on me. I trembled to think that the place where I sat in the Villa's kitchen might be set directly over a child's tomb.

CHAPTER 18

NONCORPOREAL: WHEN I SOMETIMES thought of myself as not quite a ghost, but certainly as less than material, my flesh only a dream of flesh, my sleeping dreams more real to me than the sensation in the morning when I pinched my thigh. *Nebulous:* there was a peculiar pleasure in this word too, as it suggested that anything, including me, could like a cloud shift its shape on the air and dissolve. *Nebia* means fog in Italian, a word almost as evocative to me as *sfumato:* in painting it refers to the mode employed by Leonardo to blur the borders of shapes beyond the plane of focus; a haunting effect, mysterious as smoke—*fumo*—as for example, the shadows around Mona Lisa's eyes. Sick in bed while winter ebbed, I was a mystery to myself, dreaming under the shadow of a virus for which there was no name, and for whose remedy Dr. Abraham prescribed rest and more rest.

I was home from school a solid week. I was too ill, of course, to attend mass on the morning after Carnevale—that is, Ash Wednesday—and throughout that Lenten season, rather than fasting in any traditional way, I tried being honest with myself about what I actually believed, hoping to abandon what no longer served me. My catechism taught that flesh is fated to return to earth, and believers are reminded of this on Ash Wednesday morning when at mass a sooty cross is sketched on their foreheads by the priest. The forty days of Lent are in remembrance of how Jesus fasted in the desert to prepare for his ultimate sacrifice; a period of intense prayer and soul-searching during which He defeated the Devil who tempted him in ingenious ways.

I liked it that Jesus had won by being smart and keeping cool so that afterwards despite some very human second thoughts about his destiny on the cross, he was prepared to pay his father, *Our Father,* for everybody's sins. He suffered, but he didn't really die, of course: he was resurrected and returned to life on Earth *transfigured,* staying just long enough to assure his followers of the way to eternal life. But there's more to the story, a truly mind-blowing part: at the End of Time, after the Last Judgment, the dead bodies of those redeemed in Christ's blood are to be reconstituted, not as they were when they died, say after a horrible disease or mangled by murderers, or withered with old age, but rather, in *perfected corporeal forms* they will be reunited with their nonmaterial souls, presumably already up above the sky somewhere with Jesus and the Father. Meanwhile, the sinners down below in Hell get their bodies back too, but it's only so that they can feel their suffering more terribly for all of Eternity without any hope of reprieve.

It was to me an awful thought, an awesome and incomprehensible thought, that God in His Divine Wisdom and Infinite Mercy would hand these poor souls over to the Devil forever, as if to say, you've won them. Tossing and turning under the weight of my bedclothes, I sweated my mortality and my immortality, beginning a spiritual crisis that would change me for good. Why wouldn't

God want the damned to awaken to their mistakes and have the opportunity to make amends for their sins? God was never mistaken—people made mistakes, and granted, some mistakes couldn't be undone—but not God. I was caught in a cycle of despair and doubt whenever I tried to reason my way out of this conundrum. Reason was not to be my solace, no. I needed a better story about good and evil and the triumph of love.

The Age of Aquarius was upon us, and we felt the shift in Kinderkill, which if not exactly a crossroads of the Cosmos, is only a short distance north of New York City. On the jukebox at the Villa we had all the popular music of the day, and I probably knew the Beatles and Rolling Stones well before any of my acquaintances. Furthermore, thanks to Larry Bell and the Bell Boys, I was a jazz fan, especially of Stan Getz by the age of 16. Twice a month Jim Boyd, a guy with long sideburns who was in his late twenties, restocked the jukebox his company leased to us; afterwards, he very kindly handed over to me the records he'd replaced, as well as the paper sleeves picturing the long haired musicians. (Jim was the first person I knew of who smoked marijuana, and one afternoon I overheard him asking my father if he might want to try it; he did not.)

The world was now in living color, when just a few years earlier JFK had been assassinated in black and white. Although an awful war was wiping people from the Earth over in South East Asia, another wind carried the perfume of patchouli oil to the West. Then too, there was the revival of such hoary traditions as astrology and witchcraft, connected somehow to the use of psychedelic drugs. There were over sized illustrated books available on these subjects as well as on yoga and Zen, and of course the Tarot, at a head shop cum bookstore in Poughkeepsie. Whenever possible, I stood in its aisles and filled myself with magical diagrams as well as with images of the barely clad women that were used to market such volumes. (Were they supposed to be modern day witches who took LSD and also espoused Free Love?)

And yet it was here amid this kitsch that I learned something important about the Philosopher's Stone, whose powers had always fascinated me; namely, that it represented the union of all opposites. By this power of the *Rebus*—another wonderful word to add to my vocabulary—a transmutation of base materials into their "perfected" states could be accomplished. This sounded like the transubstantiation of bread and wine into the body and blood of Jesus during mass; it sounded like the Resurrection of the Faithful on Judgment Day; it sounded like a better story than the one I'd been force-fed throughout my childhood. For the first time, alchemy made sense to me not so much as chemistry devoted to manufacturing gold, but rather as a spiritual matter. Furthermore, all the accounts of it, whether European or Arabic or Chinese indicated the necessity of intervention by some unaccountable "other" power, which Christian practitioners of the Art regarded as the Holy Ghost. The appeal was immediate, crystalizing for me many intuitions.

At this time, during my weeks of convalescence, I began to study lions and to sketch them continually: crouching, creeping, roaring, running, hunting, and devouring their prey. "The wrath of the lion is the wisdom of God," I read in a poem by William Blake, which puzzled me as much as it thrilled me. One day, when I was copying a classical picture of a lion grappling with a bull, I left my uncompleted drawing on my bedroom desk, and when I returned, discovered it had vanished. Nobody had been in the room as far as I knew, nobody at the Place said they had seen it, but the drawing was gone. It had become *noncorporeal,* I told myself, trembling with the onset of another chill.

Throughout that Lenten season and into the spring I suffered periodic returns of my stubborn virus. No medicine could completely cure my purgatorial fevers, which might soar at night but cool by day so that I could function reasonably well. I returned to school, but afterwards, at home, I would regularly collapse into my bed, to receive my mother's ministrations, chiefly cups of clear beef broth. I would fall into a heavy sleep and recommence my dreaming—wet dreams often enough. I had been told by Dr. Abraham to wash my hands as often as possible so that I might avoid contracting further illnesses or passing on my germs to others. In fact, I began to wash them compulsively. In my weaker moments, the long ago incident with Tina might rear up and instantly result in a visit to the nearest sink. Once as I was leaving the bathroom, my father caught me using pieces of toilet paper to turn the handle of the door. I couldn't explain myself, and he tried to shame me out my behavior, which had no effect except to make me feel still more ashamed of myself.

I also had to battle against the impulse to recant the curse I'd laid on George McInnis. I succeeded in assuaging my conscience by clinging to the idea that in Gracie's interest I had acted as an agent of *la Giustizia.* I don't know why I never confided anything about this to Nonna, the one person who might have given me useful advice, but during those weeks when I was in such disarray, I saw her only occasionally. I had been relieved of my caretaking duties and it was difficult for her to come upstairs to my bedroom. I didn't learn until later that this period also marked a steep decline in her health.

I'm fairly sure Gracie never knew what I had done on her behalf. My curse, if she'd heard me utter any words at all, probably would have made no sense to her, except as yet another imprecation deserved by her violent boyfriend. I have no idea what she might have told my father about the scene in the parking lot, though she was soon back at work behind the bar. Knowing Gracie, I think she would have taken on herself the responsibility for having left when my father was calling for her, and would have found some means to make up for her absence. My father never asked me what happened after he sent me to find her, and strangely, I never heard him say much about the Carnevale, except to reiterate that it had better bring in more business. Gracie obviously knew what I thought of her boyfriend, and after seeing me crumple that night, and then learning how sick I had become, she was especially sweet to me. As if I were still a little kid, she took to calling me Dino, as my grandfather used to do. And so, my infatuation with her began to wane.

As for George, it would be a while before I would even look at him. I didn't fear him and I didn't need to hate him either: I believed he was going to get what he deserved. He never apologized to me or ever mentioned what had happened between us. He had stolen Gracie's heart and stolen her away, body and soul that night, and these facts saddened me, yet I also felt inexplicably embarrassed for her. How could she continue with that prick? She was supposed to have a head on her shoulders! We might still be buddies, but after the Carnevale, I avoided the cocktail lounge and bar during the hour that had once been so precious to me, when Gracie would arrive to begin her solitary ritual.

My SELF-DOUBT OFTEN CAME back in nightmares. Mornings, while I dressed, ate breakfast and prepared for school, I sometimes felt as insubstantial as a seed of milkweed floating on the air. "Nebulous, nebulous," I repeated, hoping by this incantation to take control, imagining a white fog where I was intentionally cocooning myself, metamorphosing. I tried to rationalize that the semen drying in my pajama pants might be playing a part in my transformation, since it required of me such attention to cleanliness.

I invented a game that I called "Holding the Lion's Tail." It makes me smile now to think of this metaphor chosen with Guido-esque solemnity. My aim was to reject any sight or thought likely to arouse me sexually. I had read that in this way the power of *il sesso* could be utilized for magical purposes, and I refused to masturbate despite all the opportunities that being bedridden provided. What a contrast this was to the ways of that secret agent, that suave wraith and lady killer who crept through my dreams, darkly dangerous in a tailored tux, the one who packed a Walther PPK and who with a femme fatale performed so many heated tangoes. Gripping her thigh, the lady arching her body in his hands, her breasts were pointing up toward Heaven.

CHAPTER 19

GRAZIELLA LEFT GEORGE MCINNIS, and then she left us, saying goodbye to my mother, my father and me out front of the Villa under the maple trees. It was during a sweet and sour spring after Nonna had returned home from another stay in the hospital and was bedridden. I'd just finished my junior year in high school, and a lot was about to change for me, and I think of my last moments with Gracie as a sort of benediction. I return to this memory whenever I have doubts about myself: life is circular and certain themes recur, and these depend not only on outer events but also on what's in your heart. Beautiful, wounded, courageous Graziella Laporta lives in mine.

My parents and I were sitting together in the shade of the patio, and on this particular afternoon, the three of us were happy, like a regular family, happily sitting there on the springy metal chairs that my father had recently painted. Maybe they were expecting Gracie, because they weren't surprised when she drove up in that beat pink and white Pontiac of hers.

They stood up to greet her, and then they were all kissing each other's cheeks, keeping their voices low, as if somebody shouldn't know what was happening. Gracie's black hair was pulled into a tight bun, and she was dressed in a light blue skirt and matching jacket; she had on white, soft sandals. Her bare legs looked gorgeous as always. She had on over sized, fashionable sunglasses and she didn't remove them while she spoke; she smiled hello to me, and then started talking about her upcoming trip. She was driving herself across the country to live with her sister in Phoenix. It was the first time I'd heard anything about this and I listened closely. I felt happy for her. Since she had stopped coming in to open the bar, I'd barely seen anything of Gracie. I remembered when she and George were on a date for dinner at the Villa and then started arguing afterwards in the parking lot. I had looked on through a window of the lounge with cool detachment while she put him down; I thought I was watching my curse in action.

Now Gracie started crying while she was saying goodbye, and then both my parents hugged her and kissed her again.

Although she was sporting those Hollywood shades, while standing beside her, I couldn't miss the black and purple shiner around her left eye. She caught me staring, paused for an instant, and then casually slipped off the glasses to daub at the eye with a tissue; then, just as calmly, she replaced them. My father shook his head. My mother said, "You walked into a door. Now you can close it behind you." This struck me as funny since her last name, *Laporta*, means *the door*—but I didn't make a joke. It was too somber a moment.

My mother made some small talk in that sophisticated way that I used to call *Ann-speak*. I realize now that this was how in those days she toned down difficult situations, especially as they pertained to the Business—and of course Gracie had played a part in that over the past few years. *Carnevale*, I had already begun to call that time.

There were further embraces—a quick one for me, too—and then Gracie said, "Bye-bye," and went to her car while we three waved. My mother was dabbing at her own wet eyes, and my father stood by quietly. Indeed, I will often think of my parents at this moment, somber, but also looking as if lit from within because of some private contentment of theirs. Year later, mulling over the scene yet again, I have come to suspect that they must have made love earlier that day, and that for a change they felt rooted together in their lives. I can clearly see them with arms about each other's waist, with their free hands waving goodbye to Gracie: my parents standing before the Villa Giustovera like a pair of maples, the wind in their branches.

A moment later, from behind the steering wheel of her car, she called me over. (This moment always seems to me recalled in slow motion, but no matter how hard I try, I can't clearly bring Gracie's face back. If you can imagine what the actress Cameron Diaz looks like with black hair, wearing oversized D & G shades—but that's not quite Graziella Laporta.)

She leaned out the window toward me, her hair riffled by the breeze, a few strands coming undone across her high white forehead. With her slender fingers she pushed the tresses back into place behind her ears and whispered, "I know you tried to help, Guido, and I want you to know that Georgie and me, we tried to make it work. He even got down on his knees and begged me to stay." She reached through the open window and stroked my cheek, sending a shiver all the way down there. Placing one hand gently behind my head, she drew me close to press her lips on mine. "I've gotta go."

A dizzying kiss, her scent, my puzzlement.

Then the engine firing, the driveway crackling under the car tires.

A few moments later, when my mother asked what had passed between Graziella and me, I said she was telling me thanks for her portrait.

"I never saw it," my mother said wistfully.

I didn't reply and went inside, upstairs to my bedroom.

GRAZIELLA LEFT US AND then George took off—but not right away. What happened is that she dumped him and George got himself married to a beautiful red headed Hungarian named Martina. They had a baby girl called Juna, but soon were divorced, because, he claimed, Martina was a tramp. She had a smarty pants lawyer, one of her boyfriends, George said, who had rooked him in court, but he was glad to be done with that mess, he was goddamn glad to be rid of "the Hun." He looked drunk when he told my father and me, sounding off one day at the Villa, wearing dusty jeans and a dirty tee-shirt, on his lunch break from a brick laying job.

This was during my first year as a student at HRC, and although I was living in a dorm that my scholarship paid for, I would come home fairly often for my mother's cooking. She stocked me with trays of meatballs and lasagna that I stashed in a cooler and shared with my friends. I was famous for this during my freshman year, and also for building a man-sized sculpture from melted together swizzle sticks that I installed in the hallway of the dorm—but it's Georgie's goodbye that I need to tell about, and what happened between him and me.

"I'm startin' over," he announced that afternoon. He was bloodied but proud, he was free, he said, free of that bitch and damned if he was going to keep giving her a thousand bucks a month.

He was heading south, he could make good money down there, and afterwards he'd come back for little Juna. He'd show that red haired twat and her expensive boyfriend just what kind of man he was.

"That's-a right, Georgie. You ken do it," my father said. He lit a cigarette and Georgie lit a cigarette and I took one from my father's pack of Kents. We were standing out in front of the Place all in a row, along the cement pillars on the patio, one of the jobs that George had engineered for us, abutting the Villa's steep driveway.

He took a long draw on his weed and cast a pensive look down the hill and out the open road. "I'm goin' ta Florida," he said. "I hate New York."

"Sure, Georgie. And I'm-a gonna come see you. We'll go swimmin' at Miami Beach," my father said. "*Bella figura!*" He himself had always dreamt of hitting the big time down there, and the image of Mr. Confetti surrounded by bikini blonds made me smile. I could much more easily see a babe or two clinging to George McInnis's brawny arms.

I took a hit on my cigarette and blew out a plume of thick smoke, but then I had to keep clearing my throat so that I wouldn't break down coughing. My first year of college had had a big effect on me, but it hadn't turned me into a regular cigarette smoker. Usually I bummed them from some girl I wanted to hang out with—I've always been like that. Georgie looked over at me and gave a snort of recognition. "Look at this guy, the college guy," he said. My father rested his hand on my shoulder. "That's him," he said. I looked over at George: he was six feet two inches tall, sun tanned and muscled, his eyes bright from the drinking he'd done on his way over to see us. His sandy hair was shining with Vitalis and sweat. He was a handsome son-of-a-bitch.

JUST BEFORE THE MICK skipped town there was one last time with him at the Place, around Memorial Day when the summer season was ramping up. I'd already finished my first year at college by then, and during that summer I was living at the Villa and actually getting paid by the hour to work. My father had arranged for both of us, George and me, to help him paint the south side of the building. Every summer, one side or another was supposed to be repainted, and so the Place, in theory at least, would be kept looking fresh and full of promise. This was supposed to attract business, but it was yet another strategy that didn't really help in that department.

I had decided I could do it, play it cool and work side by side with George to help out my dad. I was happy to be on a ladder in the summer sun, my shirt off, a brush in my hand. I wanted to show my father, and George too, that I could do my share of the job—more than my share: I was a painter after all.

Georgie spoke to me first, surprising me when he asked about college life, and was there really such a thing as Women's Lib. "They don't wear bras, am I right?"

"Yeah, some of them don't," I replied, glancing down at him from my perch. I tried not to get distracted thinking about my new girlfriend, Eva Lynn Samuels—yes, *that* Eva Lynn—who often went braless under one of my own dress shirts.

"What's it all about?"

I'd expected a sarcastic smirk, but instead it seemed he was actually interested.

"Symbolic," I said. "They're free to do what they want with their bodies."

"That's *something*," he said.

He was on the ground below me, slapping white paint on the building, and I noticed he was careful to catch the drips that formed and threatened to fall in strands from the bottoms of the clapboards. I dipped my own brush into a bucket of green to work on the window frame next to me. I was tempted to accidentally spill a long snake of paint into his shining hair, but that idea seemed childish. It was important to my father to get the job done today, and the three of us were in it together.

I wouldn't ever forget how George had hurt Graziella, and who knew what his marriage to Martina was really like, or what he might actually do for little Juna, but I remember having fun with him and my dad that afternoon. When it was getting late, my father, high on his ladder started to sing in Neapolitan. I was on mine to his right and George to his left on another ladder.

"You guys," my father called out, suddenly sounding a lot like Mr. Confetti, "kenna please keep up with me? And no holidays!"

He went on like that, singing and intermittently making wise-cracks. We picked up the pace, wanting to finish before dark, to get to the dinner my mother was cooking and drink cold beer. By the end, we were all doing it, pointing out each other's holidays, the missed spots, whether actual or imaginary, and calling each other "drips," and picking up on my father's running joke about "you guys" or "this guy" or "that other guy, over there."

Graziella had forgiven him, and in this way she lifted my curse, but her compassion wasn't enough to rid George McInnis of his demon. Maybe my words had only served to reveal what was inside him. I meant them at the time, although afterwards I never cursed anyone else from the bottom of my heart. It's an awful thing, even when your intentions are good.

Maybe George was okay most of the time. My father, like Gracie, saw things in him that I just couldn't or wouldn't. He always planned to visit George in Florida, but sometime later he told me that in Fort Lauderdale, George had been shot to death when he tried to stick up a gas station.

"Un-believe-a-bull," he said, lowering his eyes.

But I believed it—I could *see* it—and I was sad that things turned out like that for George McInnis.

PART 3

CHAPTER 20

MY MOTHER HAD ALREADY made a quick trip to the hospital to see Nonna on Easter Sunday morning, and when she returned to the Villa, she and my father and I attended mass. Easter and Christmas were the only two days that we did this as a family, and while we took Christmas as a holiday at the Villa, on Easter we opened for dinner at one. Easter Sunday means big business in the restaurant world, and despite the fact that her mother was hospitalized, Anna Diamante was still in business.

At around three o'clock I overheard her on the phone with Uncle Tony, arranging a family visit to Saint Francis Hospital that evening. The Villa would close at seven, including the bar, and then Uncle Tony would drive us all to Poughkeepsie.

At seven-thirty he and Aunt Josie and Tina arrived in their brand new Country Squire station wagon. My parents and I were waiting out front, wearing our Sunday clothes, me in a blue blazer and paisley tie. We were all impressed by Uncle Tony's car and my uncle himself was dressed stylishly in a gray suit and sharp fedora, looking as if he were indeed a man about town. Who knows what he might have been, had the Villa passed from his parents to him?

Perhaps he would have turned it into an all-American country resort with a bowling alley and horseback riding and a ski slope out back—who knows how he might have adapted to the changing tastes of the general public. *Uncle Tony America*, I always thought of him. But then who would have taken care of Nonno through his seven years of illness, and of Nonna, failing one foot, one leg at a time, if not my mother—my mother, who, whatever else she was struggling to become, was bound to be the daughter she was raised to be.

As we headed down the driveway, I couldn't remember the Place ever being completely vacant. Tina and I sat in the rear seat, which had been reversed, and we watched the Villa on its hill-top shrink to insignificance. Despite our grandmother's accident, despite the palpable concern of the adults, or perhaps because of their quiet decorum, some of our childhood familiarity reawakened. I had steeled myself in advance, and I was no longer going to cringe before the Incident should it reappear, and so, with our heads inclined together we listened while my mother explained what Dr. Abraham had told her: Nonna's other leg might need to come off. Not just the foot, but the entire leg. Tina's eyes flashed at me. I nodded grimly to her and turned to stare out the window, watching the road unwind behind us.

There can be no doubt that whatever the gifts that Tina, like me, has inherited from our grandmother, she is also the heir to my aunt Josie's erratic temperament. I myself am much like my own mother, anxious and caring, careful, loyal, and I believe that my father's personality has had little to do with my own—even though I sometimes wish I could take life as lightly as he. Aunt Josie has never kept her feelings under control and even today in old age is possessed of a volcanic energy and uncanny resilience.

Tina has also always been like this, even though my headstrong cousin would probably refuse to admit that her obduracy is inherited from her mother.

But let me return to that car ride when she was in her first bloom and I was shakily passing through the door to manhood. In everyone's opinion she was now "quite the young lady," and she had dressed the part tonight: black skirt, stockings, and on her feet, the fashionable, flat, tee-straps that high school girls were then wearing. She fidgeted constantly however, and I found it disturbing that she kept plucking at the bra beneath her pink blouse, as if she wanted to, to *release* herself somehow. I had the unwelcome image of her breasts being set free and like a pair of doves flying about us in the car. Would I be the one to capture them and coax them back where they belonged? I banished the image by averting my eyes.

Also, I doubted that quite-the-young-ladies were supposed to interrupt their parents' conversations constantly. It was something I had learned not to do at a very young age, and though as a teenager I was full of opinions, I knew when to keep quiet. Now that the trip was well underway, Tina began to insert herself into the adults' conversation with questions and comments. Twice my mother cleared her throat rather dramatically when she was interrupted; the lack of discipline in Uncle Tony's household was a source of tension between our families, and my parents often remarked on it. Tina even wanted to know the name of the surgeon who would, as she put it, "cut off Grandma's last leg." It was my father who interrupted at this point: "*Basta!*" he said, raising his hand: enough!

She was silenced, we all were, although after a moment my uncle said, "You let the grownups worry about these things, honey."

Because of the difference in our ages, Tina and I then had entirely different sets of friends—indeed to me, until tonight at least, she was still a child. Sadly, she had not visited her ailing grandmother throughout the past winter when things changed so dramatically, and since I'd been waylaid with my own illness, all of Nonna's care had fallen to my mother. She could have used some assistance from her niece; at Tina's age, my mother had already taken on many responsibilities at the Place. As for her nephew, who'd been fired years earlier from his summer job at the Villa and who nowadays never came around at all, my mother had confided to me that she was afraid Cristiano was turning out "rotten." When she saw me cringe at the word, she put her hand on my shoulder, and patting it said, "We'll see, we'll see. He's still part of the family."

Nobody accused me of neglect or insinuated that if I'd been with Nonna rather than Cristiano the night before, the horrible thing would not have happened. It was this: on Saturday afternoon, she'd awoken from her nap and attempted to fasten on her false leg without assistance. She hadn't been able to do it properly, and when she stood, the stump had been dislodged from the socket of the prosthesis with the result that she tumbled badly. As always, my mother had one ear tuned to her, and from downstairs she heard Nonna's crash. She found her on the floor of her bedroom moaning in pain. She saw immediately how bruised and scraped her ankle was, and worst of all, after my mother got her back into bed and elevated the leg, saw that the ankle continued hemorrhaging under the skin. There was a problem with the circulation in that leg, *the good leg*, and everyone had been on guard for signs of the Sugar's poisonous partner, Gangrene. My mother phoned Dr. Abraham, who sent an ambulance at once to fetch her to Saint Francis Hospital.

Aunt Josie had brought a large bouquet of flowers for Nonna as well as an Easter basket, and these items were nestled in the back seat of the warm car with Tina and me, where they gave off a sickeningly sweet odor. I did my best to ignore many elements of that journey, but when Tina insisted on eating one of the hardboiled eggs that she herself had painted and therefore deserved because she was so hungry, I could hardly bear the smell. Tucked amid the green cellophane straw of the basket there was also a chocolate bunny, which I thought was an absurd gift for somebody battling diabetes, and its pointed ears suddenly seemed to me demonic. I turned away and made two fists, cutting my nails into my palms, a gesture that to this day I associate with my intractable cousin.

DOWN THE HALLS OF Saint Francis the family marched. We'd gotten special permission for six visitors; we wouldn't have taken no for an answer. I hadn't been in a hospital before and was curious about every antiseptic odor and every convalescing patient I could spy through the open doors of their rooms. Outside Nonna's room, my mother drew her breath tightly, and then all of us, bearing smiles and flowers followed her in, spontaneously forming a half circle around the bed.

Nonna was sitting upright awaiting us, and I could tell she had attempted with lipstick and hairpins to look somewhat as was expected of donna Maria Giustovera. My mother pressed out an expansive greeting, but she was on the verge of tears when with her pocket comb she began to attend to Grandma's wispy hair. I thought Nonna looked small and translucent, sickly in a way I had never known her to be, even after her first operation. Although her eyes were bright with love, the soft old skin of her cheek was dry under my kiss, and her breath smelled awful. I turned away, embarrassed by my queasiness. I looked over at the empty bed on the other side of the room. I asked if she would get a roommate.

"I had one. She died this morning. Can you imagine? On Easter Sunday!"

I smiled awkwardly, unsure of what my reaction should be. My grandmother wasn't religious in any conventional sense, but perhaps she had also hoped to fly to Heaven with Jesus today? My mother moved between us, wrapping her arms about her mother's small shoulders. She gently gestured me away.

"The sisters treatin' you good, Ma?" Uncle Tony asked. He was standing behind her, hands at his sides, his head tilted somberly to the left in that way of his. "You got everything you need?"

"Yes, Tony. Oh, yes, don't worry," she replied. She'd never asked for anything from her son.

We settled into chairs or sat on the empty bed, or stood, or wandered to the window, to the doorway and back, passing the time with inconsequential remarks, manufacturing normality. Perhaps this was precisely how you did it, perhaps this was what passing the time was all about, even as it was killing you. I inspected the room, and I noticed that Nonna's false leg was nowhere to be seen. (In fact, the prosthesis would never again be worn, and would stand with its stocking and black shoe for years in a corner of her closet at home.)

Tina stepped forward to give and receive her own cheek-to-cheek kisses from our grandmother, and then she commenced sighing and tugging at her blouse, smoothing it into her skirt waist, pulling it out and trying to fit it in perfectly. We were sitting next to each other, and from the other side of the room Aunt Josie called us over. She placed one of my hands atop her daughter's, and into

Tina's other hand put a five dollar bill. "Buy something nice at the gift shop for your Grandma."

It was a pleasure to get out of there, but as soon as we stepped into the corridor, my cousin withdrew her hand, lowered her eyes, and moped. She scuffed her new shoes along the linoleum. "They're Capezios," she said aloud, more to herself than to me. And then: "Nonna's gonna die, isn't she?"

I didn't answer. We joined two other people in the elevator. Tina pulled a face and mouthed the words at me again: *Isn't she?*

I sighed and threw my hands up in a gesture of surrender. The doors slid closed and the floor sank. We turned side by side with the other riders, facing the front of the elevator in a silent trance. I noticed how tall Tina was: for sure she had ripened early, the Giustovera blood proving itself in her as it had in Cristiano and me.

I closed my eyes. My knees gave slightly, and then I wasn't in the hospital at all. I was being lowered down the stone shaft of a castle on an ingenious device that ran with counterweights and pulleys. I was to rescue my brother Armando, I was to rescue my sister, Elena. . . But no. My vampire fairy tale and heroic self-image were to no avail. When the elevator came to an abrupt halt on the ground floor, the others stepped out and I stared at Tina. Her brown eyes were locked on mine. I tried to read her thoughts, but then I felt the Incident about to rear up. I jumped through the open door, and with Tina trailing, set off rapidly for the gift shop.

"Ten minutes till we close, kids."

We made a plan and then separated, Tina heading for a rack of stuffed animals, and I to find an appropriate card. She picked a green velour turtle, a smiling, goofy-looking thing that was actually pretty cute.

"Nice," I told her when we reunited at the store counter.

She handed it along with the five dollar bill to the cashier. The woman looked us over, smiling with approval at our Easter finery.

"Sign your name," I said to Tina, shoving the card across the counter.

Grandma is the best, the card read, *at giving kisses to the rest.* I cringed at the rhyme, but the picture on the cover was painterly and reminded me of the apple orchard, white and pink that bloomed every spring at the edge of our property on Widener Road. I thought that Nonna would like that.

Love, Christina and Guido, we wrote inside the card.

"Should we sign for Cristiano, too?" Tina asked.

"I don't care. Yeah, sure. No 'h', remember."

The cashier asked if we wanted the turtle gift-wrapped and Tina nodded yes. When the woman stepped away, she said tartly, "I know how to spell my own brother's name."

"Yeah, right."

He should be here, I thought.

"I'm not a kid anymore," Tina said. She set her hands akimbo on her hips and glared at me. She was undeniably no longer a child, although at the moment I couldn't exactly say what she was.

I looked away. I inspected the cover of a magazine in the rack beside the counter: a picture of the Crucifixion, a story about the real meaning of Easter. I stared at my shoes, pointed like a pair of black bullets. The gift wrapping continued for an absurdly long time. When I looked at her again, Tina was still glaring at me.

"I've got my period," she whispered.

I blinked and frowned—surely, quite-the-young-ladies should not be making such announcements to their cousin Guido. I whispered back, "Be careful who you tell. The world is full of *psychos.*"

"You should know," she snapped.

The cashier handed her the gift-wrapped package. Tina smiled. I stood beside my cousin silently, stupidly. "Thank you very much!" she said to the nice lady.

Now the Incident replayed itself, moving frame by frame through the projector in my mind: the little girl bouncing on the boy's knees, flickering in slow motion like the Zapruder film of JFK's assassination that made you want to shout *stop!* before the fatal moment. I had repented *ad nauseam*, and I believed I'd been forgiven, but the shame still scorched my face and neck, and a band of sweat beaded out along my hairline. Should I have said to Tina that I was sorry? And then, when she didn't remember what I was talking about, what would I say next? There was much I wished to explain, but there was also too much I myself didn't understand.

We took the elevator in silence back up to the hospital room. I began to wonder if we'd been sent out of the room so that Nonna could die, and I began to prepare myself for the worst. Whatever my fantasies, my artistic imaginings, and my genuine secret information, I had also begun to think of myself in a cocky defensive way as a realist, *a fucking realist.*

Thankfully, the mood in the room had lifted, and now Nonna was out of bed, sitting in an easy chair, a light blanket covering her elevated leg. Tina paraded up to her, back arched, chest raised, and put the gift box into our grandmother's hands. I stood beside her while our parents looked on. Donna Maria summoned her old bearing, and said, "What this could possibly be?" She shook the box beside her ear. With glittering eyes she unwrapped it, and when she pulled out the velour turtle, she rubbed it on her cheek, and then on Tina's cheek to dry her granddaughter's tears. "I love you too," she said to Tina, kissing her.

At my father's prompting, I stepped forward. I felt as if I were being treated as a child, but I handed the card to my grandmother, and like the good Italian boy I'd been trained to be said, *"Ti'amo, Nonna mia."* She read it and nodded and reached over with both hands to take mine which were hanging nervously at my sides. Her kiss brushed the skin next to my ear, and she mumbled something I couldn't quite make out.

To all of us she said in a weak voice, "I'm so happy. My children, so good." Then she pointed to a bouquet of daffodils in a glass of water on the windowsill. "Cristiano brought me these this morning. He pick 'em near the old chicken coop."

CHAPTER 21

NONNA SPENT SEVERAL WEEKS at Saint Francis Hospital, during which time she recovered as well as could be expected from the immediate effects of her second amputation. When she returned home, she was completely invalid and half the size she used to be. She regularly suffered phantom pains and required a great deal of attention from my mother and me, and yet donna Maria Giustovera, having been whittled down so greatly by the Sugar, petulant as a child, was bizarrely happy.

I resumed many of my old responsibilities, fetching her medicine, her shawl or coverlet, a fresh bottle of seltzer when she called for these things from her bed or wheelchair. Although strictly forbidden by doctor's orders, one day at Nonna's insistence I smuggled to her a bottle of schnapps that the cook, Mr. Schnock, no longer in our employ, had left in a kitchen cabinet. With thimbles full of clear fire we toasted the memory of our Carnevale night down in my grandfather's wine cellar. Nonna had banned signor Caballo from visiting because she didn't want him to see her like this, but we invoked him nonetheless, and I made a speech trying to simulate his ostentatious manner, celebrating the old days with Manaperta, also very ill of late, the days when with Grandpa we all played scopa together. Tears ran down her furrowed cheeks, precious jewels both sad and sweet.

It was my mother, of course, who suffered most the burden of Nonna's final decline. Since my grandmother could no longer be trusted to administer her own insulin injections, and despite the fact that I was ready and willing to give the needles, my mother took over this job as well as emptying the bedpan, changing the wound's dressing, and answering the midnight cries. Anna Diamante had always run when her mother called, but now that the resort season was upon us and she was so busy, I saw how awful it would be if Nonna were in such bad shape all summer.

I remember an especially poignant moment when I came upon my mother in the lounge where she had retreated to smoke. She had begun to smoke plenty, as nurses often do under the stress of constant caregiving. As another antidote to her anguish, my mother was spending a lot of attention on her looks; she had her hair done frequently and applied makeup every evening after the kitchen closed. Schnock's replacement, a woman with no idea what Continental Cuisine was supposed to taste like, wasn't working out, yet my mother wouldn't take back the kitchen: she was trying to keep Ann alive as well as donna Maria. If she stole a moment for herself to smoke and stare out through the venetian blinds in the cocktail lounge, I wasn't going to interrupt her. But I watched from the doorway of the main foyer.

When I began to back away, hoping to do so before I was noticed, I bumped into the frame. "*Vieni qua,*" she said, turning to find me. "I was just having a talk with God. He must have sent you."

I came forward and she threw her arms about me, kissing my forehead, my cheeks, my closed eyes as if I were the nine year old boy she used to take on long country drives. I tried feebly to escape.

"It won't be long, Guido."

"What?" I asked uncomfortably, though I understood.

"Either God had better take her or else he'd better take me," she said. Then she shook her head briskly. She fixed her gaze on me, and with her hands on my shoulders, began to inspect her perfect only child.

Black droplets had spilled from the corner of each eye and her lipstick was smeared, making her mouth large with an expression I found disturbing. I turned my face away and pulled back, but still she wouldn't let me go. Producing her handkerchief, she dabbed at my face where it was smudged with Royal Rose from her kiss.

"You love your Nonna, don't you?" She whispered while she worked, wetting the corner of her handkerchief in her mouth, wiping my face clean. I couldn't look at her, and although I wanted to flee, I felt petrified.

"It won't be too long now. Tell her that you love her, *hai capito?* Tell her every day."

Then she released me.

Mondays we'd always been closed. When Nonna was still healthy, my parents sometimes left the two of us at home and went out for dinner alone. Now that Nonna was failing, my father sallied forth by himself on Monday nights. "Get drunk, go ahead," my mother told him, half in disgust, half in envy. "Don't kill anybody with the car."

On one such Monday night, I had been talking with my grandmother while she sat upright in the bed we'd moved into the downstairs office. I had been assigned to sleep in a cot that was set up next to it. I'd just given her a glass of seltzer, fresh from a new bottle, and she had hiccupped and laughed about "jumping water." Handing back her glass to me, Nonna trembled and then suddenly began to gag uncontrollably. I patted her back, but it was no use, she couldn't stop. I called loudly for my mother.

She arrived quickly, asking, "*Che ce?* What is it, Ma?"

I watched my grandmother's face darken as she began to retch. My mother pointed to the porcelain bedpan nearby and I grabbed it, pulling off the flannel cover, slopping yellow urine onto my hands.

"Do you need to vomit, Ma? Go ahead, go ahead, let it come!" she urged. Nonna heaved a stream of fluid blackened by her charcoal digestives into the pan my mother was holding. She seemed relieved after that and smiled at her daughter. Once she had settled back upon her pillows, she said something I could barely make out. Then my mother smoothed the bedcovers and asked her softly how she felt, but there was no response. My grandmother was smiling, asleep and smiling. My mother put the awful bedpan aside, and I ran to wash my hands.

I have returned to this many times in order to confirm and reconfirm that I heard my grandmother, waiting in the vestibule of the next world, instruct me to "Cover the six with the seven." (Much later, when I related this to my mother, she told me that she'd heard nothing at all. "But you two were very close," she said.) I have had too many experiences since then to doubt the reality of mental telepathy, but the riddle was never in *how* I audited Nonna: it was in the reference. *Cover the six with the seven*. Was it solitaire she played? Instead, I think of the sixth and seventh trumps of the Tarot. I think of the Lovers and the Chariot; I think of myself and Gwendolyn Glass, who would soon come into my life. . .

"Call Dr. Abraham," my mother ordered. I went to the phone, roused the doctor and passed over the receiver. After a moment when my mother hung up she said to me, "Go and wait for him in the lobby. Unlock the glass door and wait out there. Pray for your grandmother, Guido." I followed her orders expressly and prayed mightily a string of Hail Mary's. I grew certain that Nonna would survive. Within minutes Dr. Abraham arrived, and I greeted him, calmly relating the details of the case. "She's resting comfortably, now," I said, like one medical man to another. Big-bellied, tall, his bald pate ringed with white curls, a mountain of knowledge, the doctor peered down at me over his wire-rimmed spectacles. "Show me where she is," he said.

I led him to the office, but when I sought to enter, I was told to wait outside. I paced the small dining room, then headed back into the main lobby, marching back and forth past the fancy wall lights, past the shadows they cast like black horses on the walls. I sat down on the main stairway and stared at my reflection in the glass panels beside the Villa's front door. I was tall, about five feet ten, my strength having returned to me after all the trials of the previous months, but the guy I saw had collapsed onto his haunches. I began to pray again. A moment later, when I heard my mother sobbing, I leapt up and ran to the office, only to find that the door was still sealed. Then I heard a great gasp, clearly my grandmother's, and I knew she was still alive.

Momentarily, the door opened on Dr. Abraham. I could hear my mother crying. I tried to look around behind him, but could see little, and then he asked me to accompany him out into the lobby. I wondered about my grandmother's future care. I wondered if I would be asked to do more, and I prepared myself to administer her shots of insulin and to empty the pans full of urine and feces. With his black case hanging heavily from one hand, the doctor rested the other on my shoulder. Wise Dr. Abraham who had escaped the

Nazis, fleeing Vienna with his family, and in Kinderkill become the friend of the Giustovera's and Diamante's, the good doctor who had delivered me and my cousins into the world.

"She's at peace," he said gently. He was leaving because there was nothing more for him to do. And still I couldn't believe my grandmother had breathed her last. As he opened the door for himself, Dr. Abraham urged me to go to my mother. I raced back, and found her wracked with sobs beside Nonna's body. My mother beckoned. "Say goodbye, Guido. Say goodbye to Grandma," she said, crossing herself. With tears running freely on my face, I kissed my grandmother's cold cheek. I stood near her bed, disbelieving her death even until the priest came to anoint her body with the holy oil. I never did actually say the word, *Goodbye.*

CHAPTER 22

"I'M THAT GUY FROM the Villa. Maybe you can come over some time—"

"*That's your line?* You actually use that on chicks?"

"Well no, not yet—"

"Kid, it's not hard to get home, but this isn't your ticket. Professional secret: what you say isn't that important, so long as it's not stupid. The way you look at them, that's gotta be, like, *I love what I see*. That's the important part. It's called *the look of love*."

"The look of love," I repeated.

"Yeah. If you do it right . . . You gotta practice in real life. Pick some girl at school. Most guys your age don't know anything about this, so now that I'm telling you, you've got the edge. Girls go for this stuff. And I'll give you another piece of advice: get close enough to touch them. Accidentally on purpose, I mean. Brush against their hands, in the hallway between classes, or maybe your leg rubs a little on hers under the lunchroom table. And very relaxed, all very natural, *capeesh?* Never show them you're hungry or nervous. Then, then you take in their *fragrance*—if she doesn't smell good, fuggetaboutit. Even if she goes to bed with you, if her smell turns you off, it ain't worth it."

I pictured myself in action, I pictured myself as Chris.

It had been weeks since I'd seen him or any other member of his family. His parents and mine only communicated by telephone, and even after Nonna's death and the funeral our families had not grown any closer. Tina had come over with her parents at Christmas, but that was the last time I'd seen her at the Villa. She now took a different bus than I to school, and I couldn't remember when we had last spoken a word to each other. In the past year it seemed to me that Cristiano had moved even further away from Widener Road, but it didn't keep me away from him, and in fact, I felt that his renewed interest in me was a sign that my loyalty was finally being rewarded.

Professional secrets. His hair was combed wet and shone dark; his sideburns were long; his shoes had zippers in back and heels sporting taps; his pants were pegged at the ankles. It was a look also affected by Larry Bell and his Voys, a smooth, hard Italian masculinity. Blue jeans and beads, sandals and ponchos were about to become all the rage, but Chris hadn't heard the news, or else he wasn't interested. He had *style,* and, as he explained, "Girls love a guy with style."

I had resolved to take a serious interest in females my own age, ones with whom I had a decent chance, like Marianne Henzbach and Karen Thiesen. I told Chris that I had done a lot of thinking lately and that I had concluded I should get married as soon as possible after high school. There were guys in Wappingers who were just a little older than me, and actually even younger than Chris, who were already married and could have sex whenever they wanted it. Besides, I reasoned, I would never be a playboy. George McInnis was supposed to be one, and maybe Chris thought of himself that way, but even with a girlfriend of centerfold quality, what did these guys and their chicks talk about? Hi-fi's and sports cars, I supposed, rather than poetry and painting—but hell, maybe they fucked all day and all night. . .

Chris was silent for a moment, and then rather seriously replied that marriage actually complicated things for a lot of people. "Because love is complicated even if it shouldn't be," he said. "If you really wanna get laid you don't have to be married." There was a surprising tone of melancholy behind his words.

We were at his digs on that most unusual day of the Church calendar, Holy Saturday, the day when Jesus was officially unaccounted for, but believed by some to have left the tomb in order to liberate the souls in Limbo. Personally, I felt as if I'd been let out of a tomb myself: I hadn't felt so good in a long time. *Seraglio*, I thought with an ironic laugh, recalling the night of the Carnevale when so much changed for me. I knew that I still had to be on guard against the Devil, because he was always waiting for a gap in my defenses, but this was yet another reason why I needed my cousin. The Devil didn't seem to bother him.

"Screw unto others before they screw unto you," Chris quipped, and seeing that I didn't get it, patting my cheek, he added, "I'm not talkin' about family or friends. But you gotta put yourself first in some cases, Guy. Like Bobby says, other people will always take advantage if you don't take advantage first."

It all had something to do with the laws of the jungle, where the lion never lay down with the lamb except to devour it. "And isn't that the most natural thing in the world?" Chris asked.

"I guess so," I said, unconvinced by this logic.

He was on his feet now, looking for something, making a small circle about his bed, tapping his pants pockets, his shirt pockets. Weeds?

"So ya had a virus again, huh?"

His keys—he found them on the floor. Cristiano's absent-mindedness had always been a family joke, as was Nonna's.

"Yeah, but I lost it," I said, playing for a laugh I didn't get.

"Good." He glanced at his wristwatch and then back at me. "Cause I'm not driving you home."

My grin vanished and I stiffened. I prepared myself for another long walk home from Wappingers to Kinderkill. It was about six o'clock and there was daylight enough to make it most of the way before dark. It might be frosty by then, but I was feeling well and so this would be a test.

"Just kiddin'. I'll take you home if you like, but I'm on my way to Poughkeepsie, to the Half Moon. Wanna come?" It had been a setup. "Call your parents and tell 'em we're going to a movie." He grabbed his jacket from a pile of clothes on the floor.

I felt a rush of guilty pleasure. They knew that I was with Chris, and there had been no objections to that—I think it even soothed my mother's conscience somewhat, since we two cousins had remained close. I rationalized that Chris and I might actually end up at a movie, that we might decide to do that while in Poughkeepsie. Or we might change our minds. We might just stop by the café to see if Bob was around. Or I might get my first chance to meet the famous painter, Leo Declare, Bob's buddy and partner at the café. I could make up all kinds of things.

"I'll phone from the Moon," I called to my cousin, already out the door.

WE WERE IN THE Chevy Uncle Tony had given him, on Route 9 at the turn for Vassar Road, a shortcut to Poughkeepise. I had gotten

Chris's attention, or part of it anyway, as he bobbed his head along while I babbled about this and that fantastic idea and discovery of mine. The fact that tonight was the mysterious Holy Saturday added to my excitement.

The Gospels are silent about Holy Saturday, when it seems that Jesus is neither a corpse nor yet the resurrected Son of God. A fable from later times says that on this day, Jesus in a *noncorporeal form* visits that suburb of Hell known as Limbo in order to rescue the good souls who were confined there before his incarnation—people like Adam and Eve, Abraham and Moses whose souls were detained because their Original Sin was never cleansed.

Had I already seen the astonishing engraving by Albrecht Durer that depicts what's called *The Harrowing of Hell?* Is that what colored my conversation with Chris that night, or is it only now, looking into my rearview mirror, that Durer tints this memory? My appetite for the painters of the Italian Renaissance had been whetted at an early age thanks to the illustrated edition of Vasari's *Lives* that signor Caballo gave me—but when did I first encounter the German master Albrecht Durer?

He did two works he titled *The Harrowing of Hell*, and I prefer the 1512 engraving. At Hell's mouth, Christ appears beatific yet also bent somehow, probably from bearing all the sorrows of the world. His face is full of pathos and yet it is triumphant. In his left hand he holds a tall slender cross from which a pennant flies, a victory banner, his scepter of universal dominion. Meanwhile, with his right hand—where you can see a nail hole clearly—he grabs the wrist of an old man and hoists him up out of a dungeon or grave; metaphorically, the tomb of the flesh. Just below, as if to show that he too, Albrecht Durer, is a prisoner of mortality, the artist has put his monogram, *A.D.*, meaning also Anno Domini, 1512.

Just behind the figure of Christ, Durer shows our first parents, Adam and Eve, due to whose disobedience we have mortality in the first place. Eve is youthful, her face round, sweet, beaming. She covers her genitals, but her breasts are bare, her body sensuous. Adam also seems surprisingly fit, except he's balding and gray and has a long beard. The Devil is looking over his shoulder while Adam gazes on the resurrected Eve. Crouching overhead on the crumbling stone lintel of Hell's blasted gate is a weird demonic-lizard-rat-thing pointing a barbed spear at Adam's bald pate, as if to signal, *Man, the Devil isn't done with you.*

I related some of what I knew about Holy Saturday to my cousin, who listened while his left arm rested, elbow crooked, at the open window of the car. He knew how much I liked this sort of stuff—and I knew that matters of religion couldn't hold Cristiano's attention for very long. So I concocted another tale, a vampire tale. I put on the voices of the characters, gesticulating out into the warm April night.

"The guy who's accused of being a vampire has this brother, see, this holy hermit who comes out of the mountains to rescue him. He puts the heart back into Armando, putting his lips right up against the scuzzy rags crusted with blood, filling him with the life of the Spirit. He pulls him out of the crypt where he was tortured. That's where they threw him because of the awful things he did."

"Like what?" Chris asked.

"Well. . .he vomited the host after communion."

"Maybe he was sick," Chris replied.

I knew I had his attention now.

"Did he suck blood?"

"Sure. His own mother's blood. Sucked it through her tit like milk. That's how come she died."

"Jesus, that's pretty bad. Where'd you learn this story?" He grinned at me. "What else?"

"He fucked his own mother's corpse."

"And what, she became a vampire too?"

"Yeah. She came back to life. Then her husband found out and cut off her head. He cored her heart out like an apple. He was the king and he went crazy. He thought the whole country was infested with vampires."

"What else did this cat, Armando, do?"

"Humped his sister."

"Maybe she wanted it."

"She was just a kid," I said. "And she didn't even know what was happening."

"Yeah, well, some kids *do* know," Chris said. "Parading around nude—it's like they ask for it. Their bodies do, anyhow."

That stopped me. There were frightening possibilities behind those words, and my imagination did not want to go in that direction. We drove on in silence for a while; then I said, "He got a second chance because he knew that he had sinned."

Chris didn't respond and the moment passed. He passed a car, flooring it on a double line just before a long curve. When we were at last slowed down by traffic at the edge of town, he said, "Who do you wanna meet on Hooker Avenue?"

An old joke.

I knew we were near the bar when we drove past Vassar College. Walled off and full of young women, back then it seemed like a convent to us, although every guy in the county wanted to believe it was just the opposite.

My mood lifted and I asked Chris about the prospects of getting served at the Half Moon.

"We'll be eating dinner," he replied. He glanced at me, a smirk on his face. "Just do what I say unless I say different."

Outside, over the lintel of the Half Moon's door, floodlit, hung a painted wooden sign. On it was a ship whose gilded sail was filled with wind to make it look like half a moon. We drove by the bar slowly and crept farther along the street, looking for a space to park. Finally, we found a spot along an alley that everybody called the Graveyard, because it bordered on a cemetery. Chris howled spookily when we got out of the Chevy.

"Deliver us from evil," I said, crossing myself, meaning to make a joke, but it came out sounding serious. We hurried down the alley. Then, growing bolder, I asked him, "Getting laid tonight?"

"Not tonight," he said matter-of-factly. He shouldered up against me, pushing me out into the street. "Your mind is in the gutter, kid. And those vampires! Who's been sucking you off?"

AT THE HALF MOON Café and Saloon, opposite the entry on a wall so that you couldn't miss it was a square unframed canvas, maybe six by six feet, by Leo Declare. The white backdrop was mercilessly slashed, heaped with black and blue crosses, like grave markers three and four deep on a hillside. This central shape occupied almost the entire canvas, but in a couple of places, lozenges of light broke through the ominous foreground. That large mass of anguish, those scattered droplets of light, took my breath when we came through the door.

"What's it called?" I asked Chris, pointing.

"I dunno. You can ask Leo. He says he wants to meet my artist cousin."

Chris steered me through the front room with a hand on the swivel of my neck, directing my eyes forward. I remember a few people on barstools turning to look at us, and a couple of girls in a booth, their arms draped around each other, oblivious of everyone else. I was nervous and the rest of the scenery became indistinct as my heart began to drum. I felt giddy and had an urge to "go Louie," acting like a smart-mouthed dummy that Chris, my ventriloquist cousin, was parading before him. *I could do it,* I thought, *right here at the Half Moon, in front of all these people*—but, no, that kind of funny stuff was over.

He guided me down to the café area, a level below the bar, toward an empty table. The place was just beginning to fill, and I remember that the Shirelles were on the jukebox warbling "Foolish Little Girl," a song I'd always liked. We took chairs in a corner, cased the joint like wise guys, eyed the street through the windows to our left. It was dark, and the headlights of cars swept by occasionally, washing through the dimly lit room and catching the feet of customers at the bar. It looked like waves grabbing at their ankles on a beach.

"Call your mother," Chris said. "There's a phone booth near the head. Figure the movie is out around ten, so you'll be home half-past."

"Cool," I said. "What are we seeing?" I was nervous and he could tell.

He smiled. "It's Italian, a comedy about crooks. Tell her we're at the Juliette in Arlington. You got ten cents?"

"Yeah. . ." I reached into my pocket for a dime and held it out to him.

"For the phone call, dummy! You know your number, sonny boy?"

"Okay," I said, loosening up a little. "Okay, man. But I'll get you for that." I stared at him.

He made the sign with his fingers to ward away *mal'occhio.* "Be careful, my little snake," he said, laughing.

On my way to the telephone, I looked around. There were several paintings here and there on the walls, also by Leo I assumed, all of them oversized expressionistic statements and infinitely fascinating to me. My own interests had always been figurative, and I had no way to judge abstract work. In fact, I had never set foot in a gallery of contemporary art, let alone a café where the boss exhibited his paintings.

The phone rang and rang until my father finally answered.

"Dad? I'm with Cristiano. . . We're going to the movies, okay? The Juliette. . .I don't know, maybe ten thirty. . . No, not *Romeo e Giulietta.* What? How sick is she? The hospital? Really? Okay. . .Bye."

Back at the table, I told Chris: "My mother's in the hospital."

"What happened?"

"I don't know. My father said she started having heart palpitations and got dizzy and so he asked one of the waitresses to drive her to the Emergency Room at Saint Francis."

"You gotta go home, kid?"

"No, no. He didn't say anything about that, but, well it takes some of the fun out of things."

"Look, if she's sick, she's in the right place. The nurses are nuns, and well, she's in the right place. You know what I'm talkin' about?"

"Yeah, I do, Chris. I do." My voice sounded surprisingly calm, and in fact I was not concerned because I knew instinctively that my mother's fit or whatever it was, had something to do with the coming anniversary of her own mother's death.

During the past winter, during another bout of my so-called "virus" (a psycho-somatic condition, I now believe), I had thought back to Nonna's final decline, to those days after her second amputation, when she had sometimes been deliriously happy. I realized that although this might be attributed to the Sugar, during those final days she was carefree—to the point where my mother would shout at her to take her insulin and then shout at me for letting her forget it. But the reason for her freedom from concerns was this: Nonna had confided to me that she didn't plan to stick around, now that the doctors had taken her other leg. "It will be a relief to everybody when I'm gone," she said. "Including me." I didn't know how to reply, but she told me not to worry, because my grandfather had assured her that death was painless. "And afterwards," she said, her gray eyes twinkling, "God tells you everything you want to know."

Cristiano broke my reverie. "We need to eat before we get any older," he said. "How about a hero? They make 'em here with spiced ham and smoked Gouda cheese—ever had that? It's from Holland."

"Sound's great." My mouth began to water, and I reached into my pocket for my wallet. Then, suddenly, I was pricked by something sharp.

I had taken up a complete fast on meat during the present Lenten season. This was a more traditional form of self discipline, unlike Holding the Lion's Tail (which hadn't really lasted very long, and had not conferred any increase in my magical powers.) Fasting, of course, had given Jesus strength of character during his forty days in the desert when he resisted the temptations of Satan. "It's still Lent," I said. "No meat until tomorrow."

"Jesus, Guido! It's exactly five hours 'til tomorrow. Out of forty days and nights, you know how close that is? You think God expects you to be perfect? Jesus had to die because people are *imperfect.* You think he won't forgive you for being hungry?"

I had never heard Chris go off like that about God, but he made sense and I was starving. "Okay. Two heroes," I replied. "I want mustard and mayonnaise and tomato on mine."

"Get *her,*" Chris said. I thought he meant the waitress, but he gestured toward a girl who was just then seating herself at the next table.

When I craned my neck around to have a look, I was surprised at how near she was behind my own chair. Her complexion was flawless, and if hair could truly hold the sheen of sun-drenched flax, hers did, just like the freshly shampooed models in TV commercials. The black beret pinned jauntily to her head complimented her black leotard top. Over this she wore a red and white tartan vest that matched her skirt. I glanced down at her hips, and my eyes followed the seam of the tartan kilt, which was sealed by a gold, overlarge safety pin. She wore soft-looking white knee socks and her feet were tucked into very new black and white saddle shoes.

"A Vassar girl?" I shaped the words with silent lips.

He pulled a face and shrugged. "*Domandi,*" he said, daring me. He looked like Nonno, jutting his chin. *Ask.*

I shook my head quickly. I was thinking about the only Vassar girl I'd ever met, Eva Lynn Samuels who had helped me into bed on the night of the Carnevale and babysat me. I flushed with embarrassment at the thought of seeing her again tonight and what she might say to Chris, whom she had told me she knew. Meanwhile, I dreaded the thought that my cousin might start something with this one, this blond *chicky,* as Mr. Schnock might have called her. She was too much, sitting there in her magazine clothes, probably thinking about hi-fis and sports cars, or all the colors of lipstick on sale at Lucky

Platt's. I couldn't bear to look at her, with her blond thighs peeping though the slit of her red and black, plaid kilt.

"What about those sandwiches?" I asked.

"Yeah, sure. Oh, Deb-o-rah!" He called over to a thin, dark haired girl in tight slacks and a bulky green sweater. To me, Chris quipped, "I told you they know me here?"

When the waitress came, he said, "Meet my cousin, Guy. This is Debby." She nodded to me, didn't notice me, turned her cute, deadpan face with its dark eyelids back to Chris. She looked like she didn't care about anything, and because of this I thought she was terribly sexy. He gave her our order and whispered something else into her ear. As she stepped up into the bar area, I watched as the headlights roped her ankles. She was wearing scuffed heeled pumps with her tight pants, and her ass looked incredibly good.

A few minutes later, she came carefully down those two steps from the bar with a small tray in her hands, two tall glasses of Coke on it. When she glanced down at her feet, I did too, noticing her dirty white pumps again, the reveal of each instep, the scallop behind the toes, the sheen of flesh-toned nylon.

As Debby approached, Chris smirking, whispered to me, "She's great in those heels. Perfect sense of balance."

"Here's for you and you," she said, serving us. "I'll be right back with the sandwiches."

"Welcome aboard," Chris said, raising his glass for a toast. I touched mine to his and took a sip. My Coke was well spiked with rum. I hadn't had any alcohol, not even wine at the dinner table during Lent, and I vowed that I wouldn't get drunk tonight.

"Did you know that Hawaii was originally the Sandwich Islands?" I said.

"Uh-huh. Everybody knows that." My cousin's attention was else-where, looking over the joint. He glanced at his watch, and a moment later when Debby returned with our food, he asked, "Seen Bob?"

She shook her head. "Nope. Leo neither."

Her skin's pallor was accentuated by the eye makeup, and close up I saw there was something decidedly unhealthy about Deborah. She was pretty, with sharp cheekbones and chin, petite and fragile-looking. Her dark hair was cut with bangs precisely at her eye-brows, the tresses hanging over her ears in a pageboy that suggested an Egyptian wig. Her eyes were glassy, but their absent gaze capti-vated me. Then I remembered someone from years ago, someone I had never met, but about whom I had fantasized often enough: the legendary Geppina Ingrasci, who'd fallen to her knees when a ball of lightning burst through the walls of the Villa Giustovera.

Deborah left and we started in on the heroes. I said to Chris, "You know that time at Grandma's birthday, when she told the story about the Lightning, and signor Caballo went on about the maid who got so scared she dropped to her knees?"

Chris chewed thoughtfully. "Yeah, I remember. Caballo had something to do with the chick. The old guy got so excited just talking about her—maybe the fire never goes out, huh?"

"Mr. Caballo, yeah. He came for a weekend right after New Year. Very strange. He stayed in his room most of the time—it was sad, man."

"None of his old bullshit?"

"No," I said. "He's not a bullshitter. . ."

Chris nodded. Distracted, his eyes left mine and he looked around, for Bob presumably.

"I like to think about her, about that girl, Geppina. Sometimes I can't *stop* thinking about her, like she haunts me. . . I don't know.

I wonder if she really was *magnetic* or something, and if maybe she attracted all kinds of *influences,* and if that's why she had a weird effect on everybody."

"Sure. Or maybe she was a zombie. I heard they really exist in Haiti."

He hadn't put me down with that sidewise look of his, and so I pressed on. "Or what if she was, you know, sick in the head like Grandma thought, and maybe when lightning struck the Villa, it set her straight."

To my surprise, he replied rather seriously, "Caballo never knew what was in that package he delivered for her. But for sure, she played him. That was the moral of the story, remember?"

I disagreed but said nothing. I was thinking of the way Caballo had been guided by his heart. In the end, he couldn't know if what he'd done was for the good or not, and yet he'd kept his promise to Geppina.

"I think she had to buy her freedom," I said at last. "And maybe she had to steal stuff to do it. Maybe her whole life she'd only had crappy choices to make." I saw it now, *The Journey of Geppina,* a major motion picture. Perhaps Deborah was just the person to star in it. I was getting excited: her trials, her beautiful soul that refused to be defeated. "After going all the way to the bottom, you can still be redeemed," I said to Chris. "You gotta believe that."

"What, like me personally?"

He seemed without irony. He leveled his eyes against me. I stopped my mouth without another word and looked down at my plate.

"Listen, Guy, you have all these ideas, these fantasies, but there are things about this Geppina you might be interested to know. I heard my mother and father talking. In fact, it was probably that same night, after Grandma's birthday party. My crazy mother goes off on a jag about how they had the same name, *Giuseppina*, but she thought the other one was really a sick little witch. She actually made the sign with her fingers and spit. *Your* mother, she was tight with the girl, your mother wanted to run away with her to California. . . Yeah, it's true. Just listen to me for a minute. Well, my father usually ignores Ma when she gets herself wound up. He has to go feed his pigeons or go outside to smoke his pipe, but this stopped him. He says his sister would never abandon her mother and father. But Ma says that's exactly what she wanted to do. She says she saw them looking at maps, planning it out, like a great escape or something. She thought your mother was under some kind of spell.

"Listen, Guido, if you ask me, Caballo was, and probably still *is*. . ." He shook his head thinking things through. "Jesus," he said. "That Geppina—who you probably whack off to—she'd be like fifty years old if she's still alive. You can't be stuck on somebody old as your own mother. It's fucked up."

After a long silence, when I raised my eyes, I saw an ambiguous smile stretched across his broad lips. He reminded me a lot of our grandfather in pictures from the family album when he was young; all he needed was a small black mustache, waxed and pointed. Thick in the arms and shoulders and neck, he was like a young bull. He reached across the table and put his hand affectionately on my back.

"You're not like other guys, Guido. Your mind is, like, *big*. It's full of wild stuff. You *really* gotta meet Leo."

Feeling somewhat vindicated, I began to blush, and in order to disguise it, I took a large bite of my sandwich. Chris scanned the room again while I began to fill myself with new ideas. We were in a movie, and once again, I was also watching it, and more than that, it was as if I were the director, too. And then this idea came to me, not for the first time: *maybe I actually have the power of mind over matter!* Holding my breath, I stared intently at the food on my plate. *Move,* I commanded the sandwich with my thoughts.

My cousin said something but I didn't hear what. The hero hadn't budged and I looked up: there was no mistaking Bob Badget, who'd arrived on the scene smiling, greeting people at another table. He gave Chris the high sign, and then, unexpectedly, Bob began talking to the blond chick sitting at the table just behind us. He apologized to her for being late.

Chris stood and went over to them while I waited to be introduced. Actually, I'd met Bob once before when he and Connie were at the Villa. Tonight he was dressed in very smooth threads: dark sport coat over a dark green Banlon shirt, poison-ivy green slacks, and side-laced torpedoes, as Cristiano called such shoes. He was in his late twenties, athletic looking, fairly tall, and not at all like any business man I had ever seen. With his sandy colored goatee, his bony forehead and lively eyes, he reminded me of some animal, although I couldn't say what. His thin hair was cut short and combed forward; Chris had told me that Bob went into the City to get it styled, a shop off MacDougal Street in Greenwich Village, where, my father had said, the "benicks" and fairies lived.

When Chris started introducing me, Bob piped up immediately, "Guido!" as if we were old friends. I hesitated when he offered his hand. "Skin me, man." This was not the voice of the man I had overheard in the office during the Carnevale with a woman I did not want to believe was my mother. Surprisingly relieved, I grasped Bob's hand, but it slid away, leaving a strange, quivering aftereffect.

His palm might be smooth as a fairy's, but there was something else, something under his skin, like electricity. My cousin's praise for his business practices ran through my mind. Time must really be money to him, I thought, but with a flash of insight, I realized what Bob Badget wanted most: he liked money all right, but what he craved was the next moment, the virgin moment, and with it the latest hip thing. It was the secret of his success, even if like a junky he was always in need of a new fix.

Chris was watching Bob with a look of admiration pasted on his face, but I could tell his thoughts were elsewhere, his eyes darting about. Then it hit me: it wasn't Leo he was scanning for, but Connie. He never said much about her, except for that time when he told me how her lips had burned his cheek. He liked Bob a lot, but right then I knew that he liked Connie a lot more.

I didn't know what to say after having been skinned by Bob Badget. I simply raised my palm speechlessly, *Hello*. He grinned and turned back to the blond girl, who was looking on in cheerful silence.

She was older than me, not by much, but there was something "finished" about her, as if she'd been buffed to a shine at an early age. The light reflecting off of her practically hurt my eyes: like the girls in glossy magazines she seemed unreal and unobtainable, and for that very reason I began to be interested.

Bob stepped aside. "This is Gwendolyn. I'm interviewing her for a job at my store. She's a whiz with numbers—" he smiled down at her when he said that—"and maybe some other things I need to find out about. Gwen, this is Chris. He works for me, my best sales-man. This is cousin Guido. Watch out for him, he's a real pirate."

I gave Gwendolyn a hesitant nod and lifted my drink with a trembling hand. She smiled vaguely in return. Meanwhile my cousin started talking about the store, and then the three of them pulled their chairs close together, excluding me from the conversation. I saw how Cristiano brushed his knee deliberately against hers, and I had to fight off the black mood beginning to descend on me. I prepared myself to be marooned once again by my cousin, and bolstered my spirits with a simple logic that would prove to serve me well on my further voyages aboard the Half Moon: *I know a good thing when I see it.*

I took another taste of my rum and Coke and searched the room: this wasn't yet my scene, but it would be, with or without Cristiano. For starters, I scrutinized Bob Badget, who spoke with Gwendolyn Glass about inventories, ledgers and accounts. I also studied my cousin, as under the table Chris continued to press his thigh against Gwen's, and I studied her legs, which remained sealed together beneath her plaid. Then, all of a sudden, Chris leaned back and whispered to me, "This one is for you, cuz. This one, not Deborah."

Chris stood and grabbing his own chair with one hand, with the other yanked the back of mine to pull me around to our table. I wanted to explain how I wasn't mooning over Deborah of the vacant gaze and black Egyptian tresses. And as for Gwendolyn—

"Debby's got fangs," Chris said. "She takes dope and hustles everybody for bread." Then Bob smiled over at us, and for some reason, looking directly at me announced that he had just hired Gwendolyn. "Now that I've gotten your cousin's approval," he said to me. "So let's celebrate."

Hired her as what? With her flaxen hair and downy cheeks, the girl reminded me of an Easter chick in a black beret. I had the momentary fantasy of squashing her, a disturbing impulse—after all, this Gwendolyn seemed nice enough and I couldn't deny how pretty she was. I thought of Schnock leering at *Chicky-poo*, his assistant with the big tits. Then something that George McInnis once said occurred to me: I'd heard him brag that some girls like to have themselves messed up. I hated any man who would hit a woman, and hated the way such unwelcome thoughts might rampage through my mind, hated how I had to battle them.

Gwendolyn threw back her head to laugh loudly at one of Bob's remarks. Her teeth were perfectly even and white, Plato's ideal teeth in the mouth of a nineteen year old beauty favored by orthodontia—teeth forever to be seen in TV commercials and magazine ads and on highway billboards gleaming hugely over America. Then she caught herself, and putting her fingers to her gaping mouth, looked at me strangely. She seemed embarrassed, but also, oddly, she looked as if she were blowing me a kiss. Or else as if she were signaling to me for some sort of help.

You're too damn pretty, I thought, *that's your problem*. Then I realized that this observation had something to do with my perverse wish, not to harm her literally, but rather to obliterate the sight of her from my imperfect life. What business did I have falling for this type of girl? But what was my type? Suddenly, it was Gwendolyn Glass.

Inclining my head a little, leaning over very slightly across the table toward her, with my eyes I said, *My God, but you're beautiful.* She seemed to be nodding *Yes* to me, her clear blue eyes meeting mine. Then she lowered her hand from her mouth very slowly and actually winked, and then, recomposing herself, returned her attention to the banter Bob and Chris had begun with Deborah of the Cleopatra bangs.

In those virgin days, I used to collect horror movie magazines as avidly as once I'd purchased *Superman* comics on Sunday mornings after mass. If the heroic Man of Steel somehow made the miraculous life of Jesus seem more real to me, well, back then I never put the two together. As for my teenage interest in the lingerie clad brides of Dracula, the attraction was obvious. Into my sketchbook I wrote several pages of a vampire story and pasted works of collage, using the faces and bodies of actors and actresses that I cut from movie magazines. But those rather innocent fantasies were about to end.

Cristiano ran his fingertip around the crystal of his watch indicating to me that it was time to go. We said goodnight, Bob reaching out for my hand, and instead of skinning it, holding it warmly. He and Chris agreed it was a shame that Leo hadn't shown. I just *had* to meet Leo, Bobby said. There was nobody quite like Leo. Leo was Bob's own teacher, he said, an inspiration for how to live. Leo had probably been kept late by one of his students—he gave private art lessons—but I would certainly have another chance to meet him. Bob told me that the next time I was in Poughkeepsie I should stop by the store, and we would go and find him.

My thoughts turned immediately to the prospect of seeing Gwendolyn again, but although at that moment she was sitting right there, I didn't have a word I could say to her.

I thanked Bob. All the drinks and our sandwiches had been on him. What a straight-up guy Bob Badget was! I wondered if someday I'd be the same. I could see why Cristiano was so impressed. *Friends,* I thought happily. *We're all going to be friends.*

In the car on the ride home I said little to Chris, who was anyway preoccupied with his own thoughts. As far as I could tell, his knee to knee with Gwendolyn had meant nothing to either of them. I didn't bring her up, even though I couldn't stop thinking about her. I mentioned Connie in a vague way and he mumbled, "Not tonight."

I understood. I could hear my cousin's problems breathing in the dark.

"I PRACTICALLY HAVE THE job already. Well, I mean, Cristiano says he talked to the owner and Leo, Leo Declare is his name, he wants to meet me."

My father was drying glasses, rubbing them bright with the white towel that hung from a ring behind the bar, the terrycloth towel used for that purpose alone. Having assumed that anything to do with Cristiano might prejudice my mother, it was to my father that I was making my case. Hadn't he left home at an age younger than mine to work as a cabin boy on the Italian Line? He listened to me without speaking. He held a tumbler up to the sunshine, turning it so that the facets of its base could catch a ray of light; he splashed one, golden onto the bar top. "Like that," he said to me. "*Com'un'artista. Barista, artista.* How much he gonna pay you?"

The pay was minimal, but more importantly, Leo Declare, a real artist who ran the Half Moon, would give me art lessons. "He's a teacher," I told my father. "At a school near Millbrook, and he gives private lessons."

My father bent down to do something at the metal sink behind the bar. I could hear pieces of silverware thumping against the walls of the tub, and his voice sounded odd, as voices do near water: "I know 'em."

I repeated what Chris had told me, that Leo could use a busboy on weekends, and if I worked out, he would probably give me regular hours during the summer. Furthermore, I could probably trade some of my labor for the art lessons—Bob Badget had said so. That is, if Leo thought my work was good enough. The first thing was that I had to show him a portfolio, just like anybody did who wanted private lessons from him.

My father knew how important my art was to me, and I was banking on this. He frowned. "You want me to pay you? Work for money here?"

I frowned. "Dad, that's not the thing. But, okay if you wanna pay me for what I already do, sure, yeah, you could start anytime." We'd hit a familiar sore point. I had never had a regular allowance or been paid wages at the Villa, but instead had always had to ask for money according to specific needs.

Now he scowled at me. "Smack you if you talk like that!"

I knew the bar was wider than his reach, and when he raised his hand as if he might, I just stood there. I continued to press my case with logic. "You once said I should take art lessons if I didn't want to be a famous actor like you." A note of sarcasm had crept into it, and I caught myself. "I mean, I'll never be a very good comedian, Dad. I'm not funny like you are. But I can draw. This guy Leo isn't even gonna ask me to pay for the lessons. I'll be his assistant, just like when Cellini or Leonardo had helpers. Geeze, Dad, whatta deal!"

"This guy. He's a fairy. You know what that means? *Omo-ses-u-ale.* You don't know this guy. I know hem."

"Maybe you do and maybe you don't," I countered. "And anyway, Dad, I'm not hung up about homosexuals. They're *people,* and I'm not afraid to be around all kinds of people. I learned that here, at the Villa, from you."

My father's eyes moved away from mine. He scanned the polished walnut of the bar, as if he were searching for something, as if he had misplaced a ray of light perhaps, something barkeeps need to have on hand. "Okay," he said at last. "Be like Leonardo, be like Benvenuto Cellini." He threw the line away, ducking down once more to the sink as he spoke, retrieving some pieces of silver from the bottom of that soapy sea.

PART 4

CHAPTER 23

L EO'S DEATH STILL BOTHERS me, especially the uncertainties that
surround it.

His drowned body was recovered from the Hudson, below
the Cliff at the edge of campus, and then later at his home the police
found a piece of tangled, forlorn writing in an envelope with my
name on it. It must have been an accident, I thought, refusing to
believe he'd killed himself and left behind a suicide note for me. Into
the Void Leo had gone, quite literally. I lit incense at my home altar
and chanted a sutra for him.

About a week after his body was recovered I received a phone
call: would I care to talk with the police about my friend? In fact, I'd
already prepared myself because David Lafferty had told me I might
be getting such a call. In fact, it was Davey, an ex-cop and private
investigator, who had mentioned to them my long association with
Leo—whether or not they knew anything about the Half Moon, the
cops never said, and I didn't volunteer a word.

That note he left behind folded into an envelope with my
name handwritten on the back, the Jumble, as I think of it, was a
pastiche of Ariel's song "Full Fathom Five" from *The Tempest*. That

Leo might have wanted me to have it made sense: at a certain time in my life, he was like my second father, a Prospero who chose me if not exactly as a son, then for sure as his apprentice. Leo called himself a fairy, and so that was another echo from *The Tempest*: Ariel is Prospero's fairy servant.

You didn't have to be psychic to know that during his last years Leo was stumbling through some bad karma. People would walk the other way when they saw him on campus, no matter the good he had once done for the Hudson River College. I too kept my distance. Karma simply means action, and of course, every action has both causes and effects, and so it's human nature to look behind an event for its reason. But sometimes hindsight is only a way to convince ourselves that things couldn't have gone differently. Foresight can be equally illusory, and I'm not just talking about clairvoyance: despite our best intentions, any event can have unexpected consequences that reach far into the future.

I'M NOT A WISE guy, but I tend to get excited around authority figures—I think it's an Italian thing, this wish I have to be of service and at the same time my resistance to subordination. Over the phone I told the cops I'd help them out, but then I was foolish and asked if I should have a lawyer with me when we spoke. There was silence, and then a calm voice replied that if I thought it was necessary I could certainly have an attorney accompany me. I made matters worse by saying I didn't have a lawyer and would the State be so gracious as to pay for one? More silence. Then I got scared. "I'm sorry," I said. "I'm truly sorry. I don't need a lawyer. My friend's death has got me. . . *discombobulated*." It's a word I would never ordinarily use, but it was the right one under the circumstances.

At the stationhouse, when they showed me the note, I said right away what I thought, that it was basically a drunken screed, a jumble of rhymes not necessarily having to do with Leo's death. He might not have even meant for anybody else to see it—sure, it was found in an envelope with my name on it, but it wasn't addressed, and who knew when he'd written it? Leo had become rather reclusive over the past few years. Despite the fact that he claimed to be working, "always working," nobody had seen anything new from him in a good long while. Months ago he'd bragged to me that soon he would be ready to mount a complete retrospective and that the entire campus would need to be commandeered for space, but I didn't have the heart to tell him how unlikely that was.

Then I went on to talk some more about the College. "Let me explain," I said to the officers. "That entire area along the river was fenced off after several people, two of them students, either fell from the Cliff or jumped into the Hudson from there. I can't believe Leo would have jumped, but he might have been up to something else. He claimed to hate performance art. He thought that vaudeville-type acts were one thing, but that a lot of so-called performance artists were only exhibitionists who ought to pay their audiences to watch. He once said his whole life was a performance and therefore a work of art, and that therefore the College ought to reward him for his life-size contribution. Life-size. He could be very ironical, very funny and he might have thought of this note—" I was holding it and waved it before their eyes—"as the gist of a jest. You know, a prop, a bit of stage business."

The Jumble was written in the old fashioned script he'd learned as a child in France, and his scrawling hand, probably jiggered by gin, had made the letters slither like snakes and leap like licks of flame across the page. In its own weird way, it was a wonderful piece of calligraphy. His handwriting was always distinctive, and I wish I'd saved the notes he'd given me on my student work, but so many of his critiques were sharp to the point of hurting.

I had previously met the chubby, black cop, Officer Daniel Parvo, when Davey introduced us at a bar. I looked at him now, and feeling rather chummy, as if I were a part of the investigating team, I said, "I can see why you might believe this is a suicide note and intended for me. Goodbye to his oldest friend at the College, right? Not the Declare style. He always wanted the last laugh, and he would have needed to be alive for that, or at least he would have wanted his final act to be recorded. Have you looked for a video?" Parvo made a note on his pad and glanced over at the other cop, a young guy, a redhead named Gerald Weeder.

Parvo raised his eyebrows and Weeder snorted. To me, the kid said, "Anything else come to mind? Anything at all?" I think he had adenoid problems, his voice was whiney like that. "You and Mr. Declare, you were very close at one time, correct?" His face turned an astonishing shade of scarlet, made all the more dramatic by the contrast to his blue uniform.

I reiterated my theory: Leo got drunk and dared himself to stare down death. He'd been out of bounds all of his life, and maybe a stroll along the lip of the famous Cliff, a cartwheel outside the fence, would mean that he still had balls. Then, for the benefit of the officers I recited the actual words of Ariel's song: "Full fathom five thy father lies; Of his bones are coral made; those are pearls that were his eyes: Nothing of him that doth fade, but doth suffer a sea-change into something rich and strange. Sea-nymphs hourly ring his knell: Ding-dong. Hark! now I hear them—ding-dong, bell."

Weeder seemed impressed that I could peal out the lyrics like that, but I had memorized whole sections of *The Tempest* back in the day. I ventured that yes, the note might have been meant as a reminder to me of how close we'd once been. Then I looked directly at Weeder and said, "But we weren't lovers, if that's what you were asking." Weeder's color deepened, and he took a long breath and straightened himself.

I smiled professorially upon him.

Then I proceeded in support of my hypothesis that the Jumble might not have anything at all to do with Leo's death. "See here where it says, those are girls that were his guys—that's his take on Shakespeare's line about pearls and eyes. Ariel, a fairy, sings this to Prince Ferdinand, to make him believe his father has drowned—which he hasn't, by the way, and which you find out later in the play."

The two cops listened attentively.

"The rest of this drivel about dongs and belles—well, that's typical of him. It's what you call doggerel." I glanced up to make sure they'd gotten that. "I think all it means is that he wasn't getting laid anymore, and yet he's laughing about it. Maybe that's his sea-change. About the last bit—school hath fooled him, tooled him, hey lonnie-la—the school has to be HRC, and maybe Lonnie is a person. Have you looked into that?"

Officer Weeder made a note.

"Leo could be very ironical," I said. But now something else was coming through to me from the paper itself, something more than the silly rhyming and wild penmanship. "You can't take it to mean that he wanted to drown himself. He thought of himself as somebody who's in charge—Prospero has Ariel create the terrible storm and the shipwreck to commence the action. At the end of the play, he says he's going to drown his magic books, not himself. You should read it, you know, if you want the whole picture."

The police station smelled like boloney—I turned my head and saw that a cop sitting nearby at his desk was eating a big liverwurst sandwich. I remembered how Leo loved to point out such cosmic humor: *We're like open windows Life looks through.* A satyr's face when he said that.

I told them that I wanted to think some more before I gave an official statement, and then, stubbornly trying to redeem my earlier haplessness, I repeated that I wouldn't be needing an attorney. Parvo gave me a look, like, *Get real, man,* and then in his cop voice told me that it wouldn't be necessary unless I were named as a suspect. I said that I'd like to go home. I asked if I could have a copy of the note to study. No, he said, it was evidence, part of an open investigation. Weeder repeated that if anything else came to mind, it should be part of my official statement.

I said, "You don't suspect a foul play, do you?"

Parvo shot me that look again and shook his head, and Weeder said, "We can't talk about it." He scribbled something on a pad. "When you're feeling less, what did you call it—discombobulated?—please make an appointment to come in."

As I was about to leave, the kid piped up with something that cut right into me: "Sometimes people kill themselves accidentally on purpose. They go to the edge, maybe trying not to slip, but then they do. It's why a lot of people do it with booze or drugs. There's something similar that happens with criminals, slipping up in stupid ways—they've got mixed feelings, and partly they want to get caught and pay for their crimes."

Weeder had short, very red hair, and splotchy, sun-burnt skin on his face and hands. He must have been all of twenty one years old, right out of the police academy. Parvo looked at him skeptically like he was out of line, although later, in one of my more paranoid moments, I thought that maybe this was some sort of ruse intended to trip me up.

Parvo handed me his card. I told them they'd be hearing from me, and then, in yet another unguarded moment, I said Leo would have probably liked it that his body was found with a wreath of green slime pasted to his forehead like a crown.

"How did you know that?" Parvo asked.

"Just a guess," I said. I could feel the blood draining from my face, pooling around my feet on the floor, running out the door, streaming across town to fall into the river. I ought to have said that Davey told me about the body, which he hadn't. I would never have been able to explain the vision of Leo's corpse that had risen behind my eyes. "You told me where he washed up. I know how green the Hudson is in that whirlpool under the Cliff. I was just using my imagination."

They both stared at me.

"Listen, Leo meant a lot to me. And he was a good person, you know? I got my start at HRC because of him."

Parvo said, "Thanks for your time, professor. And, uh, sorry for the loss of your friend."

I MOURNED ALONE SINCE I couldn't think of anyone else who'd want to share a drink with me and shed some tears for Leo Declare. I began to review my memories, or rather, the memories began pouring through me, sometimes in torrents, sometimes crashing and simmering like sea foam in a storm, or whirling out of sequence. One thing that came of so much recollecting was the confirmation of my sense that time doesn't only move in a line: the future is only a projection of the past, and both are extensions of the present—itself an indefinite construct, like a point that occupies no space.

Of course, Gwendolyn Glass returned in connection to my past with Leo. We had been his models for a painting, *Goodly Creatures*, with Gwen cast as Miranda and me as Ferdinand. Side by side we had stood before him, hour after hour in Leo's studio upstairs at the Half Moon. He was the first real artist I ever knew; she was my first lover.

A lot of things in my life changed because of that painting, and because of what happened between Gwendolyn and me, things changed in my relationship with Leo. As I've said, I never took a class with him once I was at the College, and that seemed fine at the time; we'd nod to each other crossing paths on campus, he'd see my work on display sometimes and make a couple of remarks, sharp as usual. And then later, when I myself began to teach there, we began to have even less regular contact. The Half Moon was far behind us, and eventually I stopped drinking with him because of how sour he could turn; like everybody else, I saw what a bore he'd become, a ghost of the man I once idolized.

A while ago I stopped using drugs of any kind, including marijuana, of which I had been very fond, because I began to notice too many gaps in my memory. Leo's death, for example, gave me the feeling that I was at sea, bobbing in the deep trough behind a big wave: a rather scary place to be because another wave, a bigger one, might already be advancing. I began to ask myself what were the important things to salvage, and also what might I have overlooked? When I'd taken my leave of absence from the College, writing my memoir often under the influence of marijuana, I'd avoided saying certain things, and I had begun to wonder what I might have repressed. I think I see myself honestly, but I know enough about psychology to understand how the unconscious dynamics of repression spare your ego from threatening truths.

When I first met Leo at the Half Moon Café and Saloon, I could tell immediately that he was different from anybody else I'd ever known. Only my grandmother comes to mind for a comparison, and in fact Leo does remind me of her, especially with the way he could get other people to do what he wanted without demanding. Was he a "user," as one of our colleagues has alleged? By the time of his death, he had certainly used up his credit at the College. Who else but me could the Jumble have been intended for? I am now convinced that he meant it as a joke entre nous, a sign that he did after all remember all we'd once meant to each other.

I could never be a policeman because they have to spend so much effort collecting and sorting facts—and often they act on faulty reasoning, and look at the consequences of that! The fact is, facts in themselves might be important, but they don't add up to life as it's lived. I do believe in justice, however, in Cosmic Justice, what we call in Italian *la Giustizia*, meaning that I believe the Universe gives you back what you've put into life. There's no divine judge up in the sky, but we do end up having to face ourselves and what we've made of the life we were given, whether in a heaven or a hell of our own design.

It was because of my wish to do justice to Leo that I was precise and concise as possible in my statement for the police record. I touched on some of Leo's history as an artist and on his connection to HRC, and I told them about the last two times I'd seen him alive. Around a month before his death I visited him at his apartment when he was in the midst of an alcohol binge. I thought he needed medical help, and while he refused my efforts to secure it for him, somehow, shortly afterwards, he got himself into a hospital. A short while later, when I saw him for the very last time on campus I waved hello; I was on my way to speak to him, but he hurried off, calling out puckishly, "Shipshape, matey. Aye, aye." That was only a few days before he drowned.

My statement, which I read into a microphone, would be transcribed for me to approve or further revise before I signed off. Everything was smoothly facilitated by a particularly lovely female officer, and this was the first time I ever laid eyes on Sandy Lorraine. The attraction was immediate, and I couldn't wait to come back a day later with the hope of seeing her again, but unfortunately she wasn't on duty.

THAT LAST NIGHT IN his filthy Beacon apartment Leo had no sorcery left in him. He was derelict, lying on his bunk, bemoaning his friendlessness and worst of all the fact that he was *undrunk.* I surveyed the battery of empty bottles on his bedside table. I said that he was wrong, that he still had some friends—me, for one—but he ignored that. He said it was hopeless to consume more gin. "This is water in my glass, plain water, much cheaper than booze." Then he made a flighty gesture with the fingers of his right hand. "To the elements be free, and fare thou well!" he said.

That's Prospero near the end of *The Tempest,* when he releases Ariel. In spite of myself, I laughed.

WHEN I WAS IN high school, I worked for Leo at the Half Moon Café and Saloon and took art lessons from him; I also posed for him privately and eventually modeled for his figure painting classes. An artist learns to love his obsessions rather than to try and banish them, and so it's no surprise how often I return to my formative years. I still occasionally dream about Gwendolyn Glass and I have done countless pieces that were in one way or another inspired by her. What high school boy could have been adequate to Gigi with her perfect legs, with her ass that should have won a prize? The thought of her mouth on me can still make me hard! She was too much—it was all too much.

I got my Bachelor's degree at HRC, and headed upstate for grad school, but I got booted out because of two paintings I exhibited in protest of the Viet Nam War: a dolled up Indochinese girl giving a blowjob to a soldier, side by side with a pistol pointed at the head of a peasant boy. The local D.A. didn't much like my artwork and threatened to prosecute me on obscenity charges. My graduate committee wouldn't stand up for me and thought it best that my show come down immediately, or else that I withdraw from the MFA program. Lucky for me I'd pulled number 322 in the draft lottery, and so there'd be no war for me, not that I would have gone. I split for California, learned carpentry, and eventually banked enough credits for an MAT. Then I was in Italy for a while, and then France. In Paris, my girlfriend, Hwa Luong, taught me everything I didn't know about the history of Viet Nam, which was quite a lot. When I came back to Kinderkill, I was a ball of creative energy, and pretty soon I landed a part-time position at HRC. When I tried to thank Leo for helping me get it, he demurred, saying only that my French impressed him. My greatest success as a painter was in the following years.

I've tried to leave, but I keep coming back. The last time, I thought it was for good, and I was prepared with a plan for everything I wanted to accomplish. When I bid farewell to my students I played it up, comically explaining how I was a slow learner but that finally I too was going to graduate. I mimed my exit with my belongings in a satchel slung from an imaginary staff on my shoulder. Like a picture of the Tarot's Fool, unconcerned and full of trust, I took a step out into the middle of the air. I was hoping my kids would see how much faith it takes to go forward with a life in the arts. Some of them got it, I know they did, they told me so after class, and we had tears in our eyes when we said goodbye.

Well, at least I'd made it out the door, paint box in hand, a vision burning brightly like acetylene—I actually said that. I said a lot of things. My colleagues wished me luck, reminded me that I could always come back, said that the place wouldn't be the same without me. When I did return they weren't much surprised; a few asked me if I'd gotten any work done, not that they actually cared: only two had seen my show that year in Chelsea. I told no one that I'd spent most of the time writing a memoir about my childhood.

No matter how my students address me, no matter what my "unique historical association with the College," as it's been called by my dean, I am not a professor and I have never enjoyed a paid leave to do my work. Technically speaking, I have always been an adjunct, although we don't use that word around here. I think of myself as a type of perennial flower, genus *Instructor*, species *Diamante*, and I have proven remarkably renewable. I like to teach and students like my teaching and say so on their course evaluations—which are important, since customer satisfaction is what keeps a small school like ours in business. The College has also put up with my situation, because, frankly, my job line is cheaper for them than a full-time professor's.

As I get older, however, I am more and more uncomfortable with the bind into which I've worked myself, and while some people say they envy my freedom, I hasten to assure them that it comes with a cost. I do not have the job security of a tenured faculty member, and my second class status limits my income as well as my self-esteem. Nor am I especially liked by the younger adjuncts: the health and retirement benefits I enjoy date to a grandfather clause in my earliest contract, but since then, the College has changed its mind about how it treats part-time hires, never giving them a high enough percentage of employment to qualify for such benefits.

In the beginning, when Leo and a few of his friends turned the place into an accredited college of art, the idea was to draw the type of faculty and student body who might have flourished at the Bauhaus or Black Mountain. The requirements for success both for teachers and students were fairly basic: all you really had to do was be creative. Our graduates went in a hundred directions, many, such as I, committed to their art as a way of life. But things changed. After the fall of Nixon and the US retreat from 'Nam, after the OPEC oil embargo and the Bicentennial hoopla, after Ford and Carter when Reagan was elevated by the rich and pious and credit card debt became so lucrative for the big banks, when the Soviet Union collapsed because we outspent them on weapons, when military might was once more fashionable, when the formerly young were suddenly parents whose time was consumed by the interests of parents, for many, for most, our revolution seemed lost, its idealism dated, and worse, so badly co-opted by the mainstream culture as to seem a cliché.

Nowadays, a full-time faculty member at HRC teaches four classes a term, and unless she or he has wangled course release through some "good citizen" project or other, they are expected to serve the College in many other ways as well. Besides the contact hours in classrooms and studios, there's academic advising, inter-departmental committees and college-wide committees, student internships to arrange, student tantrums to soothe, parental tantrums to soothe, visiting VIP's to entertain, and, despite a decent sized endowment, constant pressure from the administration to do more with less or to do entirely without, and this without substantial salary increases. In other words, the place owns you.

LEO'S BEST WORK, HIS figurative painting, shares something of the eerie quality you can encounter in Henri Rousseau, say *The Sleeping Gypsy*. It's as if the viewer has just happened on an improbable yet somehow completely natural scene—it's like the sensation you might have in a dream. That's how the College itself, his greatest creation, first seemed to me when I was a student there: like a vision of his that I'd walked into, a revolutionary campaign into which I, the very private Guido Diamante, had been drafted. At our campsite on the river's shore we stoked our fires, made our plans, and in those early eager days it seemed the City of New York must fall to us.

Leo was surprisingly in control of himself back then, shrewd and business-like, his head and his heart unclouded because he had a creative purpose. I remember our first convocation in 1968: he told the students that if we were so ambitious as to hope to achieve something truly transformative at "our" school, we could best begin by putting aside our individual egos and committing to a larger, long term, group effort. Most artists are like the tiny anonymous organisms in yeast that leaven the bread dough: although they perish once the loaf is baked, their individual contributions are indispensible. It's why practicing any art is a radical undertaking and why all of the unknown artists down through the ages are comrades to be respected.

We stared at him in awe.

Leo believed that artists could only reasonably hope for recognition among their peers—to be understood by others "with eyes in their heads," that was really worth something. You would still have to earn your bread, whether with your artwork or otherwise, but your life would be ennobled if you could be counted a member of this visionary company. I remember how Bob Badget, waxing with surprising eloquence, back at the Moon had once claimed that money itself could be a creative medium and that amassing it without losing your soul was The Big Test. Leo agreed, quoting the rascal philosopher G.I. Gurdjieff on this, saying that you ought to be able to earn a living with the big toe of your left foot, and that such practical matters were relatively trivial compared to the Great Work of *Being*. Gurdjieff wrote that he had once gotten himself out of a desperate situation by snaring sparrows and painting them to look like canaries, which he then sold to unsuspecting but satisfied customers. An academic education by itself couldn't prepare you to be so resolute and resourceful. If art is to be your spiritual path, you need to learn by trial and error which rules are useful and which can be bent or broken.

Leo's swing with certain wealthy people in New York brought the money upstream to inaugurate the College in '68. I don't know how he got his hands into such deep pockets, but until that time, the place was little more than some art classes conducted on the sprawling estate of a Van Buren heiress. Thanks to Leo, I applied for and won a big scholarship, and then to further ease the financial burden on my parents, I got myself declared financially emancipated from them. *Emancipation*: I loved the sound of that, and although I didn't realize it at the time, it was one of the best things I could have done not only for myself, but also for my parents whose restaurant was on the brink of failure.

A GOOD RELATIONSHIP BETWEEN a college faculty and its administrators—who are in effect "management," whatever the courts might have ruled to the contrary—is a blessing. Furthermore, whatever the legitimate premium placed on professional merit, a personal friendship with your dean is a faculty member's ace in the hole. To wit: Liotta Smythe is a big reason why I have enjoyed my peculiar, prolonged arrangement with HRC.

It was Liotta who during a conversation not long ago referred to me as "an irregular." I laughed and said that the guerilla connotation seemed fitting since I still thought of myself as a revolutionary.

"Indeed," she replied in patrician tones, "but it might make things easier for your *comrades* if you were employed as a full-time faculty member. You know, there are two tenure lines we're going to search. You could apply for a respectable position. I'd be glad to help the process along."

Respectable—I made the word do a somersault in the middle of the room and then walk backwards around her. I inflated it letter by letter until it popped soundlessly like a black balloon.

The fact that Liotta wants me here and continues to defend my unique situation is both a boon and a vexation. My whole life I have been stubborn with respect to my freedom—frankly, I think it goes beyond this lifetime. Call me an idiot for refusing her overtures—well, Liotta wouldn't, although she probably considers me naïve, a free spirit in my own mind, maybe, but doubly mistaken to believe that my arrangement with the College could continue indefinitely. I am in some ways devoted to Liotta, and not simply because I depend on her good graces; however, that day, so soon after returning from my leave, I had an inkling that she wasn't merely trying to do me a favor.

I told her, "I'm grateful for everything, Lie, and I can appreciate your position, the *College's* position. You'd probably like to cut off my, *benefits*—please, you don't have to object." My frank way with her is a special feature of our relationship: she likes to laugh with me, something I've never noticed her doing with anyone else around here.

"I'm offering you something, Guido, I'm not trying to take anything away."

I have been Liotta's confidante on various occasions, even serving as a sort of personal advisor, if I do say so myself. In return, it was she who had arranged for my unpaid leave of absence, and it was she who had made it possible for me to be rehired, not only at my former pay scale, but also under certain new terms that she was about to present me and which she clearly regarded as very favorable.

"The College is offering you a three year contract, but you should know that the President wants to do away with all part-time, temporary lines. She believes that our students deserve to be taught by a tenured faculty, and while I don't know how we'll be able to afford it, in theory I agree. Putting yourself up for tenure would show your commitment to our future."

Our future—I made the words spin in a ring around her. So long as I kept them spinning, I could feel safe.

The similarity of Liotta's name to that of my departed mentor is not lost on me; however, they are very different kinds of persons. Liotta Smythe is a collector not a creator; she arranges things, and so you might say that she's fundamentally a curator or a conductor. This has been key to her many successes: she's orderly and she knows how to get things done—to get them done *her* way—meaning whose talents she can tap for the task at hand. Leo could also recruit people to help him, sometimes making what he shamelessly called "temporary friends." He could get them to help him because he would paint all his ideas as good ideas, as the *best* ideas. He was an artist, a teacher, and yes, almost a confidence man, but ultimately he was a failure as a leader because he couldn't delegate responsibility to grateful minions, as Liotta can.

Liotta stared at me and I stared back wordlessly. (I like to look at her and I have done her portrait in charcoal from memory, something I've been holding onto for the right moment to make her a gift.) Then it seemed as if she'd reached some sort of decision, I saw it register on her face, and with professional grace, with sophisticated ease, she dropped the conversation and turned away to stride on long legs across her spacious office.

Her large window overlooks the river and she likes to stand at it, silhouetted for dramatic effect. She seemed to be peering down the Hudson toward New York as if some expected cargo soon would arrive. With her black hair, dyed and expensively coiffed, her carefully made up face and shapely legs in opaque black hose, she reminds me of a girlfriend of my father's with whom I once saw him in bed. If she weren't fifteen years older than I and weren't a lesbian, I would probably want to be her lover.

"Anyway, here you are, about to start another semester of, what did you call it, *temperate employment?* Really, Guido, if your base salary were that of a professor, and compounded by annual raises. . ." Her voice trailed off in frustration, and I felt my cheeks redden as she lowered her eyes to study the expensive watch on her wrist.

Liotta has pale, freckled skin and wonderful bones, and her facial expressions are subtle—she can communicate much without relying on many words. I've always wanted her to like me and have felt privileged when outside of the professional sphere we've been able to mix casually. I didn't have anything to apologize for that day, and yet I had to keep myself from doing so. Strong emotions in a woman always affect me, and a woman's disapproval is especially difficult for me to endure.

She made some comment about having to prepare for her next appointment and returned to her desk to gaze at her computer screen. I realized that our conversation was over, that I ought to be grateful for the terms she had outlined, that I ought to hurry over to Dade Hall with the signed contract I was holding. I told her so and took my leave.

Before I reached the door, she called to me without looking up from her desk, "See you at the Convocation."

"If not sooner," I replied, thinking, *Probably not at all.*

IT COSTS AROUND $50,000 a year for tuition, fees and housing at HRC, but the students keep coming, and so we keep assuring them and their parents that we're worth it. Now that we are also offering a select MFA program along with the BFA in a variety of majors, things have really ramped up, and we're minting almost five hundred diplomas a year. Is it because of my vantage in the margins that I am impelled to ask about the legitimacy of this enterprise? Most of them won't become artists, and only a few will probably make careers based directly on their degrees. They might have done better to invest in educations at public institutions, not exactly cheap either, but certainly a more prudent purchase for the not-especially-talented-kid whose most pressing need is four years of growing time. Still, the allure of the artist's life beckons sensitive young souls, and parents who have the wherewithal cater to their children's dreams.

With the arts, as elsewhere, I make a distinction between those in search of excellence and those who are satisfied to do hack work. Not that putting bread on the table with your honest labor is ever dishonorable, far from it: as my grandfather, an unpretentious farmer and butcher, used to say, *People gotta eat.* My point is that very few people nowadays bother with the difference between work for hire and work for love. Well-designed knives and forks and ergonomic shoes and all-cotton, wrinkle-free dress shirts (personal favorites of mine) as well as greeting cards that picture pretty paintings of flowers and offer verses for every occasion (hardly my style) have their functions, but what about the other stuff whose only necessity is to exist? In other words, *art?* Call me a snob if you like, call me old school and unrealistic (I know that some of my students do) but if I don't talk to them about subjects like 13th Century hermeticism and the sacred geometry of ancient Egypt, who will?

CHAPTER 24

OVER THE YEARS, OVER whiskey poured into and sipped out of heavy crystal tumblers at her Upper East Side apartment, Liotta has been receptive to any number of my ideas. Early on, she took my suggestion about increasing our interdisciplinary majors, and more recently I convinced her how valuable it would be to award teaching residencies for musicians and theater people, as we used to do in the old days. She's grateful to me and she is sometimes physically demonstrative of this, for example nonchalantly brushing my shoulder with her ringed fingers when she walks past.

I think that for her, Leo's vision of HRC—no grades for the core courses, no need to attend the introductory studio classes if you could produce a portfolio of acceptable work, extensive socializing between faculty and students, very extensive in some cases, scholarship money to distribute with largess—all of this must now seem quaint or downright deluded and maybe legally suspect. During the 1960s, Liotta nee Fessenden was a straight-arrow graduate student in Linguistics at Indiana University. After getting her PhD she taught at NYU, where she got tenure, she said, based on "the semiotics of the market place." Liotta never thought of herself as a member of the counterculture into which I was inducted while still a high school student working at the Half Moon Café and Saloon. However, she did always know she was a lesbian.

She was for a time married to a wealthy physician much older than she, someone who had no problem with the fact of her homosexuality. It was during those two decades, when teaching became less and less important to her, that she more and more devoted herself to her husband's art collection. When he died, she went into business as an agent-buyer for other high end collectors, and this credential especially helped to pave her way to power at HRC.

She arrived at the College in 2001, just before the Twin Towers fell. Indeed, she and I bonded while organizing a series of events to help our students cope with the horror. I had hoped we might prompt them to question why the Untied States had become so hated abroad, and I wanted to use Susan Sontag's short, sharp piece in *The New Yorker* to help educate them. Liotta didn't think so. That was not the role she wanted us to play at a time like this. She thought we should maintain our reserve and defend what she considered as our mission: to remain a bastion of high culture whatever else might be crumbling around us. My counter argument, that a big part of our job was to teach the kids how to question authority, she said she agreed with in general but not under these circumstances. I remember how she compressed her lips so tightly in dismay that for a moment I thought she must be joking. Wisely, I refrained from laughing and instead quietly went about teaching my classes as I wished to, talking to them about the symbolism of Tarot Arcanum XVI, called the Lightning Struck Tower or *La Maison Dieu.*

The Hudson River College never became the revolutionary force for education in the arts that we had hoped when it was inaugurated in 1968. We do not have a reputation to be revered in the company of Black Mountain College; however, we have persisted unlike Black Mountain and many another freewheeling school. At our best, I think we're a sort of preserve where a few real artists can thrive. The school remains both my refuge and my battleground, a place where ideas might still be regarded as important, and because I am not at heart a contentious person, a place where I have learned the value of compromise. Liotta can appreciate how serious I am about what I teach and certainly we do agree on various things pertaining to the College. HRC is a small, privately endowed institution, and as such we're not responsible to a state legislature and a tax paying public for our basic operating expenses; however, as I said to the Dean back when we were first feeling each other out, "We need to be careful that we're not merely in the business of staying in business." She had replied candidly, "But we are in business. Think of all the jobs we produce and the *capital*—all the types of *capital*—whose value we increase. Isn't that what business is for?"

Who could have guessed that the College would become a player in the New York City real estate market? Answer: a busy Alumni Office, a corps of committed benefactors, and our financially well situated Board of Trustees. Of course, HRC is a not-for-profit corporation, but like any other corporate entity, it has responsibilities to its shareholders: this means the students and their bill-paying parents, but also the banks from which loans are secured to finance the growth of the enterprise, and an ever expanding network of "friends" with various kinds of investments in our solvency.

We started emphasizing the BFA in Commercial Art fairly early in our history. Leo understood the necessity, and indeed, he had always thought that young artists should be able to earn their own way while getting established instead of trying to survive on hand-outs from the State or on grants from private foundations. We used to have a letterpress workshop on campus and an entire theater arts program, and until her death in 1984, Linda Page came up from the City every week to teach for an afternoon. Neither exists any longer, and instead our alliances foster student internships in such prized arenas as film making, couture, and software design. I suppose that my original relationship with Leo could nowadays be classified as an internship, outré as it was.

I've told my students that what we do at HRC is like selling water by the river. I'm not being cynical, but rather I'm alluding to a saying of the 13th century Zen master Eihei Dogen. He was pointing out a fundamental irony about human life: even though we're free to dip from the river of abundance, having to pay for it seems to increase its worth. Some students chuckle when they get the joke—the joke is on all of us, isn't it? But I need to stop using this metaphor: I've noticed how some kids, those for whom the bogey-man of college debt is lurking, don't laugh even after I explain it. On a course evaluation one of them wrote, "He seems not to compre-hend the economic challenges we face."

WHEN I RETURNED TO the Valley and began teaching at HRC, Leo was already losing it big time. He'd always been alcoholic, but now he reeked perpetually of juniper and oranges. He made no attempt to disguise the vapors emanating from his pores, but instead bragged that he was completing the derangement of his senses, as his boyhood hero, Arthur Rimbaud, had famously advocated. He said that at last he was reducing himself to an alchemical essence, and he blinked his brown watery eyes behind their spectacles, as if surprised at his own accomplishment. He was a short man and he was stout; his gut protruded mightily in part because of a spinal scoliosis. He had always rolled like a sea captain when he walked, but now he was much slower on his feet, occasionally dragging them, stumbling almost. This went on for years, this so-called distillation that looked more like a disintegration. I was not the only one who found it repugnant to see a drunk, fat, balding satyr flirt with college students, and I warned him. He had tenure, but nevertheless, "moral turpitude" is grounds for dismissal. He had once warned us, "the First Class," that although the path of excess was supposed to lead to the palace of wisdom, you never knew how far you would have to follow it or what might befall you along the way.

Girls and guys, lads and sighs—ah, yes. Leo was queer but he also loved girls and painted many female nudes. He was by no means a flaming faggot, and around a pretty woman he could be as stupid as any straight guy. However, he never took the girls to bed, and he reserved a particular sort of disdain for any untalented female posing as an artist. On the other hand, like many artist-sons, like me, he loved his mother furiously, and long after her death she continued to haunt him. More than once when he was wasted he blubbered regretfully about how he had treated her. I would have to turn away. Liotta once told me she had only ever had two conversations with Leo: what she remembered from both occasions was "his mawkish dissembling." I needed to consult a dictionary to make sure I knew what she was talking about.

He had a collection of erotic art books and prints of what he called, archly, his pussycat girls, pornographic in the best sense: Rodin's explicit sexual flowers, for example, and the first prints of Egon Shiele's unabashed nudes that I ever saw. Back in high school, after one of my private lessons, he caught me trying to copy Shiele, and he forced the book on me with a smirk. "Study hard," he said. When I blushed in stunned silence, he was unexpectedly gentle. I don't know what idea he got about me from this episode, but he never made a grab for my ass in spite of all the opportunities he had. That's something else that's special about our relationship.

I HAD BEEN BUSY on campus all morning, a clear, cool, August day with the first feel of autumn in the air. Surprisingly, I was enjoying the rituals of return. I mopped the dust from my office desk, powered on the new computer that was waiting there—everybody had gotten one over the summer—and considered the other signs of prosperity around me: fresh paint everywhere, new plaques memorializing donors, a remodeled entry to the library which I recognized at once as an homage to the Treasury House of the Athenians at Delphi.

It was when I stepped out of my office on the way to lunch that I understood something Liotta had alluded to during a meeting that morning in her office. She had unexpectedly brought up Leo. She knew very well that he'd been my friend and teacher, and like everybody else, she knew I was a charter member of the First Class.

Liotta and I have what I think of as a *waxy* relationship: we know how to get along smoothly and how to avoid anything that's too sticky. She's generally very discreet with everyone, but she knows how to use her considerable influence both on campus and beyond. In effect, she hired our new president after declining a request from the Board of Trustees to take the job herself. Always personable and courteous, she is nevertheless rather Machiavellian, which frankly both repels and attracts me.

I'd needed her signature on some piece of paper for a student, and near the end of my visit she got me reminiscing about Leo. I brought up the supposed suicide note and how all this time later it continued to bother me. I recalled one particular trope about "low tide" and how Leo had written that he'd "combed the muck of eternity," and then some stupid rhyme with "fuck." I couldn't remember it verbatim, I explained, and I'd never gotten another look at the note, even though it had been found in an envelope with my name on it. After the case was officially closed, when I asked David Lafferty if he could get a copy for me, he said it was no longer in police possession, but had been sequestered with the estate of the deceased.

Did I know anything about the estate, Liotta piped up, and who the executor was, and what had become of any artworks that might be part of it? I did not. There had been a cousin with whom Franklin Carr, now also deceased, made the arrangements for cremation and a small memorial service. The cousin had given us permission to pour Leo's ashes into the river at a spot he used to frequent. Leo had regularly picked driftwood out of the river muck for use in his sculptures, and he used to stash it in a shack he rented near the railroad tracks below Breakneck Ridge. "That little house and whatever might have been in it washed away during the hurricane last fall," I said.

"Tell me more about him," Liotta said, smiling, sitting back against the edge of her desk, crossing her shapely legs at the ankles. I can be quite a performer when I have an audience, and I played it up, ingratiating myself with my story telling skills, talking about the discovery of Leo's body as if I'd actually been there and seen it. I mentioned Officers Parvo and Weeder, and told her about my official statement, the bare facts I had related to a lovely lady cop. "I could have written a full-length disquisition about Leo Declare, a PhD thesis if I wanted to, an entire biography. . ."

"For sure," she said admiringly, and then, "It's curious how the College owns so little of his work."

"Not really," I replied. "The College always expects us to make gifts for its collection, which after a while Leo just wouldn't do." I paused. *"I've* given you several of mine." Another pause. "Leo would have been happy to *sell* you more, of course." I looked past her, out through her window to that exquisite view of the river and the highlands on the other shore. Reading her mind, I said, "What do you suppose he's worth now that he's dead?"

She met me with another fetching smile but remained silent. I thought she was much like a panther, awaiting my next move.

I said, "He never made bequests to *anybody* so far as I know."

She said, "You might be surprised as I was to learn that his estate has just been settled. The College was contacted for legal purposes, something about claims we might have on work he produced while using our facilities. We have no such records, and so that was that." She fixed her dark eyes on me. Then she said, "I wonder why it took so long. I'm assuming he had a will?"

"Yeah, he had quite a strong will—it's just that he wasted it. I don't know what he might have left behind or to whom. He left *this* behind." I gestured broadly to the campus. "He did a lot of good around here. People might have forgotten. You should name a building after him."

I thought I might say some more about the early days, I thought that Liotta was still interested, but then she shifted her eyes to look through her window toward the Point, where Leo's body had washed up. Suddenly I didn't want to go on and said simply, "I know how busy you must be, and I've got a lot of my own work to do before classes start."

I brushed past Liotta's smooth arm as I made my way to the door, and she patted my hand. "*À bientôt*," she said, just as Leo might have done.

I dreamt of him that night.

He was on the river, standing in a tiny skiff that was racing toward the Point. I was up above, watching him from the other side of the safety fence. "I'm going to break up!" he hollered to me. "I'm going to break!" He had on a blue great-coat and gray knickerbockers, high boots, and a tricorn hat. He was striking a pose reminiscent of some Revolutionary War portrait: the Captain holding his position even as his craft was in danger of destruction, standing in the bow, cupping a hand to his mouth, calling out to me. I could see the little boat charging over the waves, pulled by some invisible force, and the waves were huge as if this were the ocean and not the river. Then I saw him smashed to smithereens. Those were the very words that came to me in the dream.

I was helpless, it happened so fast. I had terrible feelings of loss, of vanity, of guilt. Then I climbed down to that spot on the river, the place where his body was actually found, looking less like a man than a seal, bloated, blue and black—but I couldn't see any sign of him, not even the flotsam and jetsam of the wreck.

TEN SWIFT DAYS DOWNTOWN.

Two friends from the Valley Zen Center to help me pack my show away.

Twenty six paintings, many mounted sketches, and several pieces of sculpture to haul out of the City and back to Kinderkill to store upstairs at my family's old hotel. Room Eleven: three doors down the hallway from my childhood bedroom at the now defunct resort.

My work had gotten one review in *Up Top*, which was at the time a rather prestigious publication, but which had gone out of business almost immediately after "my issue."

My mother telling me, "Two sales in New York City equals something."

Six weeks later, another term at HRC.

Just as classes were about to begin, I received an e-mail from Liotta with a reminder to make the acquaintance of the College's new president. Immediately I recognized the tit-for-tat she likes to play. I had purposely divested myself from the inauguration hoopla, because, after all, I was on a leave of absence and hoping to absent myself permanently, but I was back now. Being a good citizen, I phoned the President's office, and her secretary gave me an appointment for that very afternoon.

I found Rosa Swenson instantly likeable: a woman in late middle-age, a rangy brunette with a sense of humor and the muscled forearms of the sculptor she had been, brimming with enthusiasm for all things HRC. She asked if I'd like tea on her outdoor terrace, and so we adjourned there awaiting it while we continued to exchange pleasantries and basic biographical information. Her secretary, a young man named Gilbert whom I'd never seen before, brought a complete tea service to us; he was snappy in his white shirt and black slacks, a bowtie at his collar no less, and I thought his very demeanor was yet another token of new prosperity. Soon Rosa and I were discussing our respective visits to Florence, and then we were onto the life of Dante Alighieri.

"Middle-aged," she said, "Dante's great journey was only about to begin!"

She raised her eyes heavenward, and spreading her arms, struck a humorous attitude of transport. I'd heard she was charming, and I could tell she would be good at representing the College to the outside world, a chief function of its president.

Then she brought the conversation back around to a topic we'd touched on earlier. "You were successful as an artist while still quite young, as was I. How do you think it's affected your more recent work and your teaching?"

I said only that I liked teaching very much and was happy to be back—yet I felt something fall inside of me when I said it, as if I had knocked over a pail of water. After a moment I added, "There's always the danger of losing your way once your youthful enthusiasm wanes. In Dante's case, his profound disillusionment resulted from the politics that forced him into exile. Of course, *The Divine Comedy* was born of that ordeal. But you know, even after the Florentines forgave him and invited him home, he continued to refer to himself as *a party of one*. I can relate to that."

She was probably about my age and radiated the sort of warmth and wellbeing that I've always associated with people from the Midwest. There was something "school marmish" about her and I liked it; her eyeglasses, large lenses in flesh-tone frames, as well as her height contributed to this. I thought that Liotta, who is as tall as I, had probably measured herself against Rosa and been happy to have an advantage.

Now she gestured expressively once more, branching her pale fingers into the air, and said, "Guido, I think you're an optimist, like me. For us the glass is always half full. Am I right?"

I nodded my head yes—somewhat tentatively, I must admit, but then I thought that perhaps I did have a future at HRC.

Rosa continued talking about her own love of education. She pronounced the word with a peculiar emphasis and paused ever so slightly to note my reaction. I smiled and continued nodding, thinking how her sincerity would endear her to students and parents, and how prospective donors would be happy to listen to her entertaining presentations. She said she wanted to build the reputation of the College's permanent art collection, including more works from "our distinguished faculty."

As we were parting, I followed a hunch and asked if she perhaps spoke some Italian. Rosa hesitated, but then replied that she did, a little, yes, since years ago she had lived not only in Florence but also in Rome for a while. Her accent was poor, she said, but Italian had always meant so much to her.

Strong nimble fingers, clipped nails taking my hand. "*Ciao, Professore Diamante.*" Smiling President Swenson.

Smiling "Professor" Diamante.

AFTER I LEFT DADE Hall—it has always been called "Dada Hell" by the students—I walked down onto the main part of the campus. There was enough clarity in the air, enough river valley light to promise *vita nuova* to even the most weary of teachers at the beginning of another school year. I corrected myself: *Wary, that's what I am.*

Architecturally, the core campus is considered a minor treasure of the storied Hudson Valley. The three original structures, two of them brick homes in the colonial style, and a well preserved clapboard building, originally the family mansion and now the art museum, frame a greensward whose stand of sycamores—the Grove—is a refuge in itself. Beyond the main quad—the Green—are the newer buildings that comprise the modern campus, and nearby are a pair of dormitories, the "L" as they are known, which house the residential student population. Many students, however, commute here from New York, and there's a convenient train stop nearby, just beyond the College's rear entrance.

I was surprised to find the door of the museum locked at that hour and no one at the reception desk within. Here was a significant change to a longstanding tradition: the College likes to make much of its hospitality to the surrounding communities, and the museum has always been open year round to every visitor. I doubted that they couldn't afford the necessary staffing.

The exterior of this charming structure is plain white, but the builders left much of the interior woodwork of reddish spruce exposed. Several west facing windows on the second and third floors frame extraordinary vistas of the Hudson and its opposite shore, sights which except for the occasional cars winding on hillside roads, deny the existence of the 21st Century. Inevitably you think of the original Hudson River School: those 19th Century landscape painters, American Romantics, who found their inspiration up and down the Valley and in the Catskill Mountains beyond.

The museum's holdings are substantial for its size, the collection too large to be exhibited en masse, and so most of it is stored in an annex away from the core campus—the Vault, as we call it. Some tiny paintings by Hartley and Dove are usually on display, and one room features both a de Kooning and a Motherwell. The collection also includes several invaluable prints by Giacometti—but looking in through a window I spied none where they used to hang. Works by faculty members are generally in circulation on the walls, but most are in storage. "Accruing value in the Vault," as we sometimes say, "the less seen, the more important," amusing ourselves in spite of an acquisition policy that seems to make prisoners of its prizes. One of my paintings, one of three I've given, hasn't been seen for at least twenty five years, and therefore, as I have jested to colleagues, it must now be really worth something.

Because of its location and physical beauty, a walk across the campus usually invigorates me. The river's influence is felt in more than the proximity of the wide, moving waters. On the greensward and among the sycamores I often sense an invisible presence, an ether or spirit of the place, a *genius loci* that feeds my soul. When a sudden warmth arrives in late autumn, a haze off the river can drift magically up the cliffs and loiter amid the branchy trees throughout the afternoons. Consuming this air, a person might feel as if he will live forever, or perhaps that he has lived here before. Indian Summer: when I was growing up we used to say this meant the ghosts of the original inhabitants had returned.

The unchanging, always changing river, New York City to the south, the Catskills to the north; the heaps of stone of headlands and the majestic Highlands east and west. Breakneck Ridge, Storm King Mountain on the opposite shore. Anthony's Nose, West Point—stories of the American Revolution fill this grand valley, and behind them, when thunder rolls in the mountains, it is said that the ghosts of the explorer Hendrick Hudson and his Half Moon crew are still bowling ninepins. No wonder so many 19th Century painters loved this area and that so many industrialists built their mansions here.

Crossing the campus I was aware that I'd probably put my feet on the very same stepping stones in the very same places thousands of times before, but then I remembered how a scientist friend explained that this is virtually impossible: our planet in its orbit around the sun is constantly spinning on its axis, which wobbles slightly day in and day out, never returning anything to its exact location in succeeding rotations, and furthermore, the entire solar system is in motion, as is our galaxy like a pinwheel on its hub, expanding as part of an ever expanding universe.

Well, they seemed like the same stones I'd always known, and I was grateful to be able to locate them among the overgrown weeds adjacent to the well-manicured Green. Here had once been the mansion's flower gardens, and the flagstones had probably been laid into place by workmen about whom I have often thought: anonymous artisans who made a lasting contribution to the place. Then I found a particular favorite among the stepping stones, one that looks like a chicken in profile: had those landscapers thought so too and put it into place with a hoot and a cluck that I echoed now?

Human life is short, and as the philosopher Boethius says, even the most notable persons of history are in the end reduced to but a few anecdotes. I laughed aloud. I had come around once more to what I call my zero point, where I flatter myself to think that I really could leave behind the preoccupations of ordinary life and devote myself to *sunyata,* the blessed Void beyond all preferences. I picked my way further along the grass-hidden slab stones, my mind turning to the Wheel of Fortune that Boethius also contemplates. No one escapes the vicissitudes of ordinary life, and yet even after we are laid low, Donna Fortuna can always carry us upward. Was it possible that I might become a "respectable" member of the faculty so late in my career? What would it cost? I would need to do as I was bidden. I would need to prove that I could belong and would belong, and would do my job, turning like a little wheel inside of a bigger wheel.

Sunyata, Emptiness, the Void is the basic ground of existence, out of which all composite, interdependent things arise and decay. According to the Buddhist view, this makes existence seem rather apparitional—which really isn't a problem, since all things have never actually been apart from the Void, their essence. Because of this, all experiences are fundamentally equivalent, and therefore, the truly impartial are never disturbed.

I was at the Cliff, and at the safety fence I pressed my nose through an opening in the chain link, feeling my eyes framed, mask-like by the grid-work. I gripped the heavy wire like a cage, and it was then that I knew what they wanted of me, the Dean and the President, and everybody behind them.

BACK IN MY OFFICE, as soon as I was settled into my old chair—the seat slightly ratty but soft, the leather cracked, the back firm on its hinge, squeaking while I rocked—I rubbed and then scratched my chest in a familiar spot, almost digging, rubbing, and then scratching some more, until I was able to stop.

On the screen of my new computer I opened another e-mail from Liotta, "Re: Confidential." It was in regard to a young colleague, Jesse Leiper, who had just passed his three year review; it was presumed at HRC that if you passed your first review, in three more years you'd probably get tenure; that is, unless you did something awful. I had served on the committee that recommended Leiper be hired, and since the Dean thought that I had, as she put it so elegantly, "bonhomie" with him, I might be concerned to learn how oddly he had been reported behaving. Two separate faculty members had mentioned to Liotta "public displays" that one of them termed "disturbing gymnastics." I could hear Liotta laughing to herself when she quoted that. Jesse Leiper seemed willing to perform these "*movements*"—Liotta's word this time, her emphasis too—whenever and wherever he had an audience. Not that he wasn't ordinarily a little strange: his performance art made that abundantly clear. Liotta wondered would I mind checking up on him from time to time and then sharing with her "in confidence" my impressions?

For sure, the Dean and I had reconnected rather warmly. For sure, she would want various things from me in return for her Miami sunshine. I have from time to time wondered what Liotta would be like in bed, and I can imagine her long thighs stripped of their black support hose, her nude freckled skin—but I am remembering my dad's girlfriend Inez, a racy Argentinian who seemed to be everything my mother was not.

Leiper is a dancer turned sculptor, turned videographer: a charismatic young guy whose work is well regarded by a certain curator at the Whitney. His video installations and "live action broadcasts" captivated the hiring committee, and we were all in favor of bringing him here. Chances were that Jesse had slipped up and offended somebody—he can be outrageous, his sarcasm biting, and because it's not what you might expect from so cute and tidy a person, such contradictions can be shocking; in fact, it's this tension between his appearance and his behavior that animates much of his work. I didn't believe his nuttiness was any more pathological than mine—still there was always the chance that he'd lost a screw. This place can do that to you, pressing down on you, stripping your threads, and when you can't make any further adjustments—well, I've seen it happen.

I'll visit Mr. Leiper, I typed succinctly in reply. *Warm Regards,* I signed, just as she liked to do. I was back, *for sure,* and as I kept reminding myself, I'd been handed some gifts I should be thankful for. For one thing, I was free from a section of "Introduction to Studio Art," because, instead, I was allowed to teach a new course originally proposed before my leave, "Sacred Landscapes." And in the Spring I would able to teach an old favorite, a lecture survey of Cinquecento artists I called "Hermeticism and Renaissance Painting". *Thank you again, dear Liotta. It's a good thing our department chair does whatever you believe is best for the College. I wonder what Gordon gets from you in return?*

I was scratching through my shirt. Then, as usual, I worried that I had inherited my father's psoriasis. The psychoanalyst Wilhelm Reich, who suffered from this skin condition, concluded that it was a symptom of his suppressed rage against his father. That couldn't possibly be my problem: I'd buried my dad, and Leo too, for that matter. *My particular itch, my prurience, has more to do with the women in my life, Dr. Reich.* I went on explaining myself to myself, reasoning that even though my artwork is marked by scratches and intentional smudges, erasures and slashes of paint, *I feel that this signifies*—I pulled my fingers away from the circle they were digging around my heart.

Then I shut down the computer and got up abruptly from my desk. I left the office, taking care to lock the door behind me, watching the key turn and then checking the lock two, three times by tugging the door knob back and forth, back and forth.

CHAPTER 25

THERE'S A GOOD RESTAURANT practically across the street from the College, and a former girlfriend of mine, Donna Trabucco, works there. Her divorce is now final and with her son away at Dartmouth, where his father teaches, she's well into a new life. Donna has, however, lately been rather coy around me. I thought we were still on friendly terms and hoped that we might soon be sleeping together again, but she has instead kept her distance. I was a contributing factor to the divorce, though at the start of our affair she'd assured me that her marriage was already doomed due to her husband's "history of bad decisions." According to Donna, he always was a two-timer, an inveterate skirt-chaser who slept with his graduate students; what's more, she said that she had never really loved him. I met him once and to tell the truth I wondered if we could have been friends had I known him first. I don't sleep with my friends' wives.

My eyes were down while I mused and walked. I'd just bought myself a pair of black cowboy boots, inlaid with silver and turquoise leather diamonds: I'd had a similar pair ages ago when I was an undergrad. To the people who don't know me, I probably seem like a rather typical Italian American male, vain and fit and well dressed, the sort of guy who tears up listening to "Nessun Dorma," who stands in reverence before Leonardo's *Virgin and Saint Anne*, and who can be bewitched by the sight of a pretty woman adjusting a stocking garter.

In fact, I was thinking about the way that Donna Trabucco would sometimes dress for me, when David Lafferty stepped deliberately into my path. He came up chest to chest, thick and wide, bumping against me, mumbling excuses, pretending our encounter was a coincidence. Then, as he often does during these pantomimes, he grasped my shoulders as if to stand me upright.

"So sorry, sir."

"Excuse *me*," I replied. "I'm the one in *your* way." We've worked on this routine since high school.

Then, each of us leaned in hard against the other, and, as usual, when I tried to resist him, Davey eased me completely off the walkway. My efforts to hold my ground are a perennial source of amusement to him. We embraced, and I could well remember the last time he'd given me such a bear hug: it was at my opening, and during the act, he'd unknowingly spilled the contents of his wine-glass onto a lovely young art critic whom I'd been hoping to seduce. She'd fled the scene immediately.

Laughable Lafferty, I dubbed him back in high school, and later, *Affable Davey.* I have never clearly understood why David Lafferty, in so many ways my opposite—beefy, jovial, seemingly unreflective—originally appointed himself to look after me, but I am glad of it.

Lieutenant David Lafferty he would eventually become before he retired from the Force. Too young to put up his feet, he promptly became a private investigator, a job that sounded exotic to me, although he said it was mostly eavesdropping and sorting through people's garbage. I couldn't quite picture him as a snoop because I thought his bearing gave him away as a cop. Then again, he does have a talent for disguise: I have seen him become a fat nobody in the midst of a crowd, an anonymous tourist under a dorky baseball cap.

There are numerous small town links between Davey and me: his mother who'd been a girl with my mother in Kinderkill and later worked with her and my aunt Josie at the Bleachery in Wappingers Falls; Davey's wife Jean, who once did a summer as a chambermaid at my family's resort and whom in high school I tutored; and then there's the time when Davey dated my cousin Tina—or *thought* that he had—one of our jokes—until she ditched him at a restaurant. That was years ago when he was still on the police force and Tina, flaunting her disdain for the Establishment, was on her way to renown among its agents. I've always thought she wanted something out of him that night, and when she saw she wasn't going to get it, she left for the ladies', never to return.

"So we meet again," I said. "It must *mean* something."

He blinked and narrowed his eyes, and I saw in them the simple curiosity that made him a PI. I'd once told him that we were "others" to each other, something like brothers, only different, and when I tried explaining it, he got terribly serious and began to talk about service, brotherhood, and the Force. That's a good example of why we don't socialize very often.

"This means something. Of course it does," Davey mused. "You're the one who knows that, right?"

"Ah. I see."

This too was familiar. I put my index fingers to my forehead, taking on the character of a mentalist. "Something about my art exhibit—the detective was, ah, strangely moved by certain pieces."

"I liked it, yeah," he said. "*Of course*, I liked it, Guy." He is one of only a few people who still calls me by that name; then again, he uses it rather interchangeably with terms like "bud" and "pal" for just about everybody. I can imagine him asking a suspect in the backseat of a police cruiser, *Had yer lunch yet, guy?*

"I'm really hungry," I said. "Really," and I raised my chin, motioning toward the Patriot Arms. I started walking, and Davey kept up, his arm linking mine.

"It must've been a big deal for you, that stuff about your child-hood," he said, alluding to my small retrospective. "It's still important as we get older, am I right? Maybe even more so?"

I didn't answer. We kept walking.

"Good to see your mother the other night," Davey said, refer-ring again to the opening which was weeks and weeks ago. "Did your cousin Tina ever show? Geez, I haven't seen her in ages."

Still I said nothing.

We were at the door of the Arms, and Davey, who'd had lunch already, wondered if he could talk over something with me while I ate. If he'd just been a little quicker on the ball, he probably would have caught me at my office, right? But I didn't mind, did I? Pushing himself with his big friendly paws into my life.

The lunch hour crowd was already gone and a waiter quickly arrived to take our orders. I had the Texas Tuna Melt with green chili sauce, steak-fries, and a blanched romaine salad, which was served almost immediately as an appetizer. I like to eat my salad after the main course, it's an Italian thing, but I was hungry and dug in. Davey grinned while I chewed. The day was so pretty that almost everyone else, including Donna, was outside on the deck overlooking the river. I told Davey that if he'd come looking for me a few minutes later, I would probably have been otherwise occupied. I nodded toward Donna, who looked radiant, smiling and talkative among some customers.

"Yeah, well, I had a sort of intuition. . . Listen, Guy, I've got a proposition for you," he said, getting down to business. "You could think of it as community service—what I mean is a job, part-time. You could probably have it for the asking."

"What, with the cops?" I said.

He nodded slowly, apparently impressed at how I'd known this.

"Go on," I said.

He was asking me to apply for a position as a police sketch artist. Davey knows how quickly my pencil can move—I once did tourist portraits on the sidewalk outside the Met—but he also knows of my ambivalence, almost a neurosis, so far as cops are concerned. It's one of the reasons, and a selfish reason I admit, that I have kept our acquaintance all these years: to confront my fear. I listened while he made it sound as if what policemen really do is to clean up after people who make messes, or else try to prevent the messes from happening in the first place. I could tell he had rehearsed, and it was touching, since Davey isn't exactly eloquent. He said that if I got the job I would be deputized and placed on call throughout the Mid-Hudson region. "Community service," he reiterated. "Plus you get paid to train for it. It's a piece of cake, to coin an expression."

He was pleased with himself, and I nodded respectfully, despite the absurdity. I didn't know what to say. While daubing my lips with my napkin, I happened to make eye contact through a glass panel with Donna, who smiled back at me. She was dressed for the warm weather in a short skirt, her legs bare, her feet in fashionable canvas espadrilles. I love her lean athletic legs, had loved to run my fingers along them. Then came the memory of her foxy scent and my tongue between her thighs.

"What is it with you?" Davey said. "You want the waitress on the side?" He smirked and I smirked back. "Let's get serious. I think the job would be yours if you wanted it. They'd swear you in as a Special Deputy. Pretty cool, huh?"

I thought some more about it. Karma is simple to understand at the level of obvious causes and effects, but more complex when you think how circumstances can change so unexpectedly, shaping up like towering waves because of a trembling on the ocean's floor far off in time and location.

"You using your sixth sense? Can you read my mind right now?"

I focused my gaze between his eyes. He was clean and I had always trusted that: a bona fide Eagle Scout back in high school who'd impressed me in his uniform, sashed with badges.

"Nope," I replied. "You're an empty vessel, my friend. But maybe you're the psychic one here. You're right about Donna. I confess, I'm lonely again and my heart hurts. My year away was a failure, and so it's back to teaching children how not to follow in my footsteps."

"Geeze, and I thought you liked your life! You've got all these. . . *gifts,* these special talents. The police are looking for some-body like you." He paused to be sure I'd caught the irony, but then he added seriously, "You were never a convicted felon, were you?"

"No," I answered irritably. "You ever kill anybody?"

I saw it as a speck growing near the pupil of his left eye. It enlarged steadily until the scenario seemed to fill his entire cranium: a corpse face down on blood, a city street, broad daylight. Something about a little girl—the man had threatened, waving a revolver in the air, taking aim. Davey and another policeman had fired simultane-ously. It had taken place on a bright winter day.

"You don't have to talk about it," I said.

I knew he wouldn't. In a moment, he went on enthusiastically about a book he was reading about psychics who had helped solve baffling police cases. Some of them had been deputized especially to help—he looked at me—and others, almost against their wills, had spontaneously picked up clues that contributed to cracking cold cases. After he'd seen his buddy's "supernatural paintings" he had thought of this, and then, "by coincidence," there was this job opening. He knew I wasn't a bullshitter, and he had emphasized this when he spoke to certain people about me. He'd told them that I was a regular guy, but also that I could "knock their eyes out" with my pencil. He'd told them I was "very sensitive," and leaning forward across our table, added, "That's just the way you are, right?" He gave me a conspiratorial wink, something altogether unexpected from my forthright friend.

For my part, I can also attest that David Lafferty is not a bullshitter, and furthermore, I have long believed that he could read my mind if he tried. It takes one to know one.

"Hey," he said, concluding his pitch, "I've got a feeling that this would be good for your other work too—a new inspiration."

I never did get the opportunity to talk with Donna Trabucco that day, but somehow I associate everything that happened afterwards with her. It's like me always to want a woman in the picture, not necessarily at the center, but maybe like an accent mark, or a touch of contrasting color to make a painting more lively. Donna's smile flashed once more when Davey and I got up to leave, and I felt as if she were daring me—to do what, I wasn't quite sure, but at that moment I did first begin to imagine myself as a Special Deputy.

Would I get a badge to wear or at least a card to carry in my wallet that could fix traffic tickets? Would I get to practice shooting paper silhouettes? As a teenager, under the influence of James Bond, I had once fancied myself a secret agent at the Villa Giustovera, observing customers and covertly doing sketch portraits of them. Working for the police was perhaps not so far a stretch as I might have thought, and Davey was right on with his intuition that I needed something new in my life besides the drama of campus politics into which I was being drawn.

Outside the door before we went our separate ways, I told him that tomorrow I would let him know my decision. He practically kissed me.

BACK AT MY APARTMENT, I continued our conversation in my mind: *Sure, let's change my life—and then?*

Tina.

Oh.

I remembered something my grandmother once said about the Tarot: she wasn't reading fortunes, but rather seeing how people and circumstances are interconnected. It was like looking at a big picture with smaller pictures inside it. "Like a collage," I'd said, but she didn't understand the word and only smiled as she turned up the cards. My grandmother's Tarrochini were at that moment sleeping near the back of a drawer in my bedroom. I keep the deck wrapped in one of her ancient silk kerchiefs, so threadbare nowadays that merely to unfold the bundle encourages further unraveling. Merely to think about that deck has an effect on me.

No, I was never a convicted felon, and yes, I could take an oath to uphold the Constitution of the United States of America and sign a paper attesting to my loyalty—but what else would they want to know about me? I felt as if I had already been to confession after Leo's death, but like the over-scrupulous Catholic child I used to be, I was afraid that what I had not said might yet have serious consequences for me. A background check! I don't like to look at my student evaluations or reviews of my artwork even when they're positive. I can't stand the idea of anybody else having a say about who I am and the worth of what I've done.

When I'd given my statement about Leo to the police, I was assured by friendly Officer Lorraine it was not the same thing as a legal deposition, and that only for such a document would I be advised to have an attorney's counsel. She'd stared at me for a long moment, then said, "You don't anticipate a problem, do you?" I shook my head no, and pressing my luck, I said, "You look like a woman I could pour my heart out to." She was embarrassed and turned away, but I'd seen a smile flit across her lips.

Sitting alone at home after lunch with Davey, I was nervous, but, damn it, also curious—and I had to admit that the thought of Sandy Lorraine sweetened the entire proposition. I indulged my fantasies. I pictured a star blazing on my black lambskin vest where I would pin it—and yet the offer and the timing were so strange! Just when the College seemed so much to want me, indeed to *need* me, this peculiar opportunity had arrived alongside my Texas Tuna Melt! Perhaps my friendship with Davey Lafferty was simply bearing karmic fruit. But what else had he said? *The police are looking for somebody like you.* That was disturbing.

I sat down at the little desk in my bedroom and opened my sketchbook. In it I read, "Fuck the art market, bunch of interior decorators," something I'd scribbled after I took down my show. I turned to a fresh page. I doodled for a few moments, letting my imagination play, watching as a Beardsley-like hermaphrodite materialized at the tip of my moving pencil. Gorgeous breasts and an outsized erection. "U.S. Grade A," I wrote under the drawing inside a striped badge, as if it were stamped on a side of beef. Then I felt angry with myself.

In another moment I would turn to the cards, in another moment, they would be gliding through my fingers. Then I was thinking about my grandmother and of all the women who for one reason or another have exerted influence over me. I thought about my mother living alone in the dilapidated Villa Giustovera next door to my bereft Aunt Josie. And then there was my cousin Tina, out of sight for months, her mother a *massa confusa,* fearful that Tina might be holed up with who-knows-who, or jonesing for a fix of who-knows-what, who-knows-where. I would never turn my back on them, but I was not going to end up as one those balding Italian bachelors living into late middle age with his ancient mamma, a pathetic guy once thought of as a ladies' man, but whose luck and looks have run out and about whom everyone wonders *Just what is his problem?* I tapped the drawing I had made, poking at it, as if I might prod it to speak. My sex life at this time was centered at a club where under black lights in private booths, nude young women allowed me to graze my hands over their perfect bodies. I have always avoided prostitutes, mostly for hygienic reasons, and the dancers afforded me plenty of clean thrills in exchange for my money. At the club or later on at home, I would masturbate happily until I purged my lust. At the time, this seemed easier than getting involved with another girl-friend, yet I was afraid I might be on the verge of addiction to these easy pleasures, and so, periodically, I practiced asceticism.

I would go without orgasm for days and days in order to build *prana,* the life force, within myself. After several weeks of meditation and abstinence I felt as if I were a walking erection, filled with this energy, something more subtle than lust, a psychic power both radiant and magnetic. As a result, the world was more alive to me in every respect. Other people of both sexes were drawn to me, and I could easily read their auras. Once I watched with wonder as sparks flew off of a girl who gave me directions on a street corner, another time the singing of robins each to each made me weep, and when with my fingers I combed some grass I felt that I was stroking the very breast of Mother Earth.

The last time I reached such a state, it shattered abruptly when I went to the movies with an ex-student of mine, a woman in her late twenties, now a receptionist at an art gallery, and afterwards we made love. And so I gave up my asceticism—not because this particular lover was irresistible, but because I realized that to go further in the direction I had idiosyncratically begun, I would need to find a genuine tantric master to teach me. Instead, I've returned to more familiar ways, and just as I've done so many times in my life, have settled for what was near rather than striking off into the unknown.

I stared at my spontaneous drawing of the hermaphrodite. For the European alchemists as well as the Hindu Shaivite yogis, such a figure represents the union of male and female in one body. I thought the sketch was pretty good, yet I abruptly tore it from my book, and reciting an offering mantra, burned it in a bronze bowl on my altar. I sat in meditation, coughing occasionally due to the acrid smoke, watching the transparent layers mingle and then waft out an open window.

I was at last ready for the cards, and my hands sorted with eyes of their own through my vanity's drawer, tunneling under Tibetan *katas* and prayer books, bags of corn pollen, sachets of herbs, vials of miraculous healing earth. I grabbed the Tarot bundle, opened it while inhaling the fragrant mix of mildew and perfume that brought back my grandmother.

One card, I thought. *That's all I need.* I concentrated while I cut the little deck three times left handed. I drew the King of Cups: the sensitive man, the lover of truth, the accomplished artist. I dreamed over the card, allowing my associations to flow freely.

I knew without looking that on top of the deck, face down was the High Priestess, and I knew who that represented, and I resisted turning it over to prove my intuition. The last time Tina and I had seen each other was when her father died a few years earlier. We haven't had a wedding in our family in a while, and so, unfortunately, wakes and memorial services have begun to figure as occasions for reunions. Well into her forties at the time of Uncle Tony's death, Tina seemed to be aging badly: her face was lined, her skin pallid, her hair tinted with henna, her bust quashed under her bodice. She was wearing so much heavy jewelry at the wake that my mother referred to her as *una zing-ara,* a gypsy. "What do you think is going on with her?" she whispered to me at the back of the funeral parlor. "Josie doesn't have a clue. Go talk to her, Guido. She won't say a word to her own mother."

But before I could get near, my cousin disappeared.

What Aunt Josie told me later was that her daughter had behaved very selfishly. Angrily, she accused her also of being demand-ing, spiteful, willful, and irresponsible; in other words, *disgraziata;* that is, wretched, graceless, ungrateful. "Oooh, and it breaks my heart!" Josie moaned, standing in her kitchen with me, refusing to sit and eat the cake she'd put on plates before us. "I don't even see her when I see her! *Dio mio,* what has happened to my baby?"

I too blame Tina for being so reckless in her regard for others, but also I admire her, yes, I envy her indifference to what any of us thinks. Aunt Josie for one has always believed that Tina is, or could be, "normal," and she has tried to insist on this for all of Tina's life, as if it were merely a matter of imposing her will on her. I have seen her physically take hold of her grown daughter and attempt to sit her down for a lecture. What futility! But *disgraziata*? I don't think so. An outsider, an outlier: I contend it's what makes her so irresistible. Call it her *star quality*. And as it is with so many fascinating celebrities, I think the seed of her self-destructiveness is here too. Tina's ways both provoke and entice, but when the burden of her audience's enchantment grows too heavy for such a star to bear, she vanishes. Certain persons, those with whom our family will no longer speak, have dismissed her as insane, dropping the word like a soiled napkin from their lips. I have never believed that, nor does my mother, nor does Aunt Josie, either—whatever epithet that in her anguish she might spout.

Unlike Cristiano, who left home early and set himself up at a defiant distance with a forwarding address and telephone number, Tina's style has always been to seclude herself secretly until, as in a game of hide and seek, one of us finds her, or else, exhausted and bedraggled she surrenders and returns. Then we are all lost together again, becoming preoccupied once more with how to save the family darling from herself.

Such temperamental behavior can in fact be found in both branches of her family tree. Her mother, as I've indicated, is not the most serene person, and Nonna was certainly unusual, however much she was doted upon. But then things with Tina have been further complicated by a history of substance abuse, and at least twice that I know of she has been in rehab. Until his dying day, Uncle Tony professed that "the kid can't help herself." He forgave her for everything, including his broken heart, the one she had to fix over and over. I am trying to do the same.

All of this was brimming in the chalice before my eyes, the cup that had passed to me from the hands of a painted king. "I know who I am and I know what I'm doing," I affirmed. I was going to be of service to my community, and even if I might become so respectable that my rebellious cousin would scorn me, I was going to find her and bring her home.

My cousin Tina has always had beautiful breasts and they have always posed a problem for me—I daresay they have created problems for many others as well. In particular I remember the party that my mother finally got around to giving in honor of Nonna, well over a year past her death, but fittingly just before the Season was about to commence. May was the month of my grandmother's birth, always associated with *primavera* and all the possibilities of the summer ahead. I was almost nineteen and so my cousin was around fifteen years old. To say as one did in those days that she had "filled out" is an understatement.

I can't say how innocent my cousin was of the effect she had on everybody that day. Tina has always been the family darling, and she has beautiful eyes whose irises are almost black, genuinely piercing eyes, eyes that can glint like points of obsidian. For the first part of the afternoon, this penetrating gaze posed a danger for any who ventured too near. Not even the old Italian gentlemen, friends of the family whom she'd known her entire life, neither Mr. Manaperta, nor signor Caballo, nor old Tony Lupo could get a pinch of sugar from her dimpled cheeks. In fact, she turned away whenever she was addressed, whether by her father or mother or anyone else.

The Villa was sparkling with lamps and candlelight, filled with family and friends, all of whom shared fond memories of Nonna and of the old days, and yet to me the atmosphere could not help but feel muted. Bereft as it was of my grandmother's inimitable mirth, the Place was also lacking my father's good humor. Withdrawn all afternoon and surprisingly sober, he was undoubtedly grieving for Nonna, who had regarded him with special affection as her accomplice. My dad, an immigrant as was she, had learned his comedy on the streets of Naples, and whether or not he was aware of it, much of his clowning descended from the classical *Commedia del'Arte*, which my Milanese grandmother loved. By contrast, during the memorial, when my mother, spoke of grief and its value like water for a parched soul, her eyes shone and her tears flowed freely. I'd never known her to sound so poetical, let alone to share her melancholy so publicly, and that afternoon marked a change in my awareness of her, and more importantly, in my behavior toward her. I had always known how difficult her life had been, but now I no longer begrudged all of her efforts to be free of the obligations that dogged her. As a child growing up at the busy Place, I had often felt unimportant to my parents and even neglected, but I was a college guy now: I'd done some living and with a little distance I could see that for all their inadequacies, my mother and father loved me and had never actually abandoned me.

Tina seemed to be in constant motion that day. Evasive and fidgety, she was animated with a repertoire of mannerisms I had previously witnessed but which now seemed exaggerated. She continually raked her loose dark hair with her fingers, intertwining the shining ringlets. She played with the tails of her blouse, smoothing them inside of her skirt, reaching her fingertips down deep behind the waistline. Then with a long sigh she would raise her magnificent breasts skyward and I would need to look away.

She began to toy with the jangling copper bracelets on her left wrist, spinning them around and around, and when she caught me smiling at this, surprisingly she beckoned. A green shadow had appeared on her wrist, looking like a serpent wound about it. I broke our silence by telling her about an orphaned European girl who'd been adopted by African natives. I explained that when she was at last taken home to Belgium, she refused to remove the heavy tribal jewelry on her wrists and ankles. When this was done by force, the girl became paralyzed. "They had to bring in a witch doctor to cure her. He made her stand against a tree all night in the rain," I said.

I had made up the story but relayed it so convincingly that it had its intended effect and stopped her nervous swiveling. Then, surprisingly, she rewarded me with a broad smile, just as she'd done when she was a child and I used to concoct fabulous tales for her. Her lips were the Giustovera lips, but they weren't simply thick, as were her brother's and father's: they were the sensuous lips of a young woman in blossom. I came a step closer, resisting the urge to take her by the hand. I could smell the perfume she was wearing, a thin scent, probably something from a bottle the color of a robin's egg—and beneath that, her body's own tantalizing odor. I hated myself for feeling the unmistakable stirring between my legs, and averting my eyes from my beautiful cousin, I backed away abruptly, leaving the crowded dining room to sit alone with a glass of wine at a table in the cocktail lounge.

A few moments later I heard a rush of laughter from the ballroom. Through the doorway of the lounge, I could see Tina and my mother chatting together happily. My mother must have put aside her perennial criticism of her, and now they were embracing warmly as my aunt Josie looked on, smiling as if in benediction. My cousin had grown quite tall as well as voluptuous, and clad in a sleek dark skirt, her stunning figure was obvious.

Now she saw me at my table. Now she was coming for me, making her way through the crowd. I watched her squeeze between Mrs. Mott and Doctor Abraham, pulling her flat stomach in, raising her breasts to the sky, pressing past the doctor's huge gut, smoothing down her skirt-front with the palms of both hands. *Coming to get me.* I couldn't budge from my seat amid the welter of people and I broke into a sweat. I thought of another event in honor of our grandmother, back when we were still kids and both our grandparents were still alive, and I thought about signor Caballo's tale of Geppina Ingrasci, the fallen angel of my boyhood dreams. The fantastical ball of lightning, the crashing of the silverware, the girl on her knees—it had happened not far from where I was now sitting. And then my cousin was squeezing herself into a chair beside me and resting her head on my shoulder.

It was *that* girl I wanted to find.

CHAPTER 26

I TOLD DAVEY ABOUT my interview with the Police Chief, Howard Gottman, and how he'd offered me a position on the spot. There wouldn't be a need for a civil service exam, and I could take a short, on-line course to orient myself. "It's that simple," Gottman had said, looking away from me and out the window as if he were about to change his mind. Finally he said that all I had to do was sign on the dotted line and get sworn in by County Sheriff Linley. Then Gottman returned to the album of my drawings on the desk before him. He lifted out the pastel portrait of a little boy I'd done almost twenty years earlier, the sort of thing anybody would regard as art, I explained to Davey. He paused over it and said that my work as a sketch artist wouldn't need to be nearly so detailed, and that compendiums of typical facial features would greatly assist me. He glanced down at the portrait again and I could see the hold it had on him. I said, "It really only takes a few lines to create the impression of reality." He looked at me, knitting his brows, working his flat, broad, jaw muscles, his nostrils flaring a little. I knew he wanted that picture, but that he would not ask for it: he was waiting for me to give it to him. "I'm glad you like my artwork," I said, taking back the drawing and tucking it away in my folder.

Davey was no friend of Chief Gottman, and now he tapped my shoulder with a fist and smiled. He'd been right about my qualifications, and he'd known that Gottman, that asshole, would not be able to deny them. "You always were versatile," he went. "Remember at the senior picnic softball game when you stepped in to pitch and then you hit a homer your first time at bat? That's what I'm talkin' about, man!" We were standing outside the stationhouse in Wappingers. The afternoon sky was filling with thunderheads, and a humid wind was carrying the promise of welcome rain. We were near his car when the first heavy drops spattered down. The car was an unobtrusive Ford Taurus, dull green in color, coated with dust. I was thinking it was the sort of unremarkable looking vehicle useful to a private detective, but then when the heavens opened, it seemed to come alive under the downpour, popping as if it were effervescent. Hail stones—*tock, tock, tock*—began to pelt down hard.

"Get in, man. Hurry up!" Davey shouted as he slid behind the wheel. "Let's go get you sworn in."

As I was being delivered to the County Sheriff, not to be taken into custody, but rather to be deputized, I couldn't help remembering another such ride up Route 9: I thought about my cousin Chris driving me to meet Leo for the first time. Back then, I'd also been touted as a good guy, and good with a pencil and pad; back then I was seventeen years old and I thought I was getting away from my family, just like Cristiano. What I wanted now was to get them back, and I believed police work would help me do that—not simply to sleuth out Tina's whereabouts, which Davey could easily have done as a favor if I'd asked—but, well, *to be needed*, to have my artistic talents wanted by the cops: my mother would be proud of me, Aunt Josie too, and if Tina laughed at me, hell, that would be a start at reconnecting.

ON THE DAY THAT I actually did, finally, meet the famous Leo Declare, Chris picked me up at the Villa, and before heading to Poughkeepsie we stopped at his place to share a pizza. I ate little and said less.

"You nervous about meeting him, or just playing it cool?"

I only shrugged in response.

We finished, and while I was clearing away the box and paper plates he showed off his new switchblade: it sprang straight out from the white pearl handle; you pressed a release button to slide the stiletto back home. Once I would have coveted such a knife, but today I wondered why he needed something so obviously a weapon. I knew enough to have guessed that Chris was balling Connie Badget. Was he going to fight Bob for her? At one time, that thought might also have excited me, but today it seemed ridiculous, and Chris himself only a handsome hood without many brains.

We soon split for Poughkeepsie, me with my eyes out the passenger side window, my fingers tapping the sketchbook on my lap: I pictured Gwendolyn Glass between the sheets. I had met her on my one and only previous trip to the Moon—that night when Leo had failed to show and Bob skinned me—but I hadn't been able to get her out of my mind, especially after Chris told me she sometimes modeled for Leo "in the raw." She would be my first nude, I had promised myself.

Now he nailed the accelerator and scorched three cars in one pass. I touched Gwen's invisible body for a moment more.

"Yeah, Leo is something, all right. . . He's a fag, you know? But Bobby says he loves the guy and that without him he never would have gotten anywhere."

I was silent and in my mind I continued to stroke Gwendolyn's blond legs.

"Hey, I've been thinking about good old signor Caballo." He shot me his wise guy grin. "What if he and Nonna were secretly lovers?"

I didn't say anything. I had never spoken to him about my experiences at the Carnevale, and I wasn't about to start now. I had learned something dangerous about myself that night, and I needed to keep it to myself. I believed I could curse, *really curse* a person, and I had discovered that there were consequences for me too. I needed to keep my power hidden, like a blade in its handle. As for Nonna and Caballo, of course I had wondered if they were ever lovers and if my grandfather ever suspected or intervened. Manaperta once told me a certain story, a story for a child's ears, but after the Carnevale it made sense to me, difficult as it was to acknowledge its veiled truth.

No matter how hard my cousin might be trying to hold a conversation, I continued to remain aloof. I had other things on my mind, brighter things.

Then Chris said, "Remember that blond chick, the one that Bobby hired that night at the Moon?"

"Yeah?"

"Get this: she's now his *office manager*. She answers the phone and keeps his books. I thought you might have had a chance with her, kid, but I'm not so sure. Anyway, I think she might be frigid. You know what that means, right?"

"What, like cold?"

"*What, like cold?*" He'd gotten my attention. "Like *frozen*, man. She lives in her head and she keeps an icicle in her pussy. But she's a whiz with numbers."

Is she at the store right now? I wondered. *Yes:* I could see her.

"Get this. Leo did a painting of Gwendolyn, only it doesn't look anything like her. It's an *expression* of her or something."

"You mean Expressionist? Like de Kooning?"

"Can't say I've ever met the guy—Connie and me couldn't help laughing when Leo showed us, but Leo says she's great for a model. He says she just sits there like she's frozen. He's using her for his classes at Vassar. Leo is big time, you know?"

Now we were cruising for a parking space, and now Chris was pulling the Chevy into parallel position and then dropping her into reverse. He held his foot down motionless on the clutch and looked at me.

"Hey, relax. You'll like him, you'll see."

LEO DECLARE WAS NOT a *master.* Although he did have vision, he lacked the self-discipline that greatness requires. As a teacher, however, he applied his broad knowledge of art and literature and augmented that with keen powers of observation. When he looked at a piece of work, with only a glance he could tell you where the problem lay, and furthermore, how you might solve it. The inside of Leo's bald, round head was packed with information on any major artist who had ever lived, on all the movements and schools, and he could imitate a lot of them. (I once joked that he could make a fortune as an art forger, and he had looked at me for a long moment without replying.) He had an opinion on everything, from shoe leather to the colored ink they used in *Look* magazine, to JFK's assassination—definitely a conspiracy. He was in his late forties when I first met him, about the same age as my old man, but from an entirely different planet.

A full-blown critique of a student's work in front of a class could put all his fire-power on display, but also, he could be incredibly friendly, letting his downcast students know that he'd had to blister them, because hard work and a willingness to destroy inferior efforts are necessary for serious progress. Afterwards they would still feel somewhat singed about the ears, but grateful to have garnered so much of his attention.

When I worked for him at Vassar, on more than one occasion I witnessed the blistering of an entire roomful of young women. In one figure painting class, with my body sprawled on a chair and draped at the loins, he kept comparing me to the Velasquez portrait of the crucified Christ. Whether he was complimenting me or Velasquez in front of twenty Vassar women, I felt flattered and yet I managed to remain intensely motionless—it was my first awareness of how modeling can put you at the center of the world while also removing you from it. During the break, I followed him around the room, and what a searing show he put on as he assessed his students' canvases! Some of those girls were "teeny-weenies," he alleged, whose brains were probably filled with "thorn flowers," and had they ever actually looked at the Velazquez portrait and thought about the suffering of Jesus as he died on the Cross? Why didn't they stick to their coloring books if they weren't going to do real work? If Leo hadn't been sober, which he wasn't always for his studio classes, we might have had some real tears—from Leo, I mean. The girls were shocked and wordless, most of them thinking his performance must be a joke, which is how he got away with scenes like that.

Most of his paintings weren't great but they were good enough. Too often he fell back on his talent for imitation. Too rarely he allowed himself to love his own work as much as he did that of his masters. He had been well trained in his youth at a Parisian art salon—Paris was where his family had moved just as Leo became a teenager, because his father worked as a designer for Lambourge luggage. (When I discovered a faux Cezanne and a copy of a Picasso from that period I was dazzled; a pair nudes inspired by Matisse especially impressed me.) I met him when he was coming out of a creative funk: he himself told me that he'd basically been masturbating, splashing inky hues across large canvasses, calling himself the peer of Robert Motherwell and a Zen Buddhist like John Cage. He soon returned to a more naturalistic style with great success, selling paintings again, and then within a year he was seized by his greatest inspiration, telling everybody he was going to found "a school of fishy art."

"YOU HAVE A VERY interesting head." These were the first words he said while looking me over, shaking my hand slowly when Chris introduced us.

Whatever he might think of my physiognomy, whatever the tasks assigned to me, it soon registered that I was going to get what I had come for: busboy or dishwasher, kitchen prep or salad maker, there would also be art lessons on the side. Nothing about my pay, which Chris had already indicated would be under the table "for tax purposes, you understand." I didn't know what the hell that meant, but it didn't matter—I was here to learn from a genuine painter. When he closed my sketchbook after paging through it, I held out a portfolio containing my very best finished work. He ignored it and went on about the chores I was to start with that afternoon.

I took in the surroundings. The café was nothing exceptional in terms of its architecture, but the décor was charming, woody and dark in the Colonial style popular throughout the Hudson Valley. There were small metal-sheathed candle sconces on the tables which were supposed to suggest what might be found below decks on a ship like Henrik Hudson's own Half Moon. Behind the bar on the wall above the mirrors hung some over-sized antique kitchen items: a couple of copper cauldrons, a long handled dipper or two, some rusty iron tongs. Over the door connecting the kitchen, was a sign for "The Galley." And of course, the walls featured several large paintings by Leo, different than what I had seen previously, happy young people in hippy garb sitting at the café's very tables.

"Can you listen with your eyes wide open like that?" Leo asked suddenly. It was a tone of voice that would become familiar. He cocked his round, balding head and raised his eyebrows, more amused than angry. Leo was not tall, and in fact he was considerably shorter than I. His trunk was solid oak, however, and because of the spinal scoliosis he bulged forward and seemed always to be advancing on you. I wasn't intimidated by him, not at that first meeting or ever after.

"I get it, " I replied confidently. "Glassware, flatware, wear a white shirt, my white sneakers are okay."

He smiled. When Leo was being chummy, he showed you he had a broken tooth behind his lower lip, an incongruous baby of a tooth, although he didn't show it to anybody very often. "I meant what I said about your looks. Your ancestors posed for a lot of great pictures. Too bad that doesn't automatically make you a painter."

"It makes me Italian," I said. "You should look at my drawings." I might be getting in over my interesting head, but I continued: "I've got my best stuff right here," I said, indicating the portfolio in my hands.

"I'll look later. If you're ready to work, I can use you right away in an apron at a sink. Listen, Chris," he said turning to my cousin. "If you're going over to Bob's, I've got something you can deliver for me."

"Bob's in the City. I don't even know if Connie's there today."

"Who's minding the store?"

"*Gwendolyn*," Chris said. "Our *office manager.*"

"She's okay," Leo said, and he raised his eyebrows to give Chris a look I couldn't read.

He turned back to me and said, almost as an afterthought, that I should meet him in his studio upstairs at five o'clock. With the middle finger of his left hand, he pushed his black rimmed glasses back up the bridge of his nose. It was a gesture reminiscent of Mr. Manaperta, and a pang of nostalgia nicked me. I could smell Manaperta's shop, could hear his chisel working. And then signor Caballo came to mind, and then the day of my grandmother's funeral when he had offered a white rose at the grave. I was suddenly less sure of myself than I had pretended, and amid my confused sentiments, I wondered if I might better turn around and head back to Kinderkill.

Then I remembered that a block away, so near that the distance could be measured in feet, at that very moment on a rainy Wednesday afternoon, Gwendolyn Glass was at Badget's Bazaar.

". . .to make nice with the customers." Leo was speaking to me again. "No need to get fancy—*Nous ne sommes pas à Paris.* On the other hand, when you're out front, mind your manners."

"Cool," I said, hearing my voice quaver, letting my glance stray from his.

"Yeah, yeah, cool. Just show me you can do the job, *daddy-o.*"

I was going to have to take a lot of guff from Leo, everybody did, but I had already decided I was going to get a lot in return. I held out my portfolio yet again. "Do you want to take this with you?"

He reached out to flip it open. He studied the first thing he saw, a copy of Botticelli's *Mars and Venus* that I'd done in colored pencils.

It was the best one of several attempts. "You're ambitious," he said. "A good draughtsman. But you haven't caught the spirit Botticelli saw in his models, those two kids he cast as god and goddess."

He took everything from my arms. "We'll talk about this later. Gabby will get you started. Okay?"

"Yeah," I said. It was all I could say, but I felt that I'd been vindicated: Leo had taken my work seriously and furthermore Chris had been my witness.

To my cousin, Leo said, "Let me give you that thing for Bob. Hang onto it until you can hand it over personally."

"YEAH, BUT HAVE *YOU* ever modeled?" Leo was sitting at his desk in his overcrowded office. Behind him a pair of shrouded canvases stood on easels, and along the baseboard of the room, several other paintings were propped up. All of them looked unfinished. Before him were my portfolio and sketchbook plainly in disarray, having been leafed through. Even as he spoke he held my drawing of *Mars and Venus*, tapping it nervously with his fingernails. I thought it interesting that he had returned to this one.

My tasks as a busboy and dishwasher seemed easy compared to what I was used to doing at the Villa, and my first shift that afternoon was more boring than anything else. The hours had dragged, but I kept reminding myself that I had qualified for private lessons. I felt as if I might burst with pride.

"Would you feel comfortable? Think about this, before you give me an answer, Mr. Diamond. Your work, or Botticelli anyway, has given me an idea. I want to paint you with a girl I know. I pay her to model, and so I'll pay you, too, out of my own pocket. If you're any good you can make five dollars an hour. That's a lot of money, but it isn't easy work, and, and you have to be *nude*."

He looked me over closely. "What are you, seventeen years old?"

Nude. The word resounded within the walls of my skull—*Nude*—*Nude*—*Nude*—tolling what sounded like excommunication from the Catholic Church, from family, from school, from friends. I managed to suppress the piratical smile lurking at the corners of my mouth.

"Who, who, is she? The girl?" But I already knew.

"Gwendolyn's her name. She won't bother you, *mon cher.* Do you think you can do this? Modeling requires quite a bit of self-discipline. You'll also learn a lot about human anatomy from the inside, and you'll have to learn to manage your mind. I paid my way through college working as a model—"

"Okay."

"Wait a minute, my little diamond, wait. Maybe you need to ask your parents about this?"

"This is, like, part of my lessons, right?"

"You could say that."

"Okay," I said once more. "I'm sure it will be okay."

CHAPTER 27

O F COURSE I DIDN'T tell my parents what I was up to. And anyway, I wasn't going to model naked, but *nude*, and I learned the difference and since then have always made it a matter of principle to distinguish between them. To be nude is willful: not innocent, and not necessarily sexual, yet sensuous, a pleasurable condition. To be nude is to be free, and therefore always risky in a culture that remains puritanical at its core. And hypocritical. In America we accept such obscenities as poverty, racism and war, and in effect we sell sex everywhere, but the idea of a teenager modeling nude is likely to sound as suspect today as it would have in 1967.

"Naked is bare, stripped, exposed—perhaps by force and without aesthetic concerns," Leo had explained to me. "As a punishment for their disobedience, Adam and Eve went from nude to naked. They were forced to see themselves for what they weren't: not animals and not the gods they had wanted to become when they tasted the apple. In their human skins they were now ashamed. Nobodaddy shamed them."

"Nobodaddy?" I said.

"One of the names that William Blake calls the god of judgment and wrath. Old Nobodaddy. Didn't you say you knew him?"

"Blake, yes," I said, having no idea who Nobodaddy might be.

"Urizen is another name for him. Blake wrote a *Book of Urizen*. Illustrated. And hung-up though the old guy is, he makes you feel sad for him, because he's trapped by his own thinking—*yr reason*. Get it? That's great art for you. Then there's *The Marriage of Heaven and Hell*—you've heard of that?"

I hadn't.

"*Je te prende un editione.* Now back to polishing the silver, matey, *s'il vous plait.*" He looked at me with a friendly touch of self-mockery, his eyes bulging over the rims of his spectacles. "It's the one thing I insist upon!" he lisped exaggeratedly, turning on his heel to make his exit.

Even though the café didn't aspire to bistro elegance, Leo could be picky about details. In response to this bossy streak in him, each of his crew learned how to escape him. It is the way of pirates: to do your duty to the ship and to respect the captain, but never to lose your sense of independence. Gabby, for example, grumbled constantly about the dirty dishes that came back to the kitchen with stubbed cigarette butts poking from uneaten food, something he found "ugly as shit." So he would accidentally drop and break a few. Not a very bright reaction—he was grimy and slow-witted, nicknamed because he rarely spoke to anybody—yet Gabby's behavior seemed to make sense at the Half Moon.

Busboy, kitchen boy, boy with a brush and paints: at the Moon I was these and more. Boy, I was and wasn't. I don't pretend my folly promptly led me to a palace of wisdom in the company of William Blake, Arthur Rimbaud and Leo Declare, but that first summer and the following year, my senior year of high school, put me on a path.

On account of my job at the café, I was assigned few chores at the Villa. On account of my grandmother's death, I suddenly had abundant time to myself, and so, with considerable force of will, I pursued my passions. My parents were generous toward me in more ways than I understood or could have thanked them for. True, I took advantage of their trust in me. They were preoccupied with their struggling business and marriage, but it is also true that their many dispensations to me were forms of negligence from which I suffered.

Because I took my art so seriously, I became very modest about it, and I craved privacy whenever possible at home. I had by then discovered the landscape painters of the Hudson River School, and while the river itself was always near and the blue profiles of mountains never far from sight, I chose a secluded, forested place at which to meditate and paint *en plein air*. I took my watercolors to a favorite spring-fed, duckweed covered pond. There I also trained for my debut as a model.

That I would pose nude with Gwendolyn Glass still sounds unbelievable: it was as if Nobodaddy had changed his mind about punishing our First Parents and decided instead that their children could return to Paradise. At first, I couldn't think about Gwendolyn nude without popping a boner. That would never do, and yet I couldn't rely on my fear of embarrassment to govern *il sesso*. I could think of nobody but Leo to whom I might turn for advice, but that was impossible: I had already learned that sex was not a subject I found comfortable discussing with him.

I prepared by sunbathing *au naturale*. At a certain moment, I would with the discipline of an ancient Olympic athlete, rise nude and sweaty from my towel and walk directly, slowly into the cold water of the pond. There I would pause with the water lapping my groin, cooling my blood. At last I would bend forward and with a broad gesture, as if I were throwing open the draperies at a window, sweep away a thousand tiny pads of duckweed from the surface. Now I could see my reflection shimmering in the dark water, and if, or when, I became aroused again, I simply stared myself down in that mirror. Occasionally, my double, whom I used to call Cellini, would grin back wolfishly at me, knowing what I secretly wanted, yet was afraid to seize.

When I entered the water completely, I walked until I lost my feet and floated in a cold, pure sensation that subsumed all else: the pond and its wooded banks, the sky with its soaring birds and shifting clouds, my hunger for sex. With my heart pounding, with *il sesso* wilted and presumably under control, I came to know myself as well as to delude myself like this.

EVEN AS I HAUNTED the pastures and ponds that once belonged to my grandparents' farm, the memories of my childhood were passing away and like old storybooks were shelved. I traded my old lamps for new, and as completely as possible, between my junior and senior years of high school, I left Kinderkill behind. Like my father, I became adept especially at evading my mother, who ruled at the Villa, but who seemed content to leave me on my own.

My father meanwhile began to stay out late alone after he closed the bar to go drinking with his pals across the river in Highland. Probably they also gambled over there, for his afternoon games were now prohibited by my mother. As usual, on his hung-over mornings, my dad often incurred her wrath. Sometimes, he would seek her forgiveness by performing obvious forms of penance: for days he might allow her nothing whatsoever to criticize about his work and would meekly smile in assent to any idea of hers. I remember him climbing a three story tall ladder to tar the Villa's roof on hot summer afternoons, or swabbing the barroom floor in the dark before dawn, or mowing its vast lawns until sundown, after which he would quietly shower, shave and dress for a night of sober bartending, his jokes shelved for use elsewhere. Now that I'm around the age that he was then, I often think about his unhappiness and the constraints of his mismatched marriage. His example is one reason why I've never wed—but it is also a reason why my mother and I became so close once he was gone.

"YOU KNOW WHAT I mean by that, *monkey business*? You keep yourself out of trouble."

My mother is my passenger. We're driving north on Route 9 to Poughkeepsie when she says this. I know what she means and I bob my head.

The dream has me sweating bullets. The rolled-down window is blasting warm air past my face, but everything is sticky: the steering wheel of the Plymouth Fury, the vinyl under my left arm where I rest it on the door panel, my back inside a white shirt plastered wet against the seat's padded vinyl upholstery. It's this sensation, the fabric pulling uncomfortably from my skin when I lean forward, that makes me suddenly aware I'm dreaming.

I turn my head toward my mother; slowly, so that I don't disrupt the scene. When I attempt to speak, no sounds emerge from my mouth, and my mother noticing this, seems to panic: "What is it? What? What?" she asks.

I cannot speak, and so I use my thoughts: *This is not the way.*

My mother squints out through the windshield, takes a cigarette from her purse and lights it while she ponders. "Don't drive so fast," she says. She looks unhappy.

"They don't do things at the Moon like we do them on Earth." The words emerge with surprising ease—they are the exact words that I remember saying to her when I was seventeen years old, when I believed I was witty and sneaky and took pride in my deceits.

"I don't know what they do," my dream mother replies, just as my actual mother did at the time. "No monkey business, *hai capito?*"

I'm going to awaken and there's not enough time to say what I want. I think of an idea from Plato—had I read anything of Plato back then?—the way we remember by concealing or partially forgetting, so that memory's veil gives us the outlines of things rather than their real forms. I can't find the correct words, the dream is dissolving, and I blurt out, "*Ceci n'est pas une pipe!*"

ON A WEEKEND AFTERNOON that first summer of my employment, the Half Moon opened its doors and moved a few little tables onto the sidewalk. Leo said, "We're in Paris, kid!" and then shook his round head slowly, *no*. Within a few weeks he was in court with a lawyer to defend his freedom to seat customers on public pavement—which he argued he had a right to do, since his tax dollars had helped to lay the cement for the common good. He gathered the support of some Chamber of Commerce types and together they won "The Case of *Al Fresco*," as the newspaper called it. Other cafés and restaurants soon followed his example.

"Conceptual art," he said, beaming with victory. "It's a brave new world, kid!"

It was with this sort of enthusiasm and pure doggedness that he sold his patrons on his vision of the Hudson River College. A certain type of person could find Leo's edges very pleasant to the touch—and touch such persons he did for large sums. He was no beggar, no parasite or swindler, but playing off the beat, like a drummer attacking his kit with rim shots and splashes of brass, he could be the life of a party when he needed to be. Those friends also helped him sell his paintings and grooved with him on long weekends around Long Island. The Captain was definitely an acquired taste— perhaps he could be compared to arak, so sweet that it burns your throat, or to the pleasure of puffing an Indian bidi, its tobacco harsh but heady as grass if you held the smoke in your lungs and believed it would stone you. That summer everybody wanted some of Leo's high, everybody wanted to hang out with him drinking and smoking under imported Cinzano umbrellas, *al fresco*.

You would never compare Leo's particular flavor to junk, and he himself never used any hard stuff. He hated the thought of it being dealt at his café, although it could be found out back in the alley that belonged to everybody. I remember a certain hulking creep who came around now and then to whisper into the Captain's ear: Leo told me with disgust that he was a cop on the take, "Bobby's security blanket." I thought he must be joking. I had studied mugs like him at the Villa, but always kept my distance because my father warned me that those "big boys" were "connected." But a corrupt cop? I thought they only existed in movies.

Pot wasn't like junk—it was practically harmless, right? It arrived in shipments from the City, though not nearly in such quantities as the fresh roasted coffee beans we ground for the house espresso and sold over the counter in paper sacks. Still, lids of Mary Jane were relatively easy to acquire if you were cool like Larry and his Boys: you got a pass from Leo and then went around the corner to Badget's Bazaar. Sometimes they would give away joints—Bob referred to free sticks of grass as appetizers, I remember. One night that summer after hours at the Half Moon, Badget invited me to a party at his house in New Paltz, but it was already eleven and I had to get home. Later I heard that everybody had taken acid and danced nude until dawn.

"Boo," MY COUSIN SAID. He passed me a reefer he'd lifted from his pack of Viceroys. We were standing outside the backdoor to the Bazaar. It was supposed to be a surprise, my cousin springing the joint on me, like he might shoot the blade of his knife for a kick, yet I took it from him nonchalantly. Took my first hit like, *What's the big deal?* We'd already flirted, Mary Jane and I: she had teased me many times behind the café, her sweet scent breezing by.

The string that jerks and holds a junky fast is wound around the fingers of a slaver, but grass is like a girl who knows somebody who's dangerous: she's licking her lips while you watch and she goes, *Ummm. So I'm illegal?* Yeah, Boo could put you in prison, but she doesn't want you to leave her for the deadly stuff. Times have changed for sure, but Smack still sounds painful to me, a sucker punch to the jaw, or possibly a fatal kick to the head. One guy told me H was like a kiss from God, big enough to kill all of his suffering, but I wouldn't know. It's sad that so many try to get happy and kill their pain with heroin.

My first time with grass, I didn't believe I was high, and so I concluded that Chris must be goofing on me with some stuff he'd rolled in the kitchen. I hopped out of the doorway behind Badget's where we'd smoked and continued to hop on both feet toward Leo's studio for my afternoon lesson. It was incredibly fun to move around like this, but at three o'clock in the afternoon people on the street were gawking, and so Cristiano, laughing all the while, hustled after me. I guessed that he was going to pull a sack over my head, that he was going to *bag* me, and yet I didn't see it anywhere: how clever of him!

"I'm okay, okay, okay," I went in rhythm with my hopping.

Then Chris put an arm around my shoulders and walked me to his car, gently accommodating me into my seat, then we roared off at what seemed like a phenomenal speed. In a moment we stopped. The two of us entered a door behind the Moon and hiked a mountain of stairs to Leo's studio.

Leo was there, and he knew right away I was high. Bidding Chris *au revoir*, he settled me down to work with watercolors as if I were a six year old. *Okay, okay, okay.* I went abstract, discovered how to layer washes, did hours of skyscapes and rivers of color before I fell asleep over my paintings on the studio's sticky floor.

CHAPTER 28

I HAD BEEN PREPARING for weeks and I was ready to be tested.
I had never shared the platform with anyone else, much less a
woman, and to help prepare myself for the sight of Gwendolyn
Glass in the raw, I visited one of Leo's classes to sketch a middle-aged woman posing nude. She clearly thought I was rude for
dropping in at the easel directly before her, and chastened by her
glare, I focused on my pencil drawing. When the day came that
Gwendolyn and I finally modeled together, I wasn't going to get
shy and stiffen like a stuffed monkey or spring a raging hard-on like
a jackass. I would be relaxed and professional, as I was when sitting
studiously three feet from that anonymous model with her smooth
dark skin and lovely pendulous breasts.

But Gwen. Gwen, nude as the sun! Gwendolyn Glass
luminous as white gold—what could I possibly have done to be
prepared for her?

THEY ARE ALREADY WORKING when I arrive: she is a statue for
him, but her living eyes check me as I entered the studio, and so
I quickly avert my gaze. I nod to Leo. So focused is he, that he

doesn't acknowledge me. I strip in the bathroom and emerge wearing a towel about my waist as if I am on my way to the Villa's pool. I am able to risk but one more straight-on gander at Gwendolyn. Her eyes flash at me once more without any sign of recognition in them. Leo calls, "Break," and quickly she dons her dressing robe, pads in her bare feet around the room, loosening her limbs, stretching her arms overhead.

Leo has been working on a painting he will never complete because it is frankly so grotesque. It's not because the face, a decidedly feminine face, is at that moment only a rudimentary drawing and something like his pal de Kooning might have done. As I come near, he pulls a cover over it, but later, I will inspect it closely and decide that it is in some way a self-portrait, despite the fact that he'd begun with Gwendolyn as his model. It's because the eyes are his own brown eyes staring back at him honestly. I recognize them at once as those of the Captain who makes his crew hate him when he ruins our fun, railing about our incompetence, or wailing about that prick, his friend Bobby, and his bad business deals. This is his self-loathing. This is the Leo Declare who whines that he will have to be "smashed dead like Pollock" before people learn to love him.

Leaning the canvas at the base of a wall, he moves swiftly across the floor to take a drink from a bottle at his desk. When he finally comes around to greet me, he's almost formal, welcoming me as if I've only now set foot in the studio. He introduces me to Gwendolyn and leaves us alone while he retreats to "the lavatory."

She and I shake hands ceremonially—still no sign of recognition—while with her other hand she holds closed the blue satin robe. I can smell cigarette smoke wafting from its folds, a floor length dressing gown, probably something from a trunk at the Bazaar. Now she steps over to her things on a chair, withdraws a pack of Camels and lights one without looking at me.

I have seen her exactly three times at the Bazaar, have spoken to her twenty-two words over the course of approximately two minutes since the night at the Half Moon when I thought she needed me. Why so cold and impersonal now? Is it because she has an icicle—I don't want to think of what Chris said. But does she remember me at all? Girl with a made up face and done up hair, vogue and vague as any that might be found on the pages of a fashion magazine. Sharp girl: I can see that clearly now, now that I am standing so near, *experienced* girl—I am very nearly dispirited. What a fool I am to think we could have made it! I feel suddenly as if I'm in a broken hearted love song, yet feeling so chilled, I come into possession of myself. Under the towel I'm wearing, *il sesso* retreats.

The toilet flushes while Gwen and I continue to wait for Leo's return. Resuming his position, without a word, he lifts the cover from the canvas he'd been working on, takes one quick look, removes it from the easel and stashes it on the floor beside a still life so lovely that I have to look twice. Then he pulls onto his easel an oversized pad of newsprint. Gwen resumes the platform, and Leo, jutting his chin, motions me to join her. Heart thumping, but *avec sang-froid*, I do. When Leo reaches out a hand to take my towel, I remove it smoothly from my waist and pass it over. I turn to Gwen who has slipped off the blue dressing gown when I wasn't looking. There is no mistaking her self-consciousness, the pink roses in her cheeks and nipples, and, strangely, as on that night when we first met, I feel suddenly protective of her.

"Move very slowly around the platform. Don't even look at each other. It's like you don't know the other one exists."

He begins to dash off gesture drawings with a fat piece of charcoal, working very quickly, turning back page after page behind the easel tree. They rustle like palm fronds—it's as if a great wind has come into the room. I can feel the way that my slow controlled movements must show my muscles. It's easier not looking at Gwen, but I do when her face is averted, and I gather her profile into my memory. Her large, almost bulging blue eyes and petite nose; her fine blonde hair worn so that its pageboy tresses come to cunning points at the corners of her mouth; the downy skin along her jawline that I had once mocked, thinking her nothing but a cute little chick. She is perhaps twenty, and she seems "finished" as some girls do who from an early age are left to mature on their own.

"Very good, Diamond. He's beginning to catch on, isn't he Gwenny? No, no, don't look at him, not yet. You can feel him, though, can't you? Move your hands over your body. There's something in the air. . ." He sketches very quickly, holding in his mind individual gestures, drawing while the models in motion lead his eye and hand faster than he can think.

"Diamond, now you rest your hands very lightly on her shoulders, but stay behind her, at arm's length. Gwenny you don't look, you don't know him, and yet all along you've been awaiting this. . . *prince.* Your father has taught you many things, but he couldn't have told you about *him.* Stop now—yes, there. "

We've halted our languid dance and I remain in direct contact with Gwen's body. The heat sears my palms, and her bodily scent, a mixture of sweat and soap and cigarettes threatens to topple me. Then, as if a switch has been thrown, the heat rushes all the way through me.

"Don't pay any attention to that! *That* is a big distraction, *monsieur!*"

And in one fluid motion Leo has leaned forward with his outstretched hand to slap my penis. "Both of you, keep your minds on your work," he snaps.

My arousal vanishes instantly. Simultaneously, my upraised arms are unbearably heavy, and I struggle proudly to remain motionless. I feel as if I've passed some kind of test, however. Years and years later, I will continue to feel a peculiar triumph in connection to that swift tap, knowing too what Leo would learn from it: that this stolen touch was all he would ever have of me.

On we go until Gwendolyn and I are both shining with sweat. *"Bien."*

He closes the sketchpad, pushing the great crinkled sheets down without looking at any of the drawings. He steps around the easel toward us as we break. Gwendolyn pulls on the royal blue robe immediately. I step off the platform to retrieve my towel, and wrapping it about my waist, I feel strangely underdressed, like a dolt whom *le maître* has summoned from the hay fields to pose in his studio.

"Picasso says there isn't any difference between the artistic impulse and the erotic one. What do you think, Gwenny?" He doesn't expect an answer. I see her profile in a scowl, but Leo doesn't care. His stare fixes on me. "I hope you don't start smoking cigarettes just because she does. Your parents would never forgive me."

Is this a joke? What does he want of me, anyhow?

"Ten minutes, and then we begin to work in earnest."

WHAT IS TEN MINUTES? Time to stroll about and gaze out the window of the studio on an overcast sky? Time to dream what I would like to do when we're done here, when I might ask Gwen to have a coffee with me downstairs? A few minutes to limber my stiff muscles, whirling my arms and flexing my legs like a swimmer about to dive.

Had Leo said, *Take five*, well then, it would be time for Brubeck's classic. Instead, my memory is devoted to Stan Getz in a blue key. Getz, whose moody tone Larry Bell copped, whose saxophone injected me at an early age with a love of smoky ballads. It's a habit I've never wanted to kick.

THESE FOOLISH THINGS REMIND me of you, Gwendolyn.

SHE IS ALL BUSINESS, back on the dais now, ready to work, all but ignoring big-bellied Leo, who, in a reverie, taps with the handle of a paint brush his balding pate lightly in time to an up-tempo tune. Behind the canvas he's hoisted onto his easel he squints through a skylight at the clouded sun until the music ends. Although she barely acknowledges me, I know Gwendolyn remembers who I am—but she has removed herself from any sort of interaction with me. Meanwhile, wrapped in my towel like a swimmer, I stare at the studio's paint spattered floor. I am determined to succeed, if not as Gwendolyn's lover, then as her modeling partner. I already sense how difficult it will be to work another two hours today. She knows she can do it. She's strong. She's smart too, pretty and smart and strong. Nothing will stop her, I can tell—and her attitude gives me the strength to persevere during that first unforgettable day.

WHEN THE BLUE SATIN gown slips first from the globe of her left breast so that the baby-pink nipple suddenly juts at my eyes, I blink. *Inscrutable in her fair skin,* I think, thinking poetry for her. Staring would make me a kind of thief, easy to call out, and so I will learn to adore her only with my mind. Ready to work, now, I drop my towel and take my position beside her, stepping firmly onto the stage, planting one bare foot next to hers, so much smaller than mine. Through her translucent skin I can sees the fine vessels carrying her blood, their blue tracery. Resuming the pose, my body remembers its fatigue, the previous long minutes of work: how did I manage to move so slowly and with such control of myself? I dart my eyes toward her now, no longer able to resist temptation, and allow them to graze over the curves and planes of her body. I savor her scent. *Lilac.* I taste her.

LEO HASN'T MISSED THE flush of transport washing through me— indeed, he seems pleased. He knows Gwendolyn is disciplined, and how she will abstract herself from the strain of the passing minutes, and comply with what he asks. He's found it very easy to work with her. She's like a figurine to bend into position. What if he were to paint directly on her skin? *But no.* He shakes his round head, *no.*

"Now I want you to see him for the first time, Gwenny. Turn your head very slowly. That's right, slowly, slowly. *See him—* like Miranda when she first sees Prince Ferdinand. Shakespeare, *cherie, The Tempest?* "

WHAT DOES SHE KNOW of Shakespeare? She remembers *Romeo and Juliet*, but English class was never her strength. Nor was art appreciation. A short course of business accounting made her a bookkeeper rather than a book lover. Men she already understood like numbers, to add and subtract from her life. But Leo has asked her to act. She knows that good modeling is more than keeping still, that the best models can project a thought, an emotion, an attitude almost indefinitely. And behind the pose, behind the mask, there is a curious freedom. *If you don't go crazy.* Instead, she has learned to go blank; that's what she calls it, taking herself, *like, Nowhere.* And when it's over, moving around in your body again, there's that indescribable feeling of returning to life, and then the pleasure of that first smoke you suck down hard, and your knowledge of the power you have over their eyes.

"SHE'S EVERYTHING A YOUNG man could dream of. Say it with your eyes, *mon ami.* Face to face with her now. No touching—your hearts see each other. That's right, that's right, Ferdinand. And Miranda the same. Amazement. Your daddy Prospero couldn't have prepared you for this."

Leo's movements behind his canvas are peculiar: an elbow keeps appearing outside the vertical edge, and his bald head surfaces periodically, while his body rocks to and fro, so that when I let my eyes stray, I'm looking directly into his nostrils. And then there's the force of the brush strokes falling, a force reverberating throughout Leo's body, which is in constant motion, as if he were dancing or conducting an orchestra. When I meet his gaze, I am reprimanded:

"You see only her. This beautiful creature to whom you have instantly given your heart."

Wondrous strange: a boy, a prince, has survived a shipwreck on an enchanted island, encountered a magician and traded hearts with a creature so lovely she might well be a goddess! I am instructed to bow my head before her; I would throw myself down at her beautiful feet whose toenails are the pink of seashells. I love her thin ankles and the place behind them where her slender calves begin. Between her golden thighs is the chapel of Venus. *Oh, fortunate Ferdinand.*

"Good. Very good, you two. That's enough for today. Thank you, Gwendolyn. Mr. Diamond, you're a natural."

CHAPTER 29

Of course I like to remember the first time I worked nude with Gwendolyn Glass! Haven't I already said that long ago I learned to choose my memories, and that these *obsessions*, shall we say, generate my artwork? As for justice and truth and the Law—well, thank goodness that Sandy Lorraine came into my life.

Davey was wising me up as we rode: "Most of the work in a police station is paper work, or these days computer screens. In your job, you'll be using paper and pencil, naturally, and spending a lot of time one-on-one with your witnesses. The orientation course will answer a lot of questions about protocols."

I bowed my head once, twice in mute acceptance.

The Taurus slashed its way forward, while all around us, thunder rumbled and rain washed down on both the just and the unjust. I had a woman on my mind, and when I have a woman on my mind I have a picture of possibilities.

At the county sheriff's office, I followed Davey through a sterile narrow room, down an aisle flanked on either side with desks and computers. In this respect police work is, as Davey had indicated, like so much else today: the quantification and digestion of information, vast amounts of information, and at such astonishing speed that it can create the illusion of omniscience. Too bad for all the cop shops and secret services, too bad for all the digital marketeers and hacker racketeers that the human soul can hold so many contradictions, and that the universe doesn't only roll in one predictable direction.

There was a woman in a blue uniform sitting with her back to Davey and me, busily typing at one of the desks. Her smooth auburn hair was pinned up into a shining bun, and that glorious crown of umber and gold had the same effect on me as before. *Good,* I said to myself, relaxing a little for the first time that afternoon. *My intuition hasn't failed me.* An upturned uniform cap rested near her elbow on the desktop; I glanced into it as I walked past, as if the secret to a happy, orderly life might be contained therein. Her nails were painted platinum and because of the overhead lighting, her fingers seemed to flash as she typed. My Athena took no notice of me.

When we'd made our way through the squad room into a waiting area outside the Sheriff's door, I thumped Davey on the back with a loosely clenched fist. "Purgatory," I whispered. "Purgatory is a place to do penance."

He gave me an elbow in my ribs. "Relax, man." He nodded toward the lovely officer at the opposite end of the room. "She the one you told me about? I can see why you never forgot her. This must be your lucky day." Then he said, "Know why they call it the *penal* system?"

"The same root as penance," I said. "Not to be confused with *penial,* which as I recall means tail, and thereby hangs a tale . . ."

He shook his head, letting out a long breath between his teeth. Then he walked over to a tall bookcase, studied it for a moment, pulled a volume from a shelf and shoved it into my hands.

I opened at random and read in a hushed voice: "'Modern prisons are reformatories in a primary sense and can be compared to other institutions whose goals are the improvement of society.'" I stopped there. I thought he might be baiting me, maybe to test my resolve, for although I had been offered the job, I hadn't yet signed on. "Penitentiaries protect the law abiding public from convicted criminals, but besides this, incarceration is also intended to teach behavior that civil society depends upon. Furthermore, our system provides many sorts of educational opportunities and even the possibility of modest financial reward on the way to rehabilitation.'"

I looked up for his reaction. He had his head inclined, his ear close to my mouth, prompting me to keep my voice lowered. I thought of a priest in a confessional, and I thought too that Davey was good at his game, sliding from one guise into another; a detective would need to be.

"Lot of important stuff in here?" I asked, rapping the book sharply. My voice was trembling. "The use of force for the improvement of society is doomed to failure," I announced. "Blake says that one law for the lion and the ox is oppression."

"Sure, " he said quietly. "And maybe the prison system is a sort of hotel business. Or a source of cheap labor for the private companies that are taking it over. Some people think it doesn't do much besides giving criminals an opportunity to make new friends and learn new scams. All at the expense of the tax paying, law abiding public."

He placed one of his thick fingers on my breastbone, not quite affectionately. "So I ask you, Professor Diamante: Why do you think people aren't inhibited by the prospect of doing time?"

I was wound up and answered him straight: "We have a puerile society whose populace really would like to be *kept*. A nation of wage slaves and slave owners, and for some, the option of where they perform their servitude seems irrelevant. But if time is money, money, alas, doesn't really equal freedom. Our rulers are terrified that people might wake up to this. It's one reason why the widespread use of mind-expanding drugs is anathema."

It was hard to keep my voice at a whisper, and in my own ears it had begun to sound shrill and shaky.

"Yeah, but people from other countries still want the freedoms and security we have here," Davey replied. "You wouldn't want to get caught with even a stick of grass in Malaysia. Immigrants come to the U.S., not to take advantage or destroy our way of life, but to enjoy it along with us." He studied his wristwatch. It had stopped.

"People are mostly asleep," I said. "They buy their dreams—or try to anyhow, and instantly become afraid of losing all their precious stuff. Which is why they seem willing to sacrifice actual freedom for a police state. . ."

Davey tapped the face of his watch and looked up at me. "The fear of losing things and needing to feel protected is why I had a career with the Force, something I'm proud of, and it's why I still have an income as a PI. It's also why you and I have insurance, right? Take health insurance: with the way hospital costs keep climbing, and all. . ."

"Yeah, there's that too. All of it based on fear," I said.

"Well then we agree."

"No, we do not! That's not what I'm talking about!"

"Jesus, don't tell me you changed your mind about the job?" He seemed preoccupied with his watch, and with the time it wasn't telling.

"Capitalism is based on controlled scarcity and *fear*. It convinces people that they're inadequate—only try saying that out loud."

Davey shook his wrist and began to tap the glass of his watchface. Then he held it to his ear.

I had just raised a finger for emphasis when I saw the beautiful one in blue advancing toward us. She walked past, nodding graciously on her way into the Sheriff's office, but before she knocked at his door, she smiled at me with the pleasure of recognition. Then she slipped in, closing the door behind herself.

"Time to shut up," I said to no one in particular.

I pointed to my friend's wristwatch. "I don't want anyone to get the impression that I believe in violent revolution. Violence just pushes bad karma around and around like the hands of a clock."

His watch was running again and he looked up at me. "You talk to your students like this?" he asked seriously.

"Not anymore."

"If you're not in the mood right now," he said blandly, "you can think about it some more, come back another day. But the Sheriff will be pissed." He raised his eyebrows. "I've got two hours. Are you still interested in seeing where your cousin Tina lives?"

"Yes," I said. "Yes, I am. Thank you."

The door opened and Officer Lorraine beckoned. "He's ready for you now."

IN THE END, I could not resist the invitation to become a Special Deputy on ad hoc assignment to local law enforcement agencies as a sketch artist. And yet I see now that I would never have considered the work if it weren't for the timing. Of course Davey had located

Tina, had known that I couldn't or wouldn't be able to do it on my own, and for reasons of his own, he had drafted me into his posse.

After my uncle Tony's death, I took to visiting my aunt Josie with some regularity, whether in my mother's company or alone, which was actually more enjoyable. I would sit with her in her parlor drinking weak coffee while the TV blabbed and from the top of its faux-wood console, from their framed photographs, Uncle Tony in his World War Two army uniform and Cristiano in his Viet Nam era navy whites watched us. During the course of our conversations, Aunt Josie would invariably bless their memories and address their spirits, all the while sitting with her back to a picture of Tina that smoldered on the living room wall. I liked to sneak glances at that photograph, taken when she was around nineteen years old. I even remembered the boyfriend who did it, Cary Robbins, a guy who was a freshman at HRC when I was a senior.

My aunt had recently concluded that her daughter "needed waiting." This was not the dawning of equanimity, however, for as Josie also informed me, the waiting was "practical," since history had proven how Tina would eventually come around "unexpected." She grimaced when she said that, like somebody subject to recurring pain in her teeth. I did not mention that I thought her habit of lying in wait for her daughter might be a contributing factor to Tina's recalcitrance.

It was to Davey that I was now talking about my family as we rolled in his Taurus toward Beacon. I have had some of the best conversations of my life while cruising around in cars, maybe because while traveling I'm more open with other people; to boot, that day, after my swearing in, our conversation about Tina almost sounded like police work.

"Over the years she came to be lambasted as a member of

an outlaw tribe, those who these days might be parodied in the popular culture, but who nonetheless are still envied for their once-upon-a-time idealism. Even into the 21st Century, with its mounting disappointments and ever more toxic prospects, she and her ilk remain resistant, refusing to submit to the general catastrophe."

I was laying it on and Davey was eating it up. Getting sworn in had inspired me to be more of myself, not less, and yet I had also resolved to prevent my antiauthoritarianism from sabotaging me; realpolitik would be the order of the day, prudent compromise, whether with the police or at the College or with Tina. The Buddhist Middle Way.

"Because of the antagonism she suffered, because she is in fact rather delicate, less of an Earth Mother and more of a nymph, she has regularly needed to, shall we say, *submerge* herself. Like a genuine siren, she reappears when she will."

Davey drove slowly, almost leisurely south on Route 9. I knew that he knew a lot about the particulars to which I was alluding; I also knew how much he liked to hear me talk this way: during our school days he used to call me the Poe-man. At a certain stage in her life, my cousin achieved considerable notoriety with local law enforcement. She never did any hard time, was never found guilty of anything more than peddling some drugs—well, it was actually quite a lot of fine Hawaiian blotter acid, for which infraction, thankfully, she mostly paid with community service at a food bank. After that transgression she was also required to undergo psychiatric counseling.

"The thing, the thing with the courthouse picture, that was when? 1992?" Davey asked.

"Around then, yeah. There was the reporter who tried to make her into some kind of victim of the mental health system. She was the mainstay of his column for a while. He'd fallen for her, you know. People still remember that picture on the courthouse steps."

"Oh yeah," Davey went. "Acquitted of conspiracy charges, or some shit like that."

In the photograph my cousin throws her hands joyously into the air above her head. She has just shaken loose her thick black hair, and she resembles a folk dancer, her long skirt swinging, her waist cinched in a wide, silver-studded belt. ("Carmen," my father said, staring at the newspaper and nodding his head decisively.) Her face is turning toward us and because of its motion, the camera has blurred her features slightly—a very fetching effect. Unfortunately, my uncle Tony had one of his heart attacks after seeing it.

Tina was awarded a new social worker, after which a new and complicated scandal developed that involved a male psychiatric nurse and an off duty policeman, who, although he admitted having had intimate relations with Tina, insisted during the subsequent investigation that he hadn't known she was at the time under police surveillance—which was, of course, a violation of her rights, and as her attorney informed her, justifiable cause for a lawsuit. Within a few days, however, my cousin disappeared. Other later chapters of her saga included mandatory confinements in rehabilitation facilities, but never prison time—which would have probably finished off my uncle, and my aunt as well.

"This street, " Davey said abruptly as we turned a corner and pulled to a stop. "Listen, Guy, don't get your hopes up. What, I mean is. . ."

"Right." I stopped him before he became any more flustered.

"I'll tell you something funny. She showed up at the Villa not too long ago and absolutely charmed my mother. She brought her a cake—talk about carrying coals to Newcastle! She had baked an old fashioned *panettone*, the kind our grandmother used to make."

"So?"

"So, my mom told me Tina was on her best behavior, and what's more, she spoke some Italian with her. I've never heard a sentence of Italian come out of Tina's mouth. Of course, she revealed nothing about where she was living or what she was doing with herself."

"That's the house," Davey said, pointing to a brick apartment building.

"I'm surprised," I said. "I imagined something a little more, *cracked*. You coming in with me?"

"No, no. . . Listen, Guy. I've got a baby sister. Ellen. Remember little Ellen? Well, she's a forty two year old *woman*. Know what I mean? Go and talk to your cousin. I'll pick you up here in about an hour."

I didn't budge from the car. Through my window, I inspected the building for any sign I might detect of Tina's life within. Out front, the wet sidewalks steamed in the sudden sun. I hesitated further. "I wonder if she's home," I said.

"Use your psychic powers," he replied. "Or else just knock on the door."

CHAPTER 30

Tina pointed through the kitchen window into her back-yard garden. "*All* the nightshades are enchanters, not only belladonna. Did you know that Nonna once used it to make her eyes bright? Well, the girls in Milano did, in the old days, drugging themselves for beauty. The same family as tomatoes, peppers, nicotine, potatoes—*petunias*—" she emphasized the word strangely—"all in the family *Solanum*. Sun lovers. They like hot nights, too."

She had not been especially surprised to find me at her front door just a few minutes earlier, had greeted me happily, in fact, though without offering her cheek for a kiss. We'd settled in for coffee at the table in her tiny, neat kitchen, and she seemed so reserved, so careful in all her mannerisms, that I couldn't help wondering if she were medicated. Her interest in gardening was nothing new, and I liked seeing the tidy beds in the backyard, the handsome fence of wooden rails and wire boxing it. Indoors, her kitchen's north wall was hung with pale green and purple sprays of lavender whose odor permeated the place.

"Petunia is a sorceress, you know. Powerful in her own way."

It seemed to me she was speaking with a tone of voice that our grandmother used when, as she would say, she was *considering* things, turning them over in her mind until they became malleable and her words would reshape them. It's why Nonna never told a story the same way twice: she had *considered* and decided that it needed something new.

"Pinch a tomato's leaves to prune the suckers from the stem and then sniff your fingers: how she haunts you!"

That jabbed at me with its sexual innuendo. I tried a bit of humor, made an amusing shape with my open mouth—*ohh!*—but Tina didn't seem to notice and continued as if she were reciting from an herbal. "Work among them thinking thoughts of love or be prepared for mischief: nicotine addiction, or burning pain between your legs because you made an ointment from enchanter's nightshade hoping it would make you fly. . ."

Whether it was her voice with its odd rhythm and inflections or the perfume of lavender or the drowse of a late summer afternoon, a dreamy indifference had begun to settle on me. I felt as if my original intention for coming here was pretentious, only another example of my vanity. I remembered something that Donna Trabucco had said when we broke up, that my narcissism might be innocent, but it caused trouble. I wanted always to be right, she said.

I asked Tina if she had a cigarette. She once loved to smoke, and whether or not she still did, I hoped to interrupt the spell she was weaving.

"I do," she answered mechanically.

She *must* be on meds, I reasoned, but this didn't exactly make me happy: her monologue, her flat affect were *disappointing*, that's the only word I could find for it. I missed her flair, even if it scorched people as often as it charmed them. She reached from her chair behind herself into a cabinet drawer and passed me a red and white box of Nat Shermans. "I keep them around to stimulate digestion. One of the properties of *Nicotiana Tabacum*. You probably know that. You were always so smart, Guido."

I lit up with the matches she handed me, wondered if she would join me, wanted her to. Smoking together on the sly had once made us feel like adults; now I thought it might help us to feel like kids again. She reached over and took one of the thin brown cigarettes, fumbling for a moment to roll it up over its mates in the box. I have always loved her hands: I held them when she was a child and I've watched them change over a lifetime and they seem to me the epitome of beautiful feminine hands. I once told her she could work as a hand model—it was after she'd come out of rehab about a decade ago, unemployed and unattached—and she'd looked at me as if I were an idiot. "I did that already," she said, "and it didn't get me anywhere."

On one finger was an oblong topaz set in silver: it had been Nonna's ring, bequeathed to my mother who had never worn it but kept it in a safe-deposit box along with most of her mother's jewelry. She must have given it to Tina, and it made me smile to think of the cake-and-coffee sorcery my darling cousin had probably used on her. Not that mother would have given it unwillingly: she was eager in her old age to make peace with her wayward niece, who resembled her own mother in so many ways. I myself had coveted the ring, and I was strangely excited to see it on my cousin's finger.

I watched as the smoke from our cigarettes mingled, and I thought that it has always been like this: we can meet where we aren't exactly. Why couldn't we be together easily amid ordinary settings? Or was this what we were doing at the moment, making the best of our situation like ordinary people do?

Blowing smoke toward the open window, she turned the back of her head to me and I saw how her thick black hair was spun with strands of white. It was knotted loosely behind her head, pinned with a tooled silver clasp. Her elegant brown neck showed the curvature of a woman well into her forties. Tina looked her age, I couldn't deny that, nor was she trying to disguise it, yet she seemed healthier than I had seen her in a long while; that would be important to report to Aunt Josie.

"How's your mother doing?" she asked me, turning suddenly about.

A dozen miles away, where she had spent almost her entire life, my mother was almost certainly taking her afternoon siesta at that very moment, resting so that she could rise tomorrow morning at three a.m. and bake a day's worth of bread and cake for her customers. Down the road from the Villa, Aunt Josie would be done watching soap operas and might be offering a rosary for her dearly departed husband and son. Of course, she also prayed constantly for her lost daughter.

"My mother's fine," I said to Tina. "She told me she saw you."

"She saw what she wanted," Tina said, and for the first time that day there was a little laughter in her. She reached to tap her cigarette into the saucer of her coffee cup. She looked as pleased with herself as a cat. Her long earrings, silver and topaz, glittered like cat's eyes.

I took the saucer from beneath her cup, placed it on the table between us, flicked in some of my own ashes. I let my gaze rove about the apartment, assaying its contents and décor. It was surprisingly neat and bright, apparently renovated recently, and with the cost of living in Beacon nowadays, I wondered how she could afford the place. Within a handsome glass cabinet stood an array of liquor bottles, but that had never been Tina's style. Jealousy crept out from a chamber of my heart.

"You were always a voyeur, Guido. Artists always are, but with you it's like *predatory* or something, the way you want to eat everything with your eyes. But the worst thing is that you feel guilty about it." She blew some smoke into the air over my head, and then her gaze settled on me. There was mirth in it, and I felt some relief in meeting her eyes at last.

"Shall I show you what you don't really want to see?" she asked.

"O-kaay," I replied somewhat shakily.

"What you see here is somebody who knows herself. Someone who doesn't need any kind of fix. What your mother saw was someone who wanted her—and I did that day, honestly, because I wanted something I knew that she would be happy to give me. I don't mind playing the chameleon, if that's what you call it. But I know what's in here." She tapped her breast bone lightly with one beautiful finger, its unvarnished nail clipped to a blunt point.

Her face seemed to quiver ever so slightly, as if a tremor or twitch near the left eye were tugging at the features, hinting how soft the flesh was, how easily it might melt. There was something terrible about that unwelcome thought and the vision of how her skin could drip away or drop off like a garment whose stays have been cut. Then her obsidian eyes were laughing at me. I could hear the song of a cicada outside in the late summer heat. We were children playing hide and seek among the junipers on the Villa's lawn near dusk. We believed in magic.

"I know this game, Tina. I've even earned some bread with it, reading people at Renaissance fairs." I paused for effect, twitched an eyebrow. "There are rules, you know."

"You think it's a game?" Her eyes smiled, her mouth blew cigarette smoke toward the sky. "Like the game when you would sit me on your lap to ride your pony off to fairyland?"

"My *pony?*"

"Hiyo, Silver!" she yipped and broke out laughing.

A bead of sweat rolled from my armpit inside my shirt along my right flank. The strong cigarette I had been puffing threatened me with nausea, and taking my eyes from Tina, I stubbed it out slowly, solidly in the yellow saucer. I breathed slowly, deeply.

"You can tell everybody you found me. You can tell them I'm fine, that I'm getting older just like they are, going gray and drooping a little." She ran her hands over her ample bust. "It's true. But I know how to dress."

I blinked.

"Ha!" she said. "You always did wanna fuck me! No, no, no—don't get offended, Guido. Nonna tells me everything, and what I don't get from her. . ."

A swarm of imprecations rushed into my throat, but I resisted them and plunged into silence, drawing one breath after another, slowly, deliberately. Then I unfurled my fists. *I came here with a good heart,* I reminded myself, flattening my palms against my thighs.

"The rules are common sense," I said. "Trite as it sounds, what you do unto others you do to yourself."

"*Sure.* But what others have done unto you—like deserves like, don't you think?"

"Evil wants love," I countered.

"*Davvero.*" She closed her eyes when she said that. Then, with her eyes still closed, she said, "You're so *fucking* good, Guido."

She opened her eyes and lifted the plane of her face into the sunlight, fluttering her dark lashes. "Is this how you paint them? Your Magdalenes? Saved through their love of Jesus—or is it *your* love that saves them? I've seen your paintings, I know how you think about women."

"You came to my show? You saw the portrait of Eva Lynn?" I began, but then stopped. Eva Lynn Samuels was indeed the model for my one and only Magdalene. She'd been my lover years ago, had been dead for many years, but I retrieved her portrait for my retrospective exhibition. Flustered, I said, "Titian is your man for Magdalenes. He was obsessed, a great artist has to be. . ."

"But he was a fraud!"

"Titian? What are you talking about?" I was definitely losing my patience.

"Like all of you, he loved best what he could touch," she said. "Women of flesh and blood. His paintings are impostures."

I tried to laugh her off. "I don't have *any* problem with that. Nope," I said archly. And then affecting the tone of a supercilious *professore:* "Since I'm a guest in her house, very well, if *la signorina Tina Giustovera* is suggesting that artists are a company of frauds, and that this band includes the likes of *Tiziano da Cadore,* well then, let us entertain the possibility for a moment, although we heartily disagree."

She snorted at that, unintentionally forcing smoke from her nose and mouth, choking a little and coughing and covering that with a laugh as she extinguished her cigarette. I could see that her eyes were tearing. All at once she was up on her feet, heading for the sink faucet, brushing past me with her long skirt, pulling it aside dramatically. It was of the style she had always favored. *Quella fanciulla selvaggia,* my dad once called her. That wild girl. *Carmen.*

"Are you all right?" I asked, watching her sip water from a glass. I cast an eye toward the clock on the kitchen wall. I saw that the hour Davey and I had arranged was passing quickly.

"You're the poet in our family, Guido. And *that's* why you've come to me."

"I'm here because your mother gets crazy with missing you. Jesus Christ, Tina, why don't you visit? Lemme tell you, she's in danger of truly losing it. Why don't you let her know where you live, give her your phone number at least? We're all crazy over you."

"I knew you were coming. I saw it in my cards."

"*Si, sicuro,*" I snapped. "It's something we inherited from our grandmother." I paused for a moment and then in a softer voice, I said, "We've always understood this about each other, no?"

"You ought to feel more content, Guido. You've got every-thing you need to be happy." She said it casually, as if tossing the words over her shoulder while she strolled from the kitchen through an archway into the living room. On the back legs of my chair I pivoted about to follow her, could see her face in a wall mirror where she stood to loosen her hair. With the fingers of both hands she raked it out to fan open on her shoulders. Her blouse was cream colored, wrinkled behind and dampened with perspiration so that it clung to her skin. It looked as if she were braless, and something about her overall appearance contrasted with the tidy surroundings of her apartment. A lot of men would be attracted to Tina just because she always seemed slightly unkempt.

"Hasn't it ever seemed strange to you that neither of us got married?" She was looking at me reflected in the mirror as she con-tinued to play with her hair. "I know that you're not queer—hey, it's never too late. I'm sorry. . .That didn't come out right." She turned around to face me with an expression not quite apologetic.

"Listen," I said, taking another long breath, taking the conversation away from the rocks that threatened to tear out its bottom, "we haven't really spent any time together since your father died. I came here because I wanted you to know that your family loves you. We. . ."

"We? Who are you talking about?"

"What?" I exclaimed. She was silent, so I continued, "Your mother, my mother, *me*—who else is there? The dead who watch over us?"

"And I love you, too, Guido. You better believe it." She came near and gently touched my breast, honing in on that pain that I have never been able to cure.

Then she said, "Only I'm not so sure the dead don't also prey on us." I saw that other face of hers, the impersonal one.

"Sweet Jesus," I said, shaking my head from side to side, surrendering the effort to be rational with her.

"Don't tell me you're still devout?" she said ironically. "Don't you remember what they used to do to people like us?"

"That was a long time ago. . ."

"What do you remember?"

REMEMBER?

One winter when Tina is seven and I am eleven, I put her on my knee and bump her up and down and unexpectedly come in my pants.

One winter when I am twenty one, I'm home to celebrate Christmas at a family tree whose limbs have been severely lopped. My cousin Cristiano is dead for the second year in a row. My teenage cousin Tina, loopy with cognac, fawns on me with wet kisses. When our two mothers leave the room, with her tongue in my ear she says, "I'm going crazy! Wanna come?"

My mother, stiff as a figure snipped from the cover of a fashion magazine, still in the prime of her life, has nevertheless sworn off men. Instead, she is perfecting her role as some sort of nun or abbess—*Mother Superior*, I have begun to think of her, *jump the gu-un,* as the Beatles sing—and yet inside of her the woman she once was still murmurs—I can hear it—*Zee-Zee, come home.*

However, if my father were to return from New York on that Christmas Eve, surprising us all in his fawn-colored cashmere coat, a bundle of gifts in his arms, I know very well the scene my mother would make. It is she who left him, after all, she who in effect left *us,* as I have explained it to myself with the sagacity of a college guy who now can forgive her for wanting a life of her own. My mother and father ought never to have married: I have also reconciled myself to this in my twenty first year. But no, there will not be a surprise appearance from Nunzio Diamante tonight, *fuggedaboutit.* Instead, my mother and I and Aunt Josie and Tina are awaiting Uncle Tony, solid as a Chevrolet sedan, to arrive so that with him we can open our Christmas presents under a small twinkling tree.

At around seven o'clock, having had two cognacs and smoked some hash with Tina outside beneath the diamond sky, I begin to feel I might indeed be capable of losing my mind, and that it might not be such a bad idea. Tilt my head and from my well-tongued ear, my jellied brains might pour—and then I might grab Tina and flee with her to Canada where we could be married. Instead, I choose to fight against temptation, just as I have for my entire life, seeking to remain upright beside my beautiful cousin no matter how the ground beneath my feet heaves and rolls. Even when I'm kissed sloppily on the mouth in the cupboard among the cans of cranberry sauce which I've been sent to fetch, and been wept upon by my cousin of the lustrous hair and bounteous breasts, I bear up, believing that she doesn't know what she's doing and never has, and so, I can't in good conscience take advantage.

Before the night is over, standing before the crèche of Baby Jesus, I will silently acknowledge that hers are indeed blessed breasts, a stupendous bounty, such as what I myself would want if I were a girl of seventeen. But I would not fidget, smoothing my blouse and skirt repeatedly, unfastening my hair, retying it, my arms upraised and chest lifted high, a sigh perpetually on my moist lips. And I would not sob upon my cousin Guido's neck and dry it with my long dark hair—I know that I wouldn't, no matter how terrible I felt about Cristiano, about the war, about my mother, about myself— but what do I actually know for sure?

Before God, I will no longer deny what I feel. I have felt it my whole life, and while I am no longer bound by the fear that it is wrong to have this desire, on that particular Christmas Eve I vow never to act on it. To seal my pledge I sear my finger in a candle flame.

REMEMBER?

In another lifetime we were lovers. Something came between us, and our lives were destroyed.

WHEN I'M ABOUT TO leave her little house in Beacon, on that very same day when I was sworn in as a Special Deputy, I ask Tina directly what she does when she disappears, when she goes, as she says, *underground?*

"I change my tired skin," she replies.

And then my cousin throws her arms about my neck and kisses it with open lips. We touch and quickly fall apart and touch again and part.

CHAPTER 31

MY AUNT HAD BEEN very upset to learn from my mother about Tina's unexpected visit, and my mother told me how much she regretted ever mentioning it. I had promised Tina I would tell Aunt Josie only that we'd spoken. In return, from my cousin I'd received an agreement that she would eventually—when the stars were willing—visit "the grotto of despair" where her mother resided. As I was leaving, I said, "Mother is the important part."

She frowned at me.

I was afraid I might have jeopardized our reconciliation, but she phoned me the next day to invite me back for dinner. I accepted, and what's more, I agreed to her request that if at all possible I would bring along David Lafferty. When I asked why she wanted Davey there, she explained that she was working her way through a list of people to whom she needed to make amends. She and I had made our peace hadn't we? We'd had a tiff and scratched each other's noses, but we'd made up, and now we understood each other, didn't we? "We'll have fun together. I'll make sure of that," she purred.

IT WAS A NIGHT in late September when the calendar tells you summer has passed and the whirring of a million crickets says it hasn't. All of the windows were open in her apartment, and a fan ran on the floor pushing a strong gust of air out the door that she opened for Davey and me. Tina in bare feet, in her blown green cotton skirt with the fabric clinging to her legs looked positively sinuous. With extended arms she gestured for us to enter. There was no kiss for me, only a moment of eye contact; for Davey there was a dancer-like bow at the waist and a warm welcoming smile.

Davey was clearly taken by surprise, and he stepped back awkwardly before my cousin's curtsey. "Hello, kid," he said, beaming.

Plenty of people would cross the street to avoid Tina Giustovera, no matter how good she looked, but never David Lafferty. *She could always turn him into taffy*, I thought. Taffy: the kind of thing you remember from grade school parties.

"Guido, you look tired," she said, touching my hand. "Working for the cops must be hard, huh?"

In fact, I had had a long day, but it was because I'd graded the semester's first stack of student papers. So far all I had done for the cops was drive around two counties and introduce myself to police officers. It was like making the stations of the cross, I had mused. To Tina I said only, "I'm ready to relax." She led us to a pair of chairs in her living room.

Once again I noticed the scent of lavender that infused the apartment: it flourished in her garden and hung drying in sheaves on her walls. She probably put lavender sashays in her drawers and steeped it in her bath water and dabbed its oil on her neck when she dressed. I'd heard you could drink lavender tea, and maybe Tina also did that. She was fond of amethyst as well, lavender in color, and several large crystals sparkled about the apartment.

"I'll get some drinks. David, what will you have?"

"I don't know. . .What about grappa? You got that?"

"That's for after dinner," I said. "It's a cognac. . . "

"If David wants it, he can have it. I just bought a bottle."

"Really?" Davey said.

"I'm well prepared," she said, winking at him. "Guido, you want some?"

I had supposed that if she were clean of drugs she wouldn't be drinking either. Then I remembered the well-stocked liquor cabinet, and my jealous hunch that it was for a boyfriend, and then I thought what the hell? "*Si, lo stesso,*" I replied.

When she left the room, Davey quizzed me about the grappa. I teased him: "She's psychic. I'm sure you have other things in common, too."

Returning with our drinks Tina paused to put some music on a CD player, a black box perched atop a bookcase just inside the doorway from the kitchen. In a laser bright voice, Van Morrison lit into "Moon Dance." A moment later, she handed us each a thimbleful of clear fire. The delicacy with which she handled the tiny stemmed glasses reminded me of the graceful little show she used to make when passing a pipe of hashish. Then I had the absurd thought of turning-on Davey, and at that instant I glanced over at Tina. *Not too much at once,* I said with my mind. She nodded back.

"How's Jean?" I said to Davey. "Haven't heard you mention her in quite a while."

"She doesn't complain," he said, bouncing an open palm on his thigh in time with the music, turning this way and that to check out the surroundings.

Jean and he were one variation of the high school sweetheart story, one that had run all the way past their second child's graduation from college before it broke down and Jean gave up being his cheerleader. Davey's "black Irish" looks hadn't abandoned him entirely—there was something very compelling about his light eyes and cropped dark hair—but nowadays, he said he was worried about his weight and slowing down, consuming potato chips and Ring-Dings all day to keep going. "Always hungry," he had told me. But Jean was hungrier, I realized, and not for anything her husband could give her, not anymore.

"*Cincin*," I said, raising my glass. The spirit burned, but it wasn't coarse; my cousin had purchased a good label. She and Davey delicately clinked glasses, and I suddenly felt rather boorish, having drained mine in one shot.

"Ah, just what I remember," Davey said. "The first time I had this was at the Villa, at your high school graduation party, Guido. What a lucky guy I thought you were. Being able to drink whenever you wanted, all of that booze, wherever you looked. And the secret wine cellar you told me about, your grandfather's cellar. I bet he knew how to distill grappa. . ."

"Did you ever meet our *grandmother?*" Tina interjected.

"Once, at one of Guido's birthday parties. But we were little kids then. What did you call her, *Nanna?*"

"Nonna," I said.

"She was very old fashioned," Tina went. "A northern Italian aristocrat, right until the end. How she doted on Guido!"

"We were both her favorites," I said, and I was sad immediately, seeing the specter of Cristiano forever excluded. Davey had known Chris too, and I hoped he wouldn't bring him up. Nevertheless, I found myself echoing one of my aunt's familiar lamentations: *He wasn't supposed to die like that.* Then I was remembering his burial at Saint Mary's cemetery. I heard once more the sudden loud salutes of the rifles, saw their heavy smoke hanging in the air. Aunt Josie wailing, and the folded flag, silent as a swaddled baby, the tight bundle that one of the escort placed solidly into Uncle Tony's hands, and how his hands had sagged with its unexpected weight.

Whatta shame the way he died! That was unmistakably Cristiano's own voice, using the very words his shipmate Barry had uttered to me back then. Barry had sought me out purposely so I would know the story—one that would never be repeated to my aunt or uncle. He'd died while he was on shore leave in Thailand, hit by a car while trying to cross the street outside a bar. Barry told me that Chris, his best buddy, had literally expired in his arms while they were waiting for medical help. All this after a solid month at war when their carrier had supported countless bombing missions.

Davey snapped me out my reverie. "Nonna was your mother's mother, right? Some kind of white witch?"

"Did I say that?" I replied. I was still distracted with the voices arriving on gun-metal clouds. *It runs in the family,* I might have said. Davey had refused to believe me back then. Now he wanted it to be so.

"I owe many of my talents to her. Nonna had a very good imagination, didn't she, Tina?"

"She could make us believe impossible things," my cousin replied. "We never knew when she was fooling and we didn't care."

"Davey is very interested in psychic phenomena."

"Oooh—we should have the Ouija Board after dinner."

Davey chuckled and shifted his bulky bottom. As far as he was concerned, my cousin could do with him whatever she wanted. We all agreed the Ouija Board would be entertaining. I pinched Davey's cheek fondly, in the Italian way, as if he were a cute child. I cautioned him that we would have to make sure Tina didn't cheat.

Smiling happily he replied, "I know how the Ouija works. My daughter Brenda used to play with it. You can tell if your partner is moving the pointer."

"I'm choosing to ignore that last remark about cheating, Guido. Let's not give the detective any wrong ideas."

To Davey I said, "I only meant she's liable to, well. . ... She really does take after our grandmother."

"And I don't know what you mean by that, either. " She slapped me lightly, playfully on the shoulder. A tingle of delight spread from the spot. "I've gotta cook now. I hope you like veal cutlet Milanese. Garlic sauce on the pasta. We will be of one taste, one smell, one faith, Detective."

After she'd gone I said, "She's always liked you."

"Something else," he said, grinning. He emptied his glass.

We were silent for a little while and I watched as he continued to inspect the place. He was observant, it was what you would expect from a PI, and yet I knew how tired he was. I could see how his marriage had worn him down, how tired he was of many things in his life.

I thought of a time not long ago when he asked me if I could name the people that we passed on the street, or if I could know things about them just by tuning in. I told him that theoretically this was possible, but I didn't believe that anyone could have one hundred percent certainty. You learned to trust your intuitions, and then it was very important what you did based on them. It's why serious psychics don't go around poking into other people's business.

There's too much karma involved in that. He was talking about *perception,* he explained. "About the *meaning* of Joe Blow out there on the street. Can ESP give you that?" Although I shuddered silently at the thought of mind-reading cops, his wondering about the meaning of Joe Blow and his grasp of perception as an act of consciousness rather than something mechanical surprised me.

Near where we sat on the sofa was a little three-legged table from the Middle East. On the polished top stood a glazed clay figurine, about twelve inches tall. Davey lifted the statue carefully to examine it. It was a good copy of a goddess image from ancient Crete. Her arms were upraised powerfully, and in each fist she brandished a snake. Her breasts were bare and they bulged like white globes above her tightly cinched waist. Her attitude was one of power. The long flounced skirt and ceremonial apron were nicely detailed in blue and gold, but the cat atop her headdress was overwrought and the goddess face more beautiful than that of the original. I had described her as *indomitable* when I presented this statuette to Tina after my first trip to Greece years ago.

"Nice," Davey said, putting her down gently. "You probably know all sorts of things about this. And I see—what? The pretty tits, the small waist, eyes that never blink. Something very old, am I right?" He looked at me as a student might. "I know it's a reproduction, Professor. But there's an ancient strength here."

I nodded, but something else had come suddenly to mind. "The other day you mentioned the Half Moon. What do you remember about the place?"

Davey stretched his arms, yawning, arching his back. "I remember it back when Timothy Leary and his son were tried for possession of marijuana by the DA in Poughkeepise—boy, was that a big deal! I remember your teacher, Leo. And there was his pal, the one who got sent to prison—"

"Bob," I said. "Of Badget's Bazaar. There was all sorts of monkey business going on over there, and some of it spilled into the Half Moon."

"Oh, oh," he said with mock alarm. And then, "Pot is one thing, but the other stuff, look at what it does to people. You ought to thank God that your sister, I mean your cousin, got herself straightened out."

"The gravity of Leary's crimes and his prosecution by G. Gordon Liddy, the Dutchess County DA, might seem absurd today, but the battle was symbolic and both sides understood this. In the beginning at least, Leary and friends were seriously trying to expand human consciousness. Their aim was a spiritual revolution. That's what people forget."

I remembered the Castalia Foundation, the Hitchcock Mansion in Millbrook where Timothy Leary and his followers experimented with LSD and meditation and love. I remembered a flock of butterflies one night alighting at the Half Moon Café for supper. What did they eat? Pollen and moonbeams?

Davey came back at me with one of his simple direct questions. "So are the risks of madness and drug addiction preferable to ordinary reality?"

"Don't you think we ought to value the urge to explore consciousness?" I rebutted. "Why do you suppose Adam and Eve ate the apple?"

"I'm just asking. You know I'm interested in this stuff. I don't wanna debate you," he said, adding, "If I were you, I wouldn't talk about shit like this when you're on the job."

"I'm sorry," I said, "but you're such a big target."

It was a dumb thing to say and I started over. "The original Half Moon, you know, was a Dutch ship, and Henry Hudson was an Englishman. Verrazano, an Italian, had previously come into the narrows of the river at its mouth, but Hudson sailed all the way to Albany."

Davey warmed to the new topic, and feeling forgiven, I paused to refill our glasses with firewater.

"Hudson wasn't truly an explorer of the river or the valley, and anyway most of what we know about his trip is from the journals of his First Mate, Juet, who probably hated the Captain. After their initial voyage, Hudson never returned to the river that's named for him. He was obsessed with finding a Northwest passage through Canada to the Pacific. After a terrible winter frozen over in the ice up there, his crew rebelled at the idea of resuming the search. They set Hudson and few stalwarts adrift in a longboat. None were ever seen again. It's why their ghosts still haunt us."

"Obsessions can have strange consequences," Tina quipped, rejoining us. "Wasn't your friend Leo the obsessive type?"

"Oh, captain, my captain!" I said, loosening another sheet to the wind. "Boys and booze and *yo ho ho*. Man, would he have gotten a rise out of my working for the cops!"

"The other guy, Bob, what became of him?" Tina asked, looking at each of us in turn.

Davey said something vague about prison, and I added what I had learned from Liotta, that Bob was still alive and was in fact the executor of Leo's estate. Tina took it in with faraway eyes.

GOOD BYE—THAT IS WHAT the Ouija message was in response

to Davey's first question, "Will I lose ten pounds?" He laughed when the pointer slid to that fateful word and then off the Board. I chuckled too. Tina remained serious. She asked her partner if he had truly committed himself to a diet, or was he hoping that the Board would give him a guarantee of success? If he wasn't serious, she said, the Board would know immediately, and respond in kind to all his questions.

Davey reconsidered. He wasn't ready to diet, he explained— he had eaten so well tonight that he felt like he'd just packed on ten extra pounds. That was okay, Tina said. What if he asked about something else, he wondered. His fingertips were still next to Tina's on the heart shaped pointer, and instantly the planchette slid to the letters *O* and *K*. I was recording all the answers in a notebook.

There followed from Davey a series of short questions, which it must be said, Tina and I coaxed from him. The Ouija replied with *Yes* and *No*, and phonetic significations such as *F U T N K S 2*—i.e., *if you think it's true*.

I had wondered earlier how Tina would utilize the occasion for her own purposes, and I could see how much Davey was enjoying himself in my cousin's hands—such attractive hands, with their olive skin and silver rings, with Nonna's dazzling topaz that ruled over all. She had successfully stretched the detective like taffy, sweetened and softened him, goofed on him and gabbed him up, fed and doused and groused and little-kidded him, all on the way to "making amends," I supposed, whatever that meant. I felt no jealousy, I was beyond that, for the moment at least, nor concerned, as I am so often, about Tina's "condition." Our pilgrim cop needed his mental muscles massaged and his heart brightened, and if Tina's medicine could bring some light into the grooves of his tired brain, I was all for it.

"*U -R -M -O -T -H -E -N -W -H -O -U-T -N- K -U -R,* "
I called out, reading as the planchette glided very swiftly over the talking board. The instrument was well warmed at this stage, and Davey had ceased asking his partner if she were sure she wasn't "pushing the thing." (He had even once lifted his hands suddenly and seen it stop abruptly, and hadn't done that again after Tina acted insulted.) The pointer paused. "Is that all?" Davey asked. The heart shape moved slowly toward the moon in a corner of the board, detoured very deliberately around the word *NO,* and trailed off onto Tina's left thigh.

"Wait a minute," Davey said. "We need an interpretation from our scribe. I asked how come I haven't been aware of these psychic powers it tells me I possess. What's this about *mothen?* Is it *mother?*"

Knees tight together with the Board balanced on them, he twisted his torso carefully, leaning toward me in an effort to read what I had recorded. I corrected him: "You are more than who you think you are. That's how I read it. *Tat tvam asi.*"

"Did it say that? I don't remember that. . ."

"It's my interpretation. Sanskrit, " I said. "That art thou. It means that you're God."

"No shit?"

"That too. The Devil too. Your true self is beyond such dualities. In fact. . ."

"That's enough, Guido," Tina said abruptly. She took the board from their laps and folded it closed with a snap. "You're confusing the Ouija."

Her stern eyes softened after a moment, and then she turned toward Davey, who looked befuddled. Tina touched his chest with the fingertips of her right hand, just as she had done to me on my last visit. She pressed lightly and said, "We'll have to do this again sometime."

CHAPTER 32

To perceive is to apprehend. To apprehend is also to capture. Although I never wore a badge nor banged down the doors of wrong-doers nor risked my life in the line of duty, still my police work made me feel necessary. Mostly, I was in contact with ordinary people, listening intently as I sketched, watching their faces while they spoke: *my* witnesses they became, these witnesses to crime, so sure or else not quite sure of what exactly they had seen. On my very first case, I drew for one anxious woman such a likeness based on her description that her loud exclamations—*That's him! Oh my God, you've got him!*—shook the squad room and several people rushed over to look at my drawing. An arrest and conviction soon followed, and things took off from there. My services were in demand, and I was loaned out, so to speak, up and down the Hudson Valley.

I had originally asked Davey not to refer to my psychic capacities because I know very well how the mention of *psi* phenomena can disturb people who consider themselves rationalists. I wanted to be accepted by my new colleagues for my straight-ahead drawing skills, and when success came, I felt like the little guy out in left field who one afternoon is discovered to have a rocket launcher for a throwing arm. I didn't need to say anything about psi. Even after I learned how many cops are interested in psychics because they actually have helped them out with difficult cases, I kept secret the existence of my secret information. When a hunch of mine contributed directly to collaring a woman wanted on charges of abuse at several nursing homes, I overheard one colleague comment that I had "more female intuition than a female," and I was satisfied with that.

More importantly, this particular remark did not go unnoticed by the beautiful one in blue, she who continued to smile at me whenever we happened to encounter each other. Suddenly I saw—the vision was unbidden and resisted because it seemed so outlandish—that she, Police Sergeant Sandra Lorraine, would soon be my lover, and that I would wear the very hat I so admired, the one presently on her head and under which she kept her auburn hair carefully folded; indeed, *she* would have me wear the hat in bed.

Several instances are worth mentioning here as evidence of the inner forces I had to struggle with throughout my service. Once, while the victim of a rape, a 29 year old woman, brimming with hurt and disgust described to me her attacker as "a greasy turd," behind the pair of awful eyes I put into the portrait I was making, I could see a child locked for hours raging in a narrow closet. Then I saw the man who had once victimized him, and I felt so much pity for the alleged perpetrator that my drawing fell apart uselessly. Another time, another victim's recollection of the assault committed against him had me gulping seawater and then recoiling under a barrage of violent blows. I knew at once the source of the attacker's dismal, unrelenting anger. And, strangest of all, on more than one occasion I felt that the one whom I was sketching was somehow to play a positive role in the victim's life. It was impossible to share such insights, and after all my job was to be a medium of the most technical sort: *I listen, I draw.* This became my motto, and it usually served me well. I considered how surgeons train to do their jobs, never equating the facts of flesh and blood with the *being* of their patients, and seeking a similar detachment, I felt compelled to study human anatomy as I hadn't done since my days in life drawing classes.

An important lesson about the boundary between professionalism and personal predilection came to me when through an observation window, I sketched the portrait of a suspect locked in detention. This 47 year old former school bus driver was about to be charged with the abduction, rape and brutal murder of a high school girl. On the afternoon that he was apprehended, it seemed to me that the funereal aroma of flowers filled the stationhouse. Everybody spoke in whispers, their voices tinged with disgust, and I too became convinced that here before us was a real monster, a human being who had strayed far beyond the boundaries of our shared humanity. Surreptitiously, compulsively, I began to draw his likeness on a page of my pocket pad.

An officer who was already somewhat in awe of my talents noticed what I was about, and rather than chastising me, stood near my shoulder, egging me to "get him down, get that fucker down."

I began to feel terribly queasy, suddenly aware that this must be a violation of the man's rights, and yet I couldn't stop my pencil from performing with scalpel-like precision. My colleague and I watched while the guy worried his hands together, coughed nervously, picked his nose, wiped his hair. The reality of the crime took shape in my imagination: mundane details about the way he'd met the girl, his overtures in the name of love, her resistance, his passions escalating out of control.

A short time later he was exonerated. Another man, a more respectable looking one in corduroy trousers, plaid shirt and sport coat—he'd once been a teacher at a community college—confessed to the abduction, rape and murder. We had all been mistaken. I too with my special insights and clinical skills, I too had borne false witness against my brother. My drawing was a very good study of grotesquery, one such as Leonardo himself might have condoned, but I destroyed it. The pathos of the bus driver, his terrible fear and isolation, my guilt for abusing my privileges as a deputy of the Law, as well as the memory of that horrible crime and its actual perpetrator have never left me.

THERE WERE VARIOUS MESSAGES from Tina to me in the days that followed our reconciliation, the content and means of her communications always unique. Unasked, she delivered to me the name of the ship that my cousin Chris had served aboard during the Viet Nam War, lettering it on a scrap of paper that she rolled into an empty wine bottle and which I discovered on my doorstep. Another time, taped to my apartment door was the recipe for tripe and *cannellini* that my Uncle Tony had loved to make for us as kids. However, there was not as yet the reunion with her mother that I hoped for. To Aunt Josie I said simply, "She'll come around." My aunt replied, "I don't care anymore," which I didn't believe.

Then there were the super-ordinary messages. Some were oracles Tina had obtained from the Ouija Board, which she'd begun using regularly since our night with Davey. (In fact, as I would later learn, Davey returned alone on other occasions to collaborate with her.) I had a hard time deciphering some of these, since they were represented exactly as the Ouija had spelled them, unaccompanied by the questions that had been posed. I knew she was teasing me like this, inviting me to use my talents to decode them. Twice I opened envelopes addressed to me that contained only a sigil carefully drawn in black ink on a sheet of white paper. Once, on my telephone's answer machine I heard her recorded voice chanting, *You must become yourself the labyrinth. You must become yourself. . .*

She thought I needed help, and I did, for despite the way that things were going in my professional life, my stomach churned continually. I was excited and self-satisfied, but I was also confused about where I might be headed. As I had hoped, the police job made a very positive impression on my family: how admirable my artistic calling now seemed because it was in the service of John Law! When I received an enthusiastic letter from a young, second cousin in California who was going to attend a police academy and wanted to hear all about my life as a sketch artist, I sensed instantly that Tina had played a role in this, surprising me once more with her interest in me.

I wasn't going to do this kind of work forever, and when it was over I presumed that I'd continue at the college—I never believed I would become a policeman, and, frankly, I couldn't imagine that I might become a tenured professor either, so late in life. However, it was due to Tina as much as to any other single factor that I was again in contact with the source of my creative gifts. She had been my first student, my disciple and eventual collaborator when as children we had conjured invisible worlds and made them real, and now, once again, she was inspiring me.

As close we were growing, however, Tina's private life remained off limits to me. I discounted most of my aunt's hysterical allegations about her daughter's behavior, but I too felt clueless about such things as how she supported herself. She must have a boyfriend, I'd concluded, perhaps a sugar daddy—she'd always had one if she wanted one, and usually another one waiting in line behind him. I often wondered if she were again using drugs, whether or not of the prescription variety, but my intuition told me that she really was okay. Nevertheless, her independence stung my pride: I had always thought that it was *I* who had himself together and who was therefore *her* caretaker.

"MY DREAM LIFE," I muttered to myself as I was crossing the Green in the November twilight. I was recalling a dream from the previous night: Chief Gottman was lecturing about the importance of art therapy in the prison system, a most improbable occurrence during waking life. Then he showed me a drawing he'd done of a stick figure with a bird on its head. It was so rudimentary that it was charming, and I'd complimented him as I would have a child.

My dream life. I heard the double meaning. I was at the moment something of a local celebrity due to a recent feature about me in the newspaper. The accompanying photograph of "The Artist Cop," showed me at work with my sketchpad; it was a shot I had set up myself, posing with a pencil in my hand, looking up over my reading glasses into the camera. "Art is his beat," the caption read. (Chief Gottman, who never mentioned the story to me, had probably flared his nostrils and snorted when he'd seen it.)

That afternoon in class I'd told my students that police work confirmed for me how the administration of justice, like the recognition of beauty, depends on sensitivity to the singular circumstance.

"Justice for all is the ideal, but justice for the individual must be case specific, as is the apprehension of beauty," I said. "Consider what the Old Masters thought so worthy about the art of portraiture. They weren't merely into flattering wealthy patrons. A great portrait is more than a facsimile, insofar as it does *justice* to its subject."

I flicked on the lights dramatically as the class hour concluded. "Furthermore, they were fascinated by the grotesque as well as the beautiful and saw how nature's exaggerations broaden our perception of its truths. By contrast, today's endless reproductions of so-called beautiful subject matter dull the senses and deprive the imagination. Advertising, the spawn of capitalism, ignores nature's infinite variety and in so doing disparages it. This is one implication of Warhol's work, yes?"

My nervous stomach notwithstanding, I was animated as I hadn't been for years, and this change in me owed a lot to my work for the cops. *My dream life.* I was pleased with myself as I made my way amid my labyrinth, and striding across the darkening Green, I turned my collar up with cosmopolitan panache.

AND IN THOSE EXCITED days there was this, too: a heated meeting of the faculty, closed to all administrators, pertaining to some very wealthy friends of the College who wanted a new studio complex to be named for them and also to be built by their designated agents. Feeling coerced by this second demand, we had already wrangled for two hours about our recommendations to the Board of Trustees, when finally, out of frustration, I burst out: "Who cares who pours the cement—in the end, we're all working for the Man."

I was promptly criticized by Patrick Tremoarian, who said he was shocked that I of all people could be so cavalier about such important matters. Donors usually want their names on buildings, he conceded, but he and his expert friends had already invested considerable thought in the design and choice of an architect for the project—voilà: he produced preliminary drawings. Conversation immediately gravitated to these plans, and I had no opportunity to explain myself more fully. After the meeting, at which nothing was decided but the need for a subsequent meeting, a pair of younger colleagues, both of whom were vying for tenure, refused to speak with me when I tried to pursue my point of view with them.

In a candid, rambling e-mail to President Swenson I wondered what had become of our original vision. I ventured that we were already a finishing school for the children of the ruling classes, but now we were in danger of becoming a wholly owned subsidiary of that same set. More than ever, I pleaded, we needed to encourage the highest independent standards for how the College conducted its business, and so, what was required was a statement from her about the importance of "basics"—basics on which future developments could be founded. I'm not quite sure what I expected her to do, but I averred that these basics were more important than the names on our buildings. Let money talk, it always did, even before the fashion for outsized memorial plaques with ludicrous sounding designations like the Q. W. Durfee Parking Lot at the Helgot and Katrina Burlington Spool Studio Complex for Samytech Computer Arts. The people to whom those names were attached would pass from memory soon enough. Life is short, but art is long, I concluded.

I should never have put my spleen so hastily into an irretrievable message. However, a day later Rosa Swenson did reply with a terse note saying she would take into consideration my "passionate feelings for the College." Precisely how she would do this I did not learn, and anyway, my pique soon subsided. I couldn't remain animated about the coup that Tremoarian and his clique were plotting. I had more important things to attend to.

However, that unhappy faculty meeting had repercussions for me. I was now being referred to by some younger colleagues and a few snarky students as "The Policeman." Jesse Leiper mentioned that he'd also overheard people wondering if I were a closet fascist and a spy for the Administration. I was nettled to no end by this irony: I have never even considered myself as a reformer, much less as an enforcer. I am conservative about some things, it's true, but this is the prerogative of those with experience and taste.

The course of my life between police stations and classrooms and my contrasting urges for order and for innovation, my devotion to the classics and my opposition to the obscenities of present times, these were not always so easy to negotiate. I was a little fearful of losing my way within the folds of my own brain. I was in danger of falling prey to the monster of self-righteousness. I was becoming that curiosity of American culture, the eccentric middle-aged bachelor whose intellectual pretensions and arcane interests keep him at large in the groves of academe; in other words, The Professor. I disdained that nomenclature as much as I did The Policeman.

THIS IS WHAT I told my students at my next lecture:

"Necessity was said by the Greeks to be an ancient, ancient goddess, and was never given a face. *Ananke.* She was the formless spouse of *Kronos*, Father Time. She was the mother of the Fates and Furies, she is the one whom Leonardo calls *the mistress and guide of nature . . .the theme and inventress.*

"The Renaissance was an era of allegorical thinking when the value of metaphor was widely appreciated. It was the beginning of modernism, but also a time to recover such classical traditions as hermeticism, astrology, and alchemy. Since it was ostensibly a Christian era, any imputation of heresy was dangerous, and yet, for a while, such free thinkers as Ficino and Bruno were able to speculate how Christian theology might be amalgamated with the philosophies of Plato and Plotinus. Bruno would eventually pay with his life for wondering openly about these sorts of things. At the court of the Medici, Sandro Botticelli was for a while steeped in similar ideas, but like others in Florence, he too came under the influence of the zealot Girolamo Savonarola. It is thought that Botticelli destroyed some of his own, now unknown works in Savonarola's infamous 'Bonfire of the Vanities.'

"Whenever the focus of a culture shifts away from dogma to experiential knowledge or gnosis, attention shifts to what Christians call the Holy Spirit. Jesus told his followers that he would send the Holy Spirit to sustain them once he was gone, and in the 1200s, some sects proclaimed that a universal Age of the Holy Ghost had arrived. Dangerous sounding stuff to the establishment Church, and yet despite the great power amassed by Courts of Inquisition in the 13th Century, as if to counter their injustices, a tremendous devotion to the Blessed Mother spontaneously manifested among the masses. Great cathedrals in her honor were erected, the work of generations of anonymous artisans, and through these masterpieces, the builders passed down many secrets of hermeticism. Interestingly, at this time the cult of courtly love also arose, which strove to sublimate earthly pleasures in favor of the Divine Feminine—or so the troubadours sang.

"Astrologically speaking, it's more accurate to imagine that the current era, the Age of Aquarius, is the Age of the Holy Spirit. Think about Aquarius symbolically: it's the water carrier, but it's not a water sign; it's an air sign. The air, the wind, invisibly, formlessly carries life-giving moisture. Now what about that Holy Grail everybody is always searching for? One legend says its real purpose is to serve God—and so leap with me, Christian or not: what might it mean to you to work in concert with the principle, a feminine one, that Leonardo Da Vinci calls Necessity?"

BESIDES THE SKETCH PORTRAITS I did for the cops, I produced almost no other visual art during this period. I did write plenty in my journal, however, and I began to outline what I would need to include about Leo and Bob if I were ever to see my project through and do justice to them and to the past we'd shared. I began to doodle in the journal margins, too, as Leonardo did in his notebooks. One day, while reading through *Lives of the Artists*, I was seized by a story Vasari tells about the maestro.

While still a young man, having passed from Verocchio's tutelage and now established in his own workshop, Leonardo was visited by his father, Ser Piero, who sought of his son some work. As a favor to a farmer of whom Ser Piero was fond, he had offered to have painted by Leonardo a dragon on the man's buckler, a small round shield. The project caught the maestro's fancy, and typical of the thorough fashion with which he applied science and art in all matters, Leonardo gathered for weeks into his study the corpses of "lizards great and small," all manner of birds and insects, strange creatures of the water, bats, tortoises and so forth, whatever might serve his imagination. So long did he work on the dragon, Vasari tells us, "that the stench of dead animals in that room was past bearing, but Leonardo did not notice it, so great was the love that he bore towards art." At long last, after his father and the farmer both had forgotten the project, when Ser Piero was informed that the shield was ready, he called on Leonardo, who prepared in his room the buckler *cum* dragon on an easel. Having displayed it in the proper light in order to produce the effect that he desired, Leonardo invited his father to view it. Vasari says Ser Piero was surprised, startled, and not realizing it was the object, "nor merely the painted form upon it," retreated till Leonardo stopped him. "This work serves the end for which it was made," he said to his father. "Take it then, carry it away, since this is the effect that it was meant to produce."

Ser Piero has always struck me as a rather petty person, and the rest of the story bears this out. He was a well-off accountant of Florence, the city of gold florins, and he saw only the worth in gold of the splendid product Leonardo had made for him. He kept the object for himself, and substituted for the farmer another one painted with a heart pierced by an arrow, one that he had found in the market place. The dragon shield he sold secretly for a hundred ducats to some art dealers in Florence, who, Vasari says, sold it in turn to the Duke of Milan for triple that price. Matter-of-factly, Vasari concludes this story saying only that "Leonardo then made a picture of Our Lady," and proceeds to several other anecdotes about the maestro.

The dragon buckler is unfortunately lost, though not the story. Leonardo seems to have been a gentle man in every aspect of his demeanor, but I can imagine the satisfaction he would have felt at his father's fright. The son, who was never allowed to forget that he was a bastard sired on a Tuscan hill girl, showed up his crass old man, and did him justice literally by leaving him to his own devices.

CHAPTER 33

M Y MOTHER AND I kept a weekly appointment for lunch at the Villa Giustovera, where she lived alone amid its dilapidated grandeur. Having sold off much of the acreage from the original farm to real estate developers, she subsisted on that income combined with what she also earned as a specialty baker. Most mornings she worked at her ovens: Italian bread and layer cakes, sheet cakes, cheesecakes throughout the week except for Friday—Fridays were for her creative *panettoni. Cannoli* and trays of parti-colored cookies she produced on Saturdays and Sundays. I would visit on Mondays when she didn't work, often having stopped on my way to fill some request of hers for supplies.

Monday was always our Sabbath in the years of the family run restaurant, but unlike former times when my mother, my father, and I made a pleasurable habit of eating out, and in so doing sampled the wares of competitors, nowadays my suggestion that we do so was usually rejected. She had "heard things" about Bel'monte, and "nobody likes the cooking at Stegler's," and "Peekskill is too far to drive just for lunch," she would say. "I'll make something nice for you at home."

The Valley is often beautiful in early November, and on one particular afternoon the leaves were still golden where they'd fallen on the Villa's green lawns, the mild sun golden above the nearly naked trees. We were seated on the patio outside the main dining room, and although the cement was damp and crumbling in the shadow of a wall whose rusted rain gutter hung loose, a warm light pooled in another place where we set a cocktail table and chairs. Below the patio's edge was the weedy broken basin that had once been a tiled fishpond with a plashing fountain and colored lights.

How strange, I thought, to feel my age in the presence of my aged mother! During my youth, how often I had pleaded, *See me for who I am*, and yet whoever I have been, she has always seen me as her son. If as a child I squirmed uncomfortably with having to bear the weight of her confidences, and if as a teenager I sought to escape her with unfeeling vehemence, as a man I am grateful that she has never tried to tether me. I have always returned home of my own volition.

This was not an old lady in her buttoned cardigan, charcoal colored under a red maple losing its last leaves. This was a woman who had once been almost glamorous, as Ida Lupino and Jackie Kennedy were. *That* woman was "Ann," rather than Anna—a woman whom I had once suspected of having an affair with Bob Badget, of all people. She was not now a doddering caricature of her former self, wearing a pink elastic turban, lipstick pink as Diana Durban's, this present day Anna Diamante who had always also been "Mom" and more often "Ma" to me. I liked to remind her that she was still quite attractive, and told her that she could yet have gentlemen friends if she wanted them. Happy to be complimented, she'd reply, "Oh?" with an arch of her plucked brows over pretty hazel eyes. Then again, sometimes she'd said, "I don't believe you," and stuck a cigarette in her mouth and frowned.

How much smoke she'd made to veil that frown! Her story of how she began was that it was because of my father. "He thought I'd look good sitting with a cigarette at the bar, that it would be good for business." I told her that I thought she'd been angry since those days, back when they'd tried so many things to help the Business. And I told her, "Maybe you've been sad and mad since the first time your mother ironed you out, dressed you down, or whatever it was that Nonna did to keep you here at home with her." Smoking mad, I claimed she was, and I began to seethe a little myself over how much living my mother had missed out on. I wanted to awaken her to the fact that it wasn't too late, there was plenty of life ahead of her, she didn't have to be a hermit. Or a cigarette addict.

I pushed things a little too far one time when I asked her why she had never put a match to the Place, as she'd said so many times she wanted to do, to collect the insurance money: weren't there "certain persons" who could arrange that? As if I'd read her thoughts a little too accurately she immediately replied, "And then what would become of me?" I should have asked right then what had become of her friend Geppina.

Or she would light another cigarette and look me over with pride: I was her educated son, her passionate son, the sensitive one who cared enough to scold his mother. The Policeman. "*Hai ragione!*" she said, fumbling with her matches, mumbling something to me about "your frickin' father." She knew that she should stop her heavy smoking and promised that someday she *would*, "only this stupid habit keeps me company."

But also on those placid afternoons while we strolled the weedy walkways among the late blooming roses, I remembered my mother the-very-much-in-charge, my mother the-quite-well-accomplished, the calm one, the stoical one who accepted life's vagaries: "Not a big deal" that the roof leaked in the recreation room, since, of course, "things can always go bad." Her protective pessimism, she called it. The sill plates rotting under the office: "No problemo." Nor was huddling next to her oven to keep warm because the radiators were turned off in almost every room. Whatever might be wanting, the Villa was still her home; after the death of her brother Tony, with whom she had grown close before his final fatal heart attack, she had told me with a sigh and a laugh that she wouldn't be ready to leave the Place until "the end."

"Don't worry about me, my son." A hand on my cheek. "No problemo. Isn't that what they all say nowadays? See, I learned some Spanish."

A car raced down Widener Road squealing on a curve. "Let them straighten the damn road so everybody can speed!" she shouted after it. "Where do they have to go like that?" And another Benson & Hedges between her lips, the match in her fingers strike, strike, striking a flame.

My mother, who has chosen to stay put and make of her life more than a lamentation, and who, I must admit, lives at the Villa *sola* but contentedly. She in the gray cardigan I recognize as one that I cast off years ago, she who puffs her clouds of smoke and is satisfied with such small pleasures. A chickadee chips on a branch and she smiles up at it. She points out to me the uncut grass where a scintilla of light is reflected from a window's darkened glass; when a cloud crosses the sun and the star shape vanishes, she says, "That's something, huh?" This also is my mom.

Today we eat a salmon salad I've brought, a recipe of my own I want to show off: capers and crumbled feta cheese—"has to be the real sheep feta, you know, and a couple of smashed anchovies"—a recipe I happily share. This is the day I learn how my mother has lately "gotten a little closer to God," and that she has done it at an evangelical prayer meeting.

"It wasn't at all like a Catholic mass. And it was outside under a tent. They had hot air blowers, mind you. And what a lot of excitement. The Holy Ghost came into them and they were speaking in tongues! Dancing in the aisles. Arms like this." She raises her arms and sways back and forth in her chair.

I'm amazed that my mother has done something so unorthodox; not that she's ever been such a devoted Catholic, but the cultural gap seems to me a huge one for her to have crossed, even as a tourist. She's evidently pleased to read on my face the effect of this news. I am indeed speechless, deliberating my response. I tell her that I'm all for the Holy Spirit in whatever form it comes. She should know her son isn't stuck on the Church of Rome, but then I catch myself starting to lecture and stop. I want to hear more about her experience.

"I went with your Aunt Josie and one of her friends, Sally Long. But now Josie is afraid we could get excommunicated if the monsignor at Saint Mary's finds out. She called me twice to tell me this. We could all get excommunicated, she said. Can you imagine? That's Josie for you."

"You're not gonna get excommunicated, Ma. You can tell her I said so."

It is Aunt Josie's way to shiver with regret if she believes she might have done something so trivial as to have broken a dietary stricture prescribed by her doctor. "Making an opera," is what Uncle Tony used to call it. And then I'm off on that, spoofing in order to get my mother to laugh: "In Josie's first act, we're all sympathetic to her plight, but by the end of act two our patience has begun to wane, since by then she's worked herself into a panic. In act three, along with her, we throw our hands up to Heaven. Then we wait to see what happens in act four: is this opera a comedy or a tragedy?"

I note that my mother's smile is fading. "Josie needs a crisis just to feel alive," I conclude. "But look how well she's doing. She'll probably outlive us all."

It's the wrong note. My mother lights another cigarette. I see how she filters life and takes shelter in the smoke. Perhaps she needs to shield herself from me as well as from others? She crinkles her eyes, a light comes into them, and then my mother shakes her head and continues with her odd enthusiasm for the tent revival.

"It reminded me of the movie, *Elmer Gantry.* Only it was real—I think the preacher man was real. Somebody actually threw down her crutches and an old man stood up from his wheelchair to praise God. You know, *Praise Him! Praise Jesus!* Screaming it out, all the holy roller stuff." She wiggles her fingers toward the sky. "I tell you, it doesn't happen in a Catholic church. And all the singing. Everybody knew the words or else they just kept shouting, *Praise God!*" She blows a stream of smoke up to Heaven.

"Were there Black people?"

"Sure, Blacks, Whites. That Filipino guy from Stop and Shop that was friends with your uncle Tony. His whole family was there too."

"Anybody handle snakes?"

"No, no. But people were very sincere. They were very nice to Josie and me. Not pushy."

"You going again?"

"Could be. But your aunt Josie! Excommunicated! Can you imagine?"

"Let me know if you do go, because I might be interested."

"You? Really?"

"Sure. Why not?"

She's having trouble striking a match in the wind, and finally cups the matchbook to protect the little flame she manages to scratch up. Into the round opening of her hands—*Here's the Church and here's the steeple*—she thrusts the tip of her cigarette and pulls hard—*Open it up and see the people*—drawing her cheeks in tightly. She catches fire, shakes out the match, and then takes the cigarette, lady-like, between two long fingers. All this in one continuous motion, exhaling a plume of white smoke very elegantly. My mother tossing her head back, breathing out the smoke slowly, savoring the pleasure. She will never quit.

After a moment: "People need reassurance, especially when they get near the end." She casts a nervous eye toward me. I've occasionally heard things like this from her, but her health reports are good, she always says.

Then: "You're not gonna believe who I heard from! Mr. Manaperta's *daughter!* I told you he died, right?"

"Yes, you did. Caballo, too, both of them nearly a hundred years old. Manaperta had a daughter?"

"Margherita. She's lived her whole life on Avenue T in Brooklyn, a spinster. Manaperta was married after he left us. Did you know that? When he was almost seventy. Can you imagine? I never met the wife or the daughter, but out of the blue, she telephones me to say that inside his old trunk she found a package with your name on it, addressed here at the Villa Giustovera. He never mailed it, but he must have wanted you to have it."

I'm quiet.

"Who knows what it is? Grandpa's best friend, you remember. *S'a benedico!*" She crosses herself, blessing the soul of Carlo Manaperta, as do I automatically. When I raise my eyes, I catch a glimpse of a hawk circling, the feathers of its red tail catching sunlight.

"Let me go get it for you " she says, rising from her chair on the patio.

I rest a hand on her forearm. "Wait a second." I point to the hawk riding the air currents high above us. My grandmother once said I have eyes like a hawk, that I see everything, and that my hawk-shaped nose was like her own nose, and that her nose was also like that of her younger brother Guido who died of the Spanish Influenza back in Milano. The gliding hawk, wings outstretched, appears to be diving, and on the earth below, its shadow is sliding toward us.

Then I know what the gift is that Manaperta has bequeathed me: the tiny icon that hung for years in his work shed, the tarnished silver Christ on an ebony cross, his arms outstretched, triumphant over death, a silver skull and crossbones at his feet.

"Jesus of the Pirates."

"What?"

I watch the shadow now more closely than the hawk itself, watch the space it covers so quickly. *Saccio che saccio.* The scent of varnish and tobacco, a wooden sword too heavy for me when I first hefted it in his shop, clapping it against the legs of his bench. A veiled story about my grandmother and signor Caballo.

My mother smiles and the creases around her eyes fold softly. Her mouth looks freshly painted, the lips unexpectedly moist. I have always loved the shape of her mouth, always watched it when she spoke, watched between the lips for the tip of her tongue to emerge. When I was young, with her tongue tip she would moisten a hanky and dab at any blemish on my face, a speck of food, even a freckle, to attack with mother-love the shadow of any imperfection.

I EXPLAINED TO HER that for reasons of my own, I wanted to be alone when I unwrapped "my gift from the Beyond." I made my voice sound spooky for a laugh and waved the packet with mock ceremony. We were in the foyer of the Villa and I was on my way out. She seemed disappointed at this, knitting her brows together, but then she shrugged. She kissed me and lit a cigarette to send me off.

There was no note included with the package, and I was disappointed not to have anything more from Mr. Manaperta's last days. Within the packet that his daughter had addressed to me in care of my mother, was another one that Manaperta's living fingers had once neatly wrapped in brittle paper and tied with string. Who knows why it was left unopened and never mailed? The fact that it had lain in his seaman's trunk imbued it with further mystery, and I raised it to my face, searching for those scents I remembered from his shed behind the Villa. I detected nothing but the stale smell of the brown paper, probably cut from a shopping bag ages ago. My name had been scrawled on it with a thin, black ballpoint, as well as the address of the Villa Giustovera.

I lit some incense at my altar and unwrapped my gift. I remembered his nicotine stained fingers that now were dust. I remembered those eternal moments with him in his shed behind the Villa, where at his workbench like a monk he would raise a chalice of rum and glance at the tiny crucifix I was now holding in my hands. I blessed his memory.

"There's no going back," I said aloud.

EVEN THOUGH THE PLASTER on its walls is crumbling, and the walls themselves have buckled and its ceilings leak, the Villa is still our home, a hearth where until her last day my mother will keep a fire burning. As my father used to say, *Io saccio che saccio*—I know what I know. I love my mother, but for years I was angry with her, angry that although she never left the Villa, in effect she did leave my dad and me. It goes without saying that the Place will someday be my inheritance, but how will I ever be free of it?

It is said that August Kekulé, the chemist, dreamt of a serpent eating its own tail and then on waking solved the riddle of the benzene ring with its linked atoms of carbon. At my apartment, after Manaperta touched me from the Other Side, I took a diamond ring, and with the jewel I incised a zero on my bedroom mirror. Then I contemplated my face inside this circle, I contemplated my life that's based on carbon, and my very name, my father's family name. I passed into a reverie and saw how I have always sought to fill myself with women, how I want to drink them like milk. I saw a witch who has two faces—no, she has many faces and many names.

I GIVE YOU, MY mother, I give you back your own reflection in the gesture you have made so often, your forefinger pointing to Heaven like the exclamation made by Saint Anne, whom Leonardo sketched in charcoal behind her daughter, Mary, and the Holy Infant and his cousin, John the Baptist. Saint Anne who is almost Mary's double looking back on them.

My mother, I give you also Leonardo's portrait that once was thought to be John the Baptist when he was a wild man making ready the way for Jesus, nude save for the leopard skin draped over his loins: a rather effeminate figure seated in a dark grotto, with his right hand pointing, the index finger directing our eyes over his left shoulder into the *sfumato* of the painting's green-black woods, as if to indicate a mystery is there. His left hand along his staff is pointing too, pointing down, down toward the Earth from which we have come and to which we will return. Bacchus they call him today in the Louvre; Dionysos, I would say. Some speculate that he is modeled on a boy whom Leonardo loved.

"Now hear this," Tina's voice on my telephone answer machine. "In the Seventh place is the Devil. Not to fear, Guido D. You've got his number, no?"

I replayed the message three times. The staccato of her speech caused me to wince. What if she were stoned? What if my lost and found cousin were on the verge of what Aunt Josie calls "an episode?"

I was going to be late for work, and I gathered books into my backpack. Her message must have arrived very early, for I had checked my machine before going to sleep the previous night. I glanced at my appointment book. My life had become subsumed by routine, and my celebrity had definitely lost its luster. *The Devil, huh?*

When the gold of autumn falls and the windblown spores of moldering leaves bring tears to my eyes and redden their whites with spidery lines, when the days grow dark and cold, my devil, self-doubt, arrives. November rattles me with its bone black trees, and in anticipation of my birthday at month's end I tend to grow depressed. The nearly coinciding holiday of Thanksgiving has always overshadowed it, but what is that day lately, except for my mother, me, Aunt Josie, and an oversized turkey? Oh, there's also a pan of lasagna, for sure. But Tina hasn't joined us since her father's death. What a family! Hardly Italians, I think: there are so few of us at table.

I looked at myself in my mirror one day, proclaimed, "You look terrible," and with that malediction I fell ill. After two weeks nursing myself, sparing my voice and drinking hot tea brewed from Yerba Santa, never missing a class at school, unwanted by the cops, thank God, my symptoms ameliorated. I was still feverish some nights and although I could catch a chill from touching anything made of metal, I went on. All my life I've been subject to these visitations as if by the spirit of the Spanish Influenza that took so many of my grandparents' generation, including my grand uncle Guido.

Despite my daily routines of yoga and meditation, or maybe because of them, my back ached, my knees and elbows creaked. I berated myself as a weakling. I judged my present life, apparently so well ordered, as but a signature of my failure to have a lover. My brain was wrapped in wet gauze, and I continued to drip mucous from my nose, which was red and felt hideously large. I tried to laugh through my self-pity when by chance I glimpsed my profile reflected in a store window; the size of my nose showed I was a prevaricator, no? Who could ever love such a specimen?

My eyes ran with saltwater. I could no longer bear my reflection. I grew out my ever whitening beard, combed my hair by touch, and with closed eyes brushed my teeth because the drain hole in the bathroom sink had lately begun to revolt me. In a frenzy of despair one black Saturday, I clutched Manaperta's cross, and beating my chest with my fist, I debated whether to go to Confession, something I hadn't done in decades.

I declined invitations to socialize for fear that I would in my weakened state contract an even worse malady. Not that I had much of a social life—I spent too much time with students, and that was mainly because I could keep them as close as I wanted while I also kept them away. Why wasn't I in some kind of monastery by now, I who had always claimed to be more interested in the gifts of the Spirit than in the pleasures of the Flesh? Or was it really the opposite?

Davey learned how terrible I was feeling and kept in touch. I sought to disguise my condition from everybody else, especially Tina, although she probably knew. What more could she do for me? Oracles and herbs: thank you very much. Soon she'd be headed South as she did every winter, far away from her mother and the rest of us. I was ashamed to admit how much I had come to depend on seeing her, I, who have always believed the women of my family rely too much on me.

I broke two lunch dates in a row with my mother. Seeking some sympathy from her over the phone, coughing and wheezing, I said that I could well imagine how the Famous Flu had choked the life from our ancestors. She reprimanded me because I hadn't been dressed warmly a few weeks earlier when helping her to rake and burn leaves at the Villa. I told her angrily that not only the smoke but the Villa itself had made me sick due to its leaking roof and its unheated rooms where, sealed off from sunshine, rotting things lived.

"Thank you very much!" she said indignantly. "The Board of Health doesn't agree with you, by the way. I was just inspected last week."

"I didn't mean it like that," I whined. "I have allergies, Ma. People get them as they age. They weaken your immune system and then you get sick with some bug or other. Did it ever occur to you that some of your health complaints are related to your living situation? And your cigarettes, but let's not discuss *them*."

The telephone receiver was hot in my hand, and I reached it

away from my ear to cool. At arm's length I studied it. I felt as if I'd never seen anything quite so bizarre. I could hear my mother's voice sieved out through the pinholes of the boney thing, the distant voice of a tiny, trapped creature.

"You want me to come over there?" she said. It sounded like a threat. "Guido?"

I didn't answer her.

"Okay, then. Go to a doctor if you're sick. You hear me, Guido?"

I heard her, my mother, reacting as she had always to any illness of mine. Pinched and helpless she sounded, but also as if I were to blame not only for being sick, but also for her distress about it. I thought that her whole life she had been frightened by her capacity to love, and I felt pity for her more than for myself.

CHAPTER 34

I F I HAVE CHOSEN all my life to be on my own, that is, alone, and was not actually abandoned either by parents or anyone who loved me, still there is the feeling that I've been neglected. Many artists will know what I mean when I say that despite evidence to the contrary, I believe I haven't had the recognition I deserve. Police work satisfied some of my hunger to be of use, and my teaching does too, of course, and yet there is this *absence*. I have not been *known*. Does it originate with my parents' incomprehension of my creative gifts? Christ, it's embarrassing to suppose this—and even more disconcerting to think I substituted Leo's interest in me not so much for my father's, but for my grandmother's after she died.

IT'S IT, WE WENT, passing the word, the wink, the reefer with its glowing tip. *The happening thing.*

I prophesied: "In 1969, a man will walk on the Moon." I blew a ring of smoke to Leo who sat opposite me on the sofa in his studio. "*Really.*"

"*Le soixante-neuf,*" he said, looking up from the magazine he was paging through. His eyes were red. He pushed back his spectacles with the middle finger of his left hand. "Only one more year," he said, licking that finger, turning a page.

He passed over to me an article about John Cage, but before I could even glance at it at, he began to lecture. For starters, he said, Cage was very nice, the nicest sort of man, but his music was boring. What was more interesting was what he said about it, and it was as if his words needed to be heard in counterpoint. His scores had to be played precisely and sometimes on instruments that weren't instruments at all, like glasses of water or bananas. Prepared piano meant that keys had been muted, their hammers fitted with cotton, for example, and then you couldn't know how the music would sound until it came out, because what's *really* real can't be decided ahead of time. That was *very* interesting, and its intention was to open your ears to the life all around you. "It's it," Leo pronounced. Furthermore, Cage could hit his mark "*repeatedly.*" For emphasis he lowered the spectacles on his stubby nose and stared at me over the top. "It helps that nobody else quite knows what he's aiming at. An artist's way to success is always unique, *cheri.*

"But give me the symphonies of Mahler instead, give me some tears," he said. "With Mahler I have things to celebrate, in spite of the history of Western Civilization. Hope for the future, *eh?* Give me John Cage and I have the present, whatever it holds. He's very big on chance events, you know. That's what a Happening is. A frame, or a *cage,* if you like, for the present moment and what's happening here and now. Interesting if you add attention. The mundane plus attention becomes interesting."

He made a sad face. I zeroed in, trying to penetrate his mind. I came up utterly blank and thought that my emptiness might be a form of *satori.* I had read how such an experience could occur suddenly, unexpectedly if you were prepared to recognize it.

"Call him the daddy of the Happening, like this magazine says. Sure. Let John Cage be the pappy. But Dada was before and was always and *is*. The Zen cats know about that. When they charge their brushes with ink and draw circles, the universe *chances* to show. You dig?"

I definitely thought that I dug. I nonchalantly put the hot roach into my mouth and chewed and swallowed.

"A man with a flute plays a song," Leo continued. "A ballerina dances on the points of her toes. How does she do it? Oh yeah, lots of practice, but really, she doesn't know. Can we say that it's *because* of the music or choreography? Or is it because she was born in Moscow? Because she has good bones? Because her mother pushed her? A most improbable sort of movement and she makes it look beautiful. Because what? Because she's put all her attention into balancing on those toes. It's it. Just this."

He snatched the magazine back from me. We were concluding what was to be my final private lesson, only I didn't know it yet.

"Take Da Vinci, take his famous *sfumato* effect. Paintings so dark they look as if they're eating their own light." He leaned forward on the ratty cushions of his sofa. From behind his ear he produced another joint, lit it, contemplated the burning coal, daubed the paper with a gob of spit. "The smoke of uncertainty," he said, exhaling into my face. "Maybe tomorrow, the mushroom cloud—who knows?" He kept his eyes on me. "Men will walk on the Moon one year from now? So you say, my little psychic. We will see." His glasses were shining.

He had more than once called *me* a flirt, but I was ignorant of the implications, and as it turned out, my innocence was my shield. He laid off when he realized I wasn't going to bed with him. In those days, I didn't go to bed with anybody, and Leo, after all, did have some scruples: I never heard of him taking advantage of the unprepared or underage. When he was on the make he was very persuasive, seductive, his trump card his neediness. Afterwards, when it was over, he'd whine that nobody had ever loved him just for himself: everyone always wanted something from him.

He passed over the joint and went onto his latest favorite subject, the College, and all that it would mean for students like me, kids whose financial resources were limited, who were as he put it, "economically deprived, culturally naïve, but nevertheless gifted." I was soon to graduate from high school and a place was already reserved for me at HRC. At Leo's urging and with my high school guidance counselor's support, I had applied for a scholarship from something called the Kent Foundation—the name has always made me think of my father's cigarettes—and had won from them more money than I would have dreamed. "Why do you think I drew your horoscope?" Leo said. "Jupiter smiles on you, *cheri*. Just don't take his munificence for granted."

I was highly stoned. Reefer in hand, I stood slowly and drifted over beneath the studio skylight. *It's it*, I said to myself happily. *I'm, like, one of the* ones.

Full of himself, Leo began to describe the consortium that was bankrolling the expansion of the College. They were digging out their deep pockets, those philanthropists—"It means lovers of men," Leo reminded me—lovers of the arts who hung around with the likes of Lenny Bernstein, the Kennedys and the Kents. He explained how my family's economic limitations were actually working out in my favor. I had never thought of myself as disadvantaged in any way, and instead had believed I was lucky. I'd rolled snake eyes when I needed them, right? It hurt my pride to think of myself as underprivileged.

Leo continued, explaining how he too had started out as what he called *une ambrosie:* "No more than a weed, a piece of ragweed," just like his heroes Rimbaud and Genet. Then he had met those well-heeled women. Then he had met their husbands, and "On more than one occasion it was *monsieur* who proved the more helpful."

He looked at me sideways, raised his eyebrows. "*C'est vrai, cheri.* I can be such a whore." He wasn't laughing when he said that.

I took a step back, feeling confused but afraid to show it. My eyes were on the reefer between my fingers. Two silver threads of smoke rose from the ember, twined and split, rejoined each other, merging as one overhead. I thought of the caduceus, its pair of serpents, crowned with the wings of Mercury, the messenger. Then a sun shaft broke through the skylight, and looking up I saw a mist of gold with many tiny angels floating through it. The flesh of my hand glowed whitely for an instant. Then the sun was blocked and I saw the window glass pocked with pigeon shit and smattered soot. And yet this too was *It,* the ever happening *Now.*

And that was when I realized that whatever the future promised, something else was going to end. *He's going to break up with me.* I blushed to have used these words, ashamed to think that we'd been— what exactly had we been to each other? *Thanks to him I'm a shining star, the Kent Foundation says, and so now he doesn't want me any-more—is that it?* I contemplated the crazy sense of this. *Generous Leo,* I thought sarcastically, whom I actually loved in spite of everything.

"I saw your father in Poughkeepsie the other day. I asked him how come he never stops by the Café. He said he doesn't want to embarrass you. Your old man embarrasses you?"

"Christ, yes," I said, emerging from my reverie.

"Christ is the Son of God. We had a little talk, your daddy and me."

"What? You hung out with him?"

"Your father used to come around with Larry Bell. *Lorenzo*, as he calls him. Arm-and-arm like a couple of boys from the old country. Very cute."

Cute? Did he actually say that—I had never heard my father described as cute, and I could imagine what he would have thought about Leo's implication. My father had always evinced a stereotypical Old World revulsion of homosexuality, and yet, come to think of it, I had in fact seen him more than once drape his arm around Larry Bell, or walk hand-in-hand with him. Lorenzo Bellocielo: *Bello mio*, he sometimes called him. I was frozen under Leo's watching eyes, bummed completely out of my high. What was his angle?

A hundred years later, I'm still asking myself, and still do wonder sometimes if I ought to have had sex with him. Surely the spirit of the times condoned such experimentation, but I wasn't drawn to him like that, and furthermore I wanted my first time to be with the girl to whom I had given my heart. Gwendolyn Glass.

I didn't want to hear anymore about my father or about Larry Bell, who, like my cousin Chris, seemed above the inner turmoil I attributed to my failure at being neither completely Italian nor truly American. I thought that I was supposed to be rational and optimistic, devoted to truth and justice; I thought that I was supposed to be cool and stylish, a gentleman, except when, like a switchblade jumping from its handle, passion shot through me for reasons of its own—that was Italian and I was afraid of it. My father could be like that, and I had made a point of doing whatever it took to distinguish myself from him.

"Your father is happy, you know, about your scholarship. He's proud of you, Diamond. Don't turn your back on him. I never really knew *my* father. . ." Leo mumbled something more, but I had wandered into a far corner of the studio mulling my thoughts. I was already planning to use the Kent money to declare myself financially emancipated from my parents once I began college. This meant that they would not be responsible for the cost of my education, nor would they have much to say thereafter about my life, or so I thought. I also figured I could earn money by modeling for art classes at the College or in New York, and I knew that if I had to, I could get restaurant work to support myself.

Next to me on the wall, pinned up lopsided, there was a poster reproduction of a painting by Paul Klee. Two of Leo's canvases had been propped upright beneath it on the floor, and that print of Klee, a masterpiece, was a good visual foil for the actual Declares below it. In one, a splotch of elemental earth held something bright, like a pearl or a jewel. I wanted to pluck it out and swallow it.

"Dig me, Diamond? Like *now*."

Leo in white, white clothes: tee shirt tight across his pot belly, white slacks, new white tennis sneakers too. Full-dress captain of the joint, who orders me to drop my dish-wash-rag, tells me that I am playing cook tonight. I am being given a field promotion. I am to take the place of the ailing MacDermond, Mack-the-Knife. I am to run the kitchen.

"I know you can do it." Smiling, showing me his baby tooth.

This is the moment I have long awaited, and its value both to me and to Leo is understood. Quick as can be, to the boss I say, "And this would also include a raise per hour of some considerable sort, won'tit, Cap'ain?"

I am by now on the books at the Café, being paid to bus tables and do kitchen prep. I also get a split of the tips from the waitress pool, and *upstairs*, as I refer to my work modeling in Leo's studio, I am paid in cash also, rather than bartering my time for private lessons. So I have it good, but hell, I know I'm worth a lot, especially tonight, with Leo in a bind. I want a bigger cut of the action: it's the piratical way.

The Captain grins, his bluster gone, replaced by what else can I call it, a sense of pride in me, his protégé. *Dear Leo* he looks, the whacky father figure whom his crew loves, who juts his jaw forward, showing me that broken tooth again, a symbol for his childish heart. "Sure, Diamond. You get what Macky gets when you do his job."

His hand on my shoulder. I nod.

The menu is easy: short order grill, three kinds of specialty sandwich, pizza, spaghetti and meatballs, and the house salad, which is a chef's salad that I have great plans to improve. It's all stuff my mother or Mr. Schnock could do one-handed, simple fare that I've helped Macky prepare since last summer. I wipe both palms on my apron. Leo watches, then he winks at Gabby who is smoking a cigarette nearby, grubby and grouchy as usual.

"My how you've grown," says the Captain to me.

"Why thank'e, sir," says I.

IN THE YEAR SINCE I signed on, I've gained another inch in height, and resuming my weight lifting, I'm five feet ten inches of self-confidence. This is my senior year of high school, and despite my father's taunting that my long hair makes me look like a fairy, I grow it out, until it hangs well over my collar, long as the Beatles are wearing theirs. Also, I carefully cultivate a wispy goatee, the first of many to follow, and establish the habit of shaving it off periodically, so that I can renew the pleasure of shaping it whenever I decide to grow it back. I have started to use a straight razor for this, which with its faux-onyx handle is a thing both beautiful and dangerous. I believe that the beard makes my nose seem smaller.

According to Bob, who has lately taken a shine to me, the goatee makes me look "raffish." Bob sports some blond chin spinach himself, almost like a tassel hanging below his lower lip, and I have wondered if he might dye it. Chris has told me that Uncle Bob wants to see my artwork. I'm flattered.

I have been the beneficiary of Badget's largess in various ways, including discounts on my purchases at the store, and discounts on the nickel bags of grass he gives me for two dollars each. But I'm uncomfortable around him, always feeling that he's willing to do me his favors in return for what-I-know-not. The less I actually say to him, the better we seem to get along, and I'm enjoying this new act of mine: *Guido the Mysterious*. I have learned how keeping myself aloof and apart makes me more attractive to certain people. Perhaps this is what Bob means by raffish?

When with Badget in his T-bird we drive to New York, everybody gawks at us, girls especially, trotting past the low-slung open car at crosswalks. "Girls love this car," Bob says. He waves after the pretty skirts on 70th Street, reaching out as if to grab their legs, laughing all the while. At first I'm embarrassed, even nervous that some cop might bust us, but then I want to join in. He has something that the ladies can't resist, just like Cristiano says. And I do believe he could sell anything, because, well, as Bob himself puts it, "You're really just selling yourself."

He drops me off at the Guggenheim. I've been here once before with my high school honors class, but this is the first time I've ever been alone in a great museum of art, not to mention New York City—not even my cousin Angie over on 47ᵗʰ Street knows I'm in town. Bob says he'll be back at 3:00 PM, and he assures me I'll be home in Kinderkill by dinner time.

I'm almost eighteen and everything is going my way. The jewel in the crown is my First Prize at an all-county art competition. It's a series of drawings, three of them in pastel chalk hinged in a triptych, frames I made myself in Manaperta's old workshop. Leo has commended this as my best stuff ever. Inspired by Debussy's *Prelude to the Afternoon of a Faun*, and some photos I've seen of Rudolf Nureyev in the role, I've done two dancing nymphs—they're practically the same figure, inspired by Gwendolyn Glass, one light and one dark—flanking a prancing satyr. At the exhibition, when I am awarded my prize and the judges ask me about my inspiration, I reply, "I'm Italian. We are drawn to beauty."

IT'S NOT EASY AS I thought, manning the galley on a busy Saturday night.

Because of the high volume of business, the kitchen stays open as late as possible. Around eleven, at every break in the pace I wonder if it's closing time, but then I'm making sandwiches again to send with Debby and Karen out to customers at the bar. Gabby is no help at all. He's lazy and resents me. I try not to take it personally—he hates everybody.

"Don't give a shit whether or not you are his boy. I'm goin' on break."

"Suit yourself," I shoot back, as Gabby disappears into the alley for a smoke. Through the galley's back door comes a blast of

winter wind into my face. "Bastard," I mumble. "Motherfucker."
Shaking my head, I pull a ham out of the refrigerator.

"Party of eight! I just seated 'em and now will take their
aww-ders," Deborah squawks as she comes into the kitchen. She's
exhausted and slumps against a wall.

Under these fluorescent lights, her thin face looks especially
gaunt. In the fourteen months I've known her, she has dwindled to
a silhouette in leotards, a blank face painted "pretty." She's always
exhausted. Everybody knows she has a habit. The word is that she
didn't acquire it at the Half Moon and that she's always been able
keep it under control; the word is that a little heroin ain't so bad.
We're stupid and complacent, the crew lying to ourselves that she's
okay, that she's not really on the needle. Karen the waitress and
Macky and I joke that she must be riding a pony rather than a full
size horse. Leo's helping her, we whisper, that's why he's so strict with
her. She needs that. Chris told me that she did some hooking on
the side, but I wouldn't believe him. She has a small daughter and a
husband, although he's always out of work.

The world is fucked, I tell myself between a pair of heroes that
I'm making. *Nobodaddy fucked it up.*

"I'm on top of things," I tell her. "And by the way, the kitchen
closes at midnight."

"Says who?"

"Cook says." I give her a cocky smile, one that I've been practicing lately. "Who's this bunch that just came in?"

"Oh, yeah," she goes. "Some of Bobby's friends." She gives me
back a look that means I shouldn't ask too many questions. "Your
cousin and Connie are with 'em. No sign of Bob."

"Got it."

I am already bracing myself for what might happen next: the Captain himself will burst into the galley, flustered with a peculiar anxiety, fraught with the need to impress his friend's friends, people whom Leo can barely tolerate. Not that he's afraid of them—I don't think he is, not anymore, not now that we'll all be out of here before too long. And yet, backstage with us in the kitchen, he will vent his despair and bare his self-loathing like a secret identity, like teenage acne resurfacing to rage on his skin. On such occasions, we, his devoted crew will offer him our sympathy—this from a calculated distance, of course. We know what to do when the Captain *tumbles*, we know what a rotten time it can mean for all of us. He will shout for Sapphire, and someone will bring him his special bottle of gin. Then he will lecture about human stupidity. He will bemoan Bob Badget's "dealings with the Devil," and lament the lot of all artists betoken to moneyed fools. ("Damn the Medici!" I shouted one night, hoping to help him exorcize his demons—he looked up at me beaming, and evidently renewed, barged back out into the fray.) Having spewed his bile and tumbled like a lubber bested by a sudden blow, the Captain will eventually find his sea-legs and come about to resume his course. It's something I truly admire, this pluck and savvy, although why he is given to such inexplicable bouts of despair, just as my father is, I cannot fathom.

To Debby I say, "Stand clear, dear, of the swinging doors."

We listen for his approach. Nothing. Instead, Gabby saunters in from the alley and begins scraping a pile of dirty plates.

I smile. Coast clear. To Debby I say, "Better take their orders."

She goes, and I go after her to spy. Through the saloon doors I watch her skinny ass, a shadow of the ass I once lusted after, watch her bend at tableside, paper pad in hand. Two of the eight I recognize:

Jack and Barty. Two that my cousin has cautioned me about. There are two other men with their backs to me, rather well dressed for a visit to the Half Moon, and each of them has a woman beside him. Then there is Connie Badget. She looks especially stylish tonight in a red mini-skirt. Surprise, surprise: her eyes meet mine for an instant, but when the doors swing through and open out again, Connie's face is gone. I see Chris leaning in close to her, his handsome profile.

Connie knows me, Cristiano's younger cousin, and remembers as I do that once, as if it were in another life time, I was a fifth grade student of hers. Of course, she knows I work here now, we've seen each other plenty of times, but tonight, I have seen how disturbed she was to catch my eyes on her.

I continue to study her through a window of the kitchen doors, much as I have always done at the Villa Giustovera, pursuing my vocation as a spy. She slides her eyes past Chris toward the café's main entrance, expecting Bob at any moment, I suppose. Then I see her squeeze my cousin's leg below the table top, out of sight of all but me. His hand slides down to hers, and the fingers interlock for a moment. She stares at the jerks sitting with them. I can read her thoughts: *How could this have happened?* And more: she won't admit she knows the answer.

Chris has told me that these days Connie is less and less often present at the Bazaar. At home she sews and over the telephone she sells. Not that her college education and experience at James S. Evans Elementary School is forgotten: she could always go back to teaching, or else leave Bob and return to Puerto Rico, but that's not what she wants. "She likes the island Manhattan," Chris says. And so she measures and snips and threads and stitches. And so she schemes. Bob has Gwendolyn to help with the business; his wife, Concetta has her own life. Chris believes she will soon divorce Bob. She has told him she has grounds. Even if a wife can't be forced to testify against her husband, she would do it, she told Chris, and Bob knows why. More than that, my cousin won't say.

Crazy!

I shake my head, thinking about the life of Connie Badget.

I have the idea of making a picture to hold this very moment, an experience that enters me so deeply I recoil at first from the impact. Which is why I have to look again, and the reason why, much later, I will indeed paint Concetta Badget *nee* Acosta from my memory. That frown in her soft face: because of it I want to touch my cheek against her cheek, and like a school child, to nuzzle there. *I will make you happy, teacher*. Pretty and round with a short pointed chin, that face. The sallow skin, not brown not white: under low lighting it looks bronze. And the sad shadows about her Spanish eyes.

I step back. I have a job to do right now.

In my kitchen, the greasy pans near Gabby's elbow shine. The white suds in his sink steam under the rushing faucet. At my counter in a big salad mixing bowl, drops of water gleam on lettuce leaves.

"I won't forget," I say aloud. Gabby looks up from his pots, the stub of a spent cigarette in his mouth. *I won't forget any of this.*

Deborah returns with the orders: a sausage and pepper pie, two strip steaks rare, a cheeseburger rare with bacon and tomato. And a chef's salad for Connie, a masterpiece I will create especially for her.

Leo learns my worth that night, everybody does, and never again in the history of the Half Moon will I be referred to as *his boy*.

WHAT I WANTED, NATURALLY, was to be First Mate. Surely the Captain needed a cat such as I to depend upon. Surely, he needed all kinds of help, and anyone who knew him knew that, and Leo knew how to play on your sympathy to get it. I think that I agreed to pose nude for him and to keep it a secret because I wanted to help him out. I wouldn't have stayed around if I hadn't also been able to hang onto my self-esteem, which meant no sex with him, no how, no way. He respected me for that. As for his temper, there was often good reason that it flared at the Café. To stay afloat, his business needed more than a crew of potted merry makers.

I have always stiffened at the implication that because my family ran an Italian restaurant, there must have been some mafia connection. I have never knowingly associated with the Mob, but those pals of Bob's were surely outlaws, even if one or two of them were indeed cops. I sold some dope back then, everybody did to pay for their own stash, but I never peddled anything hard. I got my share and kept quiet. Thanks to my cousin I enjoyed many privileges, including a certain level of protection. Even if my mother didn't completely approve of her nephew, Cristiano was our blood, and she trusted that, as did I.

My father must have figured I was old enough to take some chances on my own. I could drive alone at night during my senior year, and he didn't mind if I stayed out late on the weekends. He was by then hopeless in his marriage and altogether tired of the Villa, getting fatter as his failures accumulated, his face grown rather pudgy. Lady Luck had jilted him—or so it seemed after my grandmother died and there was no one around to cheer for him and urge him onto a bigger stage.

In the off-season, when the hotel and resort were closed, he'd always left us for weeks at a time to make money in New York as a waiter at Delfino's. He said Ed Sullivan sometimes came there to eat. My father said that between courses of pasta and veal, he had cracked up Mr. Sullivan with that business of his he called *Scungili*. He said that Mr. Sullivan had laughed and that he was a big tipper and that they had really hit it off: my father thought he would soon be on the *Ed Sullivan* TV show. When my mother told me that he had a girlfriend in the City, I wasn't surprised—or disappointed. I was relieved. My father had already told me that a friend had promised she could get him on television, and so he had to be around when the call came, which was why he stayed at her apartment. I wished him luck and I meant it. I reminded him of that time when I was a kid and my pet snake had helped him to win big at craps. When I told my mother all of this she looked away. "He'll be back," I said stupidly, as if this was what she would want to hear. I didn't mention that I'd never seen him happier.

CHAPTER 35

THEN CAME THE DAY when I went up to the studio for my lesson and Leo wasn't around. The door was never locked if he were nearby, and since he was conscientious about our appointments, I simply decided to wait. My lessons had been by then distilled to a glance at my sketchbook, a comment, a shrug, a recommendation to look at something on his bookshelves. I opened *Le Mystère des Cathédrales*, but I couldn't get very far into it.

I knew where he kept his stash and if I had found some pot in his desk that day, I certainly would have gotten high. At the café we had begun toking on our breaks, and taking breaks regularly in order to toke. Everybody was buying their own at a discount from Bob, who had just recently turned us on to black Afghan hash. We didn't talk much about Uncle Bob's business except with a wink and a word to affirm that he minded it very well, and so we should mind our own. Possession of marijuana was no small crime, and dealing was definitely dangerous, and more dangerous yet were those acquaintances of Bob's whom I had started calling the Scary Men. Nobody thought that was funny.

I had on my lap the *Complete Paintings of Dante Gabriel*

Rossetti, and I opened it to a favorite, *Proserpine*. She was holding a pomegranate, and I couldn't keep my eyes off the pink slit in the globe of fruit. I knew the story: its seeds once tasted would have an irrevocable effect, and Proserpine, abducted by Pluto, rather than rejoining her mother Ceres on the sunny Earth, would be fated to spend each winter with the Lord of the Dead in the Underworld.

I thought about the party Leo had thrown for his crew the previous weekend. An after-hours affair, there was lots of booze, which I had no inhibition about consuming—I was practically of legal age, 18 in those days, and anyway the Captain had sanctioned it all, the Last Blast. There was free food too, including burnt hamburgers because I forgot to keep an eye on the griddle when it was my turn. In the bathroom mirror, talking to myself as I have always done when drunk or stoned, I went, "It's it, man. The living end." Back at the party I passed around my sad epiphany.

But where was Gwen that night? Just when we might have gotten close, she was neither present nor accounted for.

Larry Bell blew his horn sadly, working only with Sammy Keats, his piano man, and Todd somebody on bass: "Saint James Infirmary Blues." The crew began to buzz. *It's been, like, wow*, we went, and kissing on both cheeks like they do in France, and *I love you, baby—Me too, I love you*. Karen the Waitress stuck her tongue into my mouth and I Frenched her back. I could have had her that night, but no. And then Debbie, bony and small, threw herself into my arms to dance with her head pressed tight against my collar bone, never looking me in the eyes. "Keep on keepin' on, Giddy," she said. "Stay away from the bad."

"Jesus, goodbye," I replied, tears springing into my eyes.

Lucky for me, the Captain had an escape plan and I was included.

I closed the book and shelved the goddess. Growing restless, I was ready to split the studio, but then I got curious about some drawings Leo had tacked up on the walls. I saw that they were more than a series of quick sketches, as I had previously thought. They were all of this guy called Rafe, and I realized at once why Leo had seemed so distant lately, even during the party. He'd moved on to someone so pretty and obviously queer it was no wonder he'd gotten him to pose nude. He'd probably been screwing him.

He was a few years older than I, and was thoroughly inept as a waiter when Leo hired him. Ralph Mattingly, dirty blond and muscular, might someday make it as a moving picture puppet, I thought. Slow to get with anything hipper than Leo's cock, he was perfect as raw material to be recast as *Rafe*, Leo's *head* waiter, as we all called him behind his back. Soon enough, the guy was giving the rest of us orders, rather than simply taking them from the customers. Once the reality of his privileged position had sunk in, I laughed as much as everyone else at the sucking sounds Mack-the-Knife provided whenever Rafe made one of his self-important entrances and exits, tossing his long hair out of his eyes with a twitch of the head. I concluded that if there were anything to the raffishness Uncle Bob alleged that I possessed, it was definitely not of the same variety.

Alone in the studio with Leo's detailed drawings, however, I was definitely impressed. The muscular torsos were classical, stirring with life. The angelic features of Ralph's face were somehow roughened and made more attractive by shading, smudged in ever so delicately. The artistry bespoke great care: with his trained eye and hand, I thought Leo had revealed more than his model's physical beauty. I had forgotten he could be such a superb draftsman, but honestly, due to these drawings I felt something wholly new about Ralph: he was quite fragile.

"Where's the boss?"

A voice behind me. I spun about, embarrassed for reasons I couldn't have explained, neither to myself nor Gwendolyn, who was standing directly behind me. Seeing my startled face, she stopped herself from laughing, touching both hands to the corners of her mouth.

I remained speechless.

Then she said, "Don't you recognize me with my clothes on?" Smiling, she threw her arms wide, turning a three-sixty. Her skirt was blue, a snug woolen weave with a provocative slit in back, very stylish. She was wearing tangerine-colored tights and tall, white boots with kitten heels. A white blouse too. Pale eye-shadow, thick and shiny, accented her blue eyes. She was dressed as if she were ready for a night on the town.

"I do," I said stupidly.

It brought another giggle. "You do what?" she said.

"Whatever you want." Out it came, just like that. My heart beat quickened and I felt my face redden.

She seemed pleased with my reaction, and pleased also with herself in some mysterious way. Then she said, "I need to get paid. Does he bother to pay *you*?"

"Sure, yeah, he does," I sputtered. "Why?"

She glanced at the drawings of Rafe and then back to me. "He isn't worth getting jealous over, you know." She stared at me. I was doubly embarrassed.

"Listen, I just want the money Leo owes me," she said.

"Pay me for what?"

"For modeling, for whatever you do—Hey, look, I'm sorry.

Leo owes me money. I'm leaving Badget's. I'm not interested in going to jail. . ." She regarded me shrewdly and stopped her tongue. "Do people get paid on schedule at the Moon?" she asked.

"Yeah, sure we do." I was trying to come about in a sudden wind, and I reached for anything that might change the course of our conversation. "I wonder what he's going to do with our painting after we're gone," I said.

"Is it finished?" Her mind was on other things, and her gaze lanced through the studio, to the desktop with its mess of papers, to the bookshelves bursting with the history of art. Suddenly I was afraid she might rifle the desk drawers, looking for the money Leo evidently owed her. I felt a sense of responsibility for the place and I didn't know what I would do.

"Let's take a look now," she said. She was referring to the portrait and immediately went over to the draped canvas, her boot heels tapping loudly on the wooden floor. Near the gable window, where it had always stood, was the forbidden easel, shrouded with a piece of bed sheet. Before I could protest, she stripped away the cover in one motion.

"Jesus," she said.

I hurried over to see for myself. The figures were recognizably Gwendolyn and me. He had gotten her eyes, those blue gems that reflected so much light, and had even made them appear more enchanting by showing the lids partly lowered. Her entire expression was veiled and inviting. By contrast the young man beside her looked rather startled: he was smitten with love. I thought that I— that *he*—looked somewhat silly with his face turned up, his mouth open as if he were singing to the incandescent stars above.

The most surprising thing about the painting was that the

figures were clothed, fully costumed in Elizabethan style. She wore a cream colored tunic; he, a green doublet and hose. They were standing as we had been during those pure motionless hours, but they'd been set before a glorious backdrop of flowering trees under a deep blue sky studded with the lights of the zodiac. The painting recalled the work of Rousseau, but in truth it was like nothing else I had ever seen, not even another work of Leo's. White and gold apparitional forms hovered over the couple at the center of the composition as if conferring a blessing on them.

"It's it," I said.

For a moment longer, Gwen and I stood silently before our other selves. Then I took the cover carefully back over the canvas. I didn't know what Gwendolyn might be thinking. "He must have worked on this a lot when we weren't here," I said. "It's, like, a *vision*."

She said nothing and it irked me. She wasn't an artist, maybe not even an art lover. Like Rafe, she was beautiful to behold, but maybe blind to other kinds of beauty.

"I'm not queer," I said to her.

"Listen, I just thought. . .after all this time in the buff, I just thought you would have looked at me the way that other guys do."

I still couldn't look at her easily.

"It's been nice working with you, Guy." She held out her hand to shake, and I took it. "I'm glad we had this chance to say goodbye."

"What'll you do about the money he owes you?" I asked.

"Dunno," she said. She walked over to the table near the studio's open door where her coat and a large portfolio lay waiting.

"What's that?" I asked.

She was cradling the black folder to her chest with one

hand, and with the other, scooped up her shearling coat and tossed it over her shoulder.

"My pictures," she said.

"Pictures of you? Can I see?"

Silently, she unfolded the stiff covers; the portfolio was full of photographs, mounted professionally under plastic on thick pages, spiral bound. I could see immediately how the camera loved her, and I thought that she would easily find work as a fashion model. As I leafed through the pages of glamour shots, I was once more aware of the difference in our ages. The wardrobes were nothing fancy, but because of the lighting and her makeup, because of the poses she'd struck and the expressions on her face, she dazzled. The overall effect was to evoke a bygone era, rather than the mod and hippy-chic look that was current.

"Who took them?" I asked. But I already knew.

"Bob did. That fucker. . ." She stopped in midsentence. "You get the idea," she said, reaching to take the portmanteau from me.

I ignored her outstretched hands and continued to page through, more slowly now, looking more closely. There was a series of color shots in which Gwen's eyes were heavily shadowed with blue. In these, her skin looked incredibly white, as if her face held the light of snow fields on a winter afternoon. Her cheeks were flushed and her mouth pink—perhaps she'd just come in from ice-skating or skiing. In a few other shots, she was reclining on a white carpet before a brick hearth, nude obviously, with the focus on her derriere. She seemed to glow. Despite these clichés, the expressions on her face were always fresh and captivating. She had the thing, the "it" that makes a model memorable precisely because it doesn't conform to presuppositions. Her small, even teeth gleamed, and her hair was tinted a strange tone of yellow—tricks of the darkroom, I figured, more tokens of Badget's undeniable artistry.

Behind the loose-leafed pages, tucked into a pocket within the album's back cover was a bulging manila envelope. Gwen noticed my curiosity about it, and made no effort to stop me when I unfastened its clasp and carefully withdrew a stack of photographs. These were much racier than the others. She cradled her breasts and smiled saucily at the camera, she pinched a nipple between her fingernails, she raked the glowing flesh of her thighs above her stocking tops. In several shots, she reclined on a sofa, a classic odalisque, her head thrown back, her chin and throat exquisite, the look on her face haughty and irresistible.

I was nervous, and I went through the pack of pictures more quickly than I might have liked to do. She was standing beside me and I was trembling. Despite all the modeling we'd done together, I had never guessed how lovely her smile could be nor how wicked. She would never have trouble finding camera work, wherever she went, whether it was doing cheesecake or couture. The trouble would be finding a photographer as good as Bob.

The climax of the collection was in a seductive series that focused on her electric legs and feet, sheathed always in black stockings, black stiletto heels. I'd never seen anything like them, anywhere. In some of these photographs her face wasn't visible at all. The images had been lit remarkably and exploited the shadows into which the liquid forms of her flesh seemed to have been poured. In the penultimate photograph, reclining, she raised one leg, pointing the toe of a dangerous shoe skyward. A luminous crescent of thigh beckoned near the garter top of the stocking. In the very last picture, her thighs were parted, so that catching the light, the fleece between her legs looked spun from gold. The lips of her vulva looked as if they were waiting to speak the first words of Creation.

Carefully I slid the photos back into their paper sheathe, my hands shaking visibly. I knew my voice might well quaver, but at last I said, "Thanks for letting me see. They're great. *Really*. My God, you're gorgeous. " I repackaged the portfolio and handed it to her with special care as I tried to conceal my excitement.

"Thank you," she said earnestly. "Not exactly high art, are they?" She lowered her face while she fastened the clasp on the envelope.

"You're gorgeous," I repeated, leaning in very close and putting my arms around her. She looked up. Her mouth was near mine and I could taste her breath, tinged with cigarette smoke. I kissed her quickly on the lips, and then again, and was surprised by her tongue. I had French-kissed before, but Gwendolyn was not the kind of girl with whom I had made out at parties in high school, and she was not Karen the Waitress so hungry for love that she would do it with anybody. Nor was she the girl I had once worshipped, whose nude body, so impossibly close to mine, had posed such a terrible barrier to my ardor.

I was going down for the third time when Gwen sighed and tried weakly to push my hands from her shoulders. Clutching her, nuzzling her neck, I opened my eyes. I slipped my hand along the back of her thigh, and up through the slit in her tight skirt. I saw how the calf of her white boot was zippered, saw the small silver tongue of the zipper below the hollow of her knee. It filled me with indescribable desire.

"Wait. Not here."

"Where?" I said. "When? My God," I said, "I'm supposed to be at work. Macky'll kill me if I don't show up."

"Easy does it," she said, smiling, gently stroking my nose.

She knew she had me, and I didn't care what she did with me, only when and where.

"You have wheels?"

"I do."

"Ten o'clock. I've got some business to finish up at the Bazaar. Come to the alley door. You can take me home." She glittered when she said that.

CHAPTER 36

D IG AS I DO to reach the bottom of my story, I keep turning up something new—and this is one reason I've just shaved off my beard. Despite my obvious pride in it, I lose the beard every ten years or so, quite simply because I need to see what's been happening below. My most recent depilation gave me quite a shock, however: the next day, when I saw my reflection passing in the window of a darkened shop, I mistook that face for Tina's.

My autobiography could well be related as a history of my beards, of their cultivation and changing styles, of their continual graying, of their cyclic disappearances and restorations. Think of all those Van Gogh self-portraits, of how his visage bristles and flames, smolders and sulks, bearded or beardless or somewhere in between, depending on the condition of his soul. Mine was full and black by the time I headed to college, although back then, it was also quite soft and feathery to the touch. My girlfriend Eva Lynn loved to play her fingers through it, and she called it a philosopher's beard, a rabbinical beard, the beard of a desert prophet. "Are you sure you're a painter?" she teased, but seeing me wince, she added, "Why limit yourself to one thing?" Soft, smooth, and very dark was that beard, and it required so little care in order to shine.

By the time I was a junior at HRC, I was shaping it more or less like the *barbetta* of my boyhood hero, signor Caballo. Thereafter, I began to clip it intentionally to honor the revolutionary Che Guevera. I've also occasionally let the beard grow wild, especially when I am subject to a bout of the recurring influenza I regard as a family legacy. Unkempt, it is the beard of an inmate with a pair of sunken eyes, a portrait of me at my worst—not because my illness is so terrible, but rather because it is not. At times like these I feel I am the victim of my life rather than its agent, and I cling to some misguided idea of innocence, as in, *What have I done to deserve this?*

Lucky for me, the razorblade. Lucky for me that the thought of using it against my flesh, while contemplated, has always proven insupportable; my choice instead is a frontal attack on my delusions of grandeur. I can't bear for very long the thought of concealing any part of myself from myself. I love sharp edges and distinctions; I love the sensation of the razor's strokes and what they reveal. Naked of my facial hair, as I am today, I have a therapeutic clarity: is my self-love really any worse than that of other people? To suffer the disease of the ego is to be human. Losing the beard I know that I am yet intact, whatever my defects of character.

Before the final razor-work last Tuesday, I trimmed my still remaining mustache to look like my grandfather's in the old family photographs, before his hair went white. I twisted up the black tips and saw him for a moment in my glass: an unpretentious man, inquisitive, contented, optimistic.

YOUR BEAUTIFUL FACE, TINA wrote in a fax she sent to me at school—but that was a month ago; how could she have known what I was contemplating? Or was it something she herself had suggested? I was bothered that the department secretary might have read the message when it came in, and at first I felt peeved at Tina, but a while later I was almost euphoric. I hadn't seen my cousin for several weeks, and that was only in passing at a big shopping mall in Fishkill. It seemed to me a surreal experience: amid the bland and overweight masses, amid the throngs of teenagers zoned into their cells, beneath the endless lights that forbid every shadow, my flamboyant cousin in her Caribbean clothing did not belong. Across the galleria I called out, "What are you doing here?"

"Shopping," she replied, waving as she continued in the opposite direction.

At lunch today, Davey told me I look younger, and then revised that to say "renewed." He's choosing his words rather carefully nowadays—it must have to do with his voracious reading—and his vocabulary is increasing too. Is this Tina's influence? He sees her fairly often: he says, she's helping him "unfold" his "psychic gifts." Leaning across the table, taking my hands in his, he thanked me for getting him started on his lessons, and said that sometimes he didn't even need to be with Tina in person, that she was, as he put it, "in the air."

I tried to laugh him off: "Oh, Ouija Board. . ." I began, but he grunted, annoyed at my irreverence. *Okay,* I thought, *have your fun. Then get on with your life.* I said, "She's more together than either of us thought. But she still needs to see her mother. Has she told you why she stays away?"

"Family is complicated," Davy replied. He stared off as if he were perhaps in contact with her at that very moment.

I looked across the street from the Patriot Arms. Where my car was parked I thought I saw Tina, but that seemed impossible.

"AND YOUR CRIME IS what, exactly?" Davey's beefy arm is out the open window of the passenger's side of my Saturn. He thumps the roof for emphasis: he does not quite believe that I have something vile to come clean about.

It's a beautiful, warm April afternoon, the sort of day when in the Hudson Valley you can imagine you are actually much further south. We are in my new car, a black and gold Saturn sedan with horsepower to spare, and with my friend seated beside me, I've got things to talk about, man to man. I begin again. "I had to help her. Weird to be talking about it, all these years later—"

"You've been carrying this around for how long?" Once again he thumps the roof.

"*I don't forget,*" I say with emphasis, looking into the rearview mirror, changing lanes with a surge of power. "It's part of my particular crazy."

"Well, whatever you did, the statute of limitations has expired. Unless it was murder, or grand larceny, or something big like that. You can be prosecuted by the Feds. . ." His voice trails off and from behind his shades, he examines my face.

"I feel bad about it, man. I always have."

"And, what, my son? You wanna make a confession? I was an altar boy and I used to wonder if I'd be called to a *vocation*. I dreaded the thought. . . . Look, Guy, you swore you were never a convicted felon, and unless there's hard evidence to the contrary, consider the past settled. You grew up Catholic, man. That's got something to do with this, this what do they call it? *Free floating anxiety.* Were *you* ever an altar boy?"

"Never."

"I hate all this sexual abuse shit in the news. There are people who hear *Catholic* and they think about a priest with his hands on some kid's penis or up the dress of a little girl after Sunday school. Yuck."

"Did anything like that happen to you?"

"Hell, no. Once in confession the priest wanted to know all about my masturbation, where and when, and all the details—maybe he was getting off. These days, you can confess your sins directly to God and ask forgiveness. If you need help, then you go to a priest. You hope you get lucky with a half-way intelligent one."

"Just like cops. You ever need help, Davey?"

"I'm listening."

"I never told anybody about this."

"What, that you were a minor?"

"I'm not talking about my career." He doesn't get the joke. "I was seventeen, going on eighteen. The winter of our senior year. I was an accessory."

"Yeah?"

"An accessory to a girl." I thought that this would surely make him lighten up, but it didn't. "You remember Bob Badget?"

"Sure. That creep from Poughkeepise. Leo's partner. Whenever you talk about him, you don't talk about him." Davey tugs his shades half-way down his nose to look at me, like some actor on television playing a detective.

"Badget got busted. But before that, there was this girl, Gwendolyn, she was Badget's bookkeeper. We worked together for Leo as models. Bob Badget was a really good photographer and he did these terrific pictures of Gwendolyn, probably good enough to get her started doing fashion magazines, maybe even movie auditions. She was headed for Los Angeles. She's the one I helped."

"Somebody must have tidied up at Badget's place before the Feds got there," Davey says. "Any idea who?"

"Shit, for all I know, it could have been Leo. He knew what was going down. He was scared he might be implicated."

Davey whacks the doorframe with the palm of his hand.

"Please don't dent my new car."

He stretches a long arm around me, and with his powerful hand squeezes my shoulder. "This girl, this Gwendolyn: she gave you pussy?"

LIKE A SOLDIER, I thought. *No, that's awful. I'm not a soldier, I'm a lover.*

This was true, but the truth was, logic wasn't going to see me through. *Cool-lione. Balls,* Cristiano had said. *You gotta have cool-li-one.* I knew I'd be a fool if I didn't meet her as I'd promised. At ten to ten, I pulled on my pea coat, said goodnight quickly to Leo and Rafe and Debby who were sitting together at the bar, talking in low voices over a box of papers. They hardly noticed me. Neither did Larry Bell to whom I gave my usual nod *hello* when I slipped past him at the front door. Larry had his horn in its box, and there was fresh snow on top. He set down the sax, stamped his feet and brushed himself off. I took a step toward him, like *hey, man,* but Larry was already in the huddle with the others. Suddenly Larry's voice got loud, sounding as if he was mad about something; everybody seemed to be mad about something that night. I stepped out into the cold, yanking up my collar as I went.

Here was the night journey over ice fields into the storm, here were the new black Beatle boots, their leather soles very slippery and me wobbling as I walked like a man: around my neck, knotted snug, I wore a white scarf filched from my dad's closet, a touch of Continental panache under my navy blue pea coat. Surprisingly, it was my father that I was thinking about: Nunzio Diamante, a small man and rather rotund, who had for his whole life made his way forward despite the odds against him.

With my fingers, I combed my long hair out over my collar. My hair lifted like wings past my temples as I strode. At the Bazaar's backdoor I paused to examine my shoes and polished their points against my calves. I bent down to straighten the fabric pegged at the ankles, and then loosened my jacket to pull the scarf free, tossing one tail over my shoulder. I tested the doorknob: it was unlocked and it turned silently. Like a secret agent, I stepped into the store.

The lights were on, and down a short hallway in another room I could hear somebody moving about. I'd never been in the stock room before, and I was amazed at all the rows of clothing neatly arranged on steel stanchions and metal hangars. Two mannequins stood inside the doorway, partly dressed or undressed in pretty skirts pinned for alterations, and I supposed that Connie must have sometimes used the space to work. It was brightly lit by overhead fluorescents, and down an aisle, I spotted Gwendolyn, rummaging through a clothes rack, picking whatever she wanted and tossing the items toward her feet. She had an army-green duffle bag gaping near her on the floor, and into it she threw striped skirts, pastel blouses, hip-hugger slacks of wide wale corduroy.

A heavy wire hanger clanged suddenly against the rack and she froze. She turned around slowly: when she saw me, a smile thawed her face. I could see the line of her small even teeth, and I loved her like that, like a hungry child.

"This isn't what you think," she said. "He owes me."

She turned from the clothes to the shoeboxes stacked behind her on shelves against the wall. "If you see anything you want, just take it," she said, looking under the cardboard lids of the boxes. "He owes me big time."

"I know what I want," I said. "Hurry up. It's a refrigerator in here." My wet feet were cold and despite my heavy coat, I was shivering, but I was smiling. Just like that I became her accomplice.

"The heat's off because we haven't paid the bills. Cooking the books just doesn't do it. Let's go," she said, pulling the zipper on the duffle. Dragging the loot over, she put the canvas strap of the bag into my hand. She looked around the room once more, seemed satisfied. "Your cousin Chris is a good guy," she said. Tell him so long from Gigi."

"Gigi," I repeated. *Her initials.* "You need a ride somewhere?"

"That's the idea," she said grinning. She started to button her fleece lined coat. Her pretty knees were shining like small faces below the hem. Then she slid her hand down the wall, putting out the lights. She touched my lips with her fingers, laughing as she flew past.

I followed her to the backdoor. She looked at her wristwatch, doused the light and pushed me outside. I heard her turn the key in the door's lock, and then she asked, "Where's your car?"

"Near the Café. It's a short walk through the alley. But watch your step, everything is ice under this snow."

"Bob at the Café?"

"Not when I left. He might come in later, though, to hear Larry's set. Tonight's his last night. Leo's over there. You need to see him about some money?"

"Maybe another time. I sure don't need to see Bob tonight."

As I slung the bag on my shoulder, I felt how heavy it was.

How much did Badget owe her, and for what exactly? "Did you get everything you wanted?" I asked.

A funny look came over her face. "Not yet," she said. "His darkroom is locked. Ever been in there? He's got a fortune in equipment."

"Chris told me. Chris says Bob can do anything. He thinks Bob is, like, a *god* or something."

"Yeah, well, Bob sort of thinks he is too. Did Chris tell you about the fight they had?"

"Cristiano would kick his ass in a fair fight."

"Fair fight?" she said, looking at me. "You know about Chris and Connie?" I nodded and she continued. "Bob knows, but he doesn't let on. He gave me some cock and bull story about leaving Connie, about wanting to run away with *me*. Chris came in right then, and when Bob saw him he made a joke out of it. Later, when Bob wanted Chris to do some more pictures with me, your cousin laughed in his face and they started arguing. Then Bob told him something, I don't know what, but they shook hands. Chris is gonna get out. You'll see. With or without Connie. Remember to tell him I said goodbye."

Snow was coming down heavily and it was sticking. We made our way out of the alley, but the sidewalk and street were practically indistinguishable. Two cars were approaching us very slowly, one of them was Badget's, which turned onto a side street. Then the T-bird spun a complete 180, to face us on our left, and under a streetlight, I saw that Bob was talking to the driver—Cristiano.

"Shit," Gwen said. "Ignore them. Let's go this way." She pulled me by the arm toward the opposite corner.

We pretended we hadn't seen them. When I stole a quick look, I saw the car spinning circles wildly in the abandoned intersection. It was the sort of thing Chris liked to do for kicks.

A second later and they were right behind us. We kept walking, faster now, onto our looming shadows, and then I heard Chris call out my name.

"What?" I answered, looking over my shoulder, keeping my cool. I had one arm around Gwendolyn, and with my other gloved hand I gripped the duffle's strap on my shoulder. The bag weighed a ton.

Chris said, "You park your sled around here, Santa Claus?"

"I've got my mother's Fury," I said. "Excuse me, but I'm giving a ride to a friend."

"Lucky stiff," he said to me. "Hey, Gigi! Have fun!"

She gave him a quick look, a tight smile, and turned away tugging gently on my arm. I felt her hip bump against mine impatiently, but for an instant longer I stared at Cristiano. It wasn't a moment for crowing like some puffed up cock bird. Something else passed between us, and it's one of the moments I will always remember him for. *Lucky stiff,* he'd said, a touch of admiration in his voice, but also there was something else too: some kind of doubt, I think, maybe about the direction he was headed.

I didn't want to think what Bob might do if he found out how much of his stuff was in that sack I was slinging. Despite her assurances to me, Gwendolyn seemed awfully nervous as we hurried along. Uncle Bob and I did have our own peculiar relationship, but I wasn't in the mood to try and make happy with him right then.

She was pulling on my arm, yet when I saw Bob's mouth moving behind the car's windshield, I couldn't look away. He must have cracked a joke to Chris, because they both started laughing, and then with the blade of his hand, Bob made a gesture, chopping the air a couple of times. There was something I'd never seen before in Chris's face, as if he didn't know what else to do but force a laugh.

I sought traction in the snow, just in case we needed to run for it. I pictured myself grabbing Gwendolyn and her skiing along beside me, like in a James Bond movie. The snow was coming down thick and wet, and my own childishness overwhelmed me: it was all a game wasn't it? I would figure out the rules in a minute and how to play my position. I actually thought about starting a snowball fight just for fun. We were all on the same side, right?

I kept pressing forward toward the Fury, Gwendolyn on my arm, keeping up my pace. We stepped into the pelting snowfall, onto our shadows. "Don't look back," Gwen said, clutching me close.

"I LIKE YOUR STORY. I can see that guy. What he did is called petty larceny. And you weren't even eighteen. You probably would have gotten probation if you were caught," Davey said.

"My crimes don't fall very neatly into categories," I told him.

"You might not think so, Professor, but one reason for the justice system is to help us make sense of our crimes. Don't you think yours are included?"

He was grinning broadly now, and then he leaned over, putting his ear up close to my mouth. "Is there more, my son?"

CHAPTER 37

THE FURY WAS GOOD in snow. It had studded rear tires, sandbags in the trunk, and a terrific low gear, yet I still had to drive slowly. We were on our way to Hyde Park; Kinderkill is in the opposite direction, and I had no idea what time I might finally be turned around and going home, nor what kind of story I would have to invent for my parents. Then I saw how the storm itself would give me an alibi.

Occasionally I glanced at Gwen who sat quietly beside me on the green vinyl seat, smiling back whenever I caught her eye. Twice she told me how much she appreciated all the trouble I was going through. It must have occurred to me at one time or another that Gwendolyn Glass lived someplace, but I had usually thought of her in relation to Leo's studio, or sitting at a desk in the office of Badget's Bazaar. I felt stupid that I hadn't tried to know her simply as a girl who lived with her mother on a street in some housing development. Maybe we weren't going to have sex after all. Maybe she'd only wanted the ride, and I would just drop her off and plow back to Poughkeepsie to sleep on the sofa in Leo's studio. I was certain he would have to close early and that Bob and Chris would give him a lift home to

Mitchell Street. Leo was a terrible driver, and a snow storm like this one would be more than he could handle in his rusty Dart.

At last we pushed our way into a snowbound driveway at a darkened ranch house. "Good," Gwen said. "Mom's not home. She'll probably spend the night with her boyfriend, Jimmy."

I turned off the headlights, but left the engine running to keep us warm. She looked at me, inviting me, and I leaned over, putting both hands behind her head to pull her mouth to mine. Then I slipped one hand down into her skirt, down inside her panty hose, and when she arched her pelvis up, I pulled away her cotton underwear. Outside, it snowed and snowed. I dipped two fingers between her warm petals, and as she gyrated on my fingers I immediately grew hard. She wanted to say something, but I stopped her tongue with mine to kiss her more deeply.

At last she said, "Inside. The house. My bedroom is better." She took me by the wrist and literally put my arm through my coat sleeve. Then she began to bundle herself up, always holding my eyes, letting me know there was no doubt what she intended to do with me.

Dazzled, compliant, I gathered my wits and shut down the engine. I glanced at the backseat where the long duffle bag lay, our silent partner in crime. I was going to ignore it, but Gwen said, "Don't forget that, baby. And *brrr,* hurry up!" I feasted my eyes as she wiggled her panties into place. When she opened the car door, her tang drifted on the cold air, thick and flowery off of my fingers.

"And?" Shades up, voice lowered, Davey sounds serious.

His entire appearance has changed over the past winter, as if he's been recast, carved down, the way you do with a hunk of wood, whittling off what's unimportant, revealing the grain, the veins. His face has thinned considerably, his midsection too, and he's got new muscles around his shoulders. I can't help noticing his forearms and wrists whenever he pounds against my car. There's a new tattoo adorning his left inside forearm, a heart with three swords poking through and the words *Have Mercy.* He's told me a little about a new obsession of his—vampirism—but my old friend reminds me more of a husky black lab than a howling child of the night.

I want to get it over with, my spiritual deposition. I am guilty for what I did with my eyes half closed at the Half Moon, and yet this was my way away from the Villa. HRC would probably have come into existence without me in the picture, but I like to think that I might have inspired Leo to go forward with his plans and to abandon the Café when he did.

To Davey I say, "The law of karma doesn't just give you one effect at a time. Looking back, I can see there's a crooked line connecting the night I helped Gigi to where I am now. You dig?"

"I'm with you, man."

"Cool. So we went into her house. The place was a mess, stuff thrown around, boxes half packed. It was obvious that she and her mother were moving out. We went up into her room which was empty except for her dresser and bed. I'd never done it before, and she was patient with me. The first time, I came as soon as I went inside. The second time, she coached me, and she came too. Then I started to catch on, about team work. She moaned and whimpered and laughed when she came. I didn't know girls enjoyed it that much, or that I could give a girl so much joy.

"When we took a break, I remembered to call home from the downstairs living room, where there was a telephone on the floor. I told my mother a story about trying to dig the car out of a snow bank and giving up and having to spend the night in Leo's studio.

"The next morning it was brilliant outside. The snow was deep and beautiful. We had sex one more time, standing at the window, me behind her, pumping up under her gorgeous ass, both of us gazing out at the white wonderland. The fir trees were bowing to us, I said, in their royal ermine robes. She liked that, my poetry. It was sweet, Davey, one of the sweetest parts. Her mother would be home soon she said, I should go before then, and a few minutes later, after the plow came by, I shoveled open the driveway. Then I drove away in my big green car blowing kisses to her."

I pause for a long moment. I am still thinking about Santa's bag of goodies. "She got what she wanted. And you know, I never did learn what exactly was in that sack. It was heavy as hell, let me tell you."

"You can't know everything," Davey says. "You have to surmise some things. You connect some dots and make an outline. Then you try to fill that in. There's an art to being a detective," he says. "That night—you got what *you* wanted, right?"

"I've been lugging this around with me for years. You're the first person I've ever told the whole story. You good with this? No conflicts of interest or anything?"

He shakes his head. "Are you sorry for what you did? Because, you know, if you're truly sorry, your sins are forgiven. . ."

"I'm sorry I didn't love her. I'm glad she didn't love Cristiano. If Chris had wanted *her*, instead of Connie, I don't know. . ."

"You were young. You were also lucky. She was old enough to know what she was doing. She did you a favor, man. Made your first time truly unforgettable."

"Ah, but it still hurts."

We're silent again for a good long time, heading down the road together.

"Listen, Guy: now it's my turn. I'm leaving Jeannie." He stares out the window, looks back at me, pulls off the shades. I don't know what to say. *Does this have anything to do with Tina?*

"Do you think that sometimes a guy does something just to show the world that he can do it?"

"For sure, he does."

"And even if he was wrong, maybe being wrong was the best he could do at the time?"

At first I think he's talking about me, but then I say: "Jean? Your kids? What was the mistake?"

"Jeannie, maybe. Me too of course. We were both wrong a lot of the time. Not a complete mistake, no. We had some good years. My kids, I love 'em, but I let the job get in the way. My father was like that too, with my sister and me growing up. Waving goodbye from the door, a giant in his uniform. Now it's over—thanks to you, my friend."

"You blame me?" I stop at the turn for Widener Road, a woodsy spot, and pull off along the shoulder. I'd been headed for Kinderkill the whole time without thinking about it. I could drive the route to the Villa in my sleep.

"No blame, not at all, Guy. My *thanks*. You enlightened me." He is without irony. "You and Tina gave me the key, anyhow. And once a person opens the door, once he looks inside himself, well, you know, he'd better go all the way in. I never told you this, but I did psychotherapy. And Harry's Gym. A lot of good guys at that place." He tenses his arm reflexively, balling a fist, bulging some of the muscles he's cut. The tattooed heart seems to pump against the swords that pierce it.

To David Lafferty who is sitting in my car off the side of the road under a tree where a sign for the Villa once hung, to David Lafferty my oldest friend I say, "When I was a kid, I played at being a lot of things. The Villa was good for that, and my childhood seemed like a carnival. I was the snake handler, the joker, the pirate. An artist. I was a student of human nature, I like to say. I never wanted to be a cop, though. . ."

"Ever wanna be a private dick?" He cracks a smile. "I'm thinking of moving to San Francisco. Wanna come?"

FREEHAND, MY FATHER HAD painted a good grape arbor, and below that, on a sky blue backdrop, he had stenciled italic letters and festooned them with golden sequin reflectors. *Villa Giustovera Just Ahead. Best Food, Best Time of You Life.* I had tried but been unable to convince him to redo the last line before he nailed it up on a tree at the corner of Widener Road. He couldn't see the harm in leaving the spelling like that—in fact, he liked it. People would think it was one of his jokes, his broken English, they'd be reminded how funny he was. My mother told me to forget about it. He'd made up his mind, and if he were contradicted, my father could easily become angry. I never said another word about the sign, but I was embarrassed every time my school bus passed it. One day a kid pointed at it and laughed in my face. I calmly unfolded my penknife, and beginning to clean my fingernails with it, I asked him, "How do you spell antidisestablimentarianism? Because if y-o-u can do that," I said, never looking directly at him, "then I won't have to tell anybody that y-o-u can't spell."

The kid, his name was Larry Pinchot, thought about it for a while without replying and then he changed his seat, squeezing in next to a girl just behind the bus driver. The driver, Ken, his uncle or second cousin or something, scowled at me when I got off at the Villa and informed me that he was going to talk to the school principal about what I had done.

My parents were notified first thing next morning and they drove me into school that day. On the way, I told them only that I'd had an argument with Pinchot and he must have made up a story about me. In fact, I didn't think I'd done anything wrong. After a meeting with the principal, Mr. Vandebogart, at which I demonstrated how I had cleaned my fingernails using the penknife and repeated a slightly revised version of what I had said to Pinchot, I was asked to leave the room and wait in the outer office.

Later they told me I was going to have a "conversation" with the school psychologist. I was dumbfounded. Only the really screwed up kids ever had to see Dr. Kee. When my father asked me, I told him I didn't have anything to be sorry for, but he smacked me hard anyway, angry that I had brought shame to our family. I was mortified, yet refused to say how it was his stupid sign that had caused the whole mess, and how I was actually trying to defend our family honor. Nonna, always my champion, was still alive when this happened, but she and my mother both kept out of it—clearly this was something between my father and me.

At my first meeting with the psychologist, Dr. Kee, I said that I had meant no harm to Larry Pinchot, and that I hadn't actually threatened him. Pinchot had insulted me and I had gotten back at him. When Dr. Kee asked me if I was happy about that, I didn't answer, but suppressed a smile and lowered my eyes. I felt a little guilty but I was mostly glad.

Cristiano, whom I could beat at "Knivesies" and "Land," with my superior knife throwing skill, laughed when he found out about the trouble I was in. He brushed it off as an example of how fucked up school was. He told me not to let it bother me. He knew I liked school and that I was an A student, and he said I should just let it roll off my back. He grabbed me behind the neck and shook me playfully. "I couldn't spell that anti-stuff if you asked *me*," he said. "I didn't know you had it in you, Guy!"

Dr. Kee was also surprised that I was willing, as he put it, to act in a way "so obviously divergent" from my path of success in school.

I liked him, and in spite of my shame at having to see him every week, I began to enjoy the sessions. I had read how my hero Benvenuto Cellini dueled with anybody who insulted his honor, and so I told Dr. Kee that I believed I was a little like that. I explained that furthermore I was no idiot around knives, or guns for that matter, because I had had "sufficient experience" with them growing up as a country boy. He was attentive as I spoke, and I was equally attentive to him, a small Asian gentleman in a blue necktie, a starched white shirt, a maroon cardigan. Very seriously, I said that I knew how knives had lives of their own once they were drawn, and that this was why I had trained myself to use my little pen knife exclusively as "a grooming tool." I told him I had other knives, most of them too large to carry in my pocket, and that I also owned a real fencing foil, sent to me from Italy by my uncle.

Dr. Kee made some notes on his writing pad. I told him about my knife collection and how I kept it in a locked box. I didn't mention the movie magazines featuring photographs of my favorite leading ladies, which were also stashed in the same wooden box, something Mr. Manaperta had originally made to hold my childhood toys. Dr. Kee asked if I would draw a picture of my favorite knife for our next meeting. He made it very clear that I should not bring the knife itself to school with me, and emphasized that I should never again bring any knife to school.

At our next meeting I presented a fairly elaborate sketch in colored pencils. It included Dr. Kee in his blue necktie and maroon sweater, bug-eyed over the box of knives, which looked like a medical kit. In a thought balloon beside Dr. Kee's temple I'd sketched a dagger whose handle was the body of a shapely woman.

He looked at the drawing for quite a while before he spoke. I was familiar with such responses to my more inspired works; people often didn't know what to say when they saw the extras I included in my sketches. At last he said, "Were you a fan of Marilyn Monroe?"

That surprised me, and taken off guard I replied, "I was in love with her." I could feel my ears burning when I said that, but I'd meant it. Then I added, "I would have saved her if I could, but you know, the world always kills somebody so beautiful. When she died, she was about the same age as Jesus, you know?"

The doctor made another note. "Would you have saved Jesus if you could?"

"He was meant to die," I replied, "in exchange for our sins." I pointed to him and then myself. Dr. Kee had been born somewhere in the Far East, maybe China, I wasn't sure, and I thought it interesting that he spoke English so well. I believed he was a Christian, maybe even a Catholic, since he had a print of Raphael's *Ascension* framed and hanging in his office. I'd identified it the first day, to show him I wasn't a dope or just some wop with a knife in my pocket. "Sure. I'd save Jesus from the Romans if I could. But God's will be done, you know."

"You think about these sorts of things," the doctor said. It was not a question, and I've always remembered what he said next, too, because it cemented our friendship: "So do I."

CHAPTER 38

O FFICIAL RANK IN ITSELF means little to me, but I'm always keen to discover who really deserves my respect. It's something Italian, I think, something that I remember about my father too, and this curiosity also includes the wish to be noticed by admirable persons in particular. At the College, my dean, Liotta, is such a one, but in the cop shops of my ambit, there was nobody. Chief Gottman I began to avoid soon after I realized how he avoided me.

Sergeant Sandra Lorraine was another matter entirely. I wanted to be near her with the obsessiveness of a school boy crush, and so I became her student with regard to any and all police operating procedures. I exulted when my rapt attention would elicit from her a detailed explanation or demonstration. A new photocopying machine in its secluded nook proved optimal in this respect, and it was there that she also began flirting obviously with me.

Off duty, my education continued when off the cuff, Sandy laid bare her criticism of the profession in general and of her position in particular. She liked police work, she really did, but there was so much room for improvement. As for her difficulties with certain persons on the job—she knew she could trust me on this, she said, touching my hand while we were having drinks at an out of the way pub—I was a good listener, she knew that—a pat on the shoulder, to seal the connection. *Quiche Lorraine,* she said they called her, trying to turn her head, those guys apparently thinking to score with trash talk like that, but shooting air balls instead. I had already noticed how with vulpine eyes she mocked them. She told me that for reasons of her own she remained silent about various instances that sounded to me like bona fide examples of sexual harassment.

"Forget about legal recourse," she told me when I questioned her reticence. "Too cumbersome and ultimately alienating. There are other ways to get what you want." Shrewd—Sandy was shrewd too, something else I definitely admired. As far as I knew, no one suspected when we became more than friendly colleagues. She counseled professionalism at all times on the job, and I became her disciple.

Soon, I had my own observations about the men on the Force. I told her, "Some are the conventional sort who serve the status quo unthinkingly. They're joiners and followers and easily influenced by the group, and yet, and yet, because they're part of a *corps*—it means a body—this type can find the balls to put themselves at risk in the line of duty. Take the classical heroes: alone or among brothers-in-arms they triumph, even though some don't choose for themselves the hero's part. Necessity casts them in that role."

She liked it when I talked this way, enthusiastically, confidently, and one night while I was going on about the Trojan War, she began to take off her clothes. The pride of Achilles, the cunning of Odysseus excited her, which in turn emboldened me: I grabbed her uniform hat, a prize I'd coveted from the first, and by its glossy bill sailed it like a disc across my bedroom.

"A nation's image of itself is likely to take the form of an inspiring female—Lady Liberty or Columbia or the warrior goddess Athena—because women are the power that moves the patriarchs to subdue the wilderness and conquer enemies."

She sighed and shook out her glorious mane, its auburn highlights flaming.

"Mind you, women can be powerful actors themselves, but so much masculine culture defines itself *against* them at the same time that it professes to be *for* them. In the end, such men want to assign females to their 'proper' places, that is, to the rear. On the other hand, the psychologists say that whether we're male or female, we don't become our truest selves until we've dealt with the first woman in our lives: Mother."

"Women can also inspire men to self-restraint and decency," she said, laughingly, leading me by the hand over to my bed. She was partially unbuttoned and I could see the black lace brassiere she was wearing especially for me under her uniform blouse.

"Of course." I pushed my fingers up into her disheveled hair and began to massage the back of her neck. "For the classical hero, marriage to a mortal woman can reflect his contract with an immortal goddess. As a *father*—" the word stuck momentarily in my throat—"as a father, a man also pledges himself to Necessity, the goddess who rules futurity, which means the lifetimes of his children and grandchildren."

She sighed audibly under my kneading fingers and proceeded to strip off her stiff blue blouse. She did everything easily and efficiently. I loved to watch the working of her nimble fingers with their shining nails. By the time she had disrobed completely, my cock was standing at attention behind the gate of my fly. I began to undress myself as quickly and gracefully as possible.

When we first become lovers, I admitted to Sandy how much I was turned on not only by the sight of her in uniform, but also by the anticipation of her disrobing. She was happy to make me happy by doing so very slowly, just as I had requested, folding and stacking the pieces, while I in turn did what she liked, rambling on professorially about "those old Greeks." Especially her glistening duty belt, heavy with its holstered pieces, when unbuckled and laid gently aside like a trophy on my bed moved me to bliss. I was "so unusual," she told me, her hand on my cock, sliding it home between the cheeks of her ass, trying me on for the part of hero in her life.

With my tongue at her ear, with my hands gliding over the hills and into the coves of her body, I liked also to reel out a continuing tale I'd concocted about the evil Queen Polly Esther, she who had tightly bound my lover's breasts and hips and thighs. I had arrived to liberate her, I announced, and to present my sword in her service. I licked the sweat from her nipples, from her flanks, from the valley at the top of her buttocks, and tasting her uniform's synthetic odor, found it strangely aphrodisiac. She was my image of authority, none but she, I proclaimed, submitting my head on her Mons Veneris.

She liked that very much.

SANDY HAD ASKED ME over to her home on several occasions, but I had always declined. When our relationship looked like it was becoming serious, she insisted that I must meet her son, Charles. I referred to him as Charlie, but Sandy instantly corrected me.

"Charles and I would be very happy if you would come over and decorate our tree with us."

It was not anything I really wanted to do, but it was Christmas time, a time for children. The season is generally depressing to me because I always find myself asking, Where are the true Christians? I am not, nor do I pretend to be, and certainly I do not believe that I live in a Christian nation; still I can't do without the holiday, because of the way it can touch the heart of innocence.

Sandy loves Christmas. She's a non-practicing Catholic of French Canadian extraction, and, like me, at an early age the rituals of the Church were deeply imprinted on her. The last time I attended midnight mass on Christmas Eve was with her, at the end of a rather tearful evening on account of Charles being with his father and family in Montreal. But this year was different, he was home with *Maman*. The amount of effort she had invested in "making Christmas," as she called it, was apparently not so unusual; the exceptional thing was that Charles and I were finally going to meet. An entire evening together was planned, including a late candle lit dinner, and an invitation for me to spend the night.

I did not love Sandy, but I was, and continue to be, very fond of her. She is a good person, and we would have become friends even if the sex hadn't been so satisfying and full of surprises—all the stuff we did with her uniform hat, for example, its polished brim like a mirror, hanging it here and passing it there for "inspection" purposes. Furthermore, I soon learned that she could hold her own in a conversation, even if most of the time we weren't coming at things from the same direction. *That's what I said, didn't I?* she'd reply, after I'd rephrased an idea of hers. She puzzled me, and this bemusement was also a pleasure. I certainly felt that I owed her a happy Christmas.

The first cold weather of the season had arrived on schedule with a few inches of fluffy snow, the air was crystalline, the clear sky jeweled with constellations, and a young moon skated early to bed. I remember asking myself on the drive down to Fishkill, "Is this as good as any guy could ask for? Is this my best bet: the devoted love of the capable Sandy Lorraine and a fatherly role for myself in the life of little Charles? Children of our own to follow? Tenure at HRC, or maybe, my God, a full time job on the Force?" Almost immediately I got my answer, whether from the stars or elsewhere: *I could never do that.*

By the time I was parking the car, crunching it into the snow-packed driveway, I was feeling both dread and shame. I pushed shut the door of my car, hearing it *ka-chunk* in the cold air, the sound echoing against the garage door of Sandy's split-level house—a home she owned outright, she'd proudly informed me. I looked up and I saw Charles rush to the picture window and push his small blond face up to the glass. I gave him a little wave, more of a salute, and for fun blew out a lot of breath to make a small cloud. He stared at me a moment and jumped back, disappearing from sight. Sandy appeared in his place. She wasn't smiling.

When she met me at the door, the first thing she said was, "Charles has a fever. I need to keep my eye on him. But come in, come in, Guido. Merry Christmas, eh?" She brushed her cheek against mine and kissed the air.

Her hair was up, the way I loved to see it, but despite the allure of her perfumed neck, I resisted a nuzzle because Charles was staring. "Sandy, *bella*," I said, taking her outstretched hands as she brought me over to be introduced.

"*Charles*," she said, pronouncing the name in French, "please come here and say hello to our guest. This is Mr. Diamante I told you about."

The boy was small for his age I thought—or else I didn't know how tall a six year old should be. I liked his cowboy outfit, probably a special one for our Christmas party, selected by his mother, who was herself tastefully dressed with a snug cashmere top over a beige, calf-length skirt. The Paris heels were a gift I'd given her for her birthday and it was the first time I'd seen them on her. Charles wore a pearl-snap shirt festooned with bronco riders and had on a leather vest over it. He also had on tan, western style slacks with a longhorn silver buckle for his tooled belt, and maroon-colored cowboy boots. He looked awfully cute.

"*Bonsoir, Monsieur Charles.* Happy Christmas."

He shook with me shyly, wordlessly, and I could feel how hot and moist his little palm was, the fingers limp. Afterwards, the sensation lingered uncomfortably in my own hand.

"It's supposed to be *Merry* Christmas," he said. He looked at his mother to be sure he had gotten that right.

She said, "In Canada I'm sure you've heard people wish for a Happy Christmas, Charles."

"We're in the States," he said, glancing back at me as if to be sure I understood the distinction.

"In that case, *Joyeux Noel,*" I said smiling. He stared at me blankly. We were not off to a good start. I kept my eyes on him, seeking some means of rapprochement, trying to think of something more to say. He'd never be a Charlie or a Chuck. How about Cal as an affectionate nickname for the little buckaroo? But I wouldn't be the one to try it.

Sandy smiled and said, "Mr. Diamante has been all over the world and he speaks several different languages. He's very happy to be with us tonight."

Her son looked back at her in a daze. "Oooh," she said, putting a hand to his forehead and producing a tissue to wipe his dripping nose. Before she could do so, he sneezed hard, spraying mucous all over her lovely cashmere sweater. "Blow," she said, bunching the tissue around his nose, and he did, profusely.

Reflexively, I wiped my still moist palm against the outside seam of my black jeans. I glanced down to see a streak of yellow mucous and shuddered.

A thermometer proved that Charles's fever was at 102 degrees—"Not so unusual for a child," Sandy said when I expressed my concern. To Charles she said, "We hang a few ornaments and then we put you to bed, *eh?*"

The tree was nowhere to be seen. Sandy told me she'd just purchased it that afternoon, and it was still outside in the garage. Would I bring it in, please, and fit it into its stand near the picture window in the living room? "Oh, the base will have to be assembled first. You'll find that in the garage too."

SANDY WAS—*IS*—A BEAUTIFUL PERSON; however, she is not "pretty" in a conventional way. Her hair, of course, her exquisitely manicured fingernails, yes, the long muscles in her thighs, *bien sur*, but her face is not exceptionally memorable—except when she comes to orgasm. Then she is completely unrestrained, and she likes to shout, and she reddens so deeply that I can easily imagine the Native ancestor with whom her great grandfather, a Frenchman, fell in love. That shattering cry of hers is one of the main reasons we would rendezvous at my place rather than her home.

After our rapid climb into the high peaks of love making, and after our swift but gentle descent, soon afterwards, the role of connubial hero in Sandy Lorraine's life went to Detective Fred Smart.

I was happy for them when I learned they were engaged. Without a flicker of judgment against me, she said that children were something they both wanted.

My job as a Special Deputy also came to an end rather abruptly, and, if not so gently, at least the break was clean. One day I was simply informed that my position was to be terminated because I was being replaced by a computer program. In the hands of a reasonably attentive operator, this software could quickly provide whole catalogues of eyes and noses, mouths, hair styles, and so forth to create a composite portrait of a suspect. I was asked by Chief Gottman if I wanted to be trained as the system's full-time operator. Such a position came with generous health and retirement benefits, he informed me, and could open a "respectable career" in law enforcement. "Think about where you might be in a few years, Deputy," he said, as if addressing someone half my age.

I did think about it for maybe fifteen seconds, and I remembered something Gottman had told me on my first day: "Forget about the reasons why some people do bad things. Don't get distracted from your job, Deputy." I had indeed found the means to stay focused on my work, but I'd gotten into it in the first place because I thought that Justice required me to think about what I was doing. It was too late to try and explain this, and anyway, Gottman immediately perceived my lack of interest in his proposition.

At the end, I was thanked heartily for my efforts by colleagues who seemed genuinely sad to see me go. At a farewell party, complete with a cake inscribed to "The Artist Cop," I shook hands all around, and holding back some genuine emotion, I told everyone how grateful I was to have served beside them. Fred Smart was not present that day, and I didn't miss him, especially when Sandy kissed me in front of everybody, bussing me a big one just off my mouth, and bubbling something next to my ear about the Greek Islands. Fred had always kept a polite distance, in part because he believed I was gay, and I thought that if word of Sandy's display were to each reach him, he'd brush it off as meaningless. Nevertheless, I felt somewhat embarrassed for her and for myself.

Then Sandy raised a paper cup of Hawaiian Punch to toast me: "Guido is leaving us, but he will never be forgotten, and he can never be replaced!" I laughed along with everybody else, and smiling at Sandy, I noticed how tightly her hair was bound that day, and I thought that her laughter rang a false note.

"Who else recites the Greek alphabet to impress a girl?" she continued.

A moment of uncomfortable silence followed. I thought of the intense blush, the heat of her orgasms, and the fact of Fred's absence suddenly weighed heavily, ambiguously in the room with us. Then somebody said something about the punch being spiked and not to let the Chief know. We all laughed, and to no one in particular I said, "The Greek alphabet can be useful for all kinds of things." Another awkward silence. I'd once told Sandy that she was my alpha beta gamma girl, and indeed, she had liked everything Greek, including that way for sex.

The party wasn't much of an affair, and when it began to break up, I declined an invitation to head out to a bar for some genuine drinks. Various people patted me on the back, said they would miss me, that I should stop by anytime. They were glad to know I didn't resent my rather sudden termination and that I still had my teaching job. I told them that maybe now, thanks to what I'd done here, I might be ready to get back to my own painting. As we were saying goodbye, I realized that for a time I had actually belonged among them.

After the hubbub at the party's conclusion, from across the quiet room I heard Chief Gottman snorting rather loudly in that unmistakable, pneumatic manner of his. He was talking to David Lafferty who had just walked through the door, having missed the event entirely. I already knew that contrary to what Davey once told me, at some point he had mentioned to Gottman my intuitive gifts; now he was suggesting that perhaps I might yet be consulted regarding cold cases. I heard that much, as much as it took to get Gottman snorting.

Chief Gottman's angular face always looked moist and smooth, as if he had just sweated away all of his facial hair or had it cosmetically removed. When he snorted, which he did as a reaction to anything that he disapproved of or didn't want to discuss, the nostrils of his narrow nose flared mechanically, as if they were a couple of pressure releasing valves. This was how I had once described him to earn a round of laughs at a bar. All of us had had experience with Gottman's indifference and disdain.

For the first and only time with him, I let myself *see* and quietly entered the Chief's mind. It was rather like walking into a library: I soon discovered that behind a favorite book on motorboats, there were some terribly melancholy feelings about an unsolved murder. I could empathize, for I believed that my own recurring waves of sadness these past months were in part due to the horrors that police work had put me in contact with. It was an occupational hazard, and you had to manage as best as possible to cordon off whole neighborhoods of your interior: your very sanity could depend on where you let your imagination roam and where you denied it access. Doctors do something similar, desensitizing themselves to many things they must look into and smell and touch.

To the Chief I said nothing about the pictures of dismembered kids he'd stowed behind a book on motor boating. But I knew that if he would weep for them, his eyes would see more clearly, and that this particular case, which had troubled him for years, might yet be resolved.

PART 5

CHAPTER 39

I MUG, I BRISTLE, I sigh in a sensuous transport induced by the warm, soapy brush with which I lather my face. I protest. I rebut. I remind myself that my life hasn't been so bad, and if I have been threatened on some days with madness, I know what my razor is for: *Pleasure*, I say, grinning while the blade glides under my chin.

The shape of things to come: I feel it in my dreams, I hear it in my own voice humming, I smell it in my students' freshly washed hair every morning in the student union. I'm clean, I repeat to myself, my sins are repented and forgiven. I have never lost faith in the Great Whatever, but I make this distinction on the razor's edge: faith is not the same as belief, which is a wish for certainty. Faith is based on personal experience, faith gives you courage to go forward.

Belief is what my father tried to embrace, who died in the arms of the Church. He'd gotten himself remarried, and with his new wife, he began to attend mass regularly for the first time in his life. After retiring from a series of bartending jobs, he and Giulia departed the States for Sorrento, her hometown and his eventual terminus. Perhaps he had faith too? I believe he found love and that Giulia helped him to accept his death gracefully.

I flew to be beside his body in a casket and kneeled amid a room full of relatives. "So you're dead now," I whispered, touching his clean, cold cheek. "What do you know that I don't know?" His silence I took as a sign that each of us could see the other more clearly now.

Palmolive soap to lather my face, its scent that always evokes memories of Italy where I first used it on a trip in 1969. The hot water, steam rising from the sink while I shave and my mind leaping from thought to thought. The tune of "The Stripper," and the long ago TV ad featuring a Swedish beauty who beseeched every guy to take it off, *take it all off,* swiping the foam from her own face with a safety razor.

I'm looking for the blond in me. I'm still looking for Gwendolyn Glass. Ha! Whipping the razor free of suds and stubble under the faucet's running water. *Ha!* Running the tap hot on the blade's edge, preparing to resume.

Like Socrates who corrupted the youth of Athens with the love of wisdom, the other day in class I told my students that if God exists, His or Her boundless love must have already redeemed us. Buddha taught the same, yes, I averred, giving them the gist of the Diamond Sutra. But it was this bit of "religious zeal" that found its way to the ears of the Dean, who warned me rather sternly to watch what I said in class, since students nowadays are so easily offended and can so readily become litigious. *Oh, Liotta, where would I be without you?*

One last spot of shaving cream on my upper lip remains. Deft as a samurai swordsman, I close my eyes to deliver a stroke that levels Heaven and Earth. And that is why I must wear a patch of toilette paper spotted crimson near my mouth this morning.

I'M UNWANTED. THAT IS, my time is my own. I mean I'm free of every other obligation. In music, an obbligato is indispensable, an accompaniment to the principle theme, perhaps a persistent background motif. Arpeggio means harping, the notes of a chord are struck individually and rapidly. A run. *A bridge:* I see the sound thrown through the air, connecting very quickly here with there. A bird soars singing across the sky. Synesthesia: I feel its feathers with my lips, I kiss its neck as it flies by. My obligation is to myself, as a hawk naturally has no duty but to be a hawk.

"What are you working on these days?"

An ordinary question, posed to me by Jesse Leiper whom I encountered on the way to 10:10 classes. A week of warm weather had erased the memory of winter, the Green looked quite green, and crocuses were blooming.

"Circles," I replied. I'd abandoned my plans to resume portrait painting, and instead had taken up the materials of *sumi-e.* "Zeroes. Os, if you like."

"Still trying to point out the moon, huh? We've had this very conversation before, haven't we, at this very spot? Buckling your swash, you signed an O on the air. The Mark of Zero, you said. Or as they call it in Japan, the *enso.*" With his index finger, Jesse cut a circle before my eyes.

He was right; we'd been through this before, but when? I'm old enough to forget a lot of things, but for a teacher who used to depend on being able to recall immediately the telling anecdote, the source of a quotation, the picture-perfect description of a painting, such failures are an embarrassment if not a source of genuine consternation.

"Get this, " Jesse said.

I readied myself. A conversation with Leiper on a bright, warm morning might require a person to make special preparations. Jesse is a nimble guy in his late twenties: a former dancer turned sculptor and installation artist, he often dances at his exhibitions, which are video recorded and then replayed when subsequently he performs other acrobatics with these movies projected behind him, sometimes on film screens, but also on building walls, on parked automobiles, on a crowd of bystanders. He is a wiz with digital gizmos, but his physical dexterity is the thing that either wows you about him or puts you off. I remember when the Dean first asked me to check him out, to make sure he wasn't truly a lunatic. All I'd said then was, "Da kid's got chops," and like a vaudeville barker puffed my imaginary cigar. Liotta was relieved: she liked Leiper as much as I did and clearly wanted him to stick around.

Recently, he had done a thing incorporating real-time financial quotes and the World Wide Web. In a store window around the corner from Wall Street, he had traded thousands of dollars worth of commodities—or so he said—while wearing a superhero costume. He'd been wired for sound and behind a plate of armor-clad glass, had talked incessantly to passersby about poverty, greed, and social inequities. I don't know how he'd gotten permission to pull such a stunt in the very belly of the beast, but I thought his act was quite clever. He had gone on for several afternoons. In a laudatory article, Joshua Keene, an undisputed star of our faculty, wrote that the work was "very risky" and that it had successfully claimed "new genre territories." In the end, Leiper announced he would give away all his profits, which drew a sizeable crowd during the lunch hour. The profits supposedly amounted to one dollar and eight cents, which he gave to a student along with a short homily about the virtue of staying hungry. At that point he mimed a classic bit from the *Commedia dell'Arte,* looking famished and pretending to eat his own hand. I thought that was fabulous. Back when the College was deciding to hire him, I had reviewed a lot of his stuff. I dug most of it, but I had to ask how often would anyone really want to watch a video loop of Jesse Leiper with a garden hose stuffed up his ass? Not that it wasn't funny for a few seconds while he acted as if the hose were really a snake.

Thankfully, there were no gymnastics this morning. He said simply, "Leo Declare is on the Internet. What I mean is that a lot of his work is for sale. And you are there, sir: a portrait from your younger days, if I'm not mistaken."

"How did you find out about this?"

"I'm building an electronic archive for the college. I searched Leo Declare. What—you've never done that? Somebody named Badge owns a bunch of his work, and it's going to auction soon."

"Badget," I corrected him, "Bob Badget," surprising myself with how readily the name emerged from my mouth. "I used to know him."

"Great. Why don't you see if he'd like to do something nice for the College?"

It was a set up, possibly prompted by Liotta, whom I had continued to put off about the monograph she wanted me to write about Leo.

I gestured to the buildings around us. "This is thanks to Leo Declare," I said. "He drowned in the Hudson, you know, just below the Cliff. People said it was a suicide and what a shame, but hardly anybody cared or came to his memorial service. Not even his executor, Bob Badget."

"His name is Badge now," Leiper said. "Do you want to see what he's selling? The one of you, it must be you, with a beautiful girl? It's *really* good."

I said nothing, glanced at my wristwatch, saw I was late for class, picked up the pace. We were at the pillars of Memnot Hall, and we paused before going our separate ways. Jesse patted my arm and said, "I'm sorry about your friend. But, hey, let's look at the pictures together. Come over and have a drink and you can decide whether or not you want to make contact. The College is interested in acquiring some of Declare's work—it's important to our history. And this guy, Badge or Badget, has an amazing website."

ON A HUNCH THAT she would be home, I phoned Tina. Spring had arrived, and so I figured she'd be back from her annual sojourn in the Caribbean.

"What?" she said, answering after a single ring. She sounded angry, and I sensed she must have been expecting someone else.

"It's me, Guido. How are you?"

"You! I thought it was Eddy. Good. He won't be able to get through with you on the line."

I'd learned from Davey how they broke up regularly but were always on again in time to winter down South. I said to Tina, "You've gotta introduce me some time. Davey told me he's a black magician." I was teasing.

"Detective Lafferty said that?" She paused for a second. "His psychic power must be unplugged. Eddy may be Haitian, black and beautiful, but he's no witch. He wants me to marry him in a Catholic church!"

"Why don't you?"

EARLIER THAT WEEK, IN my aunt Josie's living room, when Edouard Charpentier's shadow slipped into our conversation, in serious tones Josie whispered that she thought Tina might be mixed up with some kind of voodoo. She made the sign against evil, pointing her fingers, spitting dryly. Then she said, "You're a policeman, Guido. Isn't there something you can do?"

"Aunt Josie," I replied, in an equally serious tone of voice, "I'm not working for them anymore, and anyway I never really was a cop." I had tried to explain this before. "Also, Tina is a grown woman."

With an expression on her face that looked like sympathy for my ignorance, she said, "That may be so, but she's always been involved with the wrong people."

"Eddy's the guy that got her sober, " I said. "Yes. He helped her when she was desperate. That's what I heard. And he's Catholic. Who knows, maybe they'll get married. . ."

"My daughter? Never! *Never!*" She slapped the air, as if to banish the idea or punish me for uttering it.

I leaned back in my chair at her kitchen table. Besides my mother, Josie and Tina were my two closest living relatives this side of the Atlantic, and I did not want to get between them. On the other hand, it was largely because of Josie that despite my own reservations I had originally made the effort to locate and reconnect with my cousin.

"Look, Aunt Josie, my mother always said that Tina never could make up her mind, you know, *about herself.* That's a simplification, but, well, you need to lay off. She'll come around when she's ready. She's like a cat. . ."

"A cat? Holy Mother of God, Guido, we're talking about my baby!" She blessed herself and the thought of her daughter with the Sign of the Cross.

I persisted: "Didn't everybody always make a big fuss about her? Uncle Tony actually used to call her Kitten, no? And everybody always wanted sugar from her cheeks."

I prepared myself for an opera. Tears of rage perhaps, or hysterical accusations about my failure to do the thing she had asked of me: bring her baby home. Instead, surprisingly, she worked herself down from the pitch of her excitement, and then, surprising me again, produced a pack of Salem cigarettes from her apron pouch. After she'd lit one for herself, wordlessly she pushed the green package and matches across the tabletop to me. Josie is famously hypochondriacal, and it had been years since I'd seen her smoke, but like her daughter, who had also quit long ago, she evidently made exceptions for special occasions. She motioned to me with her eyes to take one, it was an Italian thing, recalled from the old days at the Villa, when an invitation to share a smoke was almost sacred. I took one and lit it up; it was mentholated and terribly stale, but after my second hit I blew a perfect smoke ring. She smiled at me, and amid her wrinkles I caught a glimpse of her long ago beauty.

Unlike my mother who chain smoked whenever she was upset, after exactly three puffs Josie stubbed her cigarette in an ashtray that she'd also extracted from her apron pocket. I was feeling dizzy and so I also put mine out. Then she carefully swept away some stray flecks of ash that had settled on the tablecloth. The green cigarette package was also suddenly gone from the checkered yellow and white oil cloth.

"Thanks, Guido. Thanks for everything. I mean it. For finding her, you and David, thank you for all you did. I know how much you love her. I know what people say about her, the things they say about me too. But I will never abandon my baby!" She raised her hand palm out as if she were swearing an oath.

You have always been a difficult customer, I thought to myself, quoting my grandmother, the only critical thing I ever heard her say about her son's wife, Giuseppina—my aunt Josie—who has always found something not quite right with the world, and who, like most of us, does not like to admit how many of her problems she creates herself.

"WANTS TO SETTLE DOWN with me! Can you believe the man?"

"Yes, of course, I believe in Eduoard Charpentier. But do I ever get to meet him in person? Does anybody? Davey says he's never met him, but I guess you like to talk to him about Eddy."

"He's an honest cop."

She said nothing more.

I broke the silence. "You and me," I said, "it's been good to get close again. Listen, I really do want to know: are you going to marry him?"

"Living in sin is more fun. That's why I'd rather go to Miami than Haiti where his family lives." She laughed.

Changing the subject, I said, "I'm feeling much better these days. You've helped me a lot, you know."

"Great. Your mother was getting worried. But you go through this sort of shit every so often, don't you?"

I found myself rubbing the place on my chest; the scent of lavender oil rose through my shirt. It occurred to me that the itch I felt was a sign of healing.

I said to her, "What do you do in the rest of your life? Your mother thinks you're like. . . you know, that expression of hers, a piece of *flossy and gesu.* Like a survivor from a shipwreck holding onto a splinter of wood, tossed around on the waves. I told her I thought you were happy."

I got nothing in return for that compliment, and after a moment, I added, "Help me out here, kid."

"I am. I am happy. Listen, Guido, you're starting to sound. . . Why'd you call, anyway?"

I didn't have a good answer but I wanted to keep talking.

After a moment, she said, "There're some things you should keep your nose out of."

I allowed myself to feel the heat glazing the distance between us. I stiffened. My cousin and I are not of a sanguine humor, unlike some others in our family, most notably our grandmother. "Sanguine means blood," I had once explained to her. "Warm and rosy and fun to be with." Way back when she'd been a little doll, I could hush her tears by kissing her crown and with both hands on her curly hair, I'd smooth her troubles away. I had hugged and squeezed her just like everybody did until she yelped and scowled, but we had all thought this was cute and pinched her chubby cheeks until she winced.

"Why don't you say something, Guido? I can't believe what a passive aggressive fuck you can be! You still on the line or what?"

I didn't know what to say; I was hurt that we weren't connecting. Then I realized that she might hang up on me. Then I would do what I usually did. But writing about Tina doesn't cure my pain, and long ago, I gave up trying to capture her likeness in a portrait.

With her telephone slam and afterwards the line humming empty at my ear, I slipped my receiver into its cradle. I did this gently, checking to see that it fit snugly so that the electric contacts were in place. It was clear to me then as it has often been clear how much I am like my mother with her compulsive behaviors, most famously her need to check the burners on the restaurant stove. My penchant has always been to obsess about matters of conscience, poking myself again and again to see whether I am still pained, digging in further and further. Is this like the pebble in Sister Vincent's shoe?

I had phoned Tina because I was jealous of Edouard, and she'd sensed it. I believed she would marry him, and actually I thought it would be great for everybody if she did. But long after I laid down the phone, I could feel how unhappy she was with me, and how helpless I'd been to rectify that.

CHAPTER 40

"THINK OF THIS WAY: getting Mr. Badge to make a gift would be some fun." Jesse's grin was positively elfish, and his slender dancer's body swayed as he spoke. I was at his house for drinks on the first of several such occasions. "Our strategy and negotiations will comprise what I like to call a *concept fait.*"

If anyone I have ever met can truly be called *fey*, it is Jesse Leiper. I am not merely referring to his looks but also to his dexterous ability with language. In particular, he is a philologist of cyberspace, where my functional vocabulary is at about the level of an eight year old. I have liked him since I met him, but I had become suspicious of how he was insinuating himself into my life. Did he want to sleep with me? With whom *did* he sleep—I'd never heard that he was partnered and I actually wondered if the lad might be asexual. Then too I was leery of his campaign to secure tenure, something that he evidently thought I could help him with. Why would he bother when he had so much else going for himself as an artist, including one foot planted at the Whitney?

He'd been to Choate and then the Chicago Institute School, and when he mentioned his great grandfather, the inventor of an electronic device familiar to everybody, I realized that Jesse had never lived in want. Which is not to say that he didn't understand need: he needed some things passionately. His art, he professed, was a continuing search "to make things that dance in the mind." Sitting with a strong hand at the art market table, he seemed to me quite free to do whatever he liked with himself—so why decide to teach at this stage of his career? In the face of all his youthful enthusiasm, I didn't feel like trying to explain how far HRC had fallen from the heights to which it once aspired.

What I said was, "I myself don't trust the herd instinct. In my brave new world, the best would lead because their character would be demonstrably better than the rest. And I'd be sitting in the Grove under a sycamore tree like Socrates, challenging my students with *whys*."

He caught the pun and smiled. He was trying so hard to be my friend and include me in his project, but *why* was it so difficult for me to surrender? Then I answered my own question: the problem wasn't that Leiper might be too young or too cute for me, but rather, it was his fascination with Robert E. Badge, "your old friend," as he had already referred to him. And Jesse wasn't only interested in buying some of Leo's paintings for the College: he wanted to hit Bob up for a substantial bequest! I had a mind to ask Davey for some old fashioned, flat-footed snooping, yet I wanted believe in Jesse, who assured me that Mr. Badge was the real deal: an ex-con who'd reformed himself, and more than that, launched a prosperous business.

Jesse gave it to me straight: no one would be able to capitalize on Leo's legacy until his reputation was salvaged, and furthermore, he agreed with the Dean that I should be the one to do this by producing a definitive monograph. Perhaps I could do a complete biography of Leo Declare, *visionary creative*—that was one he pulled out of the air with a flourish of his hand—and this one too: "A Founding Father of the Hudson River College." We all stood to gain by his "reconstitution."

"You, sir, are a primary source for this project. You were there, man, at the beginning!" He clapped his hands together.

Taking over the museum's electronic archive had been Leiper's idea and he'd proposed it at exactly the right moment. Not only was he supervising the digital cataloguing of every piece already in the collection, but he was also acquiring new works specifically created with new technologies. This was in fact the direction Leiper's own art was headed, and two of his pieces had recently been acquired by the College, thanks to the munificence of one Mohammed Ahmed, a businessman who collected Jesse's work. The archive was the sort of years-long project an Assistant Professor needed for his tenure file. "The right idea at the right time," he said, rubbing together his thumb and forefinger, making the gesture for cash in hand.

"I'm for it," I said, trying to sound excited. "It'll benefit our students for years to come." We were onto our second round of drinks. "I have nothing against success," I said. "And I'm generally in favor of money." I raised my glass. "But let's not forget the root of all evil." I sipped my martini, but it wasn't in homage to the wisdom of Saint Paul. "An excessive love for old cold cash has undone many a fine fellow. Why, Caravaggio—you remember *il caro selvaggio*, dontcha?" I pulled two olives from my glass on a tiny pink plastic sword and waved it at Jesse. "He loved money as much as the next genius, but he had to run for his life because of a very bad, um, career choice. *Murdah,* to be precise."

Jesse doubled over, gripping his belly as if stuck by a sword. Then he bounced up from his cushion on the living room floor, made a polite bow and excused himself in order "to use the *toilette*." I poured myself another tall one, put my feet up on the white ottoman, and thought hard about Bob Badget. I had no intention of getting in touch with him on behalf of the fucking College.

"YOUR COUSIN CHRIS SAYS you've got a rocket in your pocket."

He had just parked the T-bird, that little yellow convertible Cristiano would have killed for. We were together on a daytrip to New York, one of several that year, when Bobby B. and I were something like pals. We were waiting to cross 85th street on an incredibly warm December day, a few blocks from the Guggenheim. The city looked beautiful: Christmas in July, colored lights inside the windows, and outside in their garden boxes, pink and purple flowers of impatiens, frost free all these months past summer.

Bob grabbed me by the wrist. "The most creative people learn to swim against the current. You gotta be prepared for what's coming downstream *toward* you." He gave my wrist a squeeze and pulled me into the street, through the coming traffic, across to the other side.

He was showing me around like no one else had ever bothered to do. Even if I couldn't believe in him the way Chris did, I was willing to have fun at his expense, and I didn't see the harm in that. Especially if it meant a swift trip to New York in that hot little car and a puff of Panama Red.

LEIPER RETURNED AND SAT opposite me on the floor. He began to stretch his arms and rotate his shoulders. He wore loose fitting yogi clothes tonight, his trousers tight at the ankles, his cotton blouse half open. His antics were monkey-like, and he made me smile, and because I was high on his booze, and because I knew how interested he was in any and all of my reminiscences, I opened up.

I began as I usually do when I talk about my past: I was a lucky kid, lucky to have been brought up at the Villa with its cast of characters, but happy to have left and met Leo thanks to my cousin's connections. I'd then gotten lucky with Gwendolyn Glass, too, "my first," I said, remembering that Jesse had seen the painting of us in our prime.

"What happened to her?" he asked.

"I don't know," I said. "We didn't last very long."

I told Jesse a little about the influence Bob had had on Leo's scene: "Not all of it good. He fucked up. My cousin did too. And me. It's weird to have this link all of the sudden through you."

I could see the blond tuft of beard that wagged under Bob's mouth like a second tongue whenever he gave me one of his life-lectures, could feel his hand on my shoulder alongside my neck as he steered me along the busy pavements of New York.

"You've been to the movie houses in Times Square, right?" I said this to Jesse in Bob's raspy baritone. "You know who Claudia Cardinale is? You're gonna meet her today. She'll be in your dreams tonight." That seductive voice of his.

Dropping the act, I continued, "He and Leo started out as partners at the Half Moon. Bob found the money to back them." I paused and then for effect I said slowly, "It might have been Mob money." I threw a piratical look at Leiper. "Monkey business, we used to call it."

I mentioned some of the other stupid things the crew had said to each other. The way we talked about Debbie when she got strung out on heroin. "In those days, we didn't know how bad a jones could be, and wouldn't have believed she could end up hooking full time and then going to jail for shooting her worthless husband. Bob went to prison for fraud and income tax evasion." Leiper sat in lotus posture at my feet absorbing it all.

I felt sober and went silent. Funny how booze has this effect on me: I'm drunk and then suddenly I'm not.

Jesse picked up his end of the conversation: "You know, being a criminal isn't so stigmatized as it once was, especially if it involves cheating the government. The more our society is organized as a corporate hegemony, the more that individual notoriety, *arrived at by any means*, is regarded as an end in itself. When young people are asked about this, they often reply that they just want to be known for *something*, for *anything*. Too bad about the way former felons are treated, though. . ."

"Fame," I said, "in Italian, the word *fame* means hunger. Grammatically, one does or doesn't *have* hunger. I think Bob had it, real ambition, but frankly I'm not so sure about Leo. He wasted a lot of opportunities. He could have been quite successful as a painter if he had wanted."

Leiper was on his feet now, and I knew what was coming. As he began to contort his body, I was reminded of a remark made to me by Margret Ruasch, who clearly disliked Jesse, that perhaps his "spasticity" indicted a genuine neurological disorder and that "this could be dangerous if he lost control while operating heavy machinery." In fact, Leiper had done something with a fork-lift during one of his performances, but I thought she was being ridiculous when she suggested I might use my detective skills to discover what she called "the history of his condition." I had replied that I too sometimes found his rubbery displays a bit distracting, but that I was actually interested in seeing how far he would go. Laughingly, I added that such an attitude toward Mr. Leiper might allow him to reveal something about his suitability for our faculty. Margret stared at me for a moment and then said, "You're joking, of course. Tenure is a serious matter." Then she strode off.

Now he'd risen into a shoulder stand. "To be free from need is to be wealthy," Jesse said. "To live according to one's values is success." He tumbled over and sprang on his hands into a back-arch. He bounced on elastic arms and legs, talking to me with his face upside down. The mouth looked ridiculous, all teeth and tongue, the chin like the dome of a tiny bald head. I burst out laughing.

Rolling into a cross-legged sitting position, Jesse said, "I love this bit of Zen: no matter how wonderful something is, it's more wonderful to have nothing at all. Fame is empty, like everything else, only maybe it disappears a little faster." Jesse sprang up into a standing position and wheeled a quarter turn to face me. "My head is spinning," he said, and with the back of his palm he touched his brow to mime distress.

When he'd passed his three year review and we had begun to think of ourselves as more than just colleagues, I'd told Jessie that if I were he, I would bypass HRC and jump with both feet into the theater to build my reputation. There he might eventually do what he really wanted.

He had scoffed. "I danced for five years with a company of real artists," he said. "If I thought I needed to become famous before I could do what I wanted, I'd kill myself."

We talked about fame fairly often, even though both of us attested to its relative unimportance. I told him that the school needed people like him who understood, but were unaffected by, the current emphasis on the artist as "a processor" of his or her circumstances, rather than a creator in service to individual genius. I said that I admired what he'd already accomplished and that I envied his youth.

"The process is peculiarly slow," Jessie said. He was now sitting upright across from me in his white, white living room. I had been watching his mouth rather than listening to his words, and I didn't know what he was referring to. Puckish, that mouth. I could lean in and kiss it, if I wanted to.

"Academics are notoriously resistant to new ideas, and the established elite take pleasure in chastising those they perceive as upstarts. The year I taught at Gilmont College there was a woman who showed her canines to me whenever she had the opportunity. A full professor who pretended she wasn't herself one of the herd. She who loved to snap at the hocks of strays. I've got the marks to prove it." He seemed to pull at his trouser leg to examine himself. "Somewhere." He looked both impish and angelic.

"Right," I said. "Socrates was accused of corrupting the children of the ruling class by tutoring them in philosophy."

"Haven't you ever been worried that without tenure you're not protected from attacks on your ideas?"

"No. There are people at the College who don't like me, but I've never believed that my academic freedom depended on their approval—which is what I think about tenure. Okay, okay, it *is* a form of job security and of many other benefits—that is unless the job, or the department, or the school goes under. It happened not so long ago to a small college upstate. . . But I can't equate job security with my right to free speech. And I certainly don't equate tenure with the freedom to make art; far from it."

"Maybe for some people, once they get it, they feel free to do the work they really want to, work that might have been sidelined—"

"While they were spending their time and energy, six years of it usually, trying out for the team? I suppose that for some it really does all come together on their way becoming an associate professor. They feel affirmed, and indeed they're likely to get further support for their careers because the institution wants them to keep doing whatever they've already been doing. Wonderful. The system works for some people, I'll grant you that, but for fewer and fewer. There just aren't enough faculty positions for all the MFAs and PhDs in the humanities that are turned out. I didn't have a good experience in graduate school, which as you know, is supposed to prepare you for what it takes to win that academic freedom prize."

"A graduate degree is only a ticket to freedom if you know how to cash it in," Leiper replied. "It's the means to a brave new world—not Huxley's dystopia, but the life of the mind, the life of the creative intellect."

I looked at him for a moment thinking he was right. Clearly, I had never had what it takes to stay such a course. Leo, on the other hand, a genuine maverick, had somehow managed to create a school in his own image. The timing was right for that, the conditions, the karma, whatever you call it. And then things changed. I said, "The original model of the university is the monastery. I've probably hung around academia for so long because of my past lives as a monk. Seriously, I believe this. But since the Reformation or whatever you call what happened at HRC, I am probably thought of as an apostate. You shouldn't even be talking to me, young man!"

Jesse laughed, but he had heard me out.

I woke up the morning after with a very particular kind of hangover: I could manage being thought of as a heretic but not a hypocrite. After my famous departure from the College, I'd limped back to the Green and the Grove, if not exactly disgusted with myself, then trying to accept the fact that I would eventually have to make a choice about whether I was in or out. Had I learned that I was incapable of making it in the world as an artist at large? For sure, I wasn't going to be a cop or a PI, and therefore, should I finally throw myself into Liotta's waiting arms?

Jesse respected the way I'd succeeded until now living in the margins, as it were, but I thought he was too young to grasp its continuing cost to me. This morning, my head hurt with trying to explain myself to myself. I was rubbing my eyes outside my office door, attempting to put my key into its lock. When I finally gained entrance I slumped into my friendly old chair.

In the beginning, when it was more important than I could have known, Leo had had faith in me. Whatever else had gone down between us, I owed him for that. If I could pass on to Jesse some of what we'd started out with at HRC and which, truly, I had never abandoned, that would mean something, and it would be one for the Captain too.

Susan Giles, Liotta's girlfriend, a New York City real estate agent, successful, very successful, thought that Jesse Leiper had a great future ahead of him. It was Susan who had purchased the video of Jesse with the garden hose up his ass, and the thought of her and the Dean watching it at Susan's neo-colonial palace in Westport made me laugh out loud. But I like Susan, in spite of the cost-benefit analysis she tends to bring into everything. She is smart and a patron of the arts, a lover of fine things, including fine dining and drinking. Dinner tonight on the deck at the Patriot Arms was her treat. Wine glass in hand she pronounced, "That burst bubble be damned." She was referring to the steady collapse of the housing market, something whose repercussions for the College I would begin to grasp that evening.

I am always better at assessing a woman's character if I have no erotic interest in her. Am I a sexist, or am I just being honest about myself? Hell, if I'm a sexist, then I ought to mend my ways, and rather than struggling against my impulses, banish *Eros* from my life. Right.

Susan is plump and I think her boyish face isn't complemented by her too short hair, which makes her head look small in contrast to her rather large bosom. Although she does usually try to camouflage their size, tonight she seemed to feature those breasts under a form-fitting sweater. She is typically full of herself, but she is not solipsistic, and I like that. Yet I wouldn't spend time with her if not also in Liotta's company. Voluptuous Susan is much closer in age to me than to Liotta, and while I don't like to picture them making love—well, I had just done that, and once again I began to wonder if I were a sexist and if had been drinking too much, once again.

"Excuse me," I said, still chortling over the thought of Leiper's garden hose coming to life like a serpent between them. I covered my mouth and sauntered to the deck's railing; glass in hand, I watched the red and green lights of a passing pleasure boat. It was growing late, and we three were the only diners left outside. Sue had called it "a scrumptious evening whatever awaits us tomorrow," and it had been an altogether waxy time, smooth and never sticky, made all the more pleasurable because of her benign influence on the Dean: she relaxes Liotta, and when Lie is relaxed, I am reminded why I'm fond of her. She doesn't complain when she has problems, but rather is solution oriented in the name of opportunity. With solid Sue beside her under the deck's party lights, long Liotta cut an even more attractive figure than usual.

Springtime, *la primavera*, was in the air, and I thought of Botticelli's masterpiece, perhaps my very favorite painting, a large tableaux whose beauty is obvious but whose symbolism defies every explanation. The painting has obsessed me since I first studied it in high school. As my teacher Mr. MacDonald told me back then, it must be seen in person at the Uffizi to fully appreciate its effect: the figures are practically life size, and the viewer feels as if he has come upon the Goddess of Love herself, where at twilight she presides amid a fruit filled grove. Accompanying her are various mythological personages, but each seems engaged in his or her own erotic drama and is oblivious of the others. I think the painting implies that everyone feels love's influence uniquely.

From behind me, I caught snatches of the ladies' gay conversation which was carried on a soft breeze like a musical accompaniment for my reverie. When the pitch of their voices descended into more serious tones, however, I tuned my ears more carefully.

"We've leveraged two new buildings, taking on considerable debt," Liotta was saying. "Despite the Remsen bequest, do you know how much that new performing arts center is going to cost us? We'll have to raise tuition. Again."

"Calm yourself, dear. Your Board is behind you. Put a freeze on hiring and promotions. Sell another Giacometti print at Christie's and collect some ready cash for, what did you call it, your *dispensary*? That's rich, Lie!"

There is a curious clarity that two drinks confer on me; with three I'm a sage; with four I'm weaving a little but still functional. Now I was making an effort to keep my balance while I tried to analyze what I was hearing. Sell *another* Giacometti print? Apparently the "ready cash" being collected was, among other things, financing the acquisition of works by artists whose value was being bet on to increase. I wondered how long Liotta and the Trustees had been at this: managing the museum collection like a financial portfolio whose assets might be liquidated as necessary. Did the Faculty Council approve this? Surely there would have been protests—or was there too much at stake for anybody to object?

Then I had a terrible thought, a real bummer of a thought: once the entire collection and certain pieces that had belonged to it, were available virtually on line, as Lieper was about to make possible, who would really care whether or not a couple of Giacometti's had been sold off, or whether a Dove or Bierstadt were to be found on the actual walls of our tiny museum. Those works would still have addresses in cyberspace, and, moreover, their connection to HRC would be forever preserved in digital amber. Provenance: it's what people who don't have eyes in their heads care about, because it translates into financial worth. Furthermore, if some grander establishment acquired the works, the history of their prior ownership might be a boon to the College. If private collectors acquired them, this too could have a net positive effect, drawing attention to the possibility that other works with market value were in our possession. Did I dare to think of myself in this company—but Leo Declare, oh yeah.

I was getting a headache and I wanted to dunk myself into the cool water running below me. I looked up to the sky instead, and through a break in scudding clouds spotted a diadem of stars. I thought of the figure of Hermes with his wand and eyes upraised in *La Primavera*: god of commerce, god of the crossroads. Of thieves, too.

Liotta had said we'd leveraged two new buildings. She was referring to the construction of rental properties the College owned in Manhattan. Leverage has to do with borrowing power, and it can increase your potential for gain *or* for loss. Businesses use leverage to try to increase the wealth of their shareholders, but if a financial gambit fails, the cost of interest payments or the risk of defaulting on a loan or mortgage can ruin a company and destroy the value of its shares.

Like other institutions of higher education, HRC is a not-for-profit enterprise, but its business is to *stay in business* for the benefit of its stakeholders; that is, the students, faculty, staff, alumni, and society in general. If, as Susan and Liotta foresaw, the global economy was pitching into a deep recession, to what lengths would the Board of Trustees go to insure that we stayed solvent? Objects of art are actually good investments during periods of economic turmoil, and so stockpiling them would make more sense than selling—unless you needed the cash to keep going.

Liotta motioned for me to rejoin the conversation. She was smiling warmly and had one bare, freckled arm extended along the deck railing behind Susan. My head was now reasonably clear—a shot of adrenalin will do that—but if the talk were now to gravitate to high finance I doubted I'd be able to keep abreast. And I certainly hoped I wouldn't be asked my opinion on selling *another* Giacometti.

"I've been talking to the President about you"—a big toothy smile, big dark eyes—"and I floated the idea that we might be able to consider you as already on a tenure track *retroactively.*"

I said nothing.

"In other words," she continued, rather slowly, "on the basis of what you did, you've already done for us, and do, and do what we expect you to."

A lengthy pause, her inquiring gaze.

"I told Rosa that we might. . .how shall I say. . . *grandfather* you in."

Yes, with her eyes on me, her perfectly penciled eyebrows raised expectantly—yes, I could see that the Dean was rather sloshed. Susan, also clearly soused, nestled under her arm and also watched for my reaction. They complemented each other, one fair and curvaceous, the other dark and svelte. Under the deck lights, haloed now with fog as the night began to cool, they both looked younger than their years, and, I had to admit, *très séduisant.*

I tried to laugh off my genuine surprise at what Liotta was suggesting. Susan, who was now holding her around the waist, flashed me a look as if to say I'd be a fool to pass up such an opportunity. Given what I'd previously overheard and how my thoughts had been running, I was in fact speechless. What I did in response was so typically Italian that I'm embarrassed to recall it: I drew myself upright and snapped my heels together as if I were a yeoman of the guard, proud to be commended by a superior. "Thank you, my Dean," I replied smartly.

Liotta did not doubt my gratitude, but she knew me well enough to realize that I was not simply acquiescing to her plans. She smiled, showing me the strong teeth in her lined face. "You'll think about it, I'm sure." Flavoring that with a hint of her deep South drawl. "Let the idea *perpolate*—oh, excuse me!" A hand to her lips. "*Percolate*, so that when the time is right, you, you and I can make your case."

I nodded, my smiled fixed in place. "What a beautiful night," I said, fanning an arm out over the water, since it seemed that some sort of expansive gesture was called for. Peering over the railing into the dark river I saw my head floating below.

CHAPTER 41

Despite my doubts about the future of the College, despite my doubts about my own future, I decided to help Jesse with his civics project, and so I agreed to let him take me on a complete tour of Castlefroy via his home computer system. On the appointed night, however, I found myself stalling for a long while over my scotch while he went on about the amazing experiences awaiting us in cyberspace. I'd already been to the website on my own for a short free tour, but Jesse had access to the members' areas.

He was correct that the name of company's Founder, President, and Chief Executive Officer was listed as Robert E. Badge. (Elmo was Bob's middle name, I recalled; once I'd overheard Concetta teasing, *Ale-mo needs a pocketbook,* whatever that meant.) I had the creepy premonition that I might encounter Bob's avatar or Mr. Badge himself that night.

"How much influence do you think a person's name has on his life?" I asked Jesse.

He somersaulted effortlessly across the floor and in one fluid motion regained his cross-legged posture.

"Plenty," he said. "A lot of it unconscious."

"I was named for Guido Cavalcanti, the fourteenth century poet, the lover of women and horses." I finished my drink. "Well, I also had an uncle named Guido. A great uncle who died from the Spanish Influenza. You are obviously meant to be mobile, Mr. Leiper. Whether upwardly or elsewise."

"Elsewise!" he said, reaching for his drink. "And you, Mr. Diamante, are very cool, but somewhat colder than you like to admit." For added emphasis he jiggled his glass of scotch-rocks. Some of the liquor sloshed onto his fingers and he licked them.

"Brilliant," I said. "I'm. . . brilliant. . . too," although I didn't feel that way at the moment.

Jesse had called me cold and I'd recoiled. I knew how to be calculating, if that's what he meant. And detached. To be neither for nor against, but to experience each thing in itself. I practice the Middle Way with a sense of discernment, with cool, do I not? I'm the guy who worked on three homicides, the guy whose pencil has been an instrument of *La Giustizia*, the Lady with a sword, a set of scales, and a blindfold over her eyes. Nothing wrong with cool appraisals, deft decisions, and clean cuts of a blade, is there?

There's a Zen term that covers all kinds of delusions and hallucinations: *makyo*, a Japanese word. It's said that, paradoxically, as your effort at practice intensifies, you can be more prone to delusions; it's said that the very idea of *satori* is itself a form of makyo. The literal meaning is something like "cave haunting demon." What this means is that because of our egoistic attachments, both our hopes and fears can bedevil us.

Leiper tiptoed over to the liquor caddy, treading his bone-white carpet in green merino socks that he had bought on-line from an artisan mill in Vermont. Naturally. He wheeled the table to me, all brass and glass jingling, the shelves holding bottles of booze whose contents slapped and shimmered. I handed over to him my outsized tumbler so that he could pour me another one, *neat*. He flashed me a conspiratorial look when he passed my drink to me, and taking the glass, I raised it to him, pronouncing us shipmates.

Settling into an ash-white easy chair, tossing his legs sidewise over the big arms, he proceeded: "Good citizenship requires us to be parsimonious in our expenditures." He edged his words with a Jimmy Stewart lilt. He was a good mimic, and complimenting him on that, I said I couldn't help but anticipate his next "celebrity ejaculation." Slouched in his chair, he kicked his feet gleefully in the air.

I was tight in the shoulders and had to keep adjusting the large cushion behind me. My back hadn't been treating me well lately. I'd been sleeping poorly, and that day, I had been awake since three a.m. My second large whiskey surely would relax me, I thought.

"However," Jesse continued, "there's also the necessity that we spend as much of our acquisitions fund as possible during the current fiscal year."

I didn't know how much of a player he might be in what I now thought of as the Museum Business, but I wasn't going to bring it up. Instead, I paid heed to the voices of my parents somewhere behind me intoning that familiar refrain from my childhood, *Business is bad*.

Jesse said he thought that Leo's detractors had been given time enough to get over their resentments. He said, "Who wants to hate a poor dead sonofabitch? Certainly you wouldn't want to, if you thought you could, shall we say, *capitalize* on his memory. But," he added, "you know how some people like to *niggle*—" Leiper wrinkled his nose, delighting in the word—"positively *niggle* over every nickel and dime. Thank heaven for the real artists!"

The tenor of our conversation was turning me off, and I told him frankly that I thought HRC was part of the problem making it impossible to discuss aesthetic values objectively.

He ignored my comment and started to talk about his present group of graduate students. He'd recruited them specially for his course in Internet Semiotics because things were changing so rapidly in the field that the students were often ahead of him. "A good investment—an investment in our future."

"Jesus, you're talking as if they're football players at Michigan State. Just remember, the ones who don't turn pro are likely to come back and replace us on the faculty."

"It's the way of the world," he replied with a wink.

His boyishness, his *buoyancy* was charming and inseparable from his identity as an artist—his body was after all the primary medium with which he worked—but at that moment I could clearly see why clever Jesse Leiper turned off certain people.

As my father once told me about performance, "personality" is what you're giving to an audience: whether or not it's only an act, if they like your personality, you're in. It almost doesn't matter how good or bad your jokes are. But academia is a somewhat different type of theater. An unsavory character is bound to accumulate demerits enough to be denied advancement, and yet departments sometimes discover only too late that a newly admitted member is actually rather difficult once a formerly compliant persona has been shed.

I thought Jesse was as he appeared to be, and yet what bothered me was how he might compromise himself in order to reach his goals. Tonight his quiff was combed wet, and his usual fashionable stubble had been shaven away. Two moles set asymmetrically on either side of his mouth suggested a permanent expression of impertinence. Was this the face of a future professor at the Hudson River College? Or did he have another he would wear after tenure?

"Our reputation," Jesse said—but I'd spaced out and wasn't following.

I leaned back, waved my free hand in the air, and with exaggerated nonchalance, I said, "Whatever can a girl depend upon *besides* her reputation?" I meant the College, but it came out sounding strange to my ears. I got myself another drink.

Leo was always somewhere in the background whenever Jesse and I were together, and what came into my mind unexpectedly was when I unfortunately let it slip that Gwendolyn and I had been lovers. I was with him in his office, a rat hole adjacent to the kitchen at the Half Moon, and he was cutting me a check for back pay. I asked if Gwen had stopped by to collect what was owed to her. Something about the way I phrased it caused him to look angrily at me. I remember I was playing with my mustache; I'd been doing it a lot since that night, searching for her scent on my fingers.

"We finally got it on," I said, hoping to sound cool.

"And what?" he said, staring at me, pressing back his eyeglasses. "You think you love her because she was the first?"

What he said next was devastating: "Every hole is the same hole, *cheri*. When you've been to the bottom enough times, you'll realize that." He bent to his paperwork, and without looking up at me, a moment later muttered, "Sorry, kid. I just don't think that she . . ."

I didn't hear whatever he said next.

For two days, I'd been grilling myself over whether or not I was now Gwendolyn's boyfriend, whether or not I *could* be. It felt weird to admit it, but maybe she *wasn't* right for me. I hadn't been able to reach her by phone, and although I left a message with her mother, she did not return my call. In fact, there was some relief in that, because the Gwendolyn I had once worshipped no longer existed, and I didn't know what to do with this other one, *Gigi*, who had blown my mind. Furthermore, I was now seized with a terrible fear: neither of us had said a word about birth control, and I'd blissfully assumed she was "safe." It was Cristiano's word for it: "If she doesn't say anything about it, she feels safe." Four times that night we had neglected to say anything about pills or rubbers, but by the next evening I'd begun to suffer.

I wasn't going to talk about any of this with Captain Prick. Not then, not ever.

And I wasn't going to say anything about Gigi to my hungry friend Jesse Leiper. I resumed my seat on his sofa, and sipping from my glass, I asked myself not for the first time what function was served by recollecting such pain? The act of remembering a *past* experience is simultaneously a matter of the *present*—so was this how I wanted to live, coiled around my hurts, milking them for what purpose? My art? My aloofness and self-control have often been thought by others to signify indifference, yet I have no doubt about the depth of my passions. Meditation hasn't made them go away—that isn't the point of meditation, whose only aim, if it can be said to have one, is to clarify who and what you really are.

Jesse was quiet, perhaps waiting for me to share whatever thoughts had brought on my sudden silent mood. I held my pose, propped up by the cushion of my philosophy. *Come fosse una statua.* My whole life I have practiced this talent inherited from my grandmother, becoming still as a statue and seeming to stop the forward flow of time. It's then that the present moment can open up and within my reveries I can reverse time's movement. But too much of this can destroy a person: makyo.

Leiper yawned and stretched his wiry arms above his head. In his flannel shirt and stiff blue jeans, in his stocking feet he looked as if he were about seventeen. As for me, I was tired of feeling like an adolescent who needed to face down his daddy once again. Was it possible that I could still be angry at Leo, who had helped me so much but who had also been in so many ways mistaken? Behind him stood my similarly ignorant father. Behind both was the false god who'd fucked up human beings by claiming he was in charge of everything, the Demiurge, the tyrant whom Blake called Nobodaddy.

My father's own father I had met when as a little boy we visited Italy: he was supposed to have been a tyrant, and my dad had escaped him early on. My dad had equated salvation with the love of women, but I think all of them were substitutes for Lady Luck—who probably stood for the memory of the mother he'd lost when he was very young. Late in life, a gamble took Nunzio Diamante back to Italy with Giulia, and there he had enjoyed a few months of *vita bella.* His cancer took him quickly, and at the foot of Mount Vesuvius he returned to the soil from which his people, from which *our* people sprang. I saw once again the strange picture Leo painted for me of my father holding hands with Larry Bell. "Old World," he'd called them, and although back then I'd been utterly uninterested in his guinea ways, now it made me glad to think that Zizi Diamante never abandoned them.

JESSE AND I SHARED an interest in Asian art, and more importantly, we had both done formal Zen practice, including some monastery retreats with Japanese teachers. In various ways, we probed each other's understanding of Zen, not only through philosophical

discussions, but also more playfully, with our jokes and verbal spar-
ring. I had never caught on to Zen *mondo,* the cutting remarks and
anecdotes by which the old Chinese and Japanese masters compared
their spiritual views, but then I'd never had anyone to practice with,
except, of course, my *roshi.* With the Master, even when I succeeded
in answering an apparently simple question, I'd still have my doubts,
since he refused to explain Zen to me in intellectual terms.

Leiper had wandered over to his white kitchen, and at last
I got to my feet, dancing my first step, wobbling actually, but feel-
ing relaxed, my consciousness limpid. *Prajna water:* that's what the
Master, who was particularly fond of Chivas Regal, called alcohol.
Wisdom water. Maybe. In the correct dosage.

Feeling Jessie's eyes on me, gracefully as I could manage, I
sauntered about the room, admiring his things, remarking how white
the upholstery, the carpet, the almost empty shelves, how white the
countertops in his kitchen, the narrow louvered window blinds, the
room dividers that looked like *shoji* screens. The setting contrasted
nicely with my host's crisp jeans and green plaid flannel. As usual, I
was top to toe in black, like a shadow or a disembodied consciousness. Quick as a thought, I could travel anywhere.

"It's not entirely accurate to say that Buddhists don't believe
in God. They don't believe in a supreme creator and ruler of the universe, but they do pray to deities and saints."

"In the most austere Zen centers, monks chant magical for-
mulae and pray to such figures as the enlightened Goddess of Mercy,"
Jesse added. He'd paused at the door to his computer lab, leaning
against the frame, arms folded, observing me.

I was looking at a scroll painting of that very goddess, Kannon,
tucked into an alcove that was decorated like the *tokanoma* of a

traditional Japanese home. Leiper explained that the blond wooden post propped into the corner shone because he had rubbed it with beeswax. I recognized the painting, but it couldn't possibly be an original, and close up I saw it was a copy, quite a good copy, and not a print. The goddess sat in tranquil repose, and before the scroll on a polished low table, a black ceramic vase held one white mum. The brass incense holder beside it was well used, and the entire alcove was steeped in the fragrance of plum blossoms.

"I did that," Jessie said, coming up behind me. "Copied it years ago. The original is by Sengai. I'm sure you know him, *ne?*"

Jesse switched on a tiny spotlight overhead. Then I heard some digital miracle on the ceiling click into action. It projected over the painting a transparent image of the moon as if reflected in rippling water. An elegant effect, so simple, rather like that of an old-fashioned flip-book. 21st Century *wabi-sabi.*

THERE IS A FAMOUS anecdote concerning the Florentine painter, sculptor and architect Giotto, who is among the masters who gave birth to the Renaissance. The Pope had sent throughout Italy his messenger to collect samples of the work of living artists, so that the best might be employed by the Church. Giotto was occupied with a painting when the man arrived, but hearing of his purpose, he paused, and on a piece of paper with a single brushstroke made a perfect circle. On receiving this, in appreciation of Giotto's consummate skill, the Pope naturally employed him. Much later, in appreciation of this tale, John Ruskin in his *Queen of the Air* wrote that "the practical teachings of the masters of Art was summed up by the O of Giotto."

By contrast, the beauty of the *enso* does not have to do with the circle being precisely round or the line consistently opaque, although in some cases the figure is so black that despite the centuries passed in humid monasteries or years secluded in a climate controlled gallery, years when radioactive particles have swarmed invisibly through, all of this can seem to have barely touched the quality of the hand-ground ink and superb paper. Both elements are important to such a painting's endurance, if endurance itself is thought important. The best paper is both translucent and reflective but also porous, absorbing the ink which bonds permanently with its vegetable fibers. Though some lines are heavy and very black, perhaps like the O of Giotto, the enso, which is also usually one continuous stroke, can be thin or fat, wispy, closed to form a single endless circle, or left open, as if inviting viewers to complete it in their own minds. It can be painted in any color the artist chooses and in any size. The whole universe is included in that circle, that zero, that "O." Truly, there are no mistakes here, but any hesitation of the artist will show. In Zen terms, it is a self-portrait independent of self. Because of that it can laugh in everyone's face. If it is anything at all, it is also what it is not, whether a mirror, the sun, the moon, a pond, a wheel, a hole, a round piece of cake—alongside one of them, Sengai wrote, "Eat this and have a cup of tea." Like the individual who held the brush, one enso cannot be compared to another. Like any work of art, it is an attempt to communicate a singular experience. Inclusive, unending, one circle might bristle boldly, and another fade from sight, its ink discharged before it completes its circuit, rejoining the point of origin only in the viewer's mind. Or the line might refuse to stop, becoming adamant, heading off into the void outside the circle. Equally intrepid, another enso dives into its own center. Lodged on fine silk, the ink of a Zen master would traditionally be venerated as an expression of that person's consciousness. On the wall of a simple hut amid some bamboo plants, such a scroll can serve as a focus for contemplation during *cha-no-yu,* the tea ceremony. A much venerated painting might only be viewed on special occasions, displayed in a shrine or at an altar to serve as an inspiration for students of Zen as well as for ordinary folk who might come to sit quietly in its presence, as if it were itself the moon or a Buddha image. With age, the paper might color slightly, but "foxing," freckles of mildew, can be thought to enhance the object's character, giving such a scroll the quality of living skin. Image and background, technique, provenance, a work inspired by the immortal Tao—and yet after all, what is it but a picture?

LEIPER WOULD HAVE TO wait for me a while longer at the door of his computer lab. On the screen of my mind, a familiar figure had suddenly interposed himself between us. It was no surprise that I might now encounter signor Caballo—was I not crossing the hills and dales of fatherland under a Zen moon? And earlier that very day, with the Tarot in my hands, riffling the soft oily cards, had I not cut it open to find him, a horseman on his charger? Caballo wearing a broad brimmed felt hat, festooned with a flame-like plume, and in his hand the staff of a herald. His horse's color indistinct; not white like the glorious Trentuno from the tale that Manaperta once told me, but a dark horse, very dark, galloping across the Giza plateau, as I myself once did on a lathered chestnut stallion.

What are you waiting for? he asks.

When he moves from the shadow of the Great Pyramid, I can see how red the horse is, dark and wet, flecked white about its neck and flanks. He pulls him up sharply, holding him on the bit, the horse snorting and pawing the sand. Caballo, turning aside in his saddle, points at me with his baton and cries: *Will you not see her?*

I am perplexed. I had thought that this vision pertained to another journey I was about to undertake with Jesse Leiper as my guide.

Caballo gives his mount a light touch of the heel and then he's off again behind the pyramid. In his place, the shape of a woman begins to materialize, shimmering like a desert mirage. She beckons and yet I refuse: it is Caballo whom I yearn for—and he reappears, bounding into sight.

Temperance, he counsels, raising his staff like a magician's wand. *Remember!* he commands.

CHAPTER 42

For weeks I've wasted my energies with confusion and despair, two whores who suck me dry. Perhaps my best work is behind me, and the days when it was praised are gone. My mother's passing I grieve aridly, a solitary man crossing the high desert of his middle years.

I find myself thinking often of her father, my grandfather, Antonio Giustovera, whose farm became the restaurant and resort. I remember the summer evenings of my boyhood when the cattle of a nearby dairy would gather at their barn waiting to be milked, their lowing in the twilight like a lullaby. Then I liked to sit listening with Nonno in his grape arbor behind the Villa's kitchen. I think of the story of the little Dutch girl supposed to be buried in the cellar near Nonno's winepress—the story I first heard from my grandmother on the night of the Carnevale.

Not long after my mother's funeral, I had unburdened myself to Tina. She listened attentively and patted my hand as if I were a child. "What else?" she asked, sitting opposite me at her kitchen table, small enough that we could reach across it. Between us, we'd just eaten a plate of rainbow biscotti in honor of my mother and drunk a pot of espresso, thick and black, sweetened with sugar, scented with lemon peel. Almost I expected Tina to turn my palm up and read it.

I told her of Nonno during the years of Prohibition, when besides making wine and grappa he distilled moonshine. Bathtub gin was easy to make, I explained, Holland Gin, a trace of juniper mixed into the mash. His partners in New York thought that it was "swell," thought it "the cat's whiskers," and sold it far as Elmont, where at Belmont racetrack the Pinkertons liked to swill it behind Barn Six. With his gin and *vino rosso*, with pints of grappa for his special customers, as well as crates of eggs and butchered meat on ice, he made his weekly runs into the City from Kinderkill. Then there was the Accident—whom had he offended? Whose territory might he have encroached upon? Perhaps in the end, the wreck was not such a terrible thing: it had stopped him going further down that road.

Then too, except for that famous Accident which seemed to have put an end to my mother's childhood and "pinched" so many of her later prospects, except for that, who knows, my mother might have become an entirely different person. "Now that she's gone, I should tell you what I always wished had happened," I said to Tina. "Though if it had, I wouldn't be here with you."

"Tell me so that I can remember what wasn't."

I took a Nat Sherman from its red and white box. Unlit, I played it between my lips, savoring the flavored paper. My cousin was 48 years old and I was in awe of her. No longer the fidgety girl of her youth or a medicated casualty of her own wildness, as a woman she has become practical about many things, including her looks. Her hair for example, bristling black and silver, clipped back or undone across her shoulders has no pretense about it; her clothing, her jewelry, her choices are uniquely stylish, a mix of the genuinely antique and bargain basement innovation. The glitter is not a distraction, but a foil for her natural good looks. Her mind I might call baroque, though it surely is no more so than mine, and while her moods can still fluctuate and exasperate, she is at least consistent in this. If it be madness, so too is the wild rush of water over stones and into hollow places, running water whose unfailing spirit pools and gathers where it's dammed until it overflows, water that can sublime directly into the sky and fall from a southern breeze as gentle rain or out of the north in a hail of gems. Her spirit is truly regal: for all of her life, Tina has insisted on her sovereignty.

What if we had run off together when she proposed it so many years ago? It is not unheard of for first cousins to marry, but we would have had to pay for it. *Amour fou* is often a fatal condition. Instead, I have this, this relationship across time and space that's like a shelter for my life's absurdities. This is what I thought that day, not so long after my mother died, during a day in lavender-land when Tina and I were more than kin and more than lovers.

"I'm listening," she said, turning away for an instant, while she reached back under herself to adjust the folds of her skirt. That fastidiousness was reminiscent of her adolescent tick, but now, her task complete, I noted how still she was able to sit, how attentive she could be toward me. She was wearing the same fashionable summer dress she'd had on that first night when Davey and I came over for dinner, the green one that clung to her curves and shifted across her breasts as if the fabric were alive. I wondered if she would be seeing Eduoard later on. I didn't ask, but stared at my finger tips that drummed the tabletop.

Then I said, "In my mother's unlived life, she and her girlfriend Geppina skip off with the jewels they lifted from Nonna. In that version of the story, my father comes to work at the Villa as a waiter, and it's Nonno who takes him into his confidence: he knows about the theft although his wife does not. He tells my father about his headstrong daughter and her friend. He charges him to find them, and Zizi Diamante sets out on their trail. He tracks them to California, to a motel in San Luis Obispo, but it's Geppina rather than Anna with whom he is smitten. Geppina and he take the jewels and fly away to Rio. Neither of them is ever heard from again. Betrayed and bereft, crest fallen Anna returns alone to Kinderkill. Abject and penitent, she is forgiven by her loving parents. Her mother declares that they are all better off now that the girl and the *Napolitano* have gone. And after all, she adds, those stolen stones were actually worth very little.

"This Anna will also inherit the family business and manage it until it fails, just as in the other version of my mother's tale. She will also live on alone into old age at the Villa, kind and caring and always hospitable, amiable, loved by all, just as my mother was. But then one day, miracle of miracles, she experiences a spiritual transformation. 'Anna of Kinderkill' she becomes, who leads prayer meetings upstairs in the big house, who lays on hands to heal the sick, and serves as a medium for those in need. *Angels*, she reminds her followers, *are God's messengers. We can all become angels after death.*

"Once, the angel of the Villa's ancient cellar speaks to Anna. It's the spirit of the girl who's buried there, *la Principessa Olandese* as the family has always known her, and she confides to Anna that *Your unborn child sends you love.* The angel tells her that this child loves her from the other side and that they will meet someday."

Is THIS MADNESS: I feel sober as polenta, but while studying a reproduction of the Mona Lisa, I spy behind the lady in the background the figure of signor Caballo. I call to him, "Please wait!" but my plea is—I have no better word for it—*submerged*. My speech becomes the fronds of underwater plants issuing from my mouth. When I return—I don't know where I've gone, or why—*could this be a sign of madness?*—I'm alone in an arid place. I believe that a horse was to have been left for me, that I was to saddle it and ride. The landscape is that of Leonardo's well known painting, barren save for an aqueduct or bridge that like a single wing emerges from the lady's left shoulder. On her right side, I now can see that what I'd thought of as a road is in fact a river, racing below the cliff where I stand. Along its precipice, I pick out a trail.

Once I arrive at the Villa I will have to decide whether or not to go through with my plan. Leonardo has written how the rooms of a palazzo can be made to burst into flame all at once through the employment of certain volatile spirits. To have done with the Place once and for all—it was the desperate dream of both my parents— shall I now fulfill it for them?

Business is bad, business is bad. . .

I begin to sweat profusely. The walk is longer than I had anticipated, and my step is weary. I'm carrying a saddle on my back. Caballo, whom I had expected to greet at every turn has failed to reappear, and the lady is gone entirely from sight. I must find *succulence*. I try to drink the word even as it leaves my lips. I come upon an oasis. I watch it quiver like a shadow on the desert, and when I point steadily at it with my index finger, it springs to life: date palms and flocks of goats, a communal well, several veiled women drawing water, horses tethered in the shade. A wonderful white stallion sees me and pricks his ears, whinnying sharply in recognition. I catch the drift of wood smoke and roasting lamb and my mouth begins to water.

Sapporita, Mr. Manaperta says, materializing suddenly beside me. Perhaps he is referring to a particular woman swathed in black approaching us. Two others wait with water jugs beside the well: they are waving welcome to us. My eyes begin to cross, and I see a confusing multitude of forms. I realize that I can *will* the oasis to remain or give my attention completely to Manaperta. He is thin and long and hale, no specter, but my living friend from childhood, my grandfather's best friend, the family Giustovera's *consigliere*.

"*Avvocato*," I greet him, gripping him with both my hands when we shake. "Thank you for the gift you sent."

"Look, Guido," he says pointing.

We are indoors now, a room with a high ceiling, tall windows under maroon draperies, slivered light cross-hatching the floor where the old pirate and I have been delivered. Before us are the timbers of a stout easel, holding an unmistakable portrait. At eye level, she appears luminous, like a dark emerald. I know that we are in Leonardo's private chamber and quite alone with the painting. After a stunned moment of wonder and gratitude, I'm seized by the fear that Manaperta intends to steal it. He cackles softly. "Some woman, huh?" He gestures with his leathery hands. "One time you done my pitcher, remember? *You* I called Leonardo."

Now I'm alone outdoors strolling beneath the shade of a long porch that faces on a courtyard, walking counter clockwise around a neat garden, past a dry fountain, past a series of darkened doors to my right under the long portico. I think I recognize this place, and immediately it comes clear: I'm at the Cloisters, a piece of the Old World reassembled stone by stone, now a museum that overlooks the Hudson. It houses a tremendous collection of religious art from the Middle Ages. I have been here many times. It is thanks to Bob Badget that on my first visit I also had my first experience of LSD.

Uncle Bob had laid a tiny piece of blotter acid on my tongue like a communion wafer and left me on my own, promising to return in a few hours to collect me. I wandered enchanted, then frightened, and then the wooden Bishop of St. Germaine addressed me. Bright eyed, with the voice of a sparrow, he quelled my fears and urged me to visit the unicorn: the unicorn would answer my question. A lifetime later, when Bob came back to collect me in his yellow bird, I blabbered jubilantly about my adventures. He listened and grinned and tugged the blond tassel under his lip.

On the most fabulous of the Cloisters' unicorn tapestries, the beast is corralled amid a field of flowering herbs. He's waiting for the virgin who can free him—all these years and he remains hopeful, despite his imprisonment, despite the threat that he might be destroyed by savage hunters before the virgin arrives. She has not appeared, and yet he forgives her: she is blameless, for it was he who allowed himself to be captured and imprisoned, all because he wanted to lie with his whorled horn dozing in her lap, bright as a star, wishing to be free of all earthly concerns.

"Complete," says the unicorn, and with his long horn he marks a cross in the turf. A tiny blue thing flowers there: forget-me-not.

Of course, I reply.

How solitary he is in his round paddock, subsisting only on his faith! *His sorrow is complete.* I understand. I'm wearing the crucifix Manaperta sent to me from beyond the grave, and when I wake, I know there is no cure for suffering but the will to suffer through it.

CHAPTER 43

*C*ASTLEFROY: WAS IT A pun on *froid*, the French for cold, a nod to Badget's love of "old cold cash?" Back at the Bazaar where he had traded in junk of all kinds, Bob joked that cash up front meant "better business in bureaus." He did indeed sell furniture and chandeliers at his department store, as well as work boots, galoshes, Oxfords and Beatle boots, and down at the end of aisle five, he sold to old men and women with aching feet, orthopedic shoes. Then there was the ladies' department, Connie's domain, stocked with cool fashions she'd hand picked or sewn herself. And I can't forget the section paneled off for photographs. Was there really a peep hole into the ladies dressing room, as Cristiano said?

Is it possible that rather than confronting a family curse or resisting some form of hereditary madness, is it just possible that all along what I've been doing in my labyrinth is winding a way to the monster at its core? But why should I demonize Bob? Perhaps I am the monster—I, who with such cool dispassion analyze all of my experiences as if my goal is to dispense with them.

Badget took my picture naked. *So?* He made pornography using Chris and Gwendolyn. *Yes?* He snapped up teenage girls, cheated on his wife, cheated on his business partner, sold drugs to Debby that surely did not help her, wanted me to deal drugs for him in the name of liberation, played with the mob, paid off the cops, and finally when he was caught for defrauding the United States government went to jail. *Years he spent where?* I don't know and I don't care.

Castlefroy: I had never visited a site utilizing such sophisticated, interactive software. As Jesse led the way it seemed to me we'd wandered into a video game: the front rooms had colorful interiors and window views of landscapes that recalled to me Lucerne. Someone stumbling on-line into the foyer couldn't be sure of where he was or what he might discover here, but every visitor was invited by a pleasant female voice to take a free tour. Soothing electronic music with a steady, soft, thumping bass line suggested that a party was happening nearby. To me, the atmosphere seemed like that of a real estate promotion I'd once been subjected to at a resort in Cozumel, and just as I was wondering when the margaritas might be served, a streamer ran vertically down Jesse's oversized monitor to announce that club members equipped with I-cams would be met in Gallery C by today's live hostesses.

I touched Leiper's shoulder, but he didn't notice. He touched the screen of his monitor, then swiped it broadly, which seemed to pull us down a long corridor toward the source of the music. It was as if we were in a grand hotel, or perhaps a Swiss castle. There were voices whispering all around us, just softly enough so that you couldn't quite make out what they were talking about. I assumed it was a subliminal gimmick, a means of persuading potential customers to buy in—but to buy into what?

Leiper had previously demonstrated to me how he could transfer video images from his computer and project them via two separate cameras: when the images converged on "the fountain," which misted water steadily from its base, they looked three dimensional. I was mightily impressed by the illusion as well as by Jesse's ingenuity. I was so excited the first time I witnessed it, I couldn't prevent myself from thrusting an arm into the scrim of water droplets. Seeing as I wasn't soaked, I had stepped completely forward and found myself alongside a phantom-Jesse fishing in a bathtub. "A work in progress," the flesh-and-blood Leiper announced from his control board. I laughed and danced like a kid tripping under strobe lights, whipping my arm back and forth through the mist, sending a spray of glittering droplets all over his computer lab. Jesse grabbed me by the hand and yanked me out of the picture. I apologized and quickly offered praise. "I like being fooled," I said, "even when I know how a trick is done."

I wish I could have remained so light hearted throughout our visit to the Castle. I became uncomfortable when we were confronted with the Terms of Agreement: thousands of words of legal jargon that nobody could possibly read or comprehend as they rolled down the face of the main monitor. Membership entailed specific limitations and legal liabilities, and among them was mentioned a pledge not to allow any guests to proceed further than what was included on the free tour. At the bottom of this long document where Jesse entered his code number, an Internet address presently appeared; there, we were informed, a complete prospectus of the corporation could be viewed. It seemed to me that we were being invited to buy shares in Castlefroy itself. The cascading lines and columns of tiny print left a sickly green afterimage. I rubbed my eyes and cleared my throat and mentioned to Jesse that we might want to look up Badget by more conventional means. He would have none of that.

Now we were informed by a computerized pixie in a cocktail dress that first level members were welcome in all first level galleries. Her voice sounded surprisingly fresh, as if an actual woman were interacting with us in real time. I wondered if we might be on camera, but I was embarrassed to voice my trepidation. Yet I *was* impressed, just as I was supposed to be, by this sexy arrangement of pixels with a French accent who continued to address Jesse by his user name, *Fra Lippo,* while waves of synthesizer music billowed about us. Instantly, Leiper transferred our virtual hostess into the lab: she looked as if she were standing in the fountain, a few feet from us, life-sized in her midnight blue miniskirt.

Jesse grinned at me. He touched his screen again and the cyber-doll repeated her words exactly.

"I wonder what else she does?" Jesse asked. Then he said quite seriously, "Whatever you do, don't give anybody here your credit card number."

"What exactly does being a member entitle you to?" I asked. "I saw that there are levels of membership—which are you?"

"Silver," he said. "But we're beyond that now. Ready to continue?"

"Whoa. You said you'd been here before, you saw Leo's works for sale, works of other artists also, hands on inspection possible through arrangement—I get it that this is some sort of grand emporium. Maybe it even includes a casino, right? Las Vegas came to the Web almost as soon as it was invented. Is that what Mr. Badge has here?"

"Relax," Jesse said. "We're not doing anything that anybody else doesn't do, who knows how to do it."

"What?"

"You think I would risk a hack while I'm on school business?"

I had long ago given up trying to convince my students that while poaching on the Web might be something they were all accustomed to doing, it didn't make the behavior either legal or ethical. Their argument, as is the argument of many hackers, is that they are agents for change who are helping technology to evolve. More than one of my students believes that an infrastructure for the artificial intelligence of a "global brain" is already in place.

Leiper clicked and his computer whirred and our hostess dissolved. I had gotten used to having her with us, and I felt a little sad to see her go. On the main screen, another menu appeared.

"Declare is in the big salon," Jesse said, leading the way.

Another swipe and his oversized computer monitor seemed to draw us deeper into depthless space: it felt as if we were behind the eyes of a camera moving along the hallways of a vast palace. Virtual birds were singing beautiful songs outside the virtual windows as we passed, and furthermore, it seemed as if an entire country landscape were alive "out there," a virtual Switzerland. I wondered how much all of these technological goodies had cost, but of course, money wasn't an issue for Jesse. I wondered if his classroom at the College were so well equipped.

Click: it was her again, the smiling doll in the short skirt outside a door marked *Grande Salon*. When she moved, it was with slightly jerky strides, and the illusion wilted. Click: we began a tour of "The Americans." The doll's voice, her French accent again, too familiar now to thrill, identified the artists whom Jesse selected with a touch of his finger on the monitor screen.

"Janet Bostwick," Jesse said. "She's a name."

The painting was of two dead birds along a roadway shoulder, in content and technique nothing that appealed to me, but when it materialized in the fountain, the effect was once again striking.

"Here's Dorothy Sheffield," Jesse said. "She died last year. Her prices are soaring."

A sculpture, the illusion of a sculpture, arrived within the basin's mist. It was a metal cast statue, a little less than life size, of a nude man entitled *Adam*. His gesture was hieratic, and I supposed it depicted the moment when Adam of the Genesis story is naming the animals in the Garden of Eden. The original photograph of the sculpture was sharp, and our 3-D apparition seemed solid indeed.

"A brilliant trick of light," I commented.

"That's all?" Leiper said. "Is that all we are?" He elbowed me.

"Let's find Leo," I said.

Click, whirr. The French phantom in a miniskirt: "Castlefroy has for sale a large catalogue of works by the American master, Leo Declare. Auction time and place to be announced. Works available for inspection." Our hostess rolled her r's perfectly. We followed, as on preternaturally long legs she stepped through torch light into another salon. The decor felt borrowed from a sword and sorcery game, and I half-expected to encounter an ogre or wicked wizard. I was shocked when Leo himself greeted us, Leo as I remembered him from long ago, a younger man than I am now. He was top to toe in white, the "dress uniform" he wore for special nights at the Moon.

"*Ecce homo.*"

"Yes," said Jesse. "We've already met."

No, you haven't, I thought.

As the phantom's limber jive spilled from the fountain, I trembled. But the magic didn't last, it couldn't, not without his gin breath also, and the perfume of oil paint and turpentine that clung to him like an aura. *Jesus,* I thought, *was I so drawn to the man because of how he smelled, because I put him and his studio together with Manaperta and his workshop?*

". . . nondogmatic, it can be seductive, but the carnival peep-show pay as you go, say have you met my friend Wanda, it ain't. Art is ready to fuck itself if you're not interested." He had been well lubricated—still was—". . . the price of admission. Hell is stupid suffering, why did this happen to me suffering, horrible because you want desperately for it to stop, insane because you can't end it, because it's what you yourself begot. I want the antidote—don't you? It's the end of beauty and every other sin. It's the beginning of truth."

"How he does go on!" Leiper quipped.

"Don't be concerned. It's all part of the act," I assured him. But it was a terrific performance. Rimbaud would have approved.

The video was looping now, the spiel repeating; Leo's antics replayed themselves and would replay until we moved on. To Jesse I said, "Bob must have shot the original and made the loop. It's quite true to form. That guy burned so many bitches behind him."

"Bitches?"

"Bridges."

"You said bitches."

I shrugged. "Power on, Mr. Leiper. Click the icon *Goodly Creatures.*

CHAPTER 44

IT SHOULD HAVE BEEN entirely a season of triumph. In my mother's Fury I could drive to school during the spring of senior year, could drive at night when my parents were busy at the Villa, could get away almost whenever I wanted. Davey started riding shotgun with me then. Just before our graduation, just after the Moon went down, I took him cruising past the empty place to see it dark. We spoke of Chris who had recently joined the Navy and been shipped to Southeast Asia in a jiff. I told Davey very little about my actual experiences at the Café, or about my art lessons, and nothing about my one night stand with Gigi. Broken hearted and mopey as only a teenager can be, I urged my friend to listen to Bob Dylan. The times were surely changing, I said, and I wanted my Eagle Scout to be prepared. He said he wasn't going to die in a fucked-up war, and instead of college he was choosing the police academy. He was calling me the Poe-man in those days, and he surprised me when he asked if my raven were named Nevermore.

Gigi was gone, and I tried to accept it, reminding myself that I was a realist. I'd be in college soon enough, I'd be getting laid all the time, and to hell with Gigi. Even so, that summer I refused a girl whom I'd met in Poughkeepise, a skinny fox who plainly wanted me. She was a year older, living on her own like a hippy in a rented room while working on a correspondence course in commercial art. I thought her drawing was pretty good, and I could have smoked dope with her and gotten laid, but she just wasn't my type. Instead I suffered my abandonment in solitude, thinking that what I was going through had something to do with becoming an artist.

I was definitely not a soldier or a sailor or a sous chef anymore, nor was I much of a cousin to Cristiano: I saw almost nothing of him before he shipped out. I finished high school with honors, but even the scholarship that I won couldn't lift my lugubrious spirits. *Lugubrious:* I fixated on the word. I stopped pumping iron, lost weight, and my long hair hung lank and greasy almost to my shoulders. With the way I chewed my mustache, I must have looked like a junky. I avoided my reflection at the bathroom sink and washed my eyes with damp paws like a cat.

Two salutary conditions did prevail, however. Fearing for my mental health, I stopped smoking pot and drinking alcohol. I even refused wine at the dinner table and beer on hot afternoons. Also, I returned to the style of artwork that had always come most easily to me, and for which reason I had been spurning it: naturalistic drawing and painting. I put aside my muddy experiments with abstract expressionism, and I put away my plans for driftwood sculptures, visualized while high on acid down by the river.

Speaking of acid, I owned a hundred tabs from the legendary Sandoz laboratory in Switzerland. Bob had given them to me "on consignment" not long before he was busted, with an invitation to "get in on the ground floor of something truly fabulous." I had tried to resist, but he insisted, and so I took the stash. Along with some grass and hashish, inside a glass beaker wrapped in a canvas bank-bag and packaged in a metal cashbox that wouldn't lock properly, I buried some of the world's finest LSD beneath a plank of the tumbledown tractor shed behind the Villa. I thought I might retrieve it someday if things ever calmed down, but a few years later when they had, I spent a fruitless afternoon searching for that treasure chest among the overgrown ruins.

As my high school graduation approached, I was less and less interested in other people. I was asked to the senior prom by a sweet girl whom my mother and the girl's mother wanted me to date, but I declined. I missed the salary that I'd been earning at the Half Moon, and for the first time in my life, money seemed important to me, and I thought about becoming a commercial artist. To hone my skills I began to draw a comic strip.

"Better Man Than I" was inspired by the Indian actor known simply as Sabu, star of the 1930's movie *Elephant Boy* that I'd seen on television. I combined him with my memory of another movie, *Gunga Din*, and called my hero Betuhmon. I drew him as a dark skinned, turbaned, barefoot mahout in a dhoti. The story was that he had smuggled himself airfreight into America on the trail of his beloved elephant Mapa, who had been stolen by evil circus people. Little did he know that the elephant was now in Paris, performing at the world famous *Teatro Des Betes*. Meanwhile, Betuhmon followed carnivals and circuses around America looking for Mapa and having adventures.

I showed my "Better Man" to no one. My mother and father had always respected my need for privacy in order to make art, but they nevertheless became disturbed by the various changes they could see in me. Once, despite great difficulty—so unpracticed was he at intimacy with me—my father asked if I were in some kind of trouble with a girl. I had the horrible feeling he might have heard about Gwen, but I said nothing. Frustrated, he made a derisive remark about my hair and said that until now he'd always been proud of me. As far as he was concerned, I'd become a *capellone*.

I sank deeper into my pea coat, its collar pushed high around my neck. Despite my melancholy, I felt strangely flattered, because I thought that I was definitely part of some worldwide happening thing. The spirit of the age was shaking my long locks. In Rome, the *capelloni*, wild haired guys and girls, had claimed the Spanish Steps, and in Wappingers Falls the local heads, equally hirsute and scuffed, had seized a portion of the village bridge for themselves. Together we suffered the derision of the straights for our looks. Besides my father's obvious disdain, I endured wisecracks at school from former mates as well some teachers, although my art teacher, Ben Fairchild, defended what he called my right to be my own man. I was an honors student on my way to HRC, but as a result of a surly comment I made one day to the Vice Principle, it was recommended to my parents that once again I visit Dr. Kee.

I agreed, but before that, in an earnest effort to understand what was happening with me, my parents did a most unexpected thing: they invited Leo to have dinner with us. The familiarity with which my father and mother greeted him was troubling: maybe I was overreacting, but I was truly afraid they were gathering in order to tell me that I would not be attending college next fall, and instead would be placed in a mental institution.

I had prepared for dinner that night by shaving my wispy goatee and chewed-up mustache. Borrowing some brilliantine from my father's dresser, I combed my hair back smooth. When my parents saw me, they greeted these changes with approval. I offered a wan smile in return, but I remained suspicious and spoke very little throughout the entire dinner. Leo I had greeted with a firm handshake, a nod of my head and a less than jolly, "Sir." When my mother asked me if I wanted to show him some of my recent work, I demurred, even though I would have liked to do so.

For dessert we ate spumoni ice cream, a favorite of mine. Eventually, the grownups' conversation turned to Bob's recent arrest. Leo said that he was very happy that he'd never partnered with Badget at his store. He said he was "glad all over" that he'd shut down the Café before the IRS came poking around. It hadn't dawned on me until then that it was for some kind of financial fraud that Badget was busted. I was dumbfounded that his arrest had not been for drugs, and quite relieved, too, since that meant there would not be a link to me.

My mother's voice was very tight during this conversation, and then, abruptly, after we'd finished dessert, she asked me directly, "Just how much did you know about all of this?"

I was unsure what "all of this" referred to and unsure "just how much" might be sufficient to incriminate me. My parents had trusted me with considerable independence, and she didn't have to remind me of that; I was already cut to the quick by my guilt. "Nothing," I said, poking at my plate with the tip of my spoon. This was, in its own way, an honest answer: however cool I had tried to play it, whatever I had ignorantly been embroiled in, I really didn't know very much. I kept my eyes lowered. On the white table cloth I kept seeing some photographs, large glossy black-and-whites, studio quality pictures of Gwen and Chris doing it. I felt nauseous. *Gigi is nothing to me. Chris is nothing.*

Leo stared at me. He stared at my mother, who stared back. Like a poker player, my father watched them both over the rim of his coffee cup.

"If my son or my nephew was mixed up in anything, I wish you'd explain exactly what," she said to Leo. She looked over at me, her expression well composed, but I knew how furious she could become, and it was scary to imagine what her tight voice might be holding on a leash.

Leo wiped his lips with his napkin. He took a deliberate breath through his nostrils, then he flashed me a quick, sympathetic smile. "Guido's a good kid, Ann. He'll do great in college. And I think the Navy will be good for Chris—even in the South China Sea, he'll be safe."

I knew he was stalling.

Suddenly my father burst out: "That sonofabitch Bobby!" He bunched up his napkin and threw it down with disgust on the table, as if it were a losing hand of cards.

I cringed.

"*Pazienza*," my mother said to my father. She looked again at me as if to ask *Is there something you want to say?* Then she squinted hard at Leo while she lit a cigarette.

He looked quite calm, and except for the deep crease seared between his eyebrows as he spoke, I might not have believed that he and Bob had ever been the best of friends. "That guy, whew! Whatta piece of work. Chris is lucky he got out. And Bob's wife, you know, Concetta, she left him. Hey, I'm lucky *I* got out before he brought his monkey business over to my place!"

He sounded entirely believable. He sketched out an account of Bob's "sins"—that was Leo's word, which surprised me—and admitted "confidentially between us" that because of Bob's stupidity, some Big Boys from New York had tried to muscle in at the Café. "Drugs, pornography, prostitution—who needs that?"

My father nodded. I could tell that this wasn't exactly news to him. My mother swiveled her head back and forth looking at each of them.

Just as she was about to say something to me, Leo grabbed me by the bicep of my left arm and said, "You're lucky you never knew anything about Bobby's shenanigans. Because, you see"—he was addressing my parents with this part—"Bobby has this *sickness*. I had a girl working as a model. Gwendolyn, right, Guido? Well, I almost hate to bring it up, but the story makes my point: Bobby got her to pose for some *pictures*. Know what I mean, Zizi? Next thing he tries to put the make on her, and next thing she comes crying to me."

He paused there, to check that my parents were with him. His hand was now resting on my forearm, almost patting me, as if to keep me calm. "Guido here befriends the girl, pretty girl, but she's not right for your son"—he squeezed, while his eyes slipped from my father to my mother and back to my father—"only I think that maybe Guido has some heartache from her." He released my arm and in a more gentle tone, as if he might actually care, he asked, "You wanna talk about any of this, Guy?"

My father's expression suddenly changed, as if his assumption about my girl trouble had just been validated. He looked at me with a funny kind of warmth in his eyes and nodded his head slowly.

How much did Leo know about Gwen and me? My paranoia was enflamed: *My God could she possibly have gotten pregnant?* I thought that I might scream right then. I really thought I might lose my mind right there among this unlikely trio of grown-ups who were all acting as if they cared, but who, I was convinced, under-stood nothing about me.

"Since his grandmother died, Guido has spent too much time alone. That's why we were happy he had a job with you, and the art lessons. His artwork is very important, isn't it, son?" My mother touched my cheek like she hadn't done in a long time.

"That girl. . .I'll probably never see her again," I sputtered at last.

Then my mother asked about my use of her car, gently at first, but when I refused to say much, she warned me that I would lose my driving privileges if I didn't tell the complete truth. Then she leaned over toward my father and in Italian said, "Remember the night he didn't come home because of the snow storm?"

In English to me, my father said, "This girl. You didn't, you know make her. . ." With both hands he rounded out a bulging belly.

I was mortified. I looked frantically to Leo of all people, Leo, who had hurt me so badly just when love, with its roses and thorns, had invited me into its garden. I felt feverish, and I pressed my right hand against my temple.

"I'm the one in trouble!" I cried. "I'm the one gonna go crazy!" I stood, and scowling, threw my crumpled napkin at Leo's chest. I leaned forward with both hands on the table. I spied the long knife that had been used to cut the spumoni loaf. After I cut Leo's throat with it, I would flee the cursed Villa forever—no, I would come back to burn it down. Then I would find Mapa, my elephant, the good beast who alone in all the world could comprehend me.

Taking command of the situation, my mother sprang to her feet and came around to me, covering my trembling hands with her own. "You need help, my son. It's okay if you don't want to talk with us right now. Dr. Kee says you like to talk to him. Isn't that right, Guido?"

"Ye-es," I said hesitantly, rubbing my teary eyes with both fists, ashamed most of all to let Leo see me like this.

"Ah, Guido!" my father exclaimed, shaking his head sadly. "*Figlio mio, poverino, poverino.*"

"This sort of thing happens," Leo said, "to the sensitive ones."

CHAPTER 45

Dr. Kee was interested in everything I could remember. I had told him I could go way back in my mind, even as far back as being circumcised: "The knife. The scalpel. Whatever you call it."

"And what do you feel?"

"It hurts, man."

"Hmmm. It's very rare for a person to be able to remember so early a trauma, even under hypnosis."

I was lying on the sofa in his office, and he was seated near my head, writing something, which he did a lot during our sessions. He didn't sound Chinese, or even what I imagined a Chinese American would sound like. I figured he wasn't Chinese in the way I thought a Chinese person would be, but then again I didn't know any Chinese people—except for Dr. Kee. Was he Chinese? I was somewhat obsessed with this, but I was too embarrassed to ask him about it. Perhaps this was a sign of what he called my "distress."

He had the epicanthic fold, sheathed eyelids, dark brown irises and very black pupils. He was a short, solidly built man, with short black hair, and his skin was a beautiful golden-brown. His face was exceptionally smooth, as if he massaged and oiled it, yet his square chin, always cleanly shaven, seemed nevertheless to wear a blue shadow.

I knew he was trying to read my mind, and right from the beginning I told him so.

"Can you read *my* mind?" he replied.

WE MET WEEKLY IN his private office in the village of Wappingers. I felt ashamed that I'd been sent to see him again, but also I knew that I needed him. One warm afternoon, he said to me, "You seem sleepy. How about some *relaxeration?*"

That was his funny word for it, but sure, I didn't mind taking a rest. I kept my eyes open and crossed my arms over my chest. I stared at the ceiling. He began to talk about my feet, my legs, my "small back." At some point, I heard him say, "I want to tell you a little about my friend, Ziggy. And by the way, since you and I are friends, Guy, you can call me Ricky, if you like."

I was very drowsy but I was determined not to fall asleep as I had previously, or thought that I had, because today I wanted hear everything *Ricky* said. He started telling me a story about caterpillars and butterflies—I knew the facts of life of course, and this was boring, and so in my imagination I went off to find my elephant. I would be the better man for it, a big success like my father and mother wanted. Commercial art, sure. Maybe a fashion designer, why not? I figured that my cousin Chris would get a kick out of that—I practically heard him laughing about it over on his boat in the China Sea or wherever the hell they'd sent him.

Dr. Kee droned on. Now there was some boring story about Ziggy's cigar. It was a joke, I realized, though it wasn't very funny. My eyes were closed and I thought that maybe after all I'd go sleep. Just then, I had a very clear insight: what a dope I'd been at the Half Moon!

"I don't go to confession anymore," I said aloud for no apparent reason. My own voice sounded weird, as if it were talking for me. My eyes popped open, and I sat halfway up, looking for the print of Raphael's *Assumption* that years ago I'd spotted on Dr. Kee's wall. I didn't see it and fell back onto the scratchy upholstery of the sofa.

". . .not that Ziggy and I agree on everything," he said.

I thought he must be talking to himself—his voice was very comforting, but I couldn't follow him and gave up trying, retreating instead into my own mind. Occasionally, I'd catch a few of his words, and I remember thinking this must be what it sounds like to have a conversation with yourself when you like yourself.

He went on and on, as if I'd done nothing unusual by sitting up so abruptly and making my announcement about confession, which was weird. Nobodaddy had a lot of tricks to keep you from knowing yourself, and besides spying on you, ignoring you was another one. I looked at Dr. Kee. His head was inclined forward and I thought that maybe he was boring himself to sleep. Then I realized I was watching him with my eyes closed.

I DON'T REMEMBER ALL the things we talked about, but we covered a lot of ground, and I always looked forward to our *conversations*, as Dr. Kee preferred to call them. He was coming from someplace altogether different than anybody else I knew. Leo and Bob might be far out, and Nonna might really have been a *strega,* but Dr. Kee was deep. Also, I had really taken to doing the relaxeration.

I wasn't a psycho: he assured me of that when I eventually asked him. I was an interesting young man, he said, and perhaps I was genuinely psychic, and whether or not I was, Dr. Kee thought that my artwork was very important and I needed to keep doing it no matter what. I showed him a couple of strips for "Better Man," and he was impressed, but he cautioned me not to get hung up about using my talents solely to make money. I could if I wanted, he said, but I could as easily find other work to support the art I really wanted to do.

Sometimes I felt he had the greatest impact on me with what I called his "passing shot," like in a game of tennis. For example, I was thinking about whose legs were more beautiful, Sophia Loren's or Gina Lollobrigida's, when out of nowhere he asked me why I hadn't gone to my high school senior prom. I had mentioned this a couple of weeks earlier, and told him that I actually did find Ellen Shultz, the girl my mother had tried to set me up with, to be quite nice. Later, when I mentioned that I now regretted not having asked her, he simply said that caterpillars don't know how they become butterflies.

One day I was sitting upright on his scratchy sofa opposite him. It smelled bad, and I wondered if a kid had recently wet his pants here—he probably saw a lot of kids with serious problems, I thought. The odor of ammonia was suddenly overpowering, and reflexively, in a horrified moment, I glanced down to make sure I wasn't sitting in piss.

I knew I was stupid to have let my chances with Ellen Shultz slip away. To this day I remember the color of her hair, red-gold and very fine and worn in a sophisticated style up on her head. She'd gone to the prom with Tom Doyle, who, in a little while, would become our school's first casualty in Viet Nam.

"But maybe Ellen wouldn't have liked me," I told Dr. Kee. "Girls my age usually don't get me."

After Gwendolyn ditched me, after one night of glorious fucking and sucking, hard up though I was, I refused to masturbate, and so I had plenty of wet dreams, just as I'd had in my virginal days. Sometimes twice or even three times a night, I'd awoken with my groin soaked. But I couldn't remember the dreams. I suppose I was using all my energy to stay tough and ignore how much heartache I was suffering.

Dr. Kee said to me, "Just then, when you lowered your eyes, where did you go, Guido? What did you see?"

"Everything—no, nothing."

"The *enso*," he said.

"End show?"

"En-so," he went, stretching the two syllables out.

"Oh."

"It *is* like the letter O," he said, chuckling. Then he described it, what it means to students of Zen, the empty circle.

I thought of my grandmother. I hadn't thought much about her lately. I told him this, and he asked me to talk about her, and then I sang the words of a nursery rhyme she taught me: *"Piccinin che 'era, balava volunterra, balava su'l quadrin, anche'l era piccinin."*

"What does it mean?"

"He was so small that he could dance on a little round penny, *su'l quadrine.* He did it because he wanted to, *volunterra."*

Dr. Kee repeated after me, "Because he wanted to. He could dance on a penny."

"Whenever she sang it, I imagined that I was that happy little guy. I'd be wearing a blue sailor suit with a white sailor hat, the square flap of the collar like a short cape on my back. I'd have red hair and freckles and blue eyes, like an American kid—weird, huh?"

Dr. Kee did a funny little move in appreciation of my story, wobbling side to side with his hands raised like a jack-in-the-box. The funniest part was that his face didn't change from his usual expression at all. He wore eyeglasses with flesh-toned plastic frames, which I thought were cool. Maybe they were Chinese—later I asked him, but he said no, they were from Japan. I wondered what sort of razor he used for shaving.

"Electronic," he said. "Made in America."

Dr. Kee was not, in fact, Chinese. He and his family had come to the US when he was a boy just as the Korean war began. His mother was American, the daughter of Methodist missionaries, and over there she had married a Korean. Ever since he was a boy Dr. Kee had been interested in psychology, and he had learned about Sigmund Freud from a friend of his father's back in Seoul. That man was a Buddhist priest, and he helped the Kee family to emigrate. Fortunately for them, they had missed the war, although his father was interrogated by US authorities who thought he could be a spy. Dr. Kee said that his father often recalled his interrogation with a curious sort of civic pride, as if it were his initiation into American life. Later his father became a high school teacher of science in the Bronx.

Then, unexpectedly, Dr. Kee told me about Bo Tanaka, his *kendo* teacher, a Japanese sword master, his *second* father, as he called him. He asked me if someday I might want to visit Tanaka *sensei's* school in New York City and perhaps meet the master? When I said yes, right then Dr. Kee taught me how to make a proper bow. This was as important as anything I might later learn with the sword, he said. This too was a form of Zen practice, and he showed me how to *gassho* with my palms pressed together. He told me I should try to do it perfectly when I was introduced to the master, who was very old fashioned.

"He's old, period," Dr. Kee added, his eyes glittering.

ON ANOTHER OCCASION, OUR conversation turned to the subject of vampires. Guys my age didn't actually believe that vampires existed; however, some guys liked to bite girls on their necks, not to drink their blood, but by sucking at the skin to leave their marks of love. Some girls proudly displayed these, others tried to hide them. I had never given a hickey, because, well, I'd been afraid I wouldn't know how hard to bite and I might hurt the girl or draw blood, and worst of all, like the taste of it.

"I used to have dreams about vampires," I told Dr. Kee. "And when I was a kid, for Halloween I went out as a vampire, so that the real vampires would think I was one of them and leave me alone. Or else a pirate. Or I went all in black like Zorro with a real fencing foil that my uncle sent from Italy."

"Ah, Zorro," he said, nodding sagely.

I sang a bit of the TV show theme. "*Out of the night, when the full moon is bright, comes a horseman known as Zorro.*" I whipped the air with an imaginary sword. "*And a 'Z' that stands for Zorro,*" I sang.

Dr. Kee removed his glasses and rubbed his eyes. He split open the fingers momentarily making a mask, and then lowered his hands smiling. "Superman or Batman, which do you prefer?"

"Batman, of course."

"Dracula or Frankenstein?" he asked. But before I could answer he said, "That's obvious. Lugosi or Cushing?"

"Lugosi, " I said. "But in the *Brides of Dracula* . . . I mean, the newer movies are. . .You know these movies?"

"Vampires are fascinating. The undead and ghosts in general are always of interest. They appear in the legends of all peoples, because the past never really dies. Do vampires still frighten you?"

The thing about Dr. Kee, the thing I had first liked years ago when I had to see him, was that he took me seriously, no matter how fucked up I thought I might be. For example, way back in junior high school when Larry Pynchet had made fun of my father's sign, Dr. Kee understood why I got mad. He never wheedled me about it; however, because of his influence, I eventually apologized to Larry Pynchet for "what might have frightened" him. Dr. Kee had indirectly suggested those words, and so, thanks to him, everybody was willing to let bygones be bygones.

"I can see things in mirrors. I mean besides my own reflection. My grandmother believed in ghosts, and, well, sometimes I think I might see *her* in the mirror of her old bureau. What's the real reason a vampire can't see his reflection?"

Dr. Kee answered, "The mirror confirms that he doesn't belong among the living. Similarly, sunshine is antithetical to him, and since Christ is the Light of the World, the crucifix, the symbol of Christ who conquers death, repels the demon. Do you have one? A crucifix?"

"Jesus and I aren't very tight these days," I said, squirming. After a moment I said, "I look in mirrors a lot, I have for my whole life. It's not that I'm in love with myself. It's more like I have to make sure I'm still here. But I don't always like what I see."

"Opposites do not negate each other," he said. This was a quote from William Blake, whom Leo held in high esteem, and whose art and poetry would become very important to me. "Without contraries is no progress," Dr. Kee continued.

"Did I tell you I know a little about Blake?" I asked.

He pressed his fingertips together, so that they sprang against each other. "Guido, the things of this world run together in currents, and they crystalize in patterns. But our perceptions change constantly, and so, even scientists change their minds. Whether such new perspectives are in the eye of the beholder or objective facts, our perception is our reality. It seems that some things fit together because they belong together. That's poetry as much as it is science.

"Is there anything else you think you might see when you look into a mirror?"

I was mute. I shook my head, meaning not *no*, but that I couldn't exactly say. I had always been a little afraid of mirrors even as I was fascinated by them. I looked nervously at the clock behind me on the wall of his office. Ten minutes until the end of our session. Outside, I could see how the afternoon light was bathing the stones and trees of the park across the street. I had sworn off drugs, but in a panic suddenly, I felt paranoid—or maybe it was something worse. Or was this fear of fear the actual paranoia?

"I made it with a woman," I suddenly said.

"A woman?"

"Slept over at her house, had sex, lied to my parents. Now she's gone. Maybe she got pregnant—I'm afraid of that. But I don't know. . ."

"And?"

I could hear some little kids over in the park, and without looking I knew they had baseball gloves and balls and bats. Then I heard their father, somebody's father, explaining how to play. "Nobody ever did that for me," I said to Dr. Kee, jerking my thumb toward the

people outside, "showed me how to do ordinary stuff like baseball."
I began to cry, despite my efforts to control myself. I felt awful and
looked at the clock again, hoping the hour had finally elapsed.

"We have all the time we need," Dr. Kee said gently. He passed
me a box of tissues. One hand strayed to his chin, which looked
extraordinarily square today.

Don't let 'em trap yer whistle, matey, said the pirate.

Go to hell, I replied.

"I didn't really love her. But that's not the saddest part. My
cousin had to join the Navy."

"Because of what you did with this woman?"

"Not exactly. Because of another woman. But yeah, it was
also because I got mad at him about Gigi." I was talking fast and I
couldn't cork it. I took a moment to blow my nose and dry my eyes. I
would have to make up something or other for him. Much as I liked
Dr. Kee, I had people to protect.

I began again.

"My cousin was in love with this woman, a beautiful woman
from Puerto Rico. The guy that my cousin worked for knew about
him and his wife. But he didn't stop them, because they were, I
don't know, part of some plan he had. His wife knew that this guy,
the Boss, juggled the books at their store. My cousin worked there,
and the other woman, too: she was the bookkeeper. The one I spent
the night with."

The truth was pouring out and I didn't want to stop it.

"I took art lessons. We were both models for the artist. That's
how I met her. I didn't know she liked me, but she did, she liked me
enough, and we made it. And then. She just. . . *left,* without saying
anything to me."

I shut up and sat there with Dr. Kee looking at me. Outside I could hear the man yelling, "Throw the ball to daddy!"

"But before that, before she left, I thought I could do her a favor. Pick up some things of hers so she wouldn't have to go back to this store where she worked. She didn't ask me, but I wanted to. I'm with my cousin, and I wander back to the darkroom. The Boss is a photographer, see? And he has all these files of pictures, and that day the door is unlocked, so I go in and start whipping through his files, looking for the pictures. Well, I found quite a few, but. . . I wish. . ."

"Go on."

"I wish I hadn't."

I stared at my muddy boots. They had come from Badget's Bazaar—everything seemed to come from there or lead back to it. In my mind's eye I saw Gwendolyn, half in profile, her eyes slanted, that sly expression she wore in many of her photos, her cute nose snubbing me. I wasn't going to mention anything else to Dr. Kee, but after a short pause, I continued.

"I was stopped cold by the pictures of Gigi and Chris. I just stood there, fanning out a bunch of them, big glossy black and whites of them doing it, naked and *fucking*, pictures that the Boss took. I couldn't stop myself from looking. It seemed to be *me* in the pictures, not Chris—but of course it was my cousin. Then Chris came in and saw what was happening and grabbed them away. *Get out of here, Guy. I have to lock up*, he said. I just stood there. Right then, I wanted to murder him and the Boss, and at that moment, I hated Gwendolyn too. Chris pulled me out of the darkroom and locked the door. He went and turned out the lights in the rest of the store. It was time to go, but I kept standing there. Chris came back and practically dragged me out into the street. He looked at me hard, and shook his head, he said something about having to protect everybody, that he was tired of doing it. I don't know what became of the pictures."

I stopped suddenly, hunched over, staring at the floor between the points of my boots.

"Guido?"

"Yeah. It's time, right?" Wasn't the goddamn hour over yet? My mother was probably in the waiting room, ready to pick me up.

"We have all the time we need. What else do you want to tell me?"

I sat straight up on the scratchy sofa, with my arms knotted over my chest. "I was afraid Bob would kill him."

"Bob?"

"Shit. . .the Boss, that guy whose wife I told you about. But I was so mad! Shit!" I said, pulling my voice down, thinking that my mother might be listening at the door. "The Boss knew about Chris and his wife, and I told my cousin this. Chris laughs, and I say he's an idiot because Bob is just waiting to lower the boom. Chris says shut up, you stupid kid. They have an arrangement, and anyway, Con—" I caught myself here—"the boss man's wife is all set to run away with him. He says I'd better keep my big nose out of things. I'm mad at him now, and I'm starting to think about knives, Dr. Kee. I really am, out on the street with Chris, I'm thinking about knives.

"I tell Chris to fuck off. He goes, what? He's practically laughing in my face, like he can't believe me. See this—he flicks open his blade, showing off, I don't know, he's like, look what I've got, sonny boy. Big man. He flips the knife up, end over ass in the air and I grab it. Swear to God, Dr. Kee. I just reach out and grab his knife from the middle of the air, and I point it at him. I could have done something right then. But instead I only told him he was an idiot and all his plans were idiotic. He wasn't going to get out of the draft so he had better join the Navy, I said. At least on a ship you don't get sent on suicide missions into the jungle."

My chest felt awfully tight, and I looked at the clock yet again, hoping it would save me, and now that I'd let it all spill, hoping I could stop, that the blood pouring out from the open place inside of me would stop.

He handed me more tissues. When he leaned forward I could see his bald spot and how he oiled his blue-black hair to comb it over. I felt suddenly very fond of him, and I wanted to put my palms together and bow like he had shown me he did to his sensei.

"This man," he said, "the one your cousin worked for, he was arrested, correct?"

"Right. It was in the newspapers," I said, wiping my wet nose and then wiping my eyes with another tissue.

"Did this man ever touch you?"

"Me? No."

Dr. Kee said nothing.

I said, "This man, he had his fingers in a lot of pies. But no, he never laid a hand me."

Dr. Kee said, "Not even to tell you what a nice boy you are, maybe to pat you in places private to you, or to make you put your hands on his private places?"

"Christ, no! We were friendly, but I always kept my distance."

He waited for me to say more, but I didn't have anything. We were through, but not before he added, "Your cousin, he's in the Navy. He hasn't been sentenced to death or sent to prison with Mr. Badget. Perhaps that's not such a bad thing?"

CHAPTER 46

MY MOTHER WAS A simple woman, who, whatever else she might have wanted for herself, lived with what she had quite simply. But her complicated blood wouldn't leave her in peace.

Our final hours together were spent in Vassar Brothers Hospital: she was heavily sedated, hooked on life-support devices, a piston breathing her, blue plastic tubing strung about her body. It had taken fourteen months to come so far, during which time I was quite literally reclaiming my own bloodline as I became the chief interlocutor of her disease, *vascular disease*, as it's vaguely called. During her final passage, beside her in the ICU, I monitored the range of peaks and troughs that traced the journey of her failing heart; when her end was near and I asked to have her disconnected from life-support, issues of hospital liability were cited, and rather than leave her side to argue with administrators, I acquiesced. In the end, I welcomed the medicine they pumped into her veins to slake the snakes of pain that gnawed her bowels. Meditating at her side, I saw her life shining *with* her life. She inhabited herself completely as she was departing. Her skin lightened to a pale yellow, a faded rose color that became more luminous with every passing moment.

"Do you remember the ball of light?" I whispered at her ear. "Become the Light you always were."

Her hand lay heavy on a pillow while I watched the pulse at her neck and brushed her hair from her forehead and stroked her arms, kissing her moist cheek. I glanced at her jagged heart line on the monitor and thought of her crossing through mountains into the valley of the sun.

"WE NEED TO TALK over a few things." Davey on the telephone, my first cellphone, the one I'd bought to keep in touch with my ailing mom.

This was several weeks after her death, when my life was beginning to settle into a new pattern—my mother was no longer in this world, and among other things, I was now the owner of the Villa Giustovera. Since her death I had visited it only to collect her few personal possessions.

I suggested to Davey that we meet for lunch at the Patriot Arms.

Whatever the recent upheavals in my own life, I had the feeling that in some ways his had been shaken up more. Jean and he were now divorced, which would have seemed impossible a short time ago. He'd left her, his wife of thirty six years, after her breast cancer, after her treatment and remission—after all of that, he'd been the one to walk. Meanwhile, he'd also let his PI business dwindle away, saying that he just didn't have the nose for it anymore.

We were seated at a bad table in the overcrowded restaurant, and while we waited for service, I recalled the day not so very long ago when he had first proposed that I work for the cops. Before I could remind him of this, he was thanking me effusively for all my help with his "enlightenment." Of course, he added, thanks were also due to Tina, who had *really* helped him to see. He tapped a spot in the middle of his forehead when he said that.

Changing the subject, I asked, "What's this thing you've got about vampires?" They had turned up more than once in our conversations, and I wondered if he could have actually gotten so whacky that he believed in them. At my mention of the word, I felt something brush the back of my neck, and I turned around suddenly, hoping to catch Donna Trabucco by the hand. There was no one there. "I know a few things about vampires," I said with a nervous laugh.

"There are probably walking, talking human beings who have convinced themselves that they're undead, damned and dependent on the blood of the living," I began. "But psychic parasites are more common. You know, people who latch on, who want something from you, who won't let go. Sometimes they themselves don't know what's happening, but so hungry are they for a warm-blooded connection, they don't notice what a draining effect they have on others. They talk at you nonstop, or try to eat you with their eyes. Some people believe that artists, especially photographers, are prone to being infected."

I leaned in close for my finale, taking Davey's hand across the table-top: "Psychics say the condition is actually caused by non-material entities who attach themselves to living bodies; for example, the succubus and incubus that visit adolescents in their dreams and milk their vitality. But immortal fanged humanoids who feed on blood—they aren't real." I released his hand. "At least I don't think so."

He liked my performance, his eyes told me so. He said, "A lot of my old pals, hearing us talk like this, they'd think I've really lost it. But you know, Guy, I've always been interested in the *paranormal*."

He gave the word a special inflection, as if to imply that he and I shared a certain secret information.

Now that he and Jean were separated, Davey had a lot of things to talk about. However, my friend wasn't always so easy to follow. He launched into a long riff on angels and extraterrestrials, and then he rambled into a dream he'd recently had, changing what I assumed to be the subject of his discourse several times midflight. Sometimes he paused to say, "But you already know about this stuff," which wasn't necessarily true.

He said that Jean actually approved of the changes in him, and that she'd told him that now he seemed more *solicitous* of her. Davey cocked his eyes at me to make sure I'd gotten the word. Jean liked it that he called her to ask if she needed anything. She liked it that he was growing closer to their son Jeff, who lived in San Francisco and was out of the closet. He also wanted me to know this: "I think that I might be gay, too. It's maybe even a reason that I liked being on the Force, which as you know is mostly guys." He waited a moment and then added, "Though of course there are exceptional exceptions."

I didn't believe that Davey was gay, but I wasn't going to get into that now. Fine with me, fine also if he was gay—he was into so many new things at once: divorce can do that to a person.

I kept switching my head back and forth to look for Donna or the waiter who had seated us. Slow service at peak hours is a problem at the Arms, and when the weather is nice, the staff is always busy with customers out on the deck.

"You can't ignore the sex," Davey said. "I mean with the vampires. They always want more."

"Of course," I said. "Sex means life."

I was yearning for my fried haddock special. I saw one go by on a platter destined for somebody outside. Davey ignored my dismay. I was certain he wasn't gay, but I could indeed attest that he looked happier, *looser,* so to speak.

While my mother was dying I had wound myself as tightly as I could into my daily routines, my labyrinth of turns and returns and circles and stops: I'd read that focusing on work at which you excel is good for people under stress. It was for me. But I still hadn't really wept for her.

I watched the backside of Donna Trabucco as she leaned forward at a table chatting amiably with a customer in a business suit. I remembered making love to her from behind and how I'd praised her ass, calling it a *classic ass.* She likes to be complimented on her looks, and she had especially liked me to do it in Italian while we were fucking. Sometimes she wrote down the things that I said, asking me to spell the Italian words, and I was flattered when she said I had inspired a character in one of her short stories. She gave me several of these to read—I couldn't find myself in any of them—and when she asked me what I thought, I said they were witty. In fact, I thought they were somewhat trite, and yet she had gotten a couple published in literary magazines, and now she had an entire collection she was shopping around.

"And don't forget immortal love," I said to Davey. "Vampires symbolize undying desire."

"It's a national obsession," Davey replied. "Best selling books, movies, TV series." He raised his hand politely, signaling to a waiter whose attention he failed to obtain.

I looked past him out to the deck where six suits were dining. "Bloodsuckers abound," I said sarcastically. It was what my mother used to call her creditors when the restaurant was going under. To Davey I said, "You need special tools to be rid of them."

"You mean like a stake in the heart?"

"Yeah, like that," I said, grinning, touching my chest, surprised at the surge of affection I suddenly felt for him. My *other*.

Then I changed the subject. "My aunt Josie is afraid that Tina's boyfriend wants to convert her to voodoo or something. Apparently the mere thought of him scares the crap out of her."

"It's 'cause he's black. No offense, Guido, but your aunt is, shall we say, old fashioned."

"You think he can keep my cousin happy?"

The sun was bright on the green river, and from where we were sitting, we had a clear view of its smooth water and the roadway on the other shore cutting the hillsides with little toy cars running back and forth along it. I thought of how the landscape must have looked, how lush it must have been, back when the likes of Hudson and Kidd sailed the river. The glinting light caused Davey to put on his shades, his Ray-Ban Daddy-o's, that made him look like what he wasn't anymore, a PI.

"She says he loves her. She doesn't say that she loves him."

I said nothing.

"Eddy is clean," he continued. "You asked and I checked. He's legit, and he really does want to marry her."

"And he got her straight," I said.

"True. Now she takes flower essences and homeopathy. There's a Chinese woman in Beacon who gives her acupuncture in exchange for her garden vegetables. And Tina makes money selling tinctures and flower bouquets at farmers' markets. But, well, Eddy must contribute something for her to live like she does."

"And he loves her?"

"That's what she says, Guy. Listen, he's on the level. He imports folk art from the Caribbean, has a dealer in Florida. They stay at a place down there during the winter, or else they go to the islands. Why do you think your cousin has that terrific tan all year?"

"My aunt says Edouard is so black that he has to use a flashlight to see himself in the dark. Can you believe it?" I shook my head. "It's gotta be hard for Josie, but I can't believe Tina will let her mess things up, not at this stage of her life."

"Tell me something," Davey said. "When you were kids, did you make up some story about the Mars Man and the Moon Man? She says you always told the best stories and that she believed them all. She says you should write a book."

"My cousin said that?" I was pleased.

I grew silent. I looked around for Donna, for a glimpse of her fantastic calves. I was thinking about her a lot lately, and in fact it was a reason I'd suggested to Davey that we meet here instead of the Parthenon Diner, which he preferred. Donna Trabucco had been part of the picture the day when Davey suggested I become a sketch artist, and I smiled to think of her as a representative of Lady Luck.

She was finally divorced and doing well for herself, had been promoted to manager of the restaurant. She looked awfully good with her new short hairdo, a feathered, blond, dye-job whose roots were intentionally dark. I could see how she did her charming best to please the corporate types who mobbed the place on warm, sunny afternoons like this. I was sure she checked out the eligible men, seating them at the tables with the best views. That ass—my God.

Lately our interactions were mostly relegated to word games, "flirtations manqué," I said, to which she shot back, "No manqué business here, *s'il vous plait.*" Donna is smart and sassy and she often gets the best of me in part because I tend to underestimate her. Then I feel guilty about that, afraid it's a sexist thing, and so I always leave too much of a gratuity at my table, hoping that she'll notice how well I treat her staff. Then I feel conflicted about that, because I don't believe in large tips unless the service is actually exceptional. I had tried to explain this to her back when she started waitressing here. She said, "How long since you were in the restaurant business? Do you know what I make per hour, even in a tony place like this?"

When we broke up I'd given her an excuse having to do with the difference in our ages, but that was never really an issue. The reason we broke up is that she's Italian. Donna is Calabrese through and through. One time we were at her brother's, Joseph, the younger one whose wife died in a car accident—the poor guy, five years since then, and he can't forget that she was pregnant when it happened. He's sweet and sentimental, the baby of the family, living in his parents' old house all alone. After dinner, he brought out the family photo albums. I'm the one who started crying: it was so much like looking at my own family pictures. Donna is the only Italian girlfriend I've ever had, and if we'd stayed together, well, all I could think of was how my father ended up true to type, dying in Sorrento. Long ago it was pointed out to me that I favored fair haired women, redheads and strawberry blonds especially. As far back as Sunday school, I can remember how we Italian boys liked the Irish and German girls best. No one had to tell us that getting one of them would be a step up in life.

"I'll tell you this about Eduoard, my personal impression," Davey said. "He wants Tina to be his queen. When they're together he can't take his eyes off her. He practically waits on her."

"Great," I interjected. "That's what everybody has always done, putting my little cousin on a throne. So you were with them, huh?"

"We went out for dinner. You know, he's quite a bit younger than she is, and—" He stopped mid-sentence to check that none of this was upsetting me. It wasn't. I was curious, but even if I'd been asked to join them, I would have declined. *Why wasn't I asked?*

"Tina says she's not going to be his trophy wife."

"Trophy?" I laughed aloud. And yet I could feel myself heating up, a mixture of jealousy and protectiveness prickling along my forearms. Tina wasn't young anymore and she wasn't rich, and maybe Eduoard did love her, but what if he only wanted something out of the marriage, like a clear road to US citizenship? Marrying into this country and marrying up in social status has a long tradition among immigrants—didn't my own father do something of the sort? And Haiti, *Haiti*, for Christ sake: isn't AIDS an epidemic down there? What if he's got HIV? *Jesus, I'm probably a racist as well as a sexist.*

"Yeah, trophy," Davey said. "Eddy just laughed. He said he wanted to marry her because he loves her. You know, Guy, the way they tease each other, it's how people act when they're in love. Eddy is very handsome, he's smart too, and that Caribbean accent of his— well, maybe I *am* gay. . ." He started laughing at himself, and shaking his big head slowly, he reminded me of a teddy bear.

"Opposites attract," I said. I caught myself beginning to scratch at my chest and stopped.

"Yo, Donna!" I called out across the dining room. "I've been waiting for somebody like you my whole life. Please!" I made as if I were a starving man, gesturing with both hands at my gaping mouth. It was a Neapolitan gesture, one of my dad's.

She was writing something hurriedly at the hostess station and shot me a look. I've been playing games like this with waitresses and barmaids and hostesses ever since I was a kid. (Oh, Graziella Laporta, where are you now?) Because my mother was unavailable so much of the time, *the girls*, as she always called them, were often delegated to look after me.

Donna called across the room, "I'll send somebody to help you, right away, *sir*."

What was truly sweet was how she pivoted from behind her station when she said that, signaling to a waiter with a raised hand, the skirt of her sundress flaring out and floating up. It was dark red with tiny black polka dots, and beneath it, her perfect legs were bare. She was wearing a pair of tooled black Western boots, like my own actually, only hers were decorated with red leather diamonds.

I didn't like to think about the way we'd ended—*bruta figura*—but of course I went over it again. Her husband discovered he was not alone in his infidelities. However, when he learned about Donna and me, he pretended to be shocked; what's more, out of some sort of vindictiveness—I think it was also fear, I told Donna, although she said he was just being a prick—he insisted that before he would agree to a divorce, Donna and her "Italian" would have to submit to an AIDS test. He said he and his girlfriend would too, but we had to do it first. I have always taken precautions against unwanted pregnancies and VD, especially AIDS, but the thought that I had to prove on demand that I was "clean" disturbed me greatly. The cards were of no use—they're often unintelligible when one is emotionally overwrought—and I thought of turning to Tina for help, but at the time I didn't know how to find her.

I began to grow suspicious of Donna. How many other lovers might she have had besides me, perhaps as revenge for her husband's serial infidelity? She refused to enumerate them. I felt dirty and I didn't want to know how dirty I might have become. I sat in *zazen* holding my shame and dread like a *koan*. At last I spoke to my roshi at the Valley Zen Center about my problem. He told me I should always be ready to die completely. Everything in life requires this sort of complete commitment: it's how the small self is finally killed off, he said.

Donna couldn't believe how long I delayed. I got tetchy and justified my hesitation by saying Tom was her fucking husband and it was their fucking divorce we were talking about. Why should I have to be tested? It was humiliating. However, at last I did succumb: we all passed our tests, and it was a great relief, and their marriage ended as quickly as could be expected. But my relationship with Donna was damaged. Although I think we could have patched it, I told myself that I didn't love her, and so what was the use of going on? I'm ashamed now to think about the way we let things fall apart, as if we were high school kids who didn't know how much work it can take to stay together.

That day at the Arms with Davey, talking about my cousin and Eddy and whatever they seemed to have found in spite of the odds against them, put me into a deeply reflective state. After our lunch had finally arrived and we'd hastily eaten, I said goodbye rather abruptly, said I was late for my office hours, and I left the restaurant without a word to Donna or even another glance in her direction.

Back when we broke up, Donna had told me that I needed to take a long look at my shadow, because I was keeping things in it that I didn't want to see. "Whatever your spiritual pretentions." That hurt. She had smiled and without rancor added, "You don't want to be a mama's boy, and I'm not gonna baby you."

CHAPTER 47

YOU FELT AS IF you were approaching from the air, and then you were hovering over the place, and then landing at a rooftop heliport; you heard the *chop-chop* of the propellers and felt the whirlybird wobbling in, a little too realistically for comfort. But then you were suddenly out and atop a wide turret being transported along a moving walkway to where a pair of tall wooden doors swung open. Splendid stuff. Castlefroy.

Complete access required Platinum level membership, which was very expensive, although free tours of select galleries and registration in the auction halls were available to all visitors. A view of the Platinum Range, as it was called, showed you images of what looked like a casino nestled amid the mountains, if not in Lucerne then in Monaco or someplace equally Disneyesque. Streaming adverts pitched real-world projects supposedly still in the developmental stages, and therefore offering tremendous opportunities to investors—if interested, there was a list of numbers you should call immediately. Membership at the lower levels came with bidding privileges for subcontracts having to do with software and hardware production. "Owner" was the highest status. Jesse said your credit background had to be checked before you were even allowed to apply for Owner. Although he was still at Silver, he was seriously thinking about going all the way to Platinum.

My lack of interest in all this was not a deterrent to Jesse as he clicked and commented; luckily, I was well fortified with his excellent scotch. (His own capacity was astounding, and I'd already discovered I couldn't keep up, although I tried.) We proceeded to what he called a first rate tech arcade. "It's a commercial pup," he said, "a franchise operation." Reading my perplexed expression, he explained: "Software and hardware in beta stage from other companies, but available on trial to members. All of it very cool." We were presently offered products whose precise functions were beyond both my comprehension and level of interest.

I could feel a frown settling about my mouth, could feel the crease between my eyebrows deepening the way it does whenever I spend too much time in front of a computer that's trying to sell me things. I tugged at my beard, thought about a pretty student who liked wearing black thong panties and made sure to have me notice this, but I resolved to press on with Jesse, who was determined to assuage my apprehensions. When we rather suddenly leaped from the Silver level beyond Gold into Platinum, I asked him pointedly about hacking. "Never!" he replied, placing his right hand over his heart: "We are *condoned!*"

A DAY LATER, AT school he told me that after I'd left he had succeeded in "rifling the cache."

"That sounds criminal," I quipped, glancing at my watch. Whether condoned or not, I'd already decided against joining him for another foray to the Castle.

We were together in the lobby of the campus union, waiting with a throng of students for a sudden heavy downpour to pass. It was the last week of classes of the spring term, an exciting time, and for those about to graduate, fraught with anxiety. The lightning and thunder didn't help: everyone seemed nervous as if the storm might burst into the lobby with us. In order to mitigate some of my tension with Jesse, I quipped, "The next thing you'll tell me is you can get a good deal on bazookas imported from Afghanistan."

"Don't even joke around like that! Look, I only borrow certain software for research, and I return it virtually untouched."

"Virtually?" I raised my eyebrows.

Leiper bobbed on elastic knees like a basketball player setting up a shot. I put a hand on his shoulder. He smiled and launched into a discourse on the uses of portals, wormholes, and squibs.

"What's a squib?" I asked.

"A type of program designed to explode in the middle."

Leiper lowered his voice and said that he was considering becoming an Owner at Castlefroy, although he really didn't have time for the "responsibilities." Then he was onto the interactive displays of the new galleries to which he'd been admitted. The Castle's system of "chutes and ladders" originating on these pages could link a Platinum member to the far quadrants of the Deep Web. It was the first time I'd ever heard the term, and all I could think of were science fiction movie scenes where lovely, alien ladies attended ugly, alien gangsters.

"Mr. Badge must have some first rate code monkeys writing for him," Jesse said.

Lightning has always affected me unpredictably, and rumbling thunder, like the heavy bass lines of funk music, can feel like a challenge to my intestines. I gulped for air while I watched the storm through trembling panes of glass at the front of the union. The sky flashed and crashed so loudly that all at once the kids looked up from their cellphones. Then, as if catching a collective breath, with one voice they erupted into a cheer while the rain punched down even harder.

Gurdjieff once said he would be satisfied if his students could at least notice when the sidewalks were wet. It's not so easy to remember yourself and to pay attention both within and without—it's even more difficult now that the pleasures of solitude have been replaced by the frisson of perpetual interconnectivity.

Hoping to entice my return to the Castle, Jesse whispered about a rare set of illustrations soon to be auctioned online. They were based on the literary works of Pietro Aretino, and he reminded me of a saying that I liked to quote by this 16th Century gentleman: "What evil is there in seeing a man possess a woman? Why, the beasts would be more free than we! It is the very source from which gushes forth rivers of people. It is that which has made you."

Considered by some as the innovator of literary pornography, Aretino was dubbed "divine" by his illustrious contemporary, the poet Ludovico Ariosto. I had read some of Aretino's verses, but had never seen the entire collection of the works based on them. They are frank depictions of pagan deities in *flagrante delicto*. To this day they are referred to simply as "*I Modi*"—"The Postures"—and they still carry with them a fragrance of the illicit.

Giulio Romano made the original drawings and then had them engraved by Marcantonio Raimondi. It is said that these explicit works greatly displeased Pope Clement, and as a result, Raimondi was thrown into prison and Romano had to flee to Mantua. Aretino, a person of considerable influence, secured his friend's release, but then, exulting further in the rebellious spirit that had so incited the Pope, he wrote an entire "indecent" cycle of sonnets to accompany the resurrected engravings. Unfortunately, many of these were destroyed by the Church fathers; since then, connoisseurs are always on the lookout for the appearance of a print previously unknown.

Jesse said that those for sale at Castlefroy were derived from Raimondi's original engravings, and they'd been certified as hand tinted during the late 19th Century. The Aretino sonnets were included as captions in Italian, which was unusual. The suggested minimum opening bid was only four figures a piece. "At least have a look," he said. "And you can translate for me. Tonight, okay?"

"Maybe," I said, glancing at my wristwatch. I already knew that neither the divine Pietro nor the precise Marcantonio nor the persistent Jesse could persuade me. I'd felt sick after my previous visits with him to Castlefroy, and then angry at myself for the amount of booze I had consumed, and then ashamed of the reason why.

Years and years ago Dr. Kee helped me to recognize that my dread of Bob Badget was the equivalent of a superstition. "Whatever the crimes Mr. Badget has actually committed, you have also made him into your all purpose boogieman," he said. After the Moon went down, after I started college, I rarely thought about Bob at all, and Leo never mentioned him to me. Now, here he was again.

But what if he's gone straight? I'd known it to happen, the criminal justice system was supposed to help it happen, and despite all the horror stories, good things do sometimes come out of prison.

Then too there was *Goodly Creatures.*

It had stopped raining and the sun was struggling to shine from behind a swag of dark clouds. We were all at once pressing out through the doors, but before I could slip away from Jessie, he latched onto me. "Guido," he said, holding my forearm as we splashed together through a shallow puddle on the sidewalk, "wouldn't you enjoy your inheritance more if it were translated into some of the things that you want?" He had already explained to me that I should try thinking about these in purely economic terms, that is, as *normal goods:* when people acquire enough money, it's normal for them to buy the things they want. "You're a good person," he said, squeezing my arm. "And you deserve to own beautiful things!"

I was already late for my class and I broke away with that excuse, and although the Green was soaking wet and terribly muddy, I sloshed directly across it toward Van Wyck Hall. "I'll think about it," I called to Jesse.

Goodly Creatures: before I rediscovered it online, I had never seen the painting in its completed form, had seen it only once, in fact, when Gwen plucked off its cover and we beheld it ripening on an easel tree. Now I was staring at the pixilated version that beamed from Leiper's screen. Miranda and Ferdinand, the pair of young lovers whom Prospero has brought together: beauteous Gwen and handsome Guido. Some commentators on *The Tempest* believe that Shakespeare means their conjunction to symbolize the *hierosgamos,* the sacred marriage by which the Philosopher's Stone is attained, the alchemist having realized how masculine and feminine energies complement each other "by the power of One Thing," as the Emerald Tablet says. Framed in Jesse's oversized monitor, Leo's painting seemed truly an icon.

Gazing on the image, I could smell once more the scent of turpentine and oil paint suffusing Leo's studio, and my body remembered its discipline and strength, its power as a breathing statue. How hungry the work made me! I used to imagine that carnelian red would taste like pomegranate seeds, that burnt umber would be like a crust of freshly baked bread. All those starving hours when I held my nude body close to Gwendolyn's, inhaling her essence, but in the name of art, barely touching her!

This royal pair, these immortal young lovers, what might *Goodly Creatures* fetch at auction? A few thousand dollars? No more than that—but buying the painting was out of the question. It should already have been mine! Fucking Leo should have given it to me.

Jesse saw I was transfixed, but at last he broke our silence with a burst of his irrepressible excitement. It was obvious that he'd already worked out a plan in concert with the Dean, and he let it spill: after identifying myself as the College's representative, I'd have the money behind me to bid on this and any other works by Declare. I was, naturally, the person best equipped to assess their value, and if I believed that by their acquisition they might contribute to the College's "collateral standing"—that is, its leveraging power—I would be authorized to act. I didn't need to have a membership at Castlefroy in order to register for the upcoming auction, and I didn't need to use my own name, but once I was enrolled, Jesse thought that I should contact Bob and reveal my identity; he had, naturally, already secured Bob's personal e-mail address. Furthermore, Jesse hoped that besides my purchases I might also be able to persuade Mr. Badge to make some additional gift to the College. "Maybe *Goodly Creatures*"—he waited for my reaction—"that is, if you don't buy it for yourself."

We both continued to scrutinize the image on the screen. "I'm quite moved by the expression on your face," Jesse said, but whether he was referring to the painting or to me, I couldn't say.

When I turned away, with the knuckles of both hands, I tapped at the corners of my eyes.

We resumed our reconnoitering but found no other works for which either Gwendolyn or I had modeled. I was relieved. Indeed, among the eight paintings available, there were no others from Leo's portrait period; all were rather small landscapes in a style abstracted to look like bars of color under wet skies. I'd never seen any of them before and I thought they might be late pieces. They were superb. Then too, there was the film strip of Leo: Jesse said we absolutely *must* have that for the College.

He leaned over my shoulder and pulled *Goodly Creatures* back into view. He admired it in silence for a few seconds, and then started in about the celebration we could have once our job was complete. He pressed his palms together with glee. "Imagine the party out back on the deck at the Arms: Guido, maybe you could recreate some special dishes from the Villa Giustovera!" Then he mimed how I might skin Bob's hand and with a wink remind him, "*It's it, man.*" I told him about the possibility of my being grandfathered in at the College, and Jesse said, "Wonderful!" and that our success would therefore be doubly rewarding. And if I didn't want to be a professor, maybe I could become a curator at the museum, or chief of acquisitions, or maybe even the new executive director. "I'd love to work under you," he said, leaping from one idea to the next, bouncing up and down beside me on his chair.

CHAPTER 48

MAYBE HE WAS TERMINALLY ill. Maybe his hospital stay only convinced him that he might as well keep drinking. Disease or addiction, ignominy or despair, suicide or accident, Leo's demon is what did him in.

Whatever the work he'd continued to create, it had not been enough to keep his psyche intact and afloat. He'd fallen so far from grace and his life was in such disarray that even the fantasy of a complete retrospective must at last have felt hopeless. The Jumble, the comical rhyme he left behind made of slobber and eye-blinks and visions of lasses and lads: this was no map to the palace of wisdom, and at the end of his road, he'd evidently found no pearl of great price. After a lifetime in thrall to the spirit of eternal youth, he might indeed have managed to "exhaust all poisons" within himself, which is what his hero, the immortal Rimbaud advises would be visionaries to do. It's too bad Leo took him literally: he was drained in the process.

"Those are pearls that were his eyes," sings the fairy Ariel of Ferdinand's supposedly drowned father. It's a lovely metaphor, but there's also something horrifying about it.

BOB HAD CAPITALIZED ON Leo's scene, making up his accounts as he went along and finally earning for himself a trip to the Big House. He thought he was the cool one, the smart one, and he too was mistaken about the road he chose. But evil? Evil is my girlfriend with a hole in her head, dead because some kid with a gun robs a liquor store while Eva Lynn Samuels is standing at the counter: it happened in Beacon in 1975. Maybe the kid needs bread to buy drugs from Uncle Bob or somebody like him, but is Bob to blame for that bullet?

Think of another kid that another kind of evil had set its sights on: this guy was a real sweetheart, a kid I played basketball with when I was volunteering at the Sunrise Community Center on Saturday mornings, a program that was intended to help underprivileged youth like him stay off the streets and out of trouble. After high school, this guy, Billy Biel joins the Army to fight the good fight against Communism. In South East Asia he learns to kill peasants who are trying to defend their homeland. He survives, but he comes home with a monkey on his back who eats him alive. At twenty three Billy Biel is dead from a heroin overdose. That's evil, I'd say, but whose crime exactly is it?

Given who they are, people only do what they can under the circumstances they face. That's not an excuse: it's a fact of life. Badget shot Chris and Gwendolyn fucking. They were adults, but the pictures were plainly pornographic by the standards of the day and therefore a crime. It was a time of excess and many kinds of experimentation, and if it seems now like an age of carelessness or downright stupidity, well then, look at how much more carelessness and stupidity abound today and how much less beatitude. To those who blame that high flying era, I would argue instead that many of today's problems are due to the fact that our revolution didn't go far enough. For one thing, women's sexual power is still misunderstood and feared. For another, most people can't distinguish the erotic from the crassly exploitative, and seek only novel sensations. It takes intelligence to follow your heart, as well as courage. As for the drugs, in our culture we rarely acknowledge the difference between ecstasy and anesthesia. You need eyes in your head to do that, and usually you need someone to help you open them—sometimes the help doesn't come the way you expected.

Still, it hurt to see those pictures.

Bob photographed a lot of girls, some of them quite young, dressed in the clothes he and Connie sold. Did he shoot them nude? I don't know. One image I can't get out of my mind is of a redhead, a Saint Anne's girl, bending from the waist forward, her tartan skirt hiked high; she's glancing at the camera nonchalantly while she pulls a green stocking over her knee, up to her white thigh. And there's this one too: a very young girl, a child really, dressed in Victorian era frills, heavily painted around the eyes, deep red lipstick on her mouth. Some kind of joke I thought at the time, so exaggerated was the effect. Would Edgar Degas, who from the wings of theater stages and dance studios in the early 20th Century sketched dozens of young ballerinas, have recognized a kindred spirit in Bob Badget? What about Degas' peer, Mary Cassatt? Her portrait *Little Girl in a Blue Armchair* communicates more about innocence and eroticism than a case of Sigmund Freud. Would she have admired the nonchalance and ambiguity in Bob's photographs?

I wish I had those pictures in my hands today.

One thing art can do that the law can't, is to interrogate the difference between exploitation and witness. All visual media, especially photography, invites our complicity through the act of looking, while at the same time inuring us to the content by objectifying it. A child of course is vulnerable, and although curious, inexperienced, and because of this, easily exploited. Children need adults to safeguard them from many sorts of dangers, and yet the law of the land can only define childhood based on consensus about a number of years. I wish I had Bob's pictures in my hands today; I wish I could see again those things I remember having looked at but which I was not prepared to see.

Perhaps I was a more judicious kid than some others were; perhaps I was just plain lucky. After all, I didn't become a dope dealer, a junky or a whore. Or a pedophile. Was Bob? After his books that Gwen helped him cook were opened by the Feds, he had to pay with hard time for the crime. *Felon:* the very sound of the word evokes its origins as a term once used to describe Lucifer, the Father's fallen favorite angel, the primordial rebel. The State hates to be rooked, but really, how much evil was there in that particular transgression of Bob's? What about the harm he caused for which he was never held accountable—but no, I can't go on like this as if I am appointed to judge the man's every iniquity, as if I have that right to do so because he took some pictures that made me complicit in his sordid business.

I TRIED TO REASON everything through in order to get clear about what was at stake for me, and after a couple of days, I was ready to back out of the Plan. I decided that I didn't care so very much about resurrecting Leo's reputation or about all the benefits this might shake from the sugar tree. I am not his son or artistic heir. He was a teacher of mine, I've had others who were also important. As for my loyalty to Jesse, he could advance himself well enough without my further assistance. And Liotta, well, Liotta has plenty of pieces on her chessboard.

I was done with Bob, whether called Badget or Badge. I didn't need to know if he was now a model of rehabilitation, proof that the criminal justice system can help a person rise above the circumstances of his past. Let Jesse discover what was what, let him transact the business at hand. I didn't ever need to see Uncle Bob again: there was no setting-to-rights required of me, I was not a victim who felt compelled to confront his abuser. As for *Goodly Creatures*, I am the living, breathing subject of that painting, one of them anyway, and I don't need a picture to remind me either of my youthful grace or folly.

But then I realized I had to go through with it.

WE ARRANGED FOR A preliminary meeting at a riverside park just south of Beacon. Leo's shack had once stood almost within eyesight of the spot, and like him, I too used to hunt the strand below the railroad tracks for the river's driftwood prizes. When you live in one area for most of your life, you accumulate many tokens of your time there, and time itself can seem to hang like mist or smoke in its atmosphere. Other moments, often unbidden, float through the present one, their shadows like those of drifting clouds on ground below. The *sfumato* effect of Leonardo's paintings comes to mind: how mysteriously a thing can emerge and then recede into the depths.

I have often come to this bench to meditate, and that day I came early to prepare myself for our appointment. I was going to do business with a businessman, and for this purpose I had been promised up to forty five thousand dollars with which to bargain. It was quite a vote of confidence. I also had a knife in my pocket—I'm not certain I can explain why. Bob arrived late, but when he emerged from his white Mercedes and saw me waiting, immediately he raised a hand in greeting. I could see he was smiling. I stood, raising my own right hand in return. He was dressed in casual clothes, jeans and sport shoes, and a polo shirt of the kind he used to favor, forest green with the collar turned up a little as if this smart touch were accidental. I was all in black, black leather jacket, black boots.

We shook hands firmly. We'd always been about the same height, but close up I could tell how much he'd aged. His blond hair was sparse and it was dyed, combed and slick; his blue eyes looked faded, almost to the color of stone. He still had that little beard of his, that weird waggle of hair under his lower lip, which I saw was also tinted blond. His unicorn tassel, as once I'd thought while on acid.

"Professor Diamante! Let me take a look at you, big guy!" He stepped back to run his eyes over me.

I felt nothing, said nothing.

His body looked slack, though I saw how he had kept his waistline trim, as ladies' men are wont to do even as they age. I watched him from someplace deep inside of myself; I studied him as I might a subject for a painting, or an opponent in a fencing match. I did not seek to enter his mind: long ago I'd learned that even the thought of an opponent's weakness can be a distraction. It had already occurred to me that since Bob was the executor of Leo's estate and its sole beneficiary, Leo would have had to trust him, which meant they had grown close again.

As for how he might see me, well, I wanted Mr. Badge only to know that I was representing the College in a business transaction. I had nothing I wanted to say about our past together. I wasn't going to let him bring up Chris, either. I'd laid my cousin to rest, and whatever he and Bob had meant to each other, it was outside the present moment.

We sat down, Bob Badge and I, side by side on that metal bench tattooed with graffiti near the Hudson. We began to discuss Leo, both of us noting that his studio shack had once stood nearby. I speculated that he was probably still using it right up until his death. Bob's eyes lingered on the vacant spot, and I thought he was going to say something more about it, but he did not.

What he said was that over the years Leo and he had seen each other now and then, and had gotten to know each other again. He gave me a telling look; I gave him nothing in return. Like me, he lamented Leo's heavy drinking: it was so bad, Bob said, that he had hated to be around him when Leo was wasted. He said that he himself had been sober for more than thirty years, that he'd had to go cold turkey while in prison. Again, a look at me in silence. I nodded. Then, with another wistful glance over toward the site of the shack: "All the opportunities he blew!"

I brought up the College. I'd noticed a hint of emotion in Bob's voice, and I thought that he would be in the mood to make us a good bargain, perhaps even, as Jesse had speculated, some sort of gift. "When it comes to your *ask,*" Jesse had coached me, "ask for what you really want. You might hit the mark." (The mark: it had sounded illicit, especially because of Leiper's mischievous smile.)

Bob said that he'd taken all of Leo's work off the block. Had I noticed? I shook my head no. (In fact, I'd been informed of this by Jesse, who said it was probably a good thing for our strategy.) Bob said it was because of me personally that he'd pulled the paintings from an upcoming auction in New York: once he'd learned of the school's interest and in particular with whom he would be dealing, he wanted to give a friend the best deal possible. Furthermore, he said he'd been thinking a lot about his responsibility to Leo's reputation.

"I wonder what he might be worth today? It figures that the school would be interested."

I didn't immediately reply. I looked at the river: it was running high after a week of rain, and a brisk wind was flowing with the current down the valley. The afternoon was clouding over and the air was suddenly chilly. Despite my intention not to judge him, I thought that there was something pathetic about Bob Badge—he certainly wasn't presenting himself as an accomplished entrepreneur, the sort of character I might have inferred from my visits to Castlefroy. Liotta probably would have had her people vet him, and yet I wondered if after all he might be putting up a front. His E-class Mercedes could well be leased, and like his colored hair, a performance prop.

I wondered if he had any family. He and Concetta had no children that I knew of, and I'd always assumed she left him long ago. How long was he actually locked away? When he was originally busted, how had he avoided morals charges and an investigation into his drug dealing? If he'd been exposed, he might have been charged with racketeering, and so, as Davey had concluded, someone important must have been protecting him. I wondered why he hadn't appeared after Leo's death or attended his memorial service. And when was the last time he'd seen Leo alive? That was what I asked him.

"Quite near the end," Bob said. He looked at me strangely. "You caused his death, you know."

He watched for my reaction, saw nothing, waited a moment more. "Sorry I said that, man, but he *did* think you'd lost faith in him. Said he was counting on you for the show he wanted, but you couldn't help him. Well, he was always a big dreamer. You remember, back in the day. . ."

"Back in the day, I was only a kid."

He didn't miss a beat: "We thought everybody ought to be free, and maybe get rich too—why not? *Money makes the man.* You know that one?"

"It's clothes. 'Apparel oft proclaims the man.' That's Shakespeare. Back in the day you took pictures—"

He raised his eyebrows. "Fashions, yeah. Connie had the right idea at the right time. She made a fortune in L.A. She's a grandma now—I wonder how she dresses? But money never goes out of style, am I right, Professor?"

He's going to try to scam me. I saw it as clearly as I could see Storm King Mountain on the river shore across from us. And this too: *He's got a lot more of Leo's work.*

"Hey Lonnie-la," I said.

"Leo tell you that? The old fruit!" He slapped his thigh.

He turned his body half away from me, looking down river. I remembered that Bannerman's Island wasn't very far away, with its castle's crumbling turrets. I thought of Castlefroy, of Badget's Bazaar, of the Half Moon, and Leo's lost shack full of his last paintings. Then Bob started laughing softly and tapped my shoulder. I stared at him, keeping perfectly still. I thought of the knife in my pocket.

Lifting his hand away, he said, "I'm more responsible for what happened than you could ever be." It looked like he was swearing an oath, his raised palm trembling slightly at the end of a bony wrist. "I had this idea, see, to start an auction house with him. Leo had his own idea: to hell with it."

"You last saw him when, exactly?" My heart ticked up its tempo, but I continued to sit completely still as we spoke.

"I was with him that night."

"And?"

"He must have climbed the fence."

"So you weren't actually there?"

"I went to my car to get my good camera. He told me he had a stunt in mind. It's such a shame—"

"And when you returned?"

"He was nowhere. I figured he'd lost his nerve. I didn't think he could have ever gotten over that fence by himself. It's what I told *your friends* when they asked me."

"So it might have been an accident."

"I don't think so." He paused for a long moment. "You know, people are always intrigued when an artist dies mysteriously." He was pinching his beard with two fingers, and when he raised his face to the sky, the strangest sort of expression came over it, not exactly a smile, but something like the look of an animal that's picked up a scent.

He moved his hand as if to reach for my shoulder again but thought better of it. "I read about you, Guido, 'the artist cop!' When I was a kid I wanted to be Dick Tracy. That two-way wrist radio— shades of things to come, eh?" Again he paused very deliberately. "It's a fucking shame what happened. A real waste."

It had begun to rain lightly and a steady wind was blowing down the ridge behind us. We sat in silence, watching the water begin to surge and chop. There was a patch of sunlight where the rain was peppering the surface about a hundred yards off shore, and the effect was mesmerizing.

I snapped alert and asked myself: *Do I buy this? Do I need to tell* my friends *about our conversation?*

"As you know, the College . . ."

"I'll give your college a deal," he said. "The best deal. I'll give you those paintings I was going to auction." He leveled his faded eyes on mine. Then he was turning up his collar tightly around his scrawny neck, buttoning it against the cold. He drew his thin arms close, crossing them together in an effort to keep warm. I could see his pale old skin puckering. His face looked thin and bony.

"I don't want much in return. What I do want, Professor, is for you to write something about these important works of art I'm giving your college."

"I'm not a critic."

"Hell, I'll even have my computer geeks work up some sort of interactive greeting for your museum. Like the hostess at the Castle—*just kidding, man!* Why so serious, Guy? You should be celebrating! And another thing: I want my name included, I want you to talk about my long association with the American master, Leo Declare. It'll be good for both of us—for Castlefroy and the Hudson River School."

"It's Hudson River College," I said, correcting him automatically as I have done with other people dozens of times. I was rather stunned by his offer; he saw this and let me ponder the details. Then I asked: "What about the rest? You know, whatever else he left?"

"Right."

He looked at me expectantly, as I myself might do when a student gets ahold of a thread that can unravel an entire problem. It was logical to have concluded that there was more than what was pictured on line, and logical that I would want to see it all. But there was something else I had to get straight just then, a piece of business I needed to settle within myself.

Leo might have been like my father in some ways, but he was more complicated than Zizi Diamante, more creative too: he'd dug a moat all the way around his heart. A drawbridge had been lowered for me, for some others too, but Christ, try to soothe his ailment and you were likely to be smote with savage wit or turned down cold for offering. It's that way with addicts: their pride is their shame, and furthermore you can't get between an addict and his *thing*. After my father died, I wept more for the neglected child I'd once been than for the death of my old man, but finally I saw how he had also suffered by neglecting me. Finally, I forgave him and could even thank him for the gifts he did bequeath me. At the end of his life, my father's buoyancy had prevailed, and with Giulia he was genuinely blessed. But drunk old Leo Declare had stepped off a cliff all alone. Poor Leo. Poor, poor Leo.

What came to me in a flash was the epilogue of *The Tempest*, Prospero entreating his audience for such mercy as can release the exhausted magician from his "bare island." The spell must be broken by which he has held us so long, and he says the power is literally in our hands, meaning our applause. The play's last lines beseech us: "As you from crimes would pardoned be, let your indulgence set me free." To say that I forgave Leo his contrary ways purely on account of his artistry is false, but that afternoon I knew what I was going to do.

As for Bob, sitting in the flesh beside me, I was neither for the man nor against him. We were not friends and we were not going to be friends. I told him I'd already begun to write something about Leo, and to complete it I would need to see in person the pieces we were discussing. If there were others he wanted to show me, I'd be happy to give him my professional opinion. Wonderful, he replied, we would arrange it all at our mutual convenience. We shook on it. Then I said I wanted to buy *Goodly Creatures* for myself. He began to say something about the painting, how special it must have been to Leo, how he'd kept it with him over all the years, but I cut him off. "I'll pay market value," I said.

It was getting late and the shadows under Break Neck Ridge were lengthening as we bid each other goodbye. They were the same shadows I had always known. I couldn't banish them, and I didn't need to.

CHAPTER 49

SANDY LORRAINE MARRIED LIEUTENANT Detective Fred Smart, quit the Force, and within a year gave birth to Dahlia. Sandy had never met my mother, but when she learned of her death she wanted to come to the wake. Fred and I hardly knew each other, but he came along to hold Dahlia in the funeral parlor's anteroom while Sandy paid her respects. To me, Fred Smart said only, "My condolences," as he grasped my hand. The baby had eyes like his, large and brown, not so far from the color of mine. I liked seeing how tenderly he took Dahlia from Sandy's arms and cuddled her. The thought flitted through my mind that if Sandy and I had stayed together she might have been ours.

Sandy knelt at the open casket, crossed herself, prayed in silence, crossed herself again. She got up and came over to me, took me by the arm very possessively and led me out away from everyone else into an empty parlor. Her auburn hair was tied back tightly, and her blue-gray eyes looked tired. I asked about Charles. He was fine, she said, on a holiday with his father and grandmother in Canada. It was clear that she had something she wanted to talk to me about. She cupped my chin in her right hand and kissed me fully on the mouth, a surprisingly wet kiss, her lipstick tasting like perfume.

Then she said, "Listen to me. The loss of your mother is sad, I know how sad because I lost mine and my father too in the past five years. Your parents aren't there anymore between you and Eternity— now they're standing behind you. Think about this, Guido, don't underestimate the difference it makes, even at your age. A lot of things in your life will change."

I'VE GIVEN MYSELF SEVERAL days at the Villa Giustovera to do what I am euphemistically calling spring cleaning. In fact I'm here to salvage what I can of the restaurant equipment and hotel furnishings in order to sell them off. I'm also planning to tear out some of the fine old woodwork, since there's a market for it among people fixing up old houses throughout Dutchess County. I'm encamped in my childhood bedroom. I have never in my life until now slept alone at the Place.

AUNT JOSIE, WHO CLAIMS she is nearly blind, comes over to help me and sits at a desk in the foyer to keep track of how things are packed off by their buyers. Josie keeps a checklist of her own device, huge letters on the brown paper of a shopping bag that she's flattened over the desk surface. She stashes away the old cold cash we collect in a shoe box stashed in a drawer. Occasionally she will lament the departure of such things as sets of plates and bowls, or an oversized cooking vat, or the meat cutting tools that she insists my grandpa brought with him from Palermo. Seeing how perturbed she can become, I stroke her wrinkled arm. I assure her that I won't let go of the really valuable stuff. I've made a collection, I say. I have given her two cut glass flower vases, ruby red, that my grandmother bought in Venice almost a century ago.

"Flossie and Gesu," she says, shaking her head with disbelief. "The Villa Giustovera goes too. . . ."

"Scientists say that nothing in the universe is wasted, Aunt Josie. And believe it or not, a particle of light can eventually return to where it started."

"Scientists—*Madonna*. What do they know?" She rubs a brown knuckle over her left eye. "They can't cure my sight."

Then: "Guido, you should get a satellite dish like I did. You can watch the whole world on a big screen. Oh, but I remember when your grandmother was alive, *sa benedica,* the stories she could tell and how she would make us laugh! You must have inherited your talent from her. The things you used to say to little Tina. How she loved it when her cousin Guido was her baby sitter!"

And here my old aunt pauses. Tina has in fact reconnected with Josie, my own mother's death having had something to do with this. She's also going to move in with Eduoard, although she hasn't found the right moment to inform her mom. Pensive Josie crosses herself. "*Dio mio*," and then in a surprisingly calm voice: "Why did Cristiano have to die? Why did Americans have to go in Vienam?"

"*Viet*," I whisper, "Vietnam. They went to serve the empire."

"Look at this." She wipes her eyes and points to the wooden coat stands collected together near the front door, like a grove of trees waiting to be harvested. "They want the old things made from wood, because the new ones are cheap crap. Did you know, Professor, that plastic is really oil, and oil is what the dinosaurs used to be? Did you know in Iraq there's oil oozing from the ground and that's why we went there? Dinosaurs! Can you imagine?"

She blows her nose and then waves to the friendly guy moving the coat racks out through the hallway onto his truck. His buddy herds away a flock of bent-wood chairs. It's possible that someday America will stop hungering after oil, but what are the chances of that during my lifetime? Scientists say a particle of light can come home to where it started, okay, but what are the odds on a certain lightning ball returning? What are the odds on this happening even once?

"This here," Josie says—I'm uncertain what she sees—"all of this came out of Mother Earth. Did you know the Moon did too? That's what science is good for. Discovering things. The Earth came out of the Sun and then the Moon came out of the Earth. Like a baby. That's something. You should paint a picture!" She gazes off into space, and then she asks, "How long until the teaching ends?"

I am momentarily taken aback. "Graduation is next weekend," I reply. But I hear the question in a larger sense.

"I was thinking of starting a restaurant," I say. "After a complete remodeling of the Place." It's a joke, but suddenly the idea sounds plausible.

"Oh, Guido! You really want that? Your mother, God bless her, she couldn't keep things going by herself."

Silence holds us, and we both feel it, the spirit of the Villa Giustovera stirring.

"I'll help you," she cackles. "Everybody used to help out in the old days, remember? Tina could help too. She can cook, you know? She brought me chicken saltimbocca—I prefer veal, but anyway. . . Oh, how your grandmother made everybody work!" She turns her head abruptly to the right, and it makes me think of the blind owl years ago on an apricot stump near the swimming pool. Someone would always remember to tell that story.

There's a porcelain thud among the group of bathroom fixtures departing via the ballroom door. We both turn toward the noise. "Be careful with that!" Josie shouts to the guy hoisting a pedestal sink high over his head as he enters the foyer. "You break that chandelier and my nephew will make you pay!"

She still sees above us the branch-work of lights even though it is long gone, and I remember its plastic prisms in rainbow hues that used to rustle like leaves when the front door closed. After fifty years living in the shadow of the Villa, my ancient aunt is having her day. Donna Giuseppina Giustovera: my aunt Josie. Geppina she was never called.

"SUSTAINED ATTENTION AND A steady flame are imperative, but a brief application of high heat at the beginning of the process can penetrate the matter to its core. Any cook will know what I mean."

Signor Caballo, as I remember him: pomaded hair and sculpted beard, the salt and pepper of an ageless, vigorous man—*very well preserved*, as was always said of him.

"What is this place?"

No sooner do I pose the question than my friend, with a sweep of his hand, invites me to survey the premises. He swings his arm broadly about and the sleeve of his white coat fans out like a wing. Then he slides back the cuff to show me his bare wrist, the brown skin and fine dark hair in the glass where I conjure. If I stare too long, the vision wavers, but when I step past my skepticism I have a lamp lit scene with Caballo at a laboratory table adjusting a piece of apparatus. He moves a burner in quick, circular motions beneath a flask clamped to a metal stand. In the wide-bottomed vessel, a transparent blue liquid bubbles roundly like hot oil. Neither turquoise, nor cobalt, nor lapis. Not cerulean, not indigo. It is a blue like that of the Aegean sea surrounding the island of Delos, where Apollo and his sister Artemis were born, the Sun and Moon.

"I'm not afraid of dying. I could die right now."

"*C'est vrai, monsieur.*" He strolls into a far corner of his chamber and drolly continues: "The French excel in all matters of taste, even so far as selecting which letters of a word are best unspoken, but do you know the Language of the Birds, Guido?"

I watch the glass. An endless alphabet streams through the flask: letters and glyphs, mute formations of birds in shapes and signs swiftly migrating through the bottle of blue sky. I see the symbol of Adam Kadmon, the First Man, and I think that this is the same as the one for the Tree of Life at the goal of the alchemical labyrinth.

Onto the tree many birds descend and instantly transform into blossoms. Leaves begin on the twig tips, and these in turn branch out until I realize all humanity is included on this, our family tree. I try to trace the shape of my own life, but a great wind shakes the leaves and birds and branches free: they whirl away and leave me at a wordless place. I think that any sound would suffice to return my Paradise, that a single syllable would mean every name. I wish to explain this to my companion, but then I think this might not be Caballo at all.

"One thing is inside of another," I say.

"One thing only," he replies.

Behind him, framed in ebony on the laboratory wall is a black and white print of Albrecht Durer's *Knight, Death and the Devil.* The mounted knight is shown in left profile, riding west it seems, into the last rays of sunlight, which detail his suit of armor. The helmet visor is raised: his expression is resolute. He rides a perfectly proportioned steed, a white stallion rippling with life. The cavalier carries a long spear on his right shoulder that transects the composition and frames behind him in his shadow by the roadside a comical monstrosity.

The Devil is a beast with snout and dewlaps, a pair of winding tusks, a single horn like a scimitar curving atop his head. He clutches the haft of his own barbed spear, and like a stupid beast stares at the horse and rider striding past. Beneath the horse, the rider's hound, the dog of Truth, runs faithfully, and beneath the dog, a lizard crawls away toward its monstrous lord.

Near the center of the composition, behind the cavalier, on a broken down nag sits Death. Crowned with spikes, his visage is that of a woeful rotted corpse. Snakes garland the skull-bone of his face. He holds aloft an hour glass. The intrepid knight seems not to notice or not to care. He is on the path of Virtue. Is that his castle in the distance? Is it perhaps the Grail Castle and he its king returning home?

"SHOW ME GEPPINA." I press forth the words before the bright black glass where I scry. It is my second night at the Villa.

By the sound of the heavy boots tramping the hallway behind me, I recognize the approach of a familiar specter; not the one whom I was seeking, but rather the ghost of the Patroon. As a child, I deduced that he must be the original builder of the house and a Dutchman on account of his outfit: the knickerbockers and coarse blue blouse, the boot shafts folded down at the knees. I've never been frightened of the Patroon, nor has he ever seemed especially friendly.

"That little girl I used to see beside you—is she the one my grandfather and Manaperta called *La Princepessa Olandese?*"

He shows me his bucktoothed grin. I used to think him sil-ly-looking because of it, rather than horrifying. Now I see how wan his smile is, how imploring his demeanor. He is Jakob Moore, one of William Kidd's crew, who sailed the Hudson in 1700—the very same Captain Kidd, the pirate, whose ship, the San Antonio followed the river north nearly a century after Henry Hudson explored it on the Half Moon. Kidd whose treasure has never been found, although it is supposed to have been hidden in various places up and down the entire Atlantic seaboard. A clairvoyant dreamer once declared that this fabled cache was buried on the river shore near Hughsonville, not far from Kinderkill. Considerable excavations were made during the 1800's, but nothing was discovered.

I want to ask if that vision was true, if Kidd's fabulous hoard is still waiting someplace along the river or on one of its islands, perhaps only a few miles from the Villa, but before I can do so, he speaks: "Cursed!" He means the ruby ring and sapphire brooch he looted from the hoard. It's as if that single word would throttle me. I make the sign of protection with my fingers, pointing to the earth. Damnation is like this, I think: a darkness where desire breeds the absence of its object, a fumbling over nails in search on faithless knees. *Cursed.*

I witness what young Jakob did: his plundering abroad, and sometime later how in Kinderkill he made his home with his wife. A Dutchman yes, but he was among the English in the Province of New York. His English wife, Janet, died in childbirth, and on his daughter, named for her, he then unknowingly bestowed the cursed jewels. But wretched Jakob lost his Janet twice: the child died at the age of ten. He entombed her in his cellar, along with those gems that would have been her dowry.

"Cold," he says, and I feel his cold.

I want to liberate the suffering of Jakob Moore, and I realize that because I've heard his tale, a portion of his grief is satisfied. He motions me to follow as he stamps along the corridor of the Villa's second story, but then, before my eyes he levitates, and rising through the ceiling he is gone. I find myself alone outside Room 21.

"*Dai, dai, dai!*"

The voice of a woman. In agony? I think not. *Give it, give, give it to me!* she cries. Like a wraith myself, I enter her room through the sealed door.

A gibbous moon hangs in the window, casting shadows over the narrow bed. There I see a black-haired girl with naked writhing limbs entangled in her summer sheets. Tears like pearls roll down her cheeks. She holds a crucifix and rubs it through her linens over her breasts and between her thrashing legs. She moans and prays and suffers for love. Orphan for whom the convent was a penitentiary rather than a refuge and no place to which she could return, here is the waif Geppina that Caballo could not rescue.

Servant of the wicked foster parents, Geppina with your white hands: magical baker, lovely maiden, my mother's frivolous friend with whom she never fled. You, the thief who vanished into legend, you who fooled them all, even my grandmother, you, the girl I pledged to find when I was still a boy. Geppina, whom Manaperta called *saporita,* kissing his fingertips, sounding wise as a serpent to me: my family preserved your story out of some mysterious necessity. You made me want to be a man.

Giuseppina Ingrasci, was that your real name? My grandmother doubted it and maligned you out of jealousy when Caballo compared you to Tosca and praised you as a force of nature. Nonna thought you'd stolen her jewelry. I have conjured you from a few precious memories, I have traveled back in time, but I have nothing for you, dear girl, except my witness. You too live in me.

THE WEATHER HAS TURNED suddenly hot over night, and I'm especially groggy this morning. Bed and bureau, drawing table and easy chair are long gone from my boyhood room, and I'm camping with only my sleeping bag and pillow on a musty smelling mattress. Downstairs in the kitchen, on my portable gas stove, I boil water for coffee, and for breakfast, I eat some food packed from my own home. It sounds strange to think of my apartment as my home, and yet, more strangely, I feel as if I am only visiting the Villa, a guest and not its *padrone*. I think about Cristiano's departure from Widener Road when he was twenty, when he took up digs in Wappingers, and how impressed I was that he would call it home. Home is where we know ourselves. Home is wherever *I am*.

I have prized free the hardwood baseboards from some downstairs rooms, which was difficult without splitting them, as well as the ceiling moldings, which came down much more easily, but I am nearing the end of what I can do alone. The main staircase and bannister are pieces of real beauty, and although they aren't structural components, I'll need assistance to dismantle them without damaging the finely turned and varnished pieces. Perhaps Davey will help me out some time.

Meanwhile, I relish my solitude. I'm experiencing a sense of self-possession I haven't known in years. I'm letting go of things and choosing what to keep, balancing my sentimentality with attention to objects of monetary worth—*prospecting*, I think of it, and although the real gold is spiritual, I can't deny my satisfaction at selling things off for a good price. Why has the idea of commerce seemed for so long anathema to me? Because my parents' business failed, of course, but also, wasn't it because I substituted for it some unrealistic ideas about the place of art in the world? When I believe these ideals to have been compromised—in my role at HRC, for example, which I myself wrangled—I feel I've been prostituted. Foolish to think like this. My gifts are born of imagination but also of a boldness I have too often discounted.

I write in this journal continually, but I resist the desire to sketch, sensing keenly the difference between pictures and what I can do with words. The writing comes easily; I feel free to say whatever I want about myself, my people, my past. I am beyond painter or poet, no longer professor, policeman or penitent. Maybe Eva Lynn was right when in college she called me a philosopher.

Many things vie to be remembered in my book: the crystal doorknob to my parents' bedroom, the velvet fleur-de-lis printed on that chamber's maroon wallpaper, and over the doorframe always that horseshoe wrapped with red ribbon for good luck, fixed into place by ancient square nails. Yesterday—was it just yesterday?—I wrote that *Luck is getting struck by lightning when you want it*, but I'm not so sure I believe it this morning. Being lucky means being grateful for what you have.

I HAD BEEN TELLING myself for months that I would eventually return to figurative painting but that I first needed to be done with the enso. I put aside dozens, trusting that when the time was ripe I'd strike it in a single stroke and be free of my obsession. After my second night at the Villa, that is on the third day, having returned to my apartment for some tools, I found myself irresistibly wanting to make another attempt. As Leonardo did when he painted the dragon buckler to face down his father, in my studio space I gathered about me my own peculiar inspirations, chiefly my sketchbooks whose pages I opened at random. Some of the entries dated all the way back to my childhood.

Seated in the middle of the room I worked quickly on large white sheets of poster board, and this cheap paper freed me, so that I could experiment beyond the forms of the traditional enso. I lost all sense of time, producing numerous circular designs using a luscious black paint, but since I wasn't interested in anything ornate, whenever a piece tended in that direction, I came back to zero with the next attempt. I looked up from the floor where I was working only when it began to grow dark outside, suddenly remembering the promise I'd made myself to spend three successive nights alone at the Villa. I was kneeling over my painting and raised my brush so quickly that pigment splashed from it, the droplets large and dark and bright outside the thick stroke of a nearly perfect circle. It was beautiful.

THE WEATHER WAS EXCEPTIONALLY fine on the morning after my third night. I'd slept heavily, peacefully, dreamlessly, and awoke refreshed. I wanted to be out of doors early with a survey map in hand to walk the boundaries of what property my mother hadn't sold off. As soon as I set out, however, I changed my plans and decided my rogation ought to include the original borders of my grandparents' farm. This meant I would have to trespass at the edges of a recent housing development. As boys, Cristiano and I had often shot our guns out here when it was all fields and forest, a landscape that belonged to itself. Even today, what did the hills and flats, the creeks and stones care for survey maps or titles? Asphalt driveways crumble into pebbles rather quickly if they're left alone.

It had been over a year since my mother's last healthy days, when she and I had taken what she called "a walk down memory lane." She'd even sung a bit of "Sentimental Journey," and some of the other "good old songs" that her orchestra, the Larry Bell Boys, once played in the ballroom. Today, my tears welled up and I let them run, and blew my nose field-style, flicking my fingers along the nostrils as Cristiano first taught me to do. I searched for the secret landmarks of my boyhood, wandering off the main trail, a road down which my father used to haul the Villa's garbage in a battered station wagon to the dump. There I found the rusted remnants of the garbage cans themselves, and, amazingly, a box turtle treading resolutely in his armor amid the underbrush and junk.

Where the summer annex, the Other House, once stood, the first greenery of a bramble cropped up among the foundation's ruins. The abandoned structure had been burnt down a few years earlier, probably by kids playing with fire. I remembered my mother's excitement when she told me about it, gesturing with her cigarette to evoke the scene. "Burned to the ground!" she'd exclaimed. "We were at bingo that night, and when Josie and I came home, here's two trucks and the firemen packing up to leave. Nothing they could do about it but hose the grass and trees. I would have liked to see it," she said, fanning her face as if before the imagined flames, perhaps recalling the times when she had wished to burn everything and be free of the Place. The next summer we picked buckets of blackberries there, but on my walk this time there were only some green shoots amid the cracked concrete blocks.

I remembered then that cement is an ancient Roman discovery, a humble alchemy of calcium carbonate: they mined this substance from limestone in shallow marine waters, where it was formed by the accumulation of coral and shell. All at once I shouted, "Those are pearls that were his eyes!" and I began to whirl around, laughing and crying till I lay down in the grass to watch the clouds wheel overhead.

I HAD TRIED TO forget what I had been, but I did not succeed.

Was I as a boy the victim of abuse?

I think about an animal, a horse who is *misused*: he falls, and when he's down he's whipped but cannot rise. I think about the effect that witnessing this cruelty had on Friedrich Nietzsche, who suffered a mental breakdown as a result.

This sort of thing happens to the sensitive ones.

I wasn't beaten or raped. I did allow myself to be used.

Leo's "Best Boy" I was called, and hated that, but I didn't really mind being his pet. Didn't I get what I wanted and much more than that, like Jim Hawkins who went off with Long John Silver to Treasure Island?

There were a couple of afternoons when Bob dropped by the studio while I was nude, posing solo for Leo. It wasn't unusual to see his camera hanging from his neck, a Leica in a leather case, small and heavy, an impressive piece of professional equipment. And so it didn't seem unusual that he would shoot some photos. In fact, I was flattered. Leo wasn't happy, however, to have him lurking about with his flashgun. "Get outta here!" His thumb yanked him toward the door. "Yer out!"

But Bob crept back.

"You're an amateur," Leo accused him.

"I am," Bob said. "I love what I do."

Once when Gwen and I were alone in the studio, I mentioned to her how Bob had come by and taken pictures of me.

"Did you give him your permission?" she asked.

"For what?" I said. "I was posing for Leo—he was right there."

In the early days I was never able to say much to her, whether we were working together or not, and I assumed this was a symptom of love. That day, when we were gathering our coats to leave, I felt befuddled as usual, and yet I found the courage to ask if Bob had ever photographed her.

She nodded and said, "But I know what I'm doing. Do you?"

In my defense I scoffed, "He can take all the pictures he wants. Pictures can't hurt me."

Some indigenous people believe that taking a photograph can steal a person's soul, and so they never permit anyone with a camera to come near. I've thought about this quite a lot and also something Ansel Adams said: "Not everybody trusts a painting, but people believe in photographs." Glutted as our day to day existence is with visual images, it's remarkable how a single photo can have the power to undo a career or an entire life. But if there ever was a void in me because of something that was taken or that I lost, I know that I have filled it. I am whole.

I did not discover a single print of myself when I later pillaged Bob's files on behalf of Gwendolyn. My best guess is that Cristiano got hold of any prints and negatives there might have been along with all the rest he'd promised to take care of.

I PURCHASED *GOODLY CREATURES* for a modest amount, its market value I reckoned at the time. It's worth much more at present—and if Leo's prices haven't yet soared to the Moon, then at least they are in the same orbit as Dorothy Sheffield's. For the select retrospective I curated at the College, along with the entire "Badge Bequest" and some pieces retrieved from the College's vault and others on loan, I lent my single Declare. Only Liotta remarked that the figure of Ferdinand must have been a portrait of me as a young man. "And the girl?" she asked. But I didn't answer. When I had acquired it— Bob handing the painting over without a word about its history, its beauty, or the vagaries of the marketplace—I told myself that what I'd done was ransom it. I'll only keep it for a little while, and then it belongs someplace grand.

LIOTTA WAS PLEASED, AND after the gala opening of *Leo Declare, American Master*, she hosted a small, private affair at her place in the City. There she waxed eloquently about my talents and accomplishments. (Bob did not attend, and at the opening, besides raising his hand when he was singled out among the well-heeled guests, he was remarkably reticent, though I don't doubt he collected some names.) At Liotta's party, Rosa Swenson also thanked me heartily for my "contribution," and one of the College trustees, Marshall Fapp, toasted me to the room. Then another one of the Board members offered some pompous words in honor of Leo. I could have puked, but I only raised my glass and smiled to myself about lads and sighs. I'd had a part in making everybody happy, and while I hadn't done it altogether selflessly, still I could honestly feel I'd been like the proverbial water wheel turning in the stream, giving and taking simultaneously.

In the days that followed, there was nothing from the Dean or the President about counting my years of service toward tenure, nor did I pursue this scheme. However, I did have the opportunity to decline to become the next Coordinator of Museum Acquisitions.

JESSIE LEIPER, ABOUT TO become an associate professor, says he's part of an evolving global brain; the Internet is only a stage of this planetary development, he explains. "Soon we won't need hardware or software or even bionic implants. We'll all be naturally telepathic, and more importantly, empathic." I wonder if he talks to his students this way?

"All intelligence is artificial," he says, taking me by the arm to walk the Green together one more time. "It's nothing but an accumulation of facts, and combinations of facts, and sets of systems for information storage and retrieval. The frontal part of our brains evolved because we humans need to think we have a choice in how we act. AI will simply replicate that, but the Planet has other, greater things it needs from us."

"A rock remains a rock until external forces act on it," I say. "But people can change intentionally."

He somersaults on the grass, rolling into a posture I might call the Philosopher's Stone.

Jessie Leiper, the Preposterous: he wants to film us having "word play." He wants to pass on to posterity our "past-post-modern dialogues." We must resist the vapid and the foul, he declares. He's ready to begin building a virtual future for us with Z-Pro Photon software and the Alpha-Omega processor he has just acquired. "I've got it all planned," Jesse says, tapping his temple where a portion of the global brain is evolving.

"God," he says, pursing his lips. "Just imagine what God thinks!"

I tell him I already have a future in mind. I take a step forward, so close that his features blur before my eyes. "I'm going to publish my book," I say. *"À bientôt, mon cher."* And kiss him on the mouth.

Acknowledgments

In the course of almost two decades during which this novel compelled me to complete it, many people supported my efforts. My thanks to all of them, especially to my wife, the poet Mary Gilliland. And *grazie mille* Donna Bister and Marc Estrin of Fomite Press.

About the Author

Peter Fortunato grew up in Wappingers Falls and Poughkeepsie, New York at a family run restaurant and resort much like the Villa Giustovera. His father was a stage magician and singer and his mother an extraordinary seamstress and cook. His grandparents and their friends were his earliest connection not only to Italy but also to the history of the Hudson Valley. Peter is a poet, painter, performer, ceremony maker, and hypnotherapist, and recently retired from teaching at Cornell and Ithaca College. He has been a Buddhist for many years, as well as a shaman, Reiki master practitioner, and Tarot mage.

For more info, visit www.peterfortunato.wordpress.com

Fomite

About Fomite

A fomite is a medium capable of transmitting infectious organisms from one individual to another.

"The activity of art is based on the capacity of people to be infected by the feelings of others." Tolstoy, *What Is Art?*

Writing a review on Amazon, Good Reads, Shelfari, Library Thing or other social media sites for readers will help the progress of independent publishing. To submit a review, go to the book page on any of the sites and follow the links for reviews. Books from independent presses rely on reader to reader communications.

For more information or to order any of our books, visit
http://www.fomitepress.com/

More Titles from Fomite...

Novels
Joshua Amses — *During This, Our Nadir*
Joshua Amses — *Ghatsr*
Joshua Amses — *Raven or Crow*
Joshua Amses — *The Moment Before an Injury*
Jaysinh Birjepatel — *Nothing Beside Remains*
Jaysinh Birjepatel — *The Good Muslim of Jackson Heights*
David Brizer — *Victor Rand*
Paula Closson Buck — *Summer on the Cold War Planet*
Dan Chodorkoff — *Loisaida*
David Adams Cleveland — *Time's Betrayal*
Jaimee Wriston Colbert — *Vanishing Acts*
Roger Coleman — *Skywreck Afternoons*
Marc Estrin — *Hyde*
Marc Estrin — *Kafka's Roach*
Marc Estrin — *Speckled Vanities*
Zdravka Evtimova — *In the Town of Joy and Peace*
Zdravka Evtimova — *Sinfonia Bulgarica*
Daniel Forbes — *Derail This Train Wreck*
Peter Fortunato — *Carnevale*
Greg Guma — *Dons of Time*
Richard Hawley — *The Three Lives of Jonathan Force*
Lamar Herrin — *Father Figure*
Michael Horner — *Damage Control*
Ron Jacobs — *All the Sinners Saints*
Ron Jacobs — *Short Order Frame Up*
Ron Jacobs — *The Co-conspirator's Tale*
Scott Archer Jones — *And Throw Away the Skins*
Scott Archer Jones — *A Rising Tide of People Swept Away*
Julie Justicz — *Degrees of Difficulty*
Maggie Kast — *A Free Unsullied Land*
Darrell Kastin — *Shadowboxing with Bukowski*
Coleen Kearon — *#triggerwarning*
Coleen Kearon — *Feminist on Fire*

Fomite

Fomite

Tony Magistrale — *Entanglements*
Gary Mesick — *General Discharge*
Andreas Nolte — *Mascha: The Poems of Mascha Kaléko*
Sherry Olson — *Four-Way Stop*
Brett Ortler — *Lessons of the Dead*
Aristea Papalexandrou/Philip Ramp — Μας προσπερνά/*It's Overtaking Us*
Janice Miller Potter — *Meanwell*
Janice Miller Potter — *Thoreau's Umbrella*
Philip Ramp — *The Melancholy of a Life as the Joy of Living It Slowly Chills*
Joseph D. Reich — *A Case Study of Werewolves*
Joseph D. Reich — *Connecting the Dots to Shangrila*
Joseph D. Reich — *The Derivation of Cowboys and Indians*
Joseph D. Reich — *The Hole That Runs Through Utopia*
Joseph D. Reich — *The Housing Market*
Kenneth Rosen and Richard Wilson — *Gomorrah*
Fred Rosenblum — *Vietnumb*
David Schein — *My Murder and Other Local News*
Harold Schweizer — *Miriam's Book*
Scott T. Starbuck — *Carbonfish Blues*
Scott T. Starbuck — *Hawk on Wire*
Scott T. Starbuck — *Industrial Oz*
Seth Steinzor — *Among the Lost*
Seth Steinzor — *To Join the Lost*
Susan Thomas — *In the Sadness Museum*
Susan Thomas — *The Empty Notebook Interrogates Itself*
Paolo Valesio/Todd Portnowitz — *La Mezzanotte di Spoleto/Midnight in Spoleto*
Sharon Webster — *Everyone Lives Here*
Tony Whedon — *The Tres Riches Heures*
Tony Whedon — *The Falkland Quartet*
Claire Zoghb — *Dispatches from Everest*

Stories
Jay Boyer — *Flight*
L. M Brown — *Treading the Uneven Road*
Michael Cocchiarale — *Here Is Ware*
Michael Cocchiarale — *Still Time*
Neil Connelly — *In the Wake of Our Vows*
Catherine Zobal Dent — *Unfinished Stories of Girls*
Zdravka Evtimova —*Carts and Other Stories*
John Michael Flynn — *Off to the Next Wherever*
Derek Furr — *Semitones*
Derek Furr — *Suite for Three Voices*
Elizabeth Genovise — *Where There Are Two or More*
Andrei Guriuanu — *Body of Work*
Zeke Jarvis — *In A Family Way*
Arya Jenkins — *Blue Songs in an Open Key*
Jan English Leary — *Skating on the Vertical*
Larry Lefkowitz — *Enigmatic Tales*
Marjorie Maddox — *What She Was Saying*
William Marquess — *Boom-shacka-lacka*
Gary Miller — *Museum of the Americas*
Jennifer Anne Moses — *Visiting Hours*

Fomite

Martin Ott — *Interrogations*
Christopher Peterson — *Amoebic Simulacra*
Jack Pulaski — *Love's Labours*
Charles Rafferty — *Saturday Night at Magellan's*
Ron Savage — *What We Do For Love*
Fred Skolnik— *Americans and Other Stories*
Lynn Sloan — *This Far Is Not Far Enough*
L.E. Smith — *Views Cost Extra*
Caitlin Hamilton Summie — *To Lay To Rest Our Ghosts*
Susan Thomas — *Among Angelic Orders*
Tom Walker — *Signed Confessions*
Silas Dent Zobal — *The Inconvenience of the Wings*

Odd Birds
William Benton — *Eye Contact: Writing on Art*
Micheal Breiner — *the way none of this happened*
J. C. Ellefson — *Under the Influence: Shouting Out to Walt*
David Ross Gunn — *Cautionary Chronicles*
Andrei Guriuanu and Teknari — *The Darkest City*
Gail Holst-Warhaft — *The Fall of Athens*
Roger Lebovitz — *A Guide to the Western Slopes and the Outlying Area*
Roger Lebovitz — *Twenty-two Instructions for Near Survival*
dug Nap— *Artsy Fartsy*
Delia Bell Robinson — *A Shirtwaist Story*
Peter Schumann — *Belligerent & Not So Belligerent Slogans from the
                  Possibilitarian Arsenal*
Peter Schumann — *Bread & Sentences*
Peter Schumann — *Charlotte Salomon*
Peter Schumann — *Diagonal Man, Volumes One and Two*
Peter Schumann — *Faust 3*
Peter Schumann — *Planet Kasper, Volumes One and Two*
Peter Schumann — *We*

Plays
Stephen Goldberg — *Screwed and Other Plays*
Michele Markarian — *Unborn Children of America*

Essays
Robert Sommer — *Losing Francis: Essays on the Wars at Home*

CPSIA information can be obtained
at www.ICGtesting.com
Printed in the USA
FSHW011612021019
62623FS